LOVE ON
THE DOTTED LINE

Ogugua Ajayi

LOVE LEGACY MEDIA

Published by Love Legacy Media
First published 2025

ISBN 978-978-774-464-2

A CIP catalogue record for this book is available from the British Library.

Typeset by PRAM Publications Ltd.

To Damilola, Dara and Ibukun

Chapter One

Two, three, four. Ada counted as he fiddled with the knot of his tie.

Over the years, she had taken to noting the number of times a minute he did this. On average, he did it twice, but his record was five.

Six, seven.

Ada straightened in her seat.

The air-conditioning did nothing to stop the moisture from pooling under her arms. She adjusted her *boubou* to provide a bit of circulation. Maybe it was the ever-humid Port Harcourt weather, or perhaps it was just nervous energy as she waited for a response from Mr Usoro, the school principal. He held a copy of her letter in his hands.

Mr Usoro cleared his throat. "Please, madam," he said finally. "I am not trying to be difficult. Running a private school is still a business."

Ada's heart sank. *Ask and you shall receive*, indeed. She forced a small smile through her despair.

"I understand. I am grateful to you for allowing the kids to finish the term."

"It was the least we could do," he said. "Your husband never missed a payment. And, of course, he was such a supportive parent."

Supportive. Ada resisted the urge to ball her hands into fists. Emeka had practically built the school's science block from the ground up – that effort surely went beyond mere 'support'.

But she held her tongue. She needed this man's help.

Mr Usoro peered at her over the top of his glasses. "I must admit, I am a little surprised by your request. After all, your husband was a man of means…"

He knew. They all knew. They all knew her wealthy late husband had rewritten his will. They all knew how, at the point of his cancer diagnosis, he had transferred everything he owned to his sister, leaving Ada and her four sons with close to nothing.

But no matter what was said at the water cooler, no one understood its depth.

Ada felt naked even though she was fully dressed. Even from the grave, Emeka was still managing to strip away her dignity. Under the desk, she twisted her wedding band and reminded herself that it was about the children. The poor had no business with pride.

"I understand having all three boys on a scholarship is a big ask," she said. "I shouldn't have put you in that position. For that, I apologise. But Tobenna is something, isn't he?"

The principal gave her a sad smile. He ducked his chin, as though trying to avoid the look of quiet optimism in her eyes.

"Would you at least consider a scholarship for Tobenna?" Ada shifted forward in her seat, placing her hands on the table in front of her. "Not a sympathy scholarship, Mr Usoro. You know Tobe is a genius and has been since he started in preschool here at age three – the top end of primary exam results in the entire country. This school was on the news for that. You remember?"

"I do, madam." The principal fidgeted in his seat and readjusted his tie three times in quick succession. His eyes avoided her. "Regrettably, Mrs Okeke, we are not giving scholarships at this time. I am so sorry."

Ada reeled at his words. She'd hoped fervently that at least, Tobenna's academic prowess would have counted for something. If he couldn't stay in school, what would they all do?

She felt tired, so very tired. She stood up but collapsed in the chair immediately, as pain gripped the front of her skull like a vice.

Mr Usoro came around to the other side of the desk and bent down beside her. Ada stiffened as his arm slid around her shoulder. She turned sharply to look up at him, her gaze landing on his bobbing Adam's apple.

"Mrs Okeke, are you alright?" he asked. He sounded as if he was speaking through cotton.

Ada held onto his jacket. Her response poured out in a torrent. "You need to help me," she said. "I'll get on my feet. I'll pay everything I owe, just let them continue here. I'll pay everything I owe. I promise."

The principal's look of shock was almost comical. Ada released him and looked down at her hands. Her palms stung from clutching at the fabric of his jacket.

"Mrs Okeke, your request is almost impossible," he said. "It will need the entire board's approval. I would have to put my neck on the line for you."

Ada looked up at him again. She rose from her seat, a flutter of hope in the pit of her stomach. Maybe. Just maybe. "Please." It was almost a whisper.

"Tell me something." He smoothed down his jacket and gave a slight shrug. "If I do help you, what do I get in return?"

"In... return?"

Ada's final hope died slowly as he explained how he expected to be rewarded. She sensed her face hardening, the lines of her cheeks and jaw solidifying like marble.

When he was finished, the principal leaned in towards her ear, his breath on the side of her neck. "Think about it."

As soon as he said it, Ada reached for the glass of water he'd offered her when she arrived for the appointment. She threw it in his face before smashing the glass back on the table.

At the sound of his surprised yelp, his secretary ran into the room to stand between her startled boss and an enraged Ada.

"You disgust me!" Ada was shaking.

The principal spat as he frantically tried to wipe his face. She stumbled out of the office leaving the door open.

She heard him shout after her, "I will not compromise my principles! If you can't afford to pay like everyone else, take your useless children away with you!"

It was loud enough for staff and a few milling parents to overhear. They gave her curious, misguided looks as she hurried out of the building, and as she stormed off the school grounds, she had to will herself not to scream out in despair, although every part of her body demanded it.

Ada Okeke had reached the bottom of the barrel.

Ada looked at the dried-up grounds surrounding the building that had been her tomb for the past twelve years.

It was her husband's pride, and the place where her spirit had begun to die. His five-bedroom mansion was one of the largest in the Rumuibekwe Estate when it was first built. He would roll in his freshly dug grave if he saw its state now. The soil turned to dust. The gardens in tatters. The paint had started peeling off the front-facing walls.

Ada had chores waiting for her, but she could not bring herself to lift a finger. Not now.

Instead, she leaned against the mango tree, stretched her legs, and pulled out the piece of paper her best friend, Osas, had left for her that morning. Three columns headed the page: 'Goals, Ambitions, Dreams'. Ada was supposed to fill in each one.

Goals? She scratched her left palm the way she often did when she was deep in thought. Would having more sons qualify? It seemed that was all she had ever done or tried to do since the day she'd met Emeka.

Dreams.

Ada sighed. A long, long time ago, her dream was to become a successful businesswoman like Mrs Nwafor, who owned the largest supermarket in the village. Despite her thriving enterprise, Mrs Nwafor always seemed so happy and relaxed.

She had once told Ada that the key to her success was a good education. Ada's late husband had promised her father that he would send her to the university, but after the wedding, Emeka scoffed at any mention of further education. It was like a piece of candy kept just out of her reach.

Emeka had married her so she would bear children; she didn't need a university degree for that. After Tobe and the twins arrived, Ada was sure he would back down. Three boys surely qualified her for some respite, but Emeka's cries for more heirs just grew more insistent.

"Maybe I can take a break and return to school?" she'd pleaded after two miscarriages three months apart. "I'll still be young enough to bear more children when I'm done. You already have three sons; your name is secure."

"I will have as many children as I can afford, and I can afford many more." Emeka's eyes darkened. A bead of sweat trickled down his double chin. "You will stop when I am good and ready, or when you are dead!"

Ada never asked again.

Ada stared at Osas's paper. She had no idea how long had passed when she heard the creaking of the gate. Osas drove in with Ada's children in the back of the car. Tobe, her quiet firstborn; Ikenna and Ahanna, her hyperactive twins; and her three-month-old baby, Obinna.

The children waved from the back of the car, tumbling out in excitement to hug her the moment the vehicle stopped. For them, she was getting better at forcing a smile.

"Easy, guys, don't knock her down," Osas called before unbuckling baby Obinna from his car seat. "Remember the food!" The boys rushed back to the car to pull out bags of food bought from the fast-food restaurant down the street.

"Aunty Osas said we're not cooking today!" Ikenna screamed, jumping up with a bag in his hand.

"Who is 'we'? Have you ever cooked?" Tobe teased as he carried two bags into the house.

"I'll be back," Osas said to Ada, handing over Obinna with a knowing smile. "I only need a moment to remove my shoes in peace."

Osas was tall and slender in all the places where Ada was curved. She always held her head high on her shoulders, as though the crown of her head was forever stretching toward the sky.

Ada followed her friend slowly into the house.

"Why don't you stretch your legs in the garden?" Ada said to the other three boys. "I'll call you once I heat everything up."

They didn't need coaxing, and ran shrieking and squealing past their mum, through the open door and into the front yard.

Once in the kitchen, Ada used a wrapper to secure Obinna to her back. She had started unpacking the food when Osas returned sans shoes and wig, exposing her neatly plaited cornrows.

Osas leaned against the counter. "What's the matter?"

"Who said anything was the matter?" Ada sniffed and continued unloading the bags.

"Save that story for people who don't know you. Why are you so down in the dumps?"

Ada rubbed her temples and looked away. It was useless to try to keep anything from Osas. "I can't see a way out, Osas. This afternoon, I applied to an agency that recruits housemaids."

"What? Ada, no o." Osas moved closer and held her arm, forcing her to stop what she was doing and face her.

Ada turned to her friend, her voice barely above a whisper. She grabbed Osas's hands, her body trembling. "What am I going to do? I have a three-month-old baby. I have three boys that need to go to school in January. I have nothing. No education, no skills. Where do I begin?"

What will I do? had become an unending soundbite in her consciousness. She held her head in her hands, bent over and moaned.

Osas snatched Obinna off Ada's back before his mother reached the floor, and cradled the baby while she fanned Ada with an old newspaper.

"Breathe. Ada, *abeg*, just breathe."

Ada struggled to obey. She rubbed her chest and opened her mouth but choked on the sobs that fought their way through her body.

"Ada, *na beg, I dey beg*. Please. Don't let me drop Obinna by mistake." Osas continued to fan Ada vigorously while striving to keep Obinna steady on her hip.

Ada tried to speak, punctuating her words with heavy heaves.

"Osas, see me o… This week… I have tried to look for work… There is nothing out there for a secondary school graduate… Just promises from leery men who don't even pretend to hide what they want from me."

Obinna wailed, snapping Ada out of her daze. She took him from Osas, guided him down to the floor, and bounced him on her knees, tears still flowing down her cheeks.

"Ada, hold on. I know it seems like the world is caving in right now. But, as my mum used to say, 'No matter how dark the clouds, they always have to move on'."

Ada nodded, sniffing.

Osas joined her on the floor. "Hmm, Ndidi, wherever you are, let your stomach be empty o. This thing you have cooked for your brother's children and their mother, you must eat it, one way or the other. You must!"

Ndidi. Just the sound of her sister-in-law's name made Ada's stomach sour.

"Osas, it gets worse."

Ada quickly narrated the incident at the school.

"The over-bloated pig!" Osas exclaimed when Ada explained the principal's request.

"I threw a cup of water in his face," Ada mumbled. Osas nodded in approval.

"But," Ada went on, "as I stood under that hot sun outside the school, I thought, am I not the biggest fool there is? At thirty-one? Look at my life!"

"You're not a fool. You have always done what you were told to do."

It was true. All her life, Ada had followed other people's orders. First her father's, then her husband's, and, in the last month after her husband's death, Ndidi's.

"And where did that get me?" Ada asked with red-rimmed eyes.

"Ugh. This is so depressing." Osas got up and helped Ada off the floor, careful to make sure Obinna was secure. "Somehow, something will budge. Let me go take a quick shower. I'll be back."

When Osas returned, Ada's hands were submerged in a sink full of soapsuds.

"Your phone must have been ringing off the hook next door," Osas said, holding Ada's phone in the air. "You have ten missed calls."

Ada withdrew her hands from the sink. "Ten *kwa*? No one calls me anymore." Once Emeka's associates and their wives realised Ada would inherit nothing, the phone had gone silent.

Osas held the phone up to her face.

"The number doesn't look familiar. Drop it here for me," Ada said, using her chin to indicate the spot.

"What if it's important? Won't you call back?"

"And use the tiny bit of money I have to hear, 'Sorry for your loss; he is in a better place'?" Ada hissed. "No. If they want to be sorry, they should use their own airtime."

Right on cue, the light flashed on her phone.

Ada rubbed her hands on the dishtowel on her shoulder and answered.

It was a short call, no longer than a minute. All the while, Ada tried to ignore Osas, whose eyes burned for information. When it was over, Ada took the phone from her ear and stared at it.

"Don't keep me waiting," said Osas. "Who was it? What did they say?"

Ada's brow furrowed. "A man. He says his boss was a friend of Emeka's, Mr Wande Badejo. Apparently, Mr Badejo wants to see me as soon as possible."

"Badejo?" Osas scrunched up her nose. "Do I know a Badejo? Anyway, what does he want with you?"

"He didn't say – just that I should name the time or place to meet. He has a proposal for me."

"Mysterious," Osas remarked.

"What do I do?" Ada mumbled.

She was not in the mood for mysteries. For all she knew, it could be a scam. Although, what anyone might desire from her now was a mystery in itself. What was there to take from someone who already had nothing?

Osas shrugged. "I guess it won't harm to meet him."

Ada hesitated. "Alone?"

"Of course not," Osas said. "I will come with you. Besides, I'm curious, as well."

"What about the boys?" Ada asked.

Osas was not bothered. "Invite Mr Badejo to my place."

"What if he's a serial killer?"

"He said he was a friend of Emeka's."

"Maybe it's a cover-up."

"My dear friend, do I need to remind you that you have nothing anyone would want to steal?" Osas shook her head at Ada. "I say, invite him to my place. We can scope him out from the window. If we get the wrong vibes, we tell him we have changed our mind before he even gets up the stairs *sef*."

Ada chewed her bottom lip as she mulled over her friend's words.

With dinner over and the kids busy brushing their teeth for bed, Ada came to join Osas in the guest bedroom. Osas had agreed to spend the night at Ada's house, much to the boys' delight.

As Ada sat beside Osas on the bed, she finally blurted, "Okay, I'll send him your address."

"Took you long enough to decide," Osas teased, elbowing Ada's side.

Ada shook her head, weariness seeping through her body at the thought of one more tie to her late husband. "The truth is, now that the burial is over, I don't want any more of Emeka's business hanging over my head. Let me hear what Mr Badejo wants, and get it over and done with.

Chapter Two

Ada hummed as she prepared lunch in Osas's brightly coloured kitchen. Everything from the orange cupboards to the white granite countertops made Ada feel lighter and happier; cooking was no longer a dreaded chore.

Obinna was in his usual spot on her back, snuggled in his wrapper, while Tobe and the twins were playing on the computer in the guest room. Ada was making Osas's favourite: *egusi* soup and pounded yam. After tenderising the meat, she added dry fish, palm oil, and ground *egusi*. While the soup simmered, Ada chopped *ugu* leaves to be added later.

The bustle of cooking took her mind off the impending appointment. Mr Badejo seemed in a hurry to meet; the quicker, the better, the secretary had said on the phone. The meeting was scheduled for that day. He would be there in a couple of hours.

Osas arrived around three in the afternoon to a delicious aroma permeating the house. At the sound of her arrival, Ada poked her head out of the kitchen into the living room, a cleaning cloth clutched in her hand.

Osas's living room was stylish, but sparse. The decor followed no discernible pattern or rules, but it still came together to create a hospitable and inviting space. Warm tones of brown and cream filtered through the room, pops of orange enlivening the accessories.

Though Osas's apartment could have rivalled any exclusive suburb, she refused to move to the more upscale parts of Port Harcourt like TransAmadi or Rumuibekwe, where young, upwardly mobile families lived in splendour. Instead, she stayed at Waterside in the same apartment she'd taken on her return from her Master's programme. Even as she progressed through the ranks at the oil company she worked with, she still refused to move, claiming she needed to stay connected to her roots. Osas's neighbours could never believe the amount of money the sharp-mouthed, unmarried tenant earned per month.

Before Emeka's death, Ada could never visit Osas unless Emeka travelled on business. Even when she did see her friend, the visits were brief. Now, she came often. She felt safer and slept better in this house than she ever did in the building she had called home.

As soon as Osas arrived, the twins were all over her – struggling to help carry her handbag and laptop.

"Easy guys, be careful. I'll give them to you." Osas giggled, handing over the items. She gave the boys a hug before they left, then collapsed on her couch still smiling. "Your kids are the best," she said to Ada. She sat up and inhaled the rich smell of *egusi*. "*Abeg*, move in here permanently. Let me come home to this aroma every day."

"If you want this every day, why don't you hire a cook?" Ada smiled as she dusted the little cabinet ornaments on the shelf.

"I agree. I'm thinking a male bodybuilder. My dinner served by a man in a loincloth that barely—" Osas ducked, laughing as Ada pretended to swat the cloth on her head.

"I am not interested in your wild fantasies."

"Well, better get your imagination ready. You never know, it could soon be husband number two for you."

Ada shuddered. The thought of another man taking control of her life set loose a chill from the base of her spine. She picked up a bronze elephant, polished it with vigour, then slammed it back on the shelf.

"I won't do that to myself again," she said. She picked up the next-sized elephant and subjected it to the same fate.

"Please stop!" Osas had risen from the couch and moved to stand in front of her. She pulled the cloth gently from Ada's hands. "On behalf of myself and my ornaments, we apologise for offending you."

Ada's shoulders relaxed and the corners of her mouth lifted.

Osas led her to the couch and pulled her down beside her. "When is our mystery guest coming, anyway?"

Ada's brow furrowed. "Five o'clock." Osas squeezed her hand. Ada squeezed back and sighed. "I just want to get it over with." The knot that had taken up residence in her stomach tightened. She hated going through this charade, something she had come to expect, being forced to listen respectfully as yet another person expressed their gratitude to Emeka: *Your husband was a great man, an amazing human being. One of the kindest, most generous and…"*

Whenever people started with those words, Ada allowed her mind to drift. It was true, Emeka had been a generous benefactor to many, but they spoke of a person they knew nothing about; they'd never had to live with him.

Ada jumped up and started to polish the TV stand. She couldn't help it. Old habits.

Osas snatched the cloth. "This is my house. If the man doesn't like my dust, he can leave."

"And when the boy ate the cake, his lip grew big and everybody started shouting!"

"It was as big as an orange!" Ahanna chimed in.

Ikenna, not to be outdone, cut back in. "No! As big as a watermelon."

"Even bigger." Ahanna's excitement grew. "It was so big, another boy had to help him carry his lip!"

Osas roared with unrestrained laughter, and the twins joined her. Ada resisted the instinct to shush them. This wasn't Emeka's house.

As usual, Tobe was on the couch in his own world, one hand rocking his baby brother's pushchair and the other holding a book. Ada caught Osas's eye, who tapped her wristwatch, while the twins continued to cackle. Ada wanted to soak in this scene of normality, but it was nearly five. Soon, they were shepherding the boys downstairs to play football with the neighbours' children.

A loud knock came at ten to five.

"He said five," Ada whispered as she grabbed Osas's arm.

"Well, he's early. Stop being so jumpy." Osas untangled herself from Ada's grasp and walked towards the door. Ada took a deep breath and followed a few steps behind. Osas stood for a few seconds with a bright smile as if preparing for a performance on stage, then swung the door open.

"I apologise for coming early," said the man in the doorway. "It's a nasty habit of mine."

Ada was surprised at his clipped British accent. It reminded her of the time her principal had made them sit through Prince Charles's speech in secondary school. 'To broaden their knowledge', the principal had said.

"No need, Mr—" Ada's words stuck on her lips as Osas opened the door wider to reveal the man behind the voice. Ada barely suppressed a gasp.

Wande Badejo walked into the room carrying a dark brown leather attaché case over his shoulder, his nose in the air like he owned the apartment. He had a bald head, a full, well-shaped beard, and dark glasses perched atop his very distinguished nose. He assumed a solid, military-style stance in the entryway, chin up, hands behind his back. Two large, thick scars ran down from above his right eye to his cheek.

Whatever it was this man had, Ada's late husband was not in his league.

Ada coughed. Mr Badejo turned, and gave Osas and Ada a slow smile, exposing a set of perfect teeth.

"I hope you don't mind. Your boys are very handsome." He nodded towards Osas's wall of pictures. "I have a son of my own. He is thirteen."

He was looking at them both. It was understandable that he didn't recognise Ada. Many people didn't. Emeka had never taken her anywhere, but still, couldn't he see her mourning attire?

"Thank you. The children are handsome indeed. They take after their mother," Osas said with a cheeky grin. "I hope one day, when I have mine, they will be as handsome."

Mr Badejo's eyes narrowed.

Osas smiled as she pointed to Ada. "This is Mrs Okeke."

The pair looked at Ada, who wanted to transform into one of Osas's little ornaments and stay unnoticed on the shelf. She looked at the floor to avoid seeing the inevitable disappointment that would surely arise in this stranger's eyes when he looked at her. She knew what he would see; Emeka had told her often enough. She was nothing worth looking at.

"That was remiss of me. I apologise, Mrs Okeke." He gave a slight bow.

Ada nodded. Without looking up, she signalled to Osas to take over. "Let's sit."

Osas waved Wande to the wingback chair, while she and Ada sat on the couch. Ada hid behind Osas, using her as a shield. After a few seconds of awkward silence, Osas pinched her arm.

To Ada's horror, she realised that Osas expected her to carry on the conversation. Why couldn't Osas do it? Ada swallowed hard, rubbed her sweaty palm along her cotton *boubou*, then sat forward.

"What are you here to discuss, sir?" she asked.

With her nose scrunched up, Osas faced Ada and mouthed 'sir' like it was a dirty word.

Emeka had insisted that all his friends were 'sir' to Ada, not only to remind her of her place, but also to prevent any familiarity. Ada cleared her throat, avoiding her friend's eyes.

Mr Badejo leaned forward too and brought the tips of his fingers together under his chin. "Mrs Okeke, could your friend excuse us for a minute?"

"No, please," Ada said, pulling Osas by the hand as though afraid this man would snatch her away.

"Very well." He nodded and sat back in the chair. "Mrs Okeke, I am truly sorry for your loss. Your husband and I crossed paths over business. He was a keen salesman."

Ada examined him. The cut of this man's emerald-green kaftan was perfect and made to fit. The gold wristwatch peeking out from under his cuff... He oozed class that Emeka could never have in a million years.

He placed his case across his knees and brought out two brown envelopes. "Well, I find myself in a bind. I am aware that perhaps you feel the same at present, Mrs Okeke. But I have a plan to solve both our problems."

Ada and Osas exchanged glances. What could this man know about Ada's situation?

Ada found her voice. "What is your plan, sir?"

Wande looked up from his case with ease. "Marry me."

Ada was sure her jaw made a sound as it dislodged. Surely, she didn't hear him right. "W... What?"

"My proposal is that you marry me." His face remained impassive.

"Her husband died less than three months ago." Osas's eyes were wide.

"Please. Go…" Ada's voice was a whisper. Not again. Not another man assuming her greatest need right now was another husband. She wanted to hold her head in her hands and scream. "Please just go," she said a little louder.

Wande put up both hands in front of him. "I know it sounds odd, but if you hear me out, you'll see that it makes absolute sense. Mrs Okeke… I am prepared to pay handsomely for this."

"She asked you to leave. Twice. Do we need backup?" Osas stood, arms akimbo.

Wande rose gracefully for a man his size. "There will be no need for that." Pointing at the envelopes on the table, he said, "Read the contract. See what I am offering before you toss out the idea. You can always propose changes."

"I don't want to read it." Ada wrapped her arms around herself and turned away from him. "Get out."

A few moments passed. Ada moved only when she heard the front door shut. Through the blinds at the window, she watched as Wande's driver held the car door for him.

Osas picked up the envelope the guest had left on the table.

"Throw that thing in the bin." Ada left the window to face her friend.

"You're not even a little curious?"

"Not one bit." Ada snatched the envelope from Osas's hands and tore it in two, then threw the pieces in the bin, dusting her hands as they dropped in. At least this was a nightmare she could wake up from. She sat down heavily on the couch.

"What is it about me that invites men to treat me like this? Do I have the word 'prostitute' engraved on my forehead?" Her brow knitted into a frown. The weight of worthlessness hung heavy around her. Was marriage all she existed for?

Osas sat cross-legged on the floor beside her and rubbed her back. "It's actually quite flattering."

"It's not funny," Ada snapped.

"I'm being serious. I'm thirty-four, single, and all these Port Harcourt men only want one thing." Osas gave an exaggerated sigh. "What does a girl in this century have to do to get a marriage proposal? Ada, please give me a little of what you've got."

"Whatever it is, I don't want it!" Ada's face crumpled. She asked in a tiny voice, "What is wrong with these men? Is it because I'm a widow?"

Osas shook her head. "If I didn't know you well, I would believe you were pretending."

Ada had never seen herself as conventionally beautiful, but if she had looked through Osas's eyes, she would have seen a woman with ethereal eyes – eyes that looked at a person and really saw them. She would have seen skin that glowed, a beautiful mix of mahogany and bronze that almost shimmered when she walked past. She would have seen a smile that stretched wide across her face, a smile that radiated warmth, that made everyone feel like they were the only person in the room. Ada never saw herself, truly looked at herself.

"Osas, you sound drunk," she said.

"Not drunk, my dear, it's the truth. But while you are blind to your own essence, the rest of the world isn't. Even with your *gori mapka*."

Ada's hand instinctively went to touch her headscarf, but she wasn't quick enough. Osas deftly pulled the scarf from her head and rubbed her freshly shaved skull. Ada reached out to retaliate, but they ended up in a heap on the floor, which sent Osas into hysterics. Stunned by her fall, Ada also gave into a fit of laughter that shook her entire body.

Tobe, Ikenna and Ahanna came upstairs to find the two women on the floor, consumed by laughter.

Ahanna remarked with a massive grin, "Are you both physically, emotionally and spiritually okay?" The comment sent the women into another fit of giggles. Ikenna, who loved a good rumble, joined his mum and aunt. Ahanna followed suit. Only Tobe smiled and shook his head, holding Obinna safely in his arms.

Osas was the first to get herself under control. "Phew. Whoever said laughter was medicine knew what they were talking about."

"I'm telling you, my sister." Ada moved off the floor and leaned against the couch, her chest heaving. "I can't believe I'm laughing. I needed that." She sat up, a smile still lingering on her face.

"Too much drama today. Let's take the kids out for ice cream."

"Ice cream, Aunty?" Tobe jumped on the spot.

Ada frowned. "You don't have to do that, Osas. It's not the end of the month, and you spend so much on us already."

"Stop with your whining. Boys, let's go. We will only take Mummy if she smiles. Mummy, please smile."

The boys all beseeched Ada, pulling funny faces. She smiled. How blessed she was to have Osas and the boys in her life.

As they got ready to leave, Osas noticed pieces of the envelope peeking out over the top of the bin. Ada, busy ushering the kids out the door, didn't see her friend double back, pick up the torn contract and hide it behind the cushion.

Chapter Three

Ada rolled over, clutching her pillow. The florid orange glow of the sun burned through the slits between the curtains. Turning towards the bedside table, she checked her phone, blinking at the sharp light.

6.45 a.m.

She had overslept. That hadn't happened in years. Usually, she was up by five like clockwork.

Luxuriating in the knowledge of having nothing pressing to do, she lay in bed and stretched for five extra minutes before tiptoeing out of the room, not wanting to wake Osas. She made a cup of tea and headed towards the balcony. On the veranda, Osas had built an overhead extension with wooden beams painted mahogany-brown. She'd sealed the space with a mosquito net, creating a pest-free haven and perfect hangout for the mornings and evenings. The wicker chair at the end of the balcony was Ada's favourite place to start the day.

But today, Osas had dashed Ada's plans. She was already in the coveted spot, mug in hand.

"I thought I left you asleep. I was trying not to disturb you." Ada chuckled as she took a seat opposite her friend. "Why are you up so early?"

Osas wore a slight frown.

"What is it? Did something happen?" Ada rose in a panic. "Are the boys alright?"

"The kids are fine." Osas chewed on her bottom lip. "I've been thinking, if you want Tobe to continue at The International School, I can handle his school fees. I am due for a promotion at the end of the year, so you don't have to worry about that. And if, God forbid, you need accommodation, we can sort that too. It's about time I moved out of this place, anyway. But the twins…" She pursed her lips and shook her head slowly.

Ada looked up at her best friend and smiled. Osas had always looked out for her ever since the beginning of their friendship all those years ago. Osas had refused to allow Ada to remain in her Emeka-imposed cocoon, and when things were at their darkest, she had drawn Ada out with her vivacious nature and endless charm. She was the only one who knew what life with Emeka was really like, and she had never broken Ada's trust, telling no one the true story, even though the injustice of it all irked her so. Here she was again, ready to turn her life upside down for Ada and her boys.

Ada rushed over and hugged her tight. "Thank you," she whispered. "Thank you for being my friend."

Osas hugged her back.

"Ada," Osas spoke hesitantly, "don't be mad at me…"

"Why would I be?" Ada pulled back and returned to her seat. A slight frown creased her forehead when she saw Osas holding the torn-up envelope. "What are you doing with that? I threw that away."

"Ada, hear me out." Osas's words streamed out in a rush. "Wande Badejo wants a marriage of convenience. He wants a marriage for the sake of his son, and he especially wants it for his two-year-old daughter who is sick."

"I am not marrying anyone," Ada said slowly.

"He wants a mother for his kids. It's a three-year contract."

Ada bristled at Osas's insistence. "Why can't he just marry someone he likes? Why me?"

"I think you should let him explain."

"Osas, no way! What could he say? Why should I even listen—"

"He will pay a million a month."

Ada sat down heavily. "A million what?" Her eyes were like saucers. "Ghanaian cedis?"

Osas laughed. "Don't be silly. A million naira."

"This is worse. He must be a drug dealer."

"No, he's not." Osas had a twinkle in her eye.

"And you know this how?"

"Google." Osas ignored Ada's look of shock and went on. "When you mentioned his name, I knew it sounded familiar, but I wasn't sure. So, this morning, I looked him up. He's the president of a vast conglomerate, businesses ranging from super-markets to production companies."

"So, Dangote?"

"Maybe even bigger. He's a second-generation billionaire. Grandfather handed the business down to his father and then to him. The empire has expanded with each handover. They call him 'The Beast'."

Ada was aghast. "Is it because of his scars?"

Osas shrugged. "More because of his reputation as a businessman, I think. Anyway, there are no pictures of him partying on the net. Just headings like, *'Nigerian-born billionaire aka "The Beast" closes a multi-billion-dollar transaction with blah blah'*. He's a big deal. He married a society woman who died in childbirth."

Ada couldn't continue to listen to it. She got up and went into the kitchen.

Osas stared after her. "Where are you going?"

Ada needed to do something with her hands. The children would soon be up – she could prep for breakfast. They always enjoyed potatoes with scrambled eggs. She started chopping the onions and peppers for frying.

Even so, her mind wandered back to Wande Badejo.

Ada's mother died giving birth to her. After that, money for palm wine had been her father's only goal. Nothing was off limits – not even selling his 18-year-old daughter to be married. In return, Emeka had kept his wine supply constant until he died.

Ada shook away the memory. She left the kitchen and returned to the balcony.

"I still don't understand this arrangement." She sat cross-legged and gave Osas a sour look.

"Funnily enough, it sounds like exactly the kind of clear-cut relationship I like." Osas responded as if the conversation had never stopped. She dropped the contract on the stool beside them. "Both of you enter into it without any illusions. A business arrangement. It happens all the time."

"So, why don't you do it?" Ada was put out by her attitude.

"One, I don't need his money," Osas said. "Two, he wants a mother, not a wife – and the only children I love in this world are yours. Three, marriage is a scam."

"You don't mean that."

"I do." Osas grinned.

"Don't you crave a genuine relationship? Mutual love and respect?" Ada plucked at the fringes of the cushion, her eyes dreamy. "If I did marry again, I would want to be with a man who thinks I'm amazing. Who loves me." She hugged the cushion to her chest. "Not a man that pays me, or worse!"

She couldn't help shuddering as she completed the thought: another Emeka. Osas made a goofy face across from her, oblivious to her discomfort.

"You're hoping for a Mills and Boon romance? Aunty, leave that matter. Hypothetically speaking, if you were to consider the arrangement, you should remind yourself that this is one thing, and one thing only... a job!"

"But I would be legally married. And then what? After three years, get divorced? Just like that? In this Nigeria? They will say I killed the first husband and the second divorced me before I could kill him, too." Ada blinked, her pupils bright and shiny.

"For the sake of argument," Osas said calmly, "I know our people and our judgmental, suspicious nature, but who among them is here right now asking how you are feeding your kids? How many of them have sent one thousand naira to assist you?" She hissed and waved her hand like she was shooing away flies.

"You owe no one any explanation," Osas said. "Let's do the math. Knowing you, you'll save your whole salary every month. Come 2022, after three years, you could be walking away with thirty-six million naira to start a new life with the boys."

"Another change for them." Ada rolled her head back, staring at the beams overhead.

"Those kids lost a dad, but they still have you. You're the stability they need. In three years, Tobe will be almost done with school, the twins will be in secondary school, and our baby Obinna will be ready for preschool." Osas ticked each point off on her fingers.

"So?"

"They'll be old enough for you to have a frank conversation with them. For now, it's all one tremendous adventure. Moving cities to start a new life with two other children. Uncle Wande's kids…" Osas shrugged. "That's all there is to it."

Ada closed her eyes. What was so simple to Osas seemed so complicated to her.

Why couldn't she see it as just a job?

She knew why. As much as she focused on her books at school, she had always been a romantic. She dreamt of giving love and being loved. The deep, fierce, I-can't-breathe-without-you kind of passion that had evaded her all the years with Emeka. Only she had never considered that he might die.

Osas's voice cut through her brooding. "For one million a month, I say, let's call him and hear it from the horse's mouth, don't you think? He must be awake by now." She jumped up and reached for her phone. Ada signalled frantically for her to stop, but it was too late.

When Wande answered, as Ada knew he would, Osas handed her the phone.

Ada hesitated. She felt her dream of love dissipate within her, like the last few grains of sand sinking to the bottom of an hourglass.

Nevertheless, she made an appointment with Wande for the following day.

"There we are, Ada," Osas said when it was over, "done."

One o'clock Sunday came all too soon for Ada. She and Osas rolled their eyes when they heard the knock. This time, he was fifteen minutes early.

When he walked in, his presence filled the room, just as it had during his first visit.

Ada took a minute to assess him again. He had to be in his early forties. He was dressed in similar attire – a kaftan and trousers – but this time in black. His scars were less distracting this time around. For a moment, her gaze locked with his, and even behind his glasses, his dark, piercing eyes bored holes into her.

There was a brief silence as each of them contemplated their next move.

"You called this meeting?" Wande cut through the quiet.

"Yes," Osas said. "We might have been a bit premature, cutting you off the other day. Your proposal caught us off-guard."

His expression softened a little. He clasped his hands in front of him. "I apologise. It was insensitive of me, considering…"

"We want to give you a chance," Osas said. "To hear you out."

"Thank you," Wande said to Osas. Then, he rested his gaze on Ada. "My request for marriage is urgent."

Ada's eyes were cold.

"Let me explain," he went on. "My work involves travel. I have my hand in quite a few pies, and overseeing multiple businesses doesn't give me time for anything else. I married my late wife in my thirties and had my son, Timi. My daughter, Emily, is two years old and arrived ten years later." He hesitated. "Sadly, her mother died giving birth to her."

"I am sorry for your loss," said Ada.

"Thank you for saying that. I am sorry for yours, too." Wande hesitated briefly. "Anyway, I know nothing about raising a daughter. My wife and I were the only children of our parents. We tried to avoid our cousins as much as possible."

Osas and Ada gave each other a look.

"But," Wande continued, "I was in dire straits, and I kept the children with my wife's cousin who lived in the UK. I paid a generous allowance, and she assured me the children were fine. I tried to check up on them every few months."

Ada raised her eyebrows. Every few months? For all Emeka's faults, at least he pretended to make time for his children.

"You disapprove," Wande said, disrupting her thoughts. "Understand, I was under tremendous pressure. Anyway, I made an unplanned trip to see them. I entered the house and…" He licked his lips. For the first time since she'd met him, Ada noted he was less than composed. For a few seconds, Wande did not speak. Then, quietly, he said, "My little girl lay asleep on the couch in the living room."

Ada released her breath slowly. She had imagined much worse.

"I wasn't happy about that. There was no adult in sight. If she had rolled to the floor, she could have given herself a concussion. I picked her up to take her to her room and noticed the bottle of milk beside her, leaking onto the couch. I bent to pick it up and caught an unmistakable whiff of gin."

Ada's eyes widened.

"I found her, the silly woman, in her room, passed out, an empty bottle beside her. If the cook hadn't come in at that very moment, I would have—" His face darkened and clouded his features. "Trust me, she will be paying for that for the rest of her life."

Wande did not look like someone who showed mercy.

Ada asked, "How is your baby?"

"The doctor is optimistic there won't be any lasting damage, but he says it may slow her down developmentally. She needs a bit of extra attention." Wande looked pointedly at Ada.

"So you need a nurse," she said.

"No, I need a wife."

"That you pay."

"Yes. Ours would not be a conventional marriage. The only thing we would share is a name. Money is not an incentive for compassion or care. I paid my wife's cousin handsomely, and I know how that turned out. This needs a higher level of commitment. I require someone with a stake in it."

"What stake?"

Wande cleared his throat. "I know that your husband left you in a crisis with four kids and minimal education, which limits your opportunities."

"How do you know all this?" Ada squirmed under his gaze.

"If you give my children the best care, I will sort out your children's education," Wande said. "I will enrol them in the best school in Lagos with my son. On top of this, I will pay you a handsome monthly salary, including allowances, travel and accommodation. Stability for the next three years."

Ada froze. The question left her lips unbidden, "What happens after three years?"

Wande's expression was unreadable. "You are free to leave. If we are both comfortable with the arrangement, we may renew. If we decide not to renew, the kids will go under the care of nannies. By that time, my son will be sixteen and my daughter five. There are great boarding options I could consider for Emily then."

"Boarding school? For a five-year-old?"

Wande appeared unaffected by her question. Ada felt she was beginning to understand the man in front of her. "Mr Badejo. First, you discuss marriage in such cold terms. Then, you talk about the emotional stability of your kids with almost no feeling. What will they call this new woman? Mummy? Nanny? Aunty or Mrs Somebody? And after three years, I disappear and another woman comes. Really? This is your plan?" Ada's voice had risen in volume. The veins at the side of her head were ready to pop.

Osas, who had been silent during this exchange, turned sharply to look at her friend, hoping her shock was not obvious. She'd never heard Ada speak like this to anyone.

"Children are a lot more resilient than you think," Wande continued, unperturbed by Ada's outburst. "I boarded early myself."

"No wonder!"

The words hung in the air like bullets suspended in motion. Ada and Wande stared each other down, their eyes locked across the room.

"Why marriage?" Osas cut in. "Why not a nanny, as Ada says?"

Wande's laser focus did not budge. "Apart from giving legitimacy to the arrangement, the person needs legal access to my kids in terms of movement – for schools, hospital appointments, visitations, and so on. My absences are extensive. I don't want the hassle of having to approve everything before she can make decisions."

"But marriage is so… big." Ada was still trying to wrap her head around the words.

"It is a contract between two people. That's all. We stick to the terms. We both walk away with what we want." Wande rose, picking up his phone from the side table. "I know you have a lot to…" He swept over both women in a single glance. "Talk about, so let me leave you to it. I need your answer in a week."

"Why so soon?" Ada's head snapped up.

"I have just brought the children back to Nigeria and school starts in January," Wande explained. "I'd prefer this to be sorted out before then. If you refuse my offer, I will need to look elsewhere. I'd prefer not to. Thank you for your time."

"Wait," Osas called out, holding onto her friend's arm. "Why Ada?"

Yes, Ada agreed inwardly. *Why me?*

"Surely other women would jump at the chance," Osas said. "So, why her?"

"Because she comes with a stellar recommendation," Wande said.

"From who?" Ada asked.

He looked at her pointedly. "Your husband."

"What?" The two women reacted in unison.

"Emeka suggested I marry you? For what? Money?" said Ada.

"No," Wande replied. "He said you were a great mother to his kids. The best, in fact. And I need the best."

Ada sank further into her chair. The weight of irony crushed her. Why would Emeka tell a stranger this, only to then report to his sister that he could not trust Ada with his children? What kind of conversation had the two men had about her? She imagined them gathered around their beers, analysing her abilities or lack thereof. She bit hard into her lip. Emeka was still controlling her life even from the grave.

"What else do you plan to gain from this?" Ada's eyes narrowed as she asked Wande the question. Her growing annoyance with him now bubbled over, tipping the lid off her timidity. "You say you want no part of me as a wife? Nothing at all?"

"I can assure you that, even if you were offering, I am not interested." His face darkened. "You do nothing for me."

Ada was silent.

Wande's voice lowered an octave but increased in intensity. "May I remind you that your options are limited. You are unemployable in your current state. You and your sons will end up eating from dustbins on the side of the road before a month is up. I am offering you an easy way out. You have a week to decide."

Ada felt the blood drain from her at his words.

"That's enough!" Osas's voice pierced through her frenzied thoughts. "Ada, don't even think about it. Mr Badejo, I don't care who you think you are. She doesn't need you or your dirty money."

"Osas—"

"Don't let him bully you into something you don't want to do." Osas grabbed Ada's hand, forcing her friend to look at her. "Tobe doesn't have to go to an expensive school. With his fees out of the equation, we can pay for the three boys at any local school. They will survive, and you will never be on the streets, not while I'm alive."

Wande watched them from where he stood at the side of the room. "You talk a good game, Osas Emuerewn."

The sound of Osas's second name coming from Wande's mouth sent a shiver through Ada. How much did he know about them?

Wande took a step towards the two women. "For how long will you carry the burden of a family of five before you become frustrated and even resentful?" He took another step. "How do you plan to support this family, with you on the cusp of losing your job?"

Osas's mouth fell open. Ada gasped.

Wande turned to Ada. "Your friend thinks she is Super-woman, but she is not. She will get tired of you – soon."

Osas bristled beside Ada, but Wande went on.

"Mrs Okeke, I know for a fact that the house you are living in is on the market as we speak. When your friend gets tired of you, and you are homeless, what will you do?"

"Please, stop." Ada's heart pounded with fear. He had no right to make up lies about her life. About Osas's life. "Ndidi isn't like that."

"If you believe that to be true, then you do not know human nature," Wande said. "Work for me, and I can save your house. After all, you will need a place to stay when the three years are up."

Osas finally thawed from her frozen state. She began to wave Wande towards the door. "Mr Badejo, that's enough! Get your insolent, blackmailing self out of my house! You are a Beast, indeed! We do not need you and never will."

Wande clenched his fist at his side, his jaw working furiously.

"You have one week. Goodbye, ladies."

And with that, Wande Badejo departed, leaving both women with their mouths open.

Even after he had been gone for several minutes, Ada still had her arms wrapped around herself.

"I'm sorry I ever put you up to this," Osas said. She came to sit beside Ada and pulled her into a hug.

"What he said… about your job," Ada asked, "is it true?"

"Of course not." Osas rubbed Ada's back. "Forget him, *joor*. He is inventing things."

Ada sighed in relief and thought of her house.

"Good. If he lied about that, then he lied about all of it."

The air conditioning in the Jeep did nothing to cool Wande down. He rubbed his scar – it usually throbbed when he was riled up, but today it was particularly aggravated.

So, the mouse had a backbone after all. Either her late husband had not known her well, or something else was giving her courage. He suspected the latter. Allowing her friend to remain present during the conversation had been the wrong move.

Wande remembered the conversation that had been the catalyst for this whole idea. It happened at an end-of-year event for Badejo Limited's contractors and their spouses. One of the lawyers, Ken Nwafor, had brought Emeka Okeke with him. Wande disliked the man on sight. There was something slimy about the way he smiled, something unsettling about his over-the-top laugh. He had an excessively loud habit of talking to one person but somehow managing to address a wider audience. That night Wande had to spend a customary five minutes with each person before he could make his escape from the event. When he encountered Emeka Okeke, he had politely greeted him the way he had greeted everyone else: by addressing both Mr Okeke and the tall, thin woman next to him, who he mistook for Mrs Okeke.

"No, this is not my wife o," Emeka replied heartily. "My wife is at home doing what she does best."

"And what is that?" Wande asked.

"Mothering, of course." Emeka gave a brash guffaw that caused his entire body to vibrate under his *agbada*. "She may be useless at everything else, but when it comes to those children… Ah, I can beat my chest; I have the best."

That was the only useful thing Wande learned that night. He didn't think of the moment again until he saw two-year-old Emily passed out on the couch. Right then, he made up his mind that he would get her the best mother money could buy.

Out of all the candidates he had considered for the position, he knew Ada was the one he wanted right from the first time he went around to observe his prospects. When he saw her, she was coming back from someplace or other, a baby in her arms and three young boys walking ahead of her. The boys kept turning back to smile at her. Their happiness was unmistakable. He wanted Emily to be able to smile like that. Maybe even Timi too.

But now, the woman was proving stubborn. He had thrown everything he had at her, and yet she still wouldn't budge. He would give her the week. After that, he would need a Plan B.

Ada and Osas prepared lunch, but an ominous undercurrent remained after Wande had left. It was so obvious that even Tobe shook his mother's arm at the table to ask her what the matter was.

Ada rubbed her son's head, embarrassed he had caught her brooding.

"Nothing, my big boy. Mummy has stuff on her mind."

"Is it about that man?"

Ada tried not to squirm under Tobe's intense gaze as he waited for a response. Her firstborn saw too much. He was an old soul. Quiet, but so astute when it came to the feelings of others. Even from an early age, he could read a room. Instinctively, he knew when to stay still and when it was okay to be rambunctious. His tantrums were rare. Ada had always assumed God gave him to her as a first child to console her for the two firecrackers he'd created in the twins.

She smiled. "Why do you say so?"

"Well, I overheard shouting," he said matter-of-factly.

"We were not shouting." Ada glanced at Osas who was busy feeding Obinna.

"How about *talking loudly*?" Tobe stuck his tongue out.

Ada grabbed him and tickled his sides. He let out squeals of laughter, which sparked the twins to join in the ruckus. Their joyful yelps briefly took Ada's mind off her proposal, but it was never far from her thoughts.

Later, while the boys were washing the dishes, Osas squeezed Ada's hand. With a bright smile, she said, "Let's not even consider it anymore. We will work out a plan. *God dey*."

"*God dey*?" Ada wondered. Where was he? She was feeling God had taken a trip and forgotten she existed.

Chapter Four

Later that evening, as Ada and Osas got ready for bed, Osas asked, "What about that list I gave you?"

Ada, failing to recall what Osas was referring to, shook her head.

"You know," Osas prodded. "Goals and dreams?"

Ada's sinking feeling deepened. She shrugged. "I've no idea what I want anymore."

"*Oya*, pull open the drawer beside you. You'll see a notepad and a pen. Take them out and let's work through this."

Osas took out another notepad on her side and paced the room. "I'm thinking with Obinna so young, a regular job may be difficult for you, and paying for a crèche also tough, considering no work yet."

"Obinna's brothers stayed home till they were three. I want the same for him." Osas raised an eyebrow, and Ada waved a hand at her. "I realise things will be different; I'm merely observing."

"What is the balance of the stash?" Osas asked.

Ada tilted her head and smiled at their code. Of course. *The stash*.

The day Ada returned from the hospital after Emeka had been pronounced dead, Osas didn't allow her to bemoan her fate for more than a few minutes before reminding her of pressing practicalities.

"My friend, how much is left in your account?"

Ada, curled into a knot on the couch, looked up at her friend with puffy red eyes. "Just the housekeeping money Emeka signed off last month. Why?"

"Who else knows about his death?" Osas pressed.

"Ndidi and Barrister Ken… They're on their way."

"So," Osas went on, ignoring Ada's confusion, "if they take a flight from Lagos, they will be here within a couple of hours. Come with me." She grabbed Ada's hand and pulled her to the master bedroom.

Ada hadn't been in that room since she'd given birth to Obinna. Emeka hadn't wanted his sleep disturbed, and Obinna had been a fussy baby, so she had moved to the guest room downstairs.

Osas began opening drawers and rifling through the contents.

"What are you searching for?" Ada stood in the corner; her eyes wide as she surveyed the room where Emeka had lain just a few weeks ago.

"While you are crying, I beg you to join me. Be the first person to find whatever needs to be found in this house. Because, trust me, if Ndidi finds anything here, you won't see it ever again."

"Why would Ndidi even be here?"

Osas stopped her searching. "Why were Ndidi and Barrister Ken in Emeka's hospital room that day you met them there? Has anyone told you?"

"No."

"Good. Ada, when you run out of that money in your account, what are you going to do? Where is Emeka's bank? What are his banking details? Does he have savings, investments? Does he have property outside Port Harcourt?"

Ada's lips quivered, and she sat on the bed. "You know he never told me about such things."

"Yes, and when a husband dies in a marriage such as yours, it never bodes well for the wife." Osas's tone was harsh.

"But I am the mother of his sons."

"And my mother was the mother of my father's only child – me. But his brothers didn't care. Why are you behaving as if you don't comprehend how fast things can switch? What if Emeka has another wife outside with four more sons? Please, let's see what we can find before *African Magic* happens."

Ada was reluctant, but Osas ignored her and ransacked the entire room, opening every drawer and bag, checking through every suit pocket. Everything she found – wristwatches, rings, cash – she threw on the bed. Finally, slowly, Ada joined her investigating one piece of clothing at a time.

Then, at last, Osas landed on something. "Yes! Thank you, God!"

"What is it?" Ada asked, her hand deep in one of Emeka's trouser pockets.

Osas straightened and pressed one palm into her lower back. With the other, she gestured to an unassuming-looking satchel, half-open on the floor.

"Most businessmen always keep ready cash in case of emergencies. Come and see Emeka's own."

Ada peered into the satchel and gasped. She had never seen such an amount of money in her life. "What do we do with it?"

"Keep it," Osas said. She gestured to all the other small valuables that lay strewn across the room. "And everything else, too."

"I don't feel right about that." Ada shook her head and stepped away.

"I feel perfect about it. If your conscience can't carry it, I'll carry it for you." Osas packed the small items they found into a small travel bag, zipped it up, and took it away.

Later, after the reading of the disastrous will, Osas handed the bag to Ada without a word.

"368,050 naira," Ada said.

Osas halted. "First of all, how do you know the exact figure? And second, haven't you guys been eating?"

"You know my head and numbers." Ada shrugged. "And you know I have to be careful."

"So, the kids are on Christmas holiday for the next three weeks, so you only need money to eat. I say, keep thirty thousand aside." Osas scribbled on the notepad, then paused, chewing the tip of her pen. "How can we use the balance to make more?" She sat down beside Ada. "This has to come from you. Is there a business you've always wanted to do?"

Ada stared blankly.

"How about cooking?"

Ada scrunched her face.

"But you do it so well." Osas winked. "Sewing?"

"No idea how."

"Is there anything you do enjoy? Maybe we can monetise it."

Ada sat up. "How about those cookies I started making? Less stressful than meals. Do you think people would buy them?"

"That's brilliant. Your cookies are wonderful, *kaii*. I especially love the peanut butter ones. I'll take a few samples to my office. If it takes off, it means Obinna gets to stay home with you while you bake. I can assist with transportation while you grow. It's 2018 – you don't even need a shop, just an Instagram page. Soon, you'll become a franchise: *Ada's Cookies* or *Ada's Creations*." Osas barely paused to breathe.

"Slow down, Osas." Ada's smile wavered.

"I don't mean to overwhelm you." Osas got into bed and pulled the covers up under her chin. "Okay, let's break it into chunks. Tomorrow when you get home, look at the kitchen set-up in your house. With what you have, what can we produce? This will guide us on whether to spend money on more equipment or packaging."

"Okay." Ada was still jotting as much as she could.

"*Abeg*, let's sleep." Osas snuggled under the covers. "Just remember my tithe when you become rich and famous."

Osas was soon gently snoring. But Ada tossed and turned, hope waging a war against fear.

Start a business? She had no idea what she was doing. With Osas already so busy at work, would she really have time to help?

That night, Ada dreamt she had Obinna on her back while the three boys were rummaging through the putrid dustbins at Mile One Market in search of food. The thick flies objected to being disturbed, and their wet antennae settled on their bodies. The rancid stench of garbage made Ada want to pass out. She turned towards the boys just as Tobenna flung the bin open and Ahanna turned aside to throw up.

Ada woke up shivering. No, she would never let that happen. Never!

Chapter Five

The children huddled together on the grass, their eyes darting back and forth as six hefty, rough-looking men emptied out their home, loading all the furniture onto a truck.

Ada saw her children's confusion and felt guilty for not preparing them better. Her sister-in-law, Ndidi, had called the day before to say she had sold the house, and Ada and the boys had to leave immediately. Ada had hoped that when the boys' aunt arrived and saw them sitting out on the lawn it would persuade her to reconsider.

One of the movers yelled for directions and shocked Ada out of her daze. He was struggling to dismantle Obinna's cot, so she stirred and moved to help.

"What do you think you are doing?" Ndidi shouted across the compound. "Don't touch a single thing!"

The mover threw the cot into the vehicle as it was.

Ada approached her sister-in-law, hands clasped. "Sister Ndidi, if I have offended you in any way, please forgive me. Pity us, this is the only home the kids know."

Ndidi continued to yell instructions like a drill sergeant. It would have been almost amusing, if not for the dire circumstances. Small Ndidi, with her round-rimmed glasses perched on her large nose, her wrapper firmly tied around her tiny waist, furiously gesticulated with spindly arms like an orchestra conductor.

"I beg you, give me one more year," Ada pressed.

"Ada, this ship has sailed," Ndidi said. "The new owner wants immediate occupancy. Besides, you don't need a big house. Remember, the boys are coming with me."

Ndidi walked back towards the truck. Ada told the boys to stay put, and followed her, still pleading. "Sis Ndidi, you cannot be serious about obeying the contents of the will. You are a woman like me. Why not give us six months? We will move out ourselves."

Ada became distracted by one of the movers carrying her suitcases. "Sir, leave those. They're mine."

"Throw them in the truck!" Ndidi shrieked. Her eyes flashing, she turned on Ada, advancing menacingly. "What is your own?"

The mover threw Ada a look of pity as he slung the bags into the truck.

"When you came into this house, did you have anything? Down to the underwear you have on, which he bought for you?" Ndidi sneered and spat at her feet. "You came in with nothing. You will leave with nothing."

The barb landed where she'd intended. Ada grabbed her chest. Ndidi's betrayal caused an even sharper pain than her husband's. When the will was read and Ada realised Emeka had signed over every single item of property to his sister, she was disappointed but not surprised. Emeka had called Ada stupid enough times for her to know he would not leave her with any financial responsibility.

But when she heard the stipulation that said that the boys would only inherit if they were in Ndidi's care, it had shocked her to her core. She had challenged Barrister Ken about it, but he and Ndidi had shut her down. The will had been signed and sealed. Even if she suspected foul play, she had no proof.

Despite it all, Ada still harboured the belief that Ndidi would never take her children away. It was preposterous. Ndidi would do right by her nephews.

"Get the boys in the car," Ndidi said.

"Now, why would I do that?" Ada scoffed. "I'm their mother. I'm still alive! Sis Ndidi, you know – and your brother knew – I have never given you a reason to doubt me as a mother."

"This is not about you being a good or bad mother, Ada. I cannot go against the wishes of the dead!"

Ndidi clicked her tongue and shoved past her, making her way towards the boys.

"*Ngwa*, Tobe, Ike, Ahanna…" She addressed the children for the first time. "Your daddy wanted you to come home with me."

The twins ran to their mother and held onto her gown. Only Tobe, who was carrying the baby, remained where he was.

"Aunty, we don't want to go with you," Ikenna answered from behind his mum. Ada gathered herself and put her arms around her boys.

"*Ah ahn*, why now? We are going to Lagos," Ndidi said sweetly, all signs of animosity gone while she had their attention. "That's why I have packed all your clothes and toys. We are moving. This was your daddy's wish."

"Is Mummy coming?" Ahanna asked from the other side.

Ndidi spat on the ground again. "No, just us."

"Then I don't want to go."

Ndidi turned to Tobe. "Tobe, you are old enough to under-stand. Talk to your brothers – this was what your father wanted."

Tobe did not respond. Ndidi fidgeted under his scrutiny and shifted her attention back to their mother.

"Give me my brother's children," she huffed. She grabbed Obinna from Tobe's arms, but Tobe resisted, holding tightly to his brother. Blood rushed to Ada's ears as she ran towards Ndidi, hands clenched, but Ikenna got to his aunt first and punched her in the stomach. Ndidi stumbled, let go of the baby, and fell on her backside, screeching, her face contorted in indignation.

"*Chai, Ike*! You did that to me? Let me catch you next time – I will knock your enormous head."

Obinna was screaming at the top of his lungs, but Ada could see he was only startled. She picked him up and gave him to Tobe, who shrank away, clutching even tighter to the baby. Tobe had never seen his mother so upset.

Meanwhile, Ndidi was struggling to get up, but Ada pushed her back to the ground. "I thought your brother was bad, but now I see that you are both cut from the same rancid cloth."

Ndidi was now crawling backward, fear in her eyes. Ada was gentle and pliable. Who was this crazed woman? The sound of a car pulling up came behind them. Ndidi turned in relief.

Osas spoke something to her across the lawn, but Ada struggled to hear her friend's voice above the din in her head. Within a few moments, firm hands were dragging her away from the cowering Ndidi, who was still shaking.

"Ada, this fool isn't worth it." Even though Ada was right next to her, Osas shouted for Ndidi to hear.

"Who are you calling a fool?" Ndidi tried again to get up. "Why are you poking your nose into other people's business? You won't go and marry?"

Osas faced Ndidi, her five-foot-nine-inch frame looming large over the puny woman.

"Marry like you, *abii*? And what you have at home is a husband? That drunkard? See how you look dry, like life has been sucked out of you? God forbid! I would rather stay single, *abeg*." Osas gave a long hiss. "You won't go to work and stop making yourself a nuisance? What you steal will choke you, I swear."

"Are you cursing me?" Ndidi bristled as she scrambled to her feet and dusted sand off her clothing.

Osas cocked her head and took a step towards her, anger in every word. "Ndidi, *no try me*! You think we don't know you changed that will? You and Barrister Ken? You knew Ada would never give up her children, so you created a legitimate excuse to reap where you have not sown."

Ndidi looked at Ada. "Did you think I would sit and watch you enjoy all my brother left behind? I have given you a choice. If the boys suffer, it'll be your fault." She waved a hand at both women. "I don't have time for either of you. I am going back inside."

She shouted at the men to keep working and then disappeared through the front door.

Ada stood there, shaking. Osas had placed her hands gently on Ada when she noticed the children huddled in a corner. She went over and pulled them into a group hug. "Okay, boys, get into the car."

The children obediently filed into Osas's vehicle. She was making sure they were all seated and buckled when her phone rang. She checked the caller ID; it was her line manager at work. She grimaced and stepped away from the car, lifting the phone to her ear.

"Why would you leave the office like that?" he shouted. "Especially under the circumstances!"

"So sorry, Deji. Family emergency."

"Wrong time for one. The boss was pissed! You know they have scheduled the panel enquiry for tomorrow morning?"

"What?" Osas whispered. "They won't even give me a chance to respond to their trumped-up charges?"

"The man is out for your blood, Osas. That's all I can say. Get back here as soon as you can. I have called in my lawyer. We need to weigh all our options."

"I'll be there as soon as I can."

Osas hung up and took a few deep breaths. The oil and gas industry in Nigeria was a closed circle. If the worst happened, how would she get another job?

She shook herself out of her thoughts. They needed to get out of there.

"Ada," Osas said, "let's leave this place. Where is your stuff?" She looked around for suitcases.

But there were no suitcases in sight. Ada, standing beside the passenger door of the car, surveyed the dusty front garden. Osas watched as heavy tears began to drop from her eyes.

"Ada, look at me…" Osas shook her arm. "Let's go home."

Ada slumped. For a moment, Osas feared she would topple to the ground.

"I am finished," Ada whispered. She doubled over with a quiet cry.

"You are not finished. Stand up, the kids are waiting."

Ada struggled out of Osas's grip. "My children don't have a place to live. I have nothing to offer them. I am finished."

"This is not the time to pity yourself, Ada. Not while we are outside this house. Not with the children watching you. We will re-strategise. We will make a plan."

"Out of what? Thin air? They have taken everything from me!"

Osas's impatience with her friend was beginning to simmer. The phone call from Deji had not helped matters. Osas had to get back to the office and sort out her own mess. If Ada resolved to have a full breakdown now, Osas would not have the energy to solve both problems.

"We can talk about this at home," Osas urged. "Please. Just get in the car."

"I don't want to," Ada mumbled. She began to sink further towards the ground. Osas was unable to steady her weight.

"Please," Osas begged. Now they both knelt on the ground.

"No," Ada refused. "I don't want to. I just want to…"

"Just want to what? Ada, come on."

"Die," Ada said. The word was barely audible. "I just want to die."

Osas didn't speak. She couldn't believe her. After all of this, after everything she had done to pull Ada out of the depths.

Now, the only thing Ada could think to do was throw it away?

"You want to die, Ada, and leave the boys for who?" Osas asked, all her anger and frustration wrapping itself in a torrent of words. "If you are so determined to give up, then maybe you should, *cause your matter done tire me.*"

"Osas…"

"Yes! What makes you so special? Are you the first widow? The first person to have everything taken away from her?"

"But—"

"But what? Lots of other people are going through shit, too. But you don't see us complaining. We get on with it!" Osas turned away to hide the tears that were now fighting their way down her cheeks. "Like this, you are useless," she said. "Absolutely useless."

"I…" Ada's voice trailed off, too caught up in tears to leave her lips.

Osas gave a heavy sigh as she studied the ground beneath them. "You can't always have someone carrying you and lifting you. It is exhausting! Do you hear me? Exhausting!"

The silence between the two friends stretched under the weight of what Osas had said. Both of them heaved for breath as if they had been in a physical battle.

Ada had felt plenty of misery before. She had felt the sharp but familiar sting of Emeka's abuse. She had felt the dull, constant pain of her own failure. But never had she endured such a blow as those words coming from Osas's mouth.

Osas, for her part, wished that she could erase the words as soon as they were spoken. With a few breaths, her head began to clear.

"Ada," she said, "forget what I said. Let's go home. The children need to eat. It's been a traumatic day for them."

But Ada did not budge. "Leave me, Osas."

"I don't have time for this. I am sorry. Do you hear me? I need to get back to the office."

"Then leave!"

At the sound of their exchange, Tobe got down from the car and pushed himself between the two women.

"Aunty Osas, why are you and Mummy crying?" Tobe looked from one to the other.

Osas's phone buzzed again. It was an SMS from Deji: The lawyer's here. Come now!

"I'm serious," Osas said to Ada. "I really need to go."

Now, Ikenna and Ahanna left the car, curious as to the delay. Obinna wailed from the back, so Tobe went back to fetch him.

"Please take a cab home when you are ready," said Osas. "You know where the spare key is. I really need to get back to the office." She tried to hold Ada again, but Ada wrenched her arm away.

"I'll see you later?"

Ada didn't respond.

Osas got into her car, slammed the door and drove off.

They would talk when they got home. She would tell Ada everything, and maybe she would understand.

Back at the house, the twins clutched each other and Tobe tried to put an arm around both. The bedraggled group stood outside the gate under the sun.

As Ada and the children waited for a taxi, Ada replayed Osas's words over and over in her mind. *Useless. Useless. Useless.*

It was a beautiful night. The full moon hung like a delicate ornament against the backdrop of a cloudless navy blue sky. The stars were on perfect display. It was as if every light in the galaxy were pulsing with life.

But Ada couldn't enjoy it. She had been pacing up and down the 2 x 3 foot space of the hotel balcony all night.

For the hundredth time, she stopped herself from calling Osas.

This is why you are exhausting. Do something for yourself! She willed herself to stop shaking. *The boys need you to be strong. You can do this. You can do this.*

It was the lie she repeated to herself as she made the call the next day.

Chapter Six

Wande bent over his laptop, his glasses in their usual position on the tip of his nose, as he read through the merger contract that would establish him as officially the richest man in Nigeria.

He looked up at the sound of a cough. A woman sat in a chair opposite his desk. He had forgotten he had asked for her, perhaps five, maybe ten minutes ago?

"I asked you to come." Wande stalled to gather the errant pieces of his mind. "It must have been important."

Mrs Ronke Coker, formerly Aunty Ronke, was once his father's personal assistant. She had been present when Wande was born and was one of the first people to hold him, as she never failed to remind him. Now, she oversaw his Africa operations. She was the only person in his world who was not afraid of him, and who had the boldness to stare him in the face like she was doing now with open irritation.

Finally, he remembered. "Something has been niggling me."

Ronke waited for him to continue.

"Last time we were in Lagos, I don't recall seeing that horrible man next door."

The 'horrible man next door' was always a sore point with Wande. The man had been selling fresh vegetables for over thirty years out of the house next to Wande's Lagos office. He had refused many times to sell it to Wande; Wande guessed that perhaps the old man was as stubborn as himself.

"Baba Seun? He got hit by a car."

Wande flinched. "Was it bad?"

"Well, he is still in hospital. He may not be able to walk again."

"Who did it?"

"It was a hit and run. They left the poor man in the middle of the road. It was his wife who found him."

Wande tapped his pen on the table. "And the eyesore of a shop?"

"Seun, his son, had to leave university to run it. The mother is focusing on the other children and their father."

Wande nodded. "Call Legal and let them know to make a new offer on the property. Double our last amount."

"Double?" Ronke scoffed. "You've made a very generous offer already."

"Just do it."

Wande tried to shake the image of the stubborn old man out of his mind. Baba Seun was a pain in his side, indeed, but the thought of him in the hospital touched a deep part of Wande. The sale of the property should tide the family through whatever troubles may come.

Without looking up, he said, "Get one of our charities – not connected to our brand – to offer a scholarship to the son. Tuition, board, and a good stipend. He should be in school, not selling stupid vegetables. Arrange something for the other children, too."

His voice was gruff, but Ronke knew better. She suppressed a smile as she made notes. No matter what he tried to portray, he would always be his sweet mother's son.

Suddenly, Wande's desk phone rang. He listened. He smiled. "Send me your address," he said to the caller. "I'll be there in ten mins."

He cut the call to see an inquiring look on Ronke's face. "Change of plans. Move all my meetings back to Lagos. I'm done in Port Harcourt."

He walked over to the coat stand, and in one swoop, pulled his suit jacket over his frame.

"And where are you off to now, sir?" Ronke asked.

"To get married."

"She needs to do what? Why?" Wande's frown deepened. "That's fine. Sort that out. I need her here by 6 p.m."

It was five-thirty in the evening. Wande sat in the office of the officiating minister of the Port Harcourt Marriage Registry musing over what his PA had just told him. They had no luggage and she needed to buy clothes for her children?

He would have his PA find out the details from the sister-in-law later. Right now, he hoped Ada wasn't one of those women who shopped for hours on end. He didn't have that time. Or patience.

He could hear the bustle as the last couple and their families were ushered out of the adjoining hall. The staff were also leaving promptly, as per the arrangement he had reached with the Registry. Not even the individuals who had signed his blank marriage certificate as witnesses knew who was getting married after-hours. Not that they cared. The fat envelope they received with very generous thank you cash was all they needed.

His phone buzzed. The driver and Ada were five minutes away. She was not a shopper, then. Good.

He went into the now-empty hall and walked towards the window to see them arrive. A few hours ago, the hall had been full of couples and their families. Each pairing had been getting married for their own reasons, but he was sure none of the brides arrived all in black as his did just now.

After she got out of the car, he saw her bend down and say something through the window. Then, she approached the building with as much enthusiasm as a prisoner approaching the gallows.

When she saw him, she shrank even more. Wande shrugged it off. What he was offering would be a million times better than anything she could have ever dreamed for herself. He used that thought to stomp down the guilt that rose when he remembered the methods he used to get her there.

Wande waited for her to reach him before acknowledging her presence with a sharp nod.

"Tell him we are ready," he said to his PA, who hurried into the back office.

Wande looked down at Ada and noticed her sway.

"Are you okay?" he asked, but she didn't respond. She swayed again. This time, Wande gripped her arm to stop her from falling on him.

"Hey, what's going on?" He led her to a chair and allowed her to slump into it. "Is this some sort of game to get out of the deal?"

Wande felt his ire rising. He bent down to her level to meet her eye. He wasn't going to be played with. He lifted her face, ready to tell her what he thought of her act.

But her eyes held a pool of tears ready to spill. Wande frowned as her breathing became even more ragged. Beads of sweat rolled down the sides of her face.

The officiating minister rushed in, full of apologies. "I am so sorry for keeping you waiting. Now if you are both ready, we can—"

A look from Wande silenced him. "Give us a few minutes." The minister quickly withdrew.

"Mrs Okeke." Wande frowned. Perhaps it would be better to use her first name. "Ada. What's wrong?"

She didn't acknowledge Wande's hand on her shoulder. He could see she was losing a war with her tears.

Suddenly, a sound erupted from her diminutive frame. It was a wail like Wande had never heard before, and it carried with it such grief and despair that something cracked inside him. She looked so small, so miserable, so lost.

Gently, he sat beside her, put his arms around her, and held her. Her whole body vibrated as she finally burst into tears.

"God! What am I doing? Everything is gone; everyone is gone. I don't know what I'm doing!" She began pounding her chest like she needed to help her heart beat again.

Wande caught her hand and held it. He drew her closer, wrapping his other arm around her, imprisoning her in his embrace. She continued to cry, and Wande let her. He wished he could detach from the moment, but her sorrow sank its claws into him and dragged him down with her.

"Please stop. Don't cry." He spoke softly over her head. "I will take care of everything." Soon, Ada's sobs subsided, and her head rested on his chest as if she were asleep.

After a while, he checked on her, and for a second, he couldn't breathe. She was looking at *him* – not staring at his scar as people often did, or even worse, beyond him, as if to be polite.

She looked at him with those eyes, as if he were whole. He felt the crack widening.

"Do you promise?" Her voice was barely above a whisper. It sounded less like a question and more like a plea.

Wande knew that in business, you never make promises. Even so, he followed the unfamiliar rhythm of his heart as he cupped her face in his hands and answered, "I promise."

The look of death she had worn into the Registry began to disappear, and for one crazy millisecond, he wondered what it would be like to kiss her.

A rap on the door sent Wande jolting up. He poked his head gingerly around the door frame and focused to hear the magistrate's words.

"Are we ready to proceed?"

Wande looked down at Ada. She was gazing at him again. Wande couldn't speak. He didn't like the way his insides were twisting.

"We are ready," she said.

Chapter Seven

The drive from the airport dragged on forever. Ada took deep, sharp breaths. The past twenty-four hours had passed by in a blur.

She must have gone through with the wedding because she had a ring on her finger: a glistening reminder of the insanity she was living through. She was married, again.

Try as she might, she could not bring herself to remember the actual ceremony. She remembered making the call to Wande as she stood outside the Rumuokoro market, trying to calm her distraught boys. Even Tobe, usually so stoic, cried with the twins. As for Ada, she didn't know herself. She was sure she was about to lose her mind when the large black car pulled up.

After that, the haze got worse. The next thing she recalled was walking out of the Registry as a wife. Now, they were all in the car on the way to the Badejo mansion.

Ada kept parroting Osas's words to the boys: *adventure, fun, new home.* It worked on the twins, but Tobe didn't say much. The excitement had knocked all of them out. They sat in a huddle in the back of the car.

The elderly driver looked at Ada with kind eyes in the rear-view mirror.

"Ten minutes more, madam, and we will arrive at Banana Island." He smiled.

Ada nodded, her outward calm belying her inner turmoil. "Banana Island. What sort of name is that?" Saying the name almost pushed a smile through her stiff features.

"I hear the shape of the island from above roughly looks like a banana. Is this your first time in Lagos, madam?"

"Yes," said Ada. The plane. Lagos. Everything was a first.

The driver chuckled and kept his eyes on the road. "Ah, don't let the name fool you. It's the most exclusive area of Lagos."

Ada brought out the new phone the driver had given her on arrival. A gift from Wande, he'd said. She wasn't yet accustomed to it; the phone Emeka had bought her had limited usage, but with this one, she had access to the world. She googled Banana Island – it existed. It was in a suburb called Ikoyi. The article referred to it as a 'billionaire's paradise'. Her breath caught in her throat.

They passed through a wrought-iron gate, and then another, before they entered the estate. The enormous car glided over the wide, tarred street so smoothly, they might as well have been back in the air.

Ada looked out through the window. The blackness of the tar contrasted with the white and yellow road markings; everything looked brand new. There was no sign of the dust that seemed to coat the rest of the city. Palm trees lined the driveway to the estate, dancing in the winds from the ocean nearby. They passed colourful high-rise buildings and terraced houses, all constructed with elegant, modern lines, not an inch of space wasted. A man was jogging with his dog on a leash.

Children cycled on a bike path. Ada shook her head. She had seen these images only in movies.

"Rounding the corner of Love Legacy," said the driver.

A black gate loomed large as they approached. Two armed guards stood to attention as the car whizzed through without stopping.

Ada's eyes widened as the Badejo mansion came into view. The building rose high and wide above them, the stucco walls, an almost blinding shade of white. A fleet of cars lined the side of the immense drive, parked against a tall, thick, perfectly trimmed hedgerow. A fountain decorated the front of the property: six stone lions stood with water gushing from their mouths around its perimeter. The driver was forced to navigate slowly around the masterpiece, as if its owner wanted any new arrivals to take a moment to appreciate its majesty.

Ada tried to wrap her head and eyes around what she was seeing. This was their new home? This... magnificent... She struggled to find a word to describe it. Prison?

She got down from the car on shaky feet and held onto the door while staring up at the lavish building. Could this really be their life?

Marble steps led up to a front door shadowed by two stately columns. While she ruminated, the large door flung open, and Wande stepped out. Ada was glad to see someone familiar. Even his scowl, which seemed permanently etched on his handsome face, brought her some relief.

He wore a navy blue suit with a pale blue shirt. The wind blew the jacket open, exposing a patterned silk lining. He looked immaculate, from his gleaming bald head to the tip of his polished black shoes.

He saw her, but he moved on with a passing glance to the line of cars. An older woman, wearing oval-shaped glasses hurried after him with a notebook, her hair packed tight in a bun.

Ada caught up with them both. "We're here."

Wande turned to her, not hiding his irritation. "I can see that. I'm off to Singapore. I've been waiting for you to show up."

Ada recoiled. Why did he sound like it was her fault the flight had been delayed? More importantly, *Singapore*? Ada shook her head, blinking.

"You're leaving?" she challenged. "What about your children? How will we settle in?"

Just then, Wande picked up a call and spoke a few lines in a language Ada could not decipher. He handed over his briefcase to another driver, who currently stood talking to a woman in a maid's uniform near the entryway to the house. The woman with the glasses doubled back to issue a few quick instructions to them both. Ada inhaled. She had never seen so much action around one household.

Wande finished his brief conversation and faced Ada. The woman with the glasses returned to his side.

"This is Mrs Coker," Wande said. "You have spoken to her on the phone." The lady stepped up and smiled. "She will stay and take you through the house and introduce you to my kids."

"Hello," Ada said tensely to Mrs Coker.

"She will come to check on you and the house every month, and she will give me reports on the state of my children. She has a keen eye. Nothing gets by her." Mrs Coker kept a straight face. She pushed her glasses up the bridge of her nose and smoothed the front of her cream-coloured two-piece suit.

Wande went on, "She handles the finances, and she will sort out accounts with you for salary, household allowance, and things like that."

"What about you?" Ada asked Wande.

"Me?" Wande cocked his head. His eyes narrowed.

Ada drew in a deep breath. "Won't *you* tell me what to do? Or will it all be done through other people?"

The look Wande gave her would have frozen liquid.

"Your role is to mother," he said. "How can I help you with that?"

Wande opened the door to one of his many cars and got inside. He shut the door, ignoring Ada's gaping mouth. The window descended.

"I'm sure you'll get used to it," he said.

Wande refused to look back. He had almost faltered at the hurt expression she wore when he got into the car.

This was how it was going to be. This was how it had to be. A business arrangement only worked when both parties stuck to the principles of the agreement. If he misstepped, it could ruin everything. The children came first. He needed to get this woman out of his system as quickly as possible, and the crisis in Singapore was a great place to start.

The driver got in on the other side, and the car's engine hummed to life. Within seconds, the car sped away through the gates. Ada watched it go, feeling as though she was going to melt into the driveway.

"Ma'am?"

Ada spun around. She had forgotten the elderly woman was still standing there.

The woman smiled as Ada turned. "I know Mr Badejo introduced me as Mrs Coker," she said, "but my name is Aderonke. Please, call me Ronke."

"Ronke, yes, thank you." Ada stretched out her hand and gave a small curtsy. Ronke looked puzzled.

"I am Ada, as you know already. Thank you for the call this morning, and for all your assistance."

"It's my job, Madam," Ronke said matter-of-factly. "May I offer you my congratulations? You are a newly-wed, after all."

Ada gave a dry laugh. "Congratulations?" She twisted the ring on her finger as she glanced at her surroundings. "I do not think so."

Ronke raised one eyebrow. "Well, be that as it may, you are the new Mrs Wande Badejo and the mistress of this empire."

Ada shuddered at the thought. "Do you know when he will return?"

"It's always difficult to say. He keeps his plans close to his chest, but please, do not worry. Everything will be alright," Ronke said gently. "This is Mr Badejo's way."

Everything will be alright. That gave Ada a warm feeling again.

"Come with me," Ronke invited her, walking towards the front door. "Let me welcome you and your children to your new home."

Ada had nearly forgotten the boys until Ronke reminded her they were still in the car. She herded them and their meagre belongings – a single suitcase for them all – onto the driveway.

As they spilled out of the car one by one, they squinted against the gleam of the mansion.

"Mummy, is this our house?" Tobe whispered.

"Yes, I think so." Ada unbuckled Obinna from the car seat.

Ronke then motioned for them all to follow her. The twins sprinted up the marble staircase to the massive double doors at the top. Ronke typed in a code into a panel at the side. There was a click, and she pushed the doors open.

"You can find the door codes in a folder by your bed," Ronke said to Ada. "Memorise them as soon as possible. We don't want details like that lying around."

Ada could only nod as she surveyed her surroundings.

They stepped into an echoing space that was as high as it was wide. Bright polished marble tiles lined the circular foyer. A large, elegant chandelier hung down from a high vaulted ceiling. The rising walls were covered with artwork. *Shiny* was the word that popped into Ada's head.

The family stood at the base of a curving marble staircase. Several closed doors lined either side; Ada wondered what lay behind them.

Ronke's voice broke through her thoughts. "I'll show you to your rooms first, then we can take a tour."

The staircase was so wide and grand that the two adults and three boys could walk up side by side without jostling one another. Two ladies in maids' uniforms were waiting for them on the first-floor landing. They curtsied as Ada and Ronke approached.

"Mrs Badejo, please meet the girls employed to assist you in any way you require. They come vetted and highly recommended by the best agency." Ronke turned to address the girls. "Mary, Cynthia – meet your Madam, your boss's wife."

Ada wanted to meet 'Madam' as well, as she certainly did not fit such a description. But the two ladies were looking at her. They curtsied with their heads bowed low, hiding whatever first impressions of her they may have formed in those few seconds.

"Good morning, Ma," they chorused.

"How… um… are you?" Ada asked. She tried to wrap her head around the fact that she now had nannies to assist her. She didn't even know what to say to them. "Tobe, Ahanna, Ikenna – won't you greet the aunties?"

The boys did as they were told.

"Can we see our rooms, Mummy?" Ikenna's eyes twinkled.

The ladies looked to Ada. Ronke coughed and whispered in her ear, "The girls are waiting for you to tell them what to do."

"Oh… okay." Ada looked at their faces blankly for a second.

What world was this where she was telling other people what to do? They would soon find out she was a fraud, no better than them. In fact, she was them. Ada swallowed hard. "Do… do… you know the boys' rooms?"

"Yes, Ma," they said.

Ada released a sigh. Perhaps this was not so bad.

She addressed the boys. "*Oya*, follow Aunty Mary and Aunty Cynthia. Ahanna and Ikenna, be good, okay? Tobe, I trust you to sort yourself out."

"Yes, Mummy," Tobe said with pride as he followed the twins who were dragging both nannies by the hands, talking nonstop as they went. Ada smiled after them. After a few seconds, Cynthia returned and asked if she could take Obinna. Ada willingly handed him over and shook her arms at her sides, enjoying the relief.

Clearing her throat, Ada leaned in closer to Ronke. She eyed the single suitcase that was looking rather lonely on the marble floor of the foyer. "I will need to shop for the children. We couldn't bring much from Port Harcourt."

"All sorted, ma'am." Ronke smiled. "Of course, the boys will need to check the clothes for fit. Anything that doesn't suit them can easily be exchanged."

"I don't understand," Ada said. "Sorted, how?"

"Yesterday evening, Mr Badejo urgently asked that we stock the children's rooms with everything they might need. He said to hold off buying anything for you so you could choose what you wanted."

Ada felt the beginnings of tears sting her eyes. What kind of man had she married? She did not know what to make of him.

Ada squeezed Ronke's arm. "Thank you very much."

Ronke smiled warmly. As the silence stretched, Ada slowly grew more uncomfortable. Finally, she could no longer avoid the question.

"Where are his kids?"

Ronke gave a knowing nod. "Emily will be in her room. Timi, most likely in the gaming den. Who do you want to meet first?"

"The little girl."

Ronke led the way down the wide hallway. Paintings lined the walls, and potted plants, the floor. The light through the windows was soft and bright.

When Ronke showed Ada into Emily's room, Ada felt like she had entered a picture book: pale pink walls, fluffy pink carpet, large stuffed animals surrounding the king-sized bed, and in the corner, a life-size rocking horse. Soft music played in the background and the mellow hum of the air-conditioning added to the serenity. The room was easily twice the size of the master bedroom in Emeka's 'mansion'.

Ada's eyes instantly fell on the tiny child in a pushchair. Beside her sat an older woman with a pinched look on her face. She rocked the little girl back and forth.

"This is Ruth," Ronke explained. "The agency assigned her strictly to Emily because of her years of experience. Ruth, this is your new Madam."

A third member of staff? Ada found it hard to believe. She had looked after four boys by herself; now, she had not one or two but three staff to help.

The nanny, Ruth, acknowledged the introductions with a curt nod – a far cry from the effusive welcome from the other two ladies. Ada ignored her, caught up in the sight of Emily.

Her frown deepened. The little girl looked so small, not like a two-year-old or even a one-year-old – just an enormous head with legs.

"Ronke, what's the matter with her?" Ada asked.

Ronke's tone was dire. "He said he told you of the state he found her in a month ago?"

"Yes."

"Pure evil," Ronke hissed. "The doctor says there is no damage. But the problem is, she rarely speaks, and she doesn't eat..."

"Doesn't eat?"

"She will only take milk in a bottle. Wande is at his wit's end. The doctors prescribed multivitamins to support her diet. All the people we have employed so far can't seem to do anything to help her. I think he's hoping you'll do the trick."

Ada gasped. "Me? What can I do?"

The sleeping child lay with her head inclined, a scrunched-up blanket in her little fist. The irony of the circumstances didn't escape Ada. She'd always wanted a daughter. When the scan showed Obinna was a boy, she was disappointed. She'd dreamed of a girl with whom to do all the things mothers and daughters did together, one she would protect and make sure no one took advantage of, a daughter she would never sell to the highest bidder just for her own gain. Ada wanted to give her daughter the care and protection her own mother would have given her, had she lived.

Those were her dreams. Now, she had a chance to be a mother to a little girl, temporarily, and she didn't know if she could do it.

Ada sat on the floor to study Emily. Even asleep, the baby looked unhappy.

Ronke sighed. "Since her birth, she has been pushed from one hand to another, each person exploiting her because of her father. Not loved for herself, just…"

Ada touched Emily's forehead, running her fingers through the wisps of hair. "My poor girl." *Me, too, Emily.*

Suddenly, the baby's eyes flickered open, and she held Ada's gaze.

In that instant, Ada felt a connection so powerful she was glad she was sitting down. She knew, as clearly as she knew her name, that she would move heaven and earth for this little one, just as she would for her sons. She swallowed the lump forming in her throat.

Ruth's brusque voice broke the moment. "Please stop touching her." Ada pulled her hand back. "I have just managed to put her to sleep."

Ada looked up, irritated, but was distracted suddenly by the boys calling. She turned away from Emily and stepped out into the corridor just in time to see the twins barrelling towards her. Ada was grateful for the thick carpeting that covered the hallway. What a ruckus her children could cause. Ronke followed Ada out of the room, and Ada motioned to Ronke to shut the door.

"Mummy! We have our own rooms!" Ahanna yelled.

"And we have brand new clothes in our cupboards!" Ikenna joined in.

"Mummy, like, we have new shoes and stuff and toys and everything!"

"I already said that, Ahanna."

"I don't care. I can say it, too. You are not the boss of me!"

"Okay, okay!" Ada burst out laughing at her twins' excitement. They were jumping around her, the potential argument now forgotten.

"Mummy, come and see." Ahanna pulled her hand.

"Give me a few minutes, okay? Play with your new toys and I'll join you soon."

The boys didn't need to be told twice.

Ada still had a grin on her face as she turned to Ronke. "We have brought our noise to this house."

"I, for one, think it's great," Ronke said. "The house needs some livening up."

"If you say so." Ada shrugged. "Now that I have met our princess, where is the prince? Little Timi, right?"

"Little?" Ronke chuckled. She started walking down the hallway. "That lad is his father's son. At thirteen, he is already taller than me. Come this way. He is a permanent fixture on the couch in the game room."

Ronke led the way to the top of the hallway. As they passed closed doors, Ada could hear her sons' screams of excitement.

She longed to join them but had to get this introduction over with first.

"This is the game room. At the end of the hall is the home-theatre room. There's also a lounge with a pool table, a piano, a bar, a few chairs."

"A game room, a theatre area, and a lounge? Mr Badejo takes his relaxation seriously."

"Oh, the irony," Ronke said. "Wande only relaxes when he is completing business deals. His parents were the real entertainers." She paused, a wistful look in her eyes. "Oh, the parties they held here. There were always people in this house, coming or going. That was how Wande met his first wife. She hung around here a lot. So, when his parents insisted he choose a partner, she was already pretty much part of the family—" Ronke stopped herself. "I shouldn't say so much about that to you."

"Don't say that," Ada said. "I would love to hear more. It makes this world seem more human. You talk like you've been around a long time."

"Ah, yes. Sir Wilson and Lady Eleanor Badejo. I started my career straight from university as Lady Eleanor's personal assistant. When Lady Eleanor realised I had a 'good head' as she called it, she moved me to the company's head office, and that was how I began my career." Ronke knocked and swung open the door to the game room.

Ada's eyes bulged. Flashing game machines lined the wall, and there was a mini-bowling alley along the back of the wide space. To the side was a massive screen, a couch, and two bucket chairs. It looked like the VIP section of an arcade.

Sprawled on the couch was a young man. Ronke was right: Timi looked older than his age. Ada couldn't tell whether he had dreadlocks, or if his hair was in a twist.

"Timi." Ronke tried to raise her voice above the din. "Timi!"

He didn't budge. Ada signalled to Ronke – he was wearing headphones. Ronke went over to shake his shoulder.

Timi Badejo jumped, panting. He pulled the headphones off his head and turned around.

"Aunty Ronke, you scared me."

Ronke laughed. "I'm sorry, Timi. I tried calling you, but you didn't hear me."

"That's okay, Aunty. It's all good."

He was a handsome boy, much like his dad would have been without the scar and the frown. Timi smiled with his whole face and had a straightforward way about him as he chatted with Ronke. It was obvious he had good manners, but when his eyes met Ada's, a deep scowl crossed his face.

Ronke hesitated. "Er, Timi, this is—"

"He told me," Timi interrupted. "I know *what* she is."

Ada felt the force of his hostility and steeled herself from stepping back.

"Hello, Timi." She smiled as brightly as she could. "It's nice to meet you. I met your baby sister. I have four boys."

He stared at her, the scowl still etched on his face, a defiant tilt to his head. Ada wondered where the amiable young man she'd seen a second ago had gone.

Ronke coughed to break the standoff. "Ada, let me show you to your room."

Ada went into the hallway, and Ronke closed the door after them.

"I don't understand," Ronke said. "He really is a pleasant boy. Please be patient."

Ada shrugged. "What else can I do? This is strange for all of us. His father should have been here to smoothen things out." She seethed slightly at the memory of his departure.

Ronke patted her shoulder and led her towards the stairs. "What has happened, has happened."

Ada followed Ronke up another flight of stairs.

"This is for the exclusive use of the *Oga* and Madam of the mansion." Ronke winked as they reached the top.

Ada held her breath as the wide-open space came into view. The sitting room was tastefully furnished with lush furniture and finely painted walls. On the left was a kitchenette, a bar, and a dining area with seating for two in the corner. Ada walked through a sliding glass panel that led to a balcony spanning the full length of the top floor.

Strategically placed patio furniture and potted plants gave the place the tranquil feel of an outdoor garden, but the most captivating thing was the view. Ada gasped as she beheld it: the ocean seemed to rise to greet her and go on forever. She leaned against the balcony and inhaled, drinking in the sight.

"The senior Badejos built this as their sanctuary. A place to get away from business and everyone. They designed it so they could spend whole weekends up here without needing to go downstairs," Ronke explained from the doorway.

"It's truly lovely," Ada remarked. From there, she almost felt at peace.

"Let me present to you, Madam's chamber." Ronke walked back into the sitting room and opened a double door on the right.

Ada's mouth dropped open again. Large windows fitted with lace curtains graced the perimeter of the room. The gentle wind blew the curtains ethereally back and forth. In the centre of the room was a king-sized bed with a canopy of more lace draped over its enormous frame. Ada went to the far corner, a small alcove with a bay window and a velvety loveseat. She sank into the plush cushions and peered briefly out at the view of the garden.

Everything was decorated in a colour palette of soft baby pink and white. Ada's favourite colour was pink. The innocent teenage Ada, before Emeka came into the picture, used to imagine sleeping in a place like this. Now she sat at the edge of the room she had always desired.

"It's beautiful, isn't it?" Ronke's voice broke through her thoughts.

"Yes." Ada breathed, but her chest felt heavy. She could build a city with all the pieces of her broken dreams. This would be one more layer. Ada turned to Ronke as she wiped her eyes with her sleeves. "I can't stay here."

Ronke pushed her glasses up her nose. "Why not?"

"Two reasons. One, I am not comfortable being so far from the children, and two…" Ada wrapped her arms around herself as she took in the room's loveliness again. "I should preserve this room for Wande's proper wife. She deserves that respect, whoever she may be."

Ronke looked Ada full in the face, smiled warmly, and nodded.

"Yes, Ma'am. In that case, what would you like to do now?"

Ada hesitated. "I know it's a lot to ask, but could you rearrange the rooms for me? The twins don't need their own; they can share. My first son can have his own space. Then another room for my baby, Emily and me."

"But—"

"Please." Ada reached out to touch Ronke's arm. "It will be good for Emily and me, and the boys will be close to us."

Ronke jotted the changes in her book. "Noted. I'll sort it out today. Unfortunately, ma'am, I will shortly need to bid you goodbye. There is another matter I need to attend to off the site."

The thought of Ronke leaving caused Ada to break out in a sweat. Ada didn't know the rules of this new world, and she had no idea her responsibilities. What would it be like without anyone around to guide her?

Ada followed Ronke downstairs as she listed a few final pointers. Ada wanted to grab her and beg her to stay, to beg her to show her what to do, but Ronke was already walking out the front door, telling her she would see her tomorrow. As the door glided shut with a gentle click, Ada wanted to cry, but then she heard a scream.

Chapter Eight

Ada knew it was Emily immediately. She ran in the direction of the cry, following the sound to the kitchen. The cook and the nannies loitered at the edge of the room. One of the nannies cradled Obinna in her arms. They all watched Madam Ruth, who sat on a bar stool with Emily trapped between her beefy thighs. The little girl's head was pulled back, and Ruth was pouring a thick substance down her throat. Ada guessed it was pap.

Emily sputtered, trying to spit the porridge out of her mouth, but her struggles only made her choke, and she coughed in pain. Once her airways were clear, she let out a blood-curdling scream, and Madam Ruth repeated the process. Ada remembered older women in the village doing this to children who refused to eat. It was a torturous process; she wasn't going to let Emily go through it.

"Stop it, right now!" Ada grabbed Emily from between the legs of the surprised Madam Ruth. One of the nannies stepped aside and pointed in the direction of a large sink.

Ada stripped Emily of her clothes and grabbed a cloth to wipe the little girl down. Emily's screams subsided, but her lips curved downwards, her little body pulsing with aftershocks from her ordeal.

"It's okay, princess, don't cry. It's okay," Ada cooed.

Soon, Emily stopped shivering, but she continued to whimper. Her enormous eyes stayed fixed on Ada as Ada cleaned her. Once finished, Ada lifted her out of the sink. Emily lay with her head in the crook of Ada's neck and gradually quieted as Ada rocked her.

A shuffle near the doorway caught Ada's attention. She saw the faint outlines of her boys in the archway. With a quick wave, she shooed them away, but they only shrank back a few inches.

Once Emily was quiet, Ada faced Madam Ruth. Ruth was large and confident in the corner, while Ada was full of indignation, her concern for her new charge giving her courage. The two women squared off like lionesses in the middle of the kitchen.

"What were you doing?" Ada asked.

Emily, seeing the towering presence of Madam Ruth, tightened her grip around Ada's neck.

"My job, Ma-dam!" Ruth dragged out the last word with disdain.

The two nannies glanced at each other. Obinna fussed quietly.

"How will this help her to enjoy food?" Ada questioned. "Besides, what nutrition is in *ogi* that you will make her suffer so? What if she choked to death?"

"What do you take me for?" Madam Ruth bristled. "I have over forty years' experience in childcare, having to deal with others like her. She is at death's door; the situation requires extreme measures."

Her ominous words sent a chill up Ada's spine. Ada pinched the bridge of her nose, biting her bottom lip.

"How about we try a different way? What worked for three hundred children may not work for her."

Madam Ruth's cat-like eyes narrowed under hooded lids.

She took a menacing step forward.

"The insult!" Her scowl deepened. "You imagine you can do better, don't you? Think of other ways?" She sneered. "Well, you do it, then!"

Ada lowered her gaze and stepped back. "Madam Ruth, that's not what—"

"I refuse to work in an environment where people question my methods and undermine my authority." She glared at Ada. "Especially someone who has been here only an instant."

Ada drew a sharp breath. "No, no, wait… I meant nothing by it. I'll need your help with her."

"You should have considered that before waltzing in here like Superwoman, telling me how to do my job!"

With that, Madam Ruth pushed past the two cowering nannies, yelling in her thunderous voice as she stormed up the stairs, "Whatever happens to her, her blood is on your head!"

Ada sat heavily in the nearest chair with Emily on her lap, all the fight gone from her. She refused to cry in front of the children and staff, but it was a struggle. What had she done?

"For what it's worth, I believe that was the right thing, Madam."

Ada looked up to find the owner of the gentle voice. It was the cook. He was not a young man, as she'd thought earlier, but he carried himself almost regally with a straight back and a lifted chin.

Ada gave a weak smile.

"I really don't know what to do. She is the expert." Ada rose, panicked again at the enormity of the implication if Madam Ruth was to leave. "Maybe I should run after her? Beg her to stay?"

"Madam, wait." Michael's gentle smile was reassuring, and Ada sat back down with Emily. "See how the little one clings to you? It is a good sign. In the time that lady has been here," he said, jutting his chin in the direction in which Madam Ruth left, "I have not seen one ounce of affection from her. And when she does that… that horrible process she does once a day, my heart always broke for the little one. I am glad her ordeal is over." He placed his hand on his chest and gave a slight bow. "My name is Michael. I am the chef of the Badejo residence. It is a pleasure to meet you, Madam, and welcome."

"Please, call me Ada." She continued to stroke Emily's back and arms and looked down at the broad top of the little one's head. "What do I do with her?"

"I'm assured you will find a way." Michael patted Ada's shoulder and gave her a mischievous grin that made his face look younger. He returned to the steaming pots on the stove.

A clarity from deep within suddenly surfaced in Ada's mind. Emily was a baby like any other. Loving her would be a good start – they could take it from there. She tightened her arms around the baby, allowing the warmth of her tiny body to seep into her soul.

Now that the brouhaha was over, her children braved the kitchen. Tobe stepped in first, wearing a cautious expression.

"Hey, guys. Come and meet your…"

Your sister? Your friend? The boys did not know the details of the arrangement. There was no need to confuse them more.

"Come over and meet Emily," she said finally.

"Ikenna and Ahanna, come," Tobe urged his brothers as he stood behind his mother and peeped over her shoulder.

The twins came reluctantly. The more they studied the bundle in their mother's arms, the less scary the baby seemed. Soon, they were holding Emily's hands.

"Can she play?" Ikenna asked.

"I'm sure she can," said Ada. "But you must be gentle, okay?"

Ada placed Emily on the ground, uncertain of her physical capabilities. Emily held on for a minute, then took a step. The twins erupted in cheers that startled her, and she fell and let out a wail. Ada scooped her up in her arms again.

Ahanna gave an exaggerated eye roll. "Girls," he muttered. Ikenna shook his head in disappointment.

Ada smiled, her eyes crinkling at the corners.

Michael rummaged around his side of the kitchen, taking things out of the fridge. Ada took a deep breath and turned to the nannies, who still waited silently for instruction at the edge of the room with Obinna.

"Mary and Cynthia, right?"

They nodded. Mary was the chubby darker one with an underlying Yoruba accent. Cynthia was lighter in complexion and slim, with a boyish, close-cropped haircut.

"Thank you for helping me with Obinna," Ada said.

"Ah, no problem, ma, he is a good baby. No crying at all," said Mary, boosting Obinna in her arms.

Ada paused. "When did you ladies start work here, anyway?"

"We were both employed on the same day, ma," Cynthia explained. "We arrived from the agency last week."

So, these ladies did not know her or anything about her. They didn't know she was Emeka's wife, who had never been allowed to voice her opinion; they didn't know she felt completely out of place in this house and had never had anyone serve her before. She could start with a clean slate and be herself – whoever that was.

"To be honest, I have never had help before, so I don't know what to say to you, ladies." Ada shrugged, ruefully. "But if you watch me and pick up on the routine, then we will be okay. For me, one thing is paramount: the children before anything else. Before a clean house, before burning food."

"Yes, ma," they agreed.

"Good." Ada grinned. "Luckily, my firstborn," she winked at Tobe, "does not need supervising, but my twins…" Ada closed her eyes and gave an exaggerated heave. "May God help us."

Both ladies chuckled, and even the twins laughed at their mother's drama.

"Obinna, in your arms, will be five months soon. Mary, please sit, you are carrying Obinna. Cynthia, can you take the twins outside? Just allow them to run around. Let them get tired a little."

Cynthia smiled and nodded. She urged the twins towards the door. Tobe followed, curious to explore.

Ada held up Emily in her arms and put her in a sitting position on her lap, facing her.

"Little madam, so what is your problem with eating? If I cook and you don't eat, we will fight o…" Emily's expression was deadpan. "Oh, no response for me?" Ada laid Emily on her back across her lap and blew hard on her tummy. Emily shrieked in delight, eliciting a smile from everyone in the room. Ada repeated this a few times and laughed along with her. Michael stopped his meal preparations for a minute to enjoy their play. When he returned to his work, he, too, was grinning from ear to ear.

When they took a break from the game, Ada allowed Emily to curl up in her arms. She was so light, not much heavier than Obinna. As Ada rocked her body and Emily's eyes closed, Ada studied her. Once she looked past Emily's size and hairlessness, she could see the baby had pretty features. She was not as dark as her father or brother, and she had a cute nose and full lips. Her face did not fit now, but it was nothing a little extra flesh couldn't fix.

"Okay, Emily, you rest now. It's been a tough day." Ada gave her a tiny peck on her forehead. "Emily, Emily. Does she have a local name, Mary?"

"No idea, ma."

"Hmm, Mary, are you Yoruba?"

Mary nodded.

"What do your people call your first daughters?"

"Nothing specific, ma. You just give them the name what you want."

"Oh. In Igboland, only the first daughters can bear the name Ada." She turned to the sleeping Emily and smiled. "And you are the first daughter – that means you are my namesake. You'll be my little Ada."

Ada had just dropped the sleeping Emily into bed when the intercom sounded. Michael asked if 'Madam' would like a late breakfast, which reminded Ada that they hadn't eaten all morning.

"Thank you, *Oga* Michael. And, remember, it's Ada." Ada would not allow a man old enough to be her father to address her as 'Madam', regardless of her so-called status.

When she got downstairs, the boys were waiting with Michael. Ada instructed everyone to wash their hands.

"*Oga* Michael, where is the food?"

"All set up in the dining room, madam." Ada gave him a mock glare. He smiled. "I mean, Ada."

Ada stood at the entrance to the dining room, where three chandeliers hung over the length of a table that could easily seat over twenty people. Michael had set the food at one end. Silver cutlery and crystal glassware graced each glass plate. It was a delicate spread unlike any she had experienced.

Ada made a quick decision.

"I'd prefer for us to eat in the kitchen, please."

"The kitchen?" Michael sounded confused.

"Don't be angry – this looks incredible, but what if we spilled food or broke something? I would be too worried to appreciate your delicious food. Please?" Ada smiled sweetly.

Michael threw his head back and laughed. It was a laugh that pulled Ada in and embraced her. She knew she was going to like this man. "Your wish is my command." He bowed with a flourish.

"Children, *oya*, grab your plates, let's move ourselves," Ada said.

Soon, everyone was seated. Even Emily had a plastic plate and spoon, her eyes dancing at all the commotion as everyone settled around the marble-topped island.

Someone's missing, Ada thought, and her heart sank. She knew she had to do the proper thing.

"Where is Timi?" she finally asked.

"He hasn't come down, ma," Mary said hesitantly.

"Please call him. Let's all eat together," Ada said. She asked her boys to wait to eat, which was met with a grumble from the twins and some fidgeting even from Tobe.

Mary rang Timi on the intercom. Five minutes later, he finally arrived. He surveyed the kitchen but stood by the door with his arms crossed. Ada thought again how very much like his father he was.

"We are having a late breakfast. Would you care to join us?" Ada hoped her smile would help him let down his guard.

Timi, ignoring her, gave Mary a fixed stare. "Must I eat here?"

Mary averted her eyes.

"Timi, come and eat with us." Ada strained to hold her smile in place. "Let us all get to know each other."

"What makes you think I want to know you?" His words were clipped, his British accent giving them more of an edge. "To know any of you. I didn't ask you to come here."

He turned and left the room.

Ada recoiled. Her smile dropped at the sound of Tobe's intake of breath beside her. Ahanna's mouth hung open. What worried Ada most, however, was the look of admiration on Ikenna's face.

Ada drew everyone's attention back to the meal and tried to keep the levity, but the incident had doused the excitement, and her heart wasn't in it. Ada didn't even notice when Emily took each piece of her chopped egg and watched in delight as they fell to the ground one by one from her highchair.

Timi's attitude had created a fresh problem to occupy Ada's mind. What were the parameters for disciplining Wande's child? Should she call Wande to report Timi's behaviour? So soon?

She decided she would give him a little more time.

Ada smiled as the twins zipped back and forth between rooms, jumping on and off the beds. Normally, this would earn them a reprimand from her, but not today. After the sleepless night and the early morning trip, the shock of Wande's departure, Timi's hostile reception, the state of Emily, and the enormous house that everyone expected her to take charge of, she was hiding out in the twins' room to avoid doing anything else.

The rooms, just like the hallway, had wall-to-wall carpeting and a warm feel. Cosy. Ada had never understood how one could choose cold tiles in a bedroom, but as trends changed, Emeka had insisted they renovate their house, ripping out carpets and replacing them with ceramic flooring. Ada had hated it.

Tobe walked in, and the twins flew on him at once to play-wrestle. As usual, Tobe pushed them off, and the twins climbed on him again and again.

Ada thought it best to help him this time. "Ikenna and Ahanna, that's enough, now. Leave your brother alone. Tobe, how do you like your room?"

"Mum, it's amazing." He got up to sit beside her, his smile wide. "You say one person owns all this?"

"Yes, my boy."

"Wow. He must be rich!"

Ada laughed.

"Mummy, let us show you outside," Ikenna, her bossy one, said loudly.

Ada knew she couldn't hide forever, and she needed to familiarise herself with their new home.

"Okay, but please, let's be careful not to break anything. Remember, you are not the only children here."

"Yes, that other boy is big. Bigger than Tobe." Ikenna stood on his tippy-toes, raising his hand as high as he could and laughing as he dodged Tobe's arm, which was aimed at his head. "But, Mummy, is that little girl sick?"

"She looks funny and weird…" Ahanna said, scrunching his nose.

Tobe stopped him. "You shouldn't use words like that for a person. How would you like it if someone called Obinna weird?" He turned to Ada. "She is not well, right, Mummy?"

"Yes, and hopefully while we are here, we'll help her get better. Come on, let's walk around and see the place."

They followed a brick path through the backyard lined with trees, neat shrubs, and flowerbeds. The back area was set up like a stadium, with an Olympic-sized swimming pool, a tennis and basketball court, each complete with spectator stand. The curving walkway led to a *lapa* with a thatched roof. They peeped in to find a bar with a fridge-freezer for drinks and a barbecue set. Right at the back of the property was a well-equipped gym with showers.

The front lawn of the building was a party planner's dream. Immaculately trimmed hedges lined the oval-shaped expanse of perfect green lawn, punctuated with rose bushes in deep reds, yellows, and pinks. Ada could easily imagine the glittering events that had taken place there, just as Ronke described.

Ada and the boys waved to two gardeners who were hard at work. One was pruning the roses, and the other was mowing the grass.

"Mummy, this is as large as the soccer field at school," Ikenna said as he zoomed past her, pretending to be an airplane. Tobe and Ahanna were doing somersaults across the lawn. The twins urged her to join in, but Ada stood back and watched. She wished she could catch a little of their excitement, but she was filled only with a cold sensation of dread.

Two days ago, they had been in Port Harcourt being thrown out of their house. Today they were… what? Where? What kind of dream was this? A nightmare or a fairy tale? Ada couldn't be sure.

The twins had worn themselves out with all their running around. Even Tobe, who usually liked to read before bed, was asleep before Ada left his room.

Ada rolled around in bed. Her body was tired, but her mind was restless. She smiled at the little bundle beside her. Emily lay on her back, her legs sprawled, her face towards Ada's. Dried milk had crusted in the corner of her mouth, but Ada decided not to wipe it off in case it woke her.

"You will run and play like the big boys. So help me God," Ada whispered to the sleeping figure. She marvelled at how one could have a connection with another human so quickly.

But then her mind went to Timi, and her mood deflated. He had refused to come down for dinner, saying he wasn't hungry, even though Ada had later seen him with a packet of biscuits at bedtime. Timi reminded her of his father, and annoyance burned in her veins.

How could Wande do this? Drag her across the country and just leave her to fend for herself? Ada took a deep breath; anger wasn't going to help. Wande would most likely return in a few days. She wasn't sure if that was a good or a bad thing, and she decided not to think about it.

Ada checked on Obinna in his cot and watched the steady rise and fall of his chest, his cheeks squashed against the mattress. She still felt guilt over him. Ever since his birth, the family had been subjected to one drama or another. She had not been at peace long enough to enjoy him as a baby.

Ada stroked his head. "Obinna, I am so sorry. Bear with me this last time." She readjusted his covering before heading out to the balcony.

Ada swung the double door open and smiled as the breeze caressed her. There was something about the natural breeze that an air-conditioning unit could never achieve. Ada inhaled, enjoying the fresh air, stunned by the absolute silence. She gazed at the majestic trees near the building and imagined their branches reaching towards her in welcome.

Mesmerised, she stretched out her hands to see if she could touch their leaves when the piercing sound of sirens cut through the night like an electric saw.

Chapter Nine

The blare of sirens was coming closer and growing in intensity. Someone was banging on a door downstairs, and the shrill ringing of a doorbell added to the chaos. Before long, the babies woke up screaming.

Back inside the bedroom, Ada's phone buzzed on the nightstand. She reached for it, struggling to keep the headset steady as she ran towards the door. The boys!

Bewildered, they stood outside their rooms in the hallway. When they saw her, they rushed towards her. She signalled to them to get on the floor with her. Even Timi obeyed.

When she looked at the caller ID on the phone, she sighed with relief. Ronke's voice came in strong and urgent: "Don't panic, Ada."

"I don't know what's going on o. I can hear people shouting and noise everywhere. What do we do?" Ada couldn't keep the tremor out of her voice.

"It's okay. It's the security unit doing a check – an alarm went off. If they cannot gain access in ten minutes, they have orders to get in by any means necessary."

"What? How can we be sure it's them?"

"They called Wande who contacted me. Open up for them, please. They need to ensure everyone is safe."

Ada left the boys in a huddle on the carpet. She ran down the hallway and, peeping down the stairs, saw Michael walking towards the front door. When he heard her footsteps on the staircase, he gave her a thumbs up and opened the door.

Over the next few minutes, burly men dressed in black and armed with guns stormed into the house, slamming open doors, searching everywhere. A tall, broad-shouldered man stood apart from the rest. Ada concluded he must be the leader.

"Madam, can you please bring out the children? I would prefer if everyone were in one place."

The older boys came down on shaky feet; the twins, still disoriented from sleep, followed like tiny lambs. The babies were still crying. One of the armed men bundled them all into the library.

"What's happening?" Ada asked.

The man held up a finger. The hiss of multiple voices came through his walkie-talkie.

"I apologise, madam," he said when finished. "We received an alarm alerting us to a security breach on a second-floor balcony."

"Wait a minute. Second floor? That's where the children and I are. What alarm? I heard nothing."

Ada listened while he explained how the silent system worked, intermittently breaking off to speak to an agent clearing the grounds. Trying to understand his technical jargon with her tired brain was like trying to catch the wind with her hands.

Spotting her unfocused gaze, he slowed. "Madam, I will explain everything to you once I am done."

It took almost an hour for the team to give the all clear. By that time, the kids were all wired with excitement at the thought of men in the house with guns. Michael saved Ada's sanity when he appeared with cookies and juice packets, which distracted the children for a while. Even Timi forgot to be disagreeable.

After the process was complete, Ada requested the nannies put the children to bed while she had a conversation with the security chief.

"So, you said that I am housebound after 9 p.m.?" she clarified.

"Not completely, ma'am. We activate the alarm at 9 p.m. by default. It covers the outside perimeter of the building. In every room, behind the curtain leading to its balcony, is a security box. The system generates a different code daily and sends it to your app. You can use that code to deactivate the alarm as needed. Three of us have access to the codes: me, your husband, and you."

"Me?" Her eyebrows lifted.

"Yes, ma'am. Your husband updated your details, and we cleared you for access. You should have downloaded the app already."

Ada wished she could disappear. What kind of wife didn't even know the basics of her home-security system? She remembered Ronke mentioning the security folder, which she had neglected to review.

"I haven't. This whole thing is new to me." She forced a laugh as she massaged the back of her neck.

The chief assured her, "That's okay, ma'am, happy to help. We prefer to err on the side of caution."

Ada didn't know whether this made her feel safe or even more exposed.

"Just a question." She hesitated. "Why so much security? Are there many break-ins in this area?"

"No, there aren't, but we don't want anyone getting ideas. Your husband is a very important man."

After the security team left, the house was quiet once again.

The events of the night had strung out Ada's last nerve. While she had felt hopeful and confident only an hour ago, now she crawled under the covers, despondent, fear of the unknown opening a hole in her heart. Who was she fooling? Maybe she was as dumb as Emeka always said. All of that nonsense had taken place just because she'd been too distracted to learn the fundamental rules of the house.

Besides that, there was no one to talk to about any of it.

Painful sobs shook her whole body. She held them in, not wanting to wake the children. She pressed her hands over her mouth, squeezed her eyes shut and curled into a tight ball. God seemed further away from her than ever, but at this moment, she hoped with all her heart that He was listening.

"Father, can you hear me?" she whispered into the night. "I don't know what I'm doing. If you remember me, please help me. Don't be far away, I beg you."

Soon, a quiet presence enveloped her. *Give all your worries and cares to me, for I care about you.*

The familiar scripture came like a balm to her wounded heart. Emotions she'd tried to bury in the past few months pushed up to the surface, raw and painful. She held nothing back. All her feelings of abandonment, loss, fear, resentment, disappointment, and anger, she brought to His feet. It had been a long time since she had last prayed, but Ada unburdened her soul completely.

Hours later, she woke to the sight of large, round eyes peering down at her.

"Little Ada? Are you awake?"

Ada spread her arms, and silently, Emily crawled into the space. Ada savoured the warmth of the little girl's body.

"My little Ada, did you have a good night? Are you wondering what I'm doing in your bed?" Ada giggled. She felt lighter.

For a second, the memories of last night's escapade came rushing at her, and she wanted to hide back under the covers. But then, she remembered her time of prayer, and her emotions shifted from embarrassed to hopeful. There was even joy simmering beneath the surface.

Ada got up with Emily in her arms and twirled the little girl in the air, laughing.

"Father, thank you for a new day." She pulled Emily in close and breathed the words into Emily's shoulder. "You are so so kind, merciful. Please help me make good decisions for the family. Give me wisdom for this little one and Timi. I pray for my boys. Help them settle in. Amen."

No sooner had the prayer passed Ada's lips than Ikenna and Ahanna raced past her room, screaming about who was faster.

"Well, they seem right at home," she murmured. She caught sight of their flight down the stairs and shook her head. She would need to caution them against such speed.

Still holding Emily with one arm, she returned to her room and peeped into Obinna's cot, where he slept soundly. She left the door ajar in case he cried and went in search of the twins. Emily clung on with her legs wrapped around Ada's waist and her head nestled in her neck.

The twins and their nannies were out on the front lawn. The two ladies were busy trying to catch the boys as they zigzagged between them. Poor Mary. Ada laughed out loud. She always thought of the twins as the spice in her life: Ahanna the salt, and Ikenna the pepper.

"I hope you're enjoying your morning exercise," she called out as she approached.

The twins squealed in delight, "Mummy, Mummy!"

Ada sat on the grass quickly, bracing for impact. True to form, they landed on her, ignoring the fact that she had Emily in her arms. The sudden weight startled the baby, who let out a piercing wail.

Ahanna, suitably contrite, got up from his mother's lap.

"Sorry, sorry, sorry, baby."

Ikenna refused to placate Emily and instead teased her with the cry-baby song. *"Cry, baby, you no go cry pass your mother."* Ikenna started clapping to the beat and his brother joined him, gleefully dancing around the crying baby.

"Stop it, boys," Ada warned. "That's not nice."

But she couldn't help herself from smiling above Emily's head. Emily, not receiving the attention she desired, cried even harder. This made the boys take their singing and clapping a notch higher.

Emily was no match for the duo, but her cries soon died down as she focused her attention on the twins. She angled her head, first looking at one brother, then the other, the corners of her mouth turned down in a perfect semicircle. Ada imagined Emily's little mind struggling to make sense of what she was seeing: the same face, the same hands, the same person, but in two places at once.

Smiling as the boys clapped and danced, Emily now arched her back, trying to copy them. Ikenna and Ahanna, oblivious, collapsed in a heap, laughing. Emily joined in as the three adults looked on in wonder.

Mary nudged Cynthia, and the nannies stared. In the entire week they had been there, Emily had shown only two emotions: misery or nothing. But in the past twenty-four hours, she had laughed twice.

Ada looked at Emily, an idea sparking in her head. *God, please let it work.*

She hurried them all into the house for breakfast. Michael was already at his workstation, concentrating on an electric mixer. Diverse aromas filled the kitchen. On the counter was a breadbasket with toast and croissants, along with a bowl of scrambled eggs and another dish laden with chopped fruit. Dainty glass bowls held homemade jams. Another tray displayed pork and beef sausages arranged in a line like soldiers. All the dishes were garnished with sprigs of green.

The boys shrieked at the sight of the spread. Ada couldn't get over the fact that breakfast was ready, and she'd had nothing to do with it. Her whole body wanted to dance.

"*Oga* Michael, this is amazing, but you really don't have to go through all this for us." Her fingers trailed on the tablecloth as she admired the intricate details of the lace covering. "We are simple people. Bread and eggs on a plate works fine."

Michael smiled. "This is how I have done it for forty-five years. My presentation is as important as the taste. The talented Chef Lawrence Barnes, God rest his soul, under whose tutelage I had the pleasure of learning, would roll in his grave if I served you on a plate like an animal." He wagged his wooden spoon. "You laugh, madam, but it's serious business. My job is to create the magic and display the spread, and yours is to enjoy."

Ada's smile didn't leave her face as she curtsied. "And we will carry out our duty to the best of our ability. But what about the excess? We can't finish all of this." She waved a hand over the table.

"That's okay. We cater for the security guards and drivers, too. This is what the senior Mrs Badejo instructed when she was alive, and we have done it that way for over twenty years. All her staff ate what she ate from her kitchen." Michael's smile dipped. "Unless you would like to change things."

"Of course not!" Ada rushed to assure him. "I agree with it wholeheartedly."

It relieved her when he smiled again and went back to mixing a pancake batter.

Ada turned to the nannies. "Mary, please call Timi and the other children to come and eat. Cynthia, can you please stay with Obinna upstairs in case he wakes up? Little Ada and I are going to try an experiment." She scrunched her nose at Emily who tried to copy her.

Within a few minutes, Mary was back and stood at the door, the boys squeezing past her as they ran in.

"Timi says he doesn't want to come. He asked if I could bring his food to him." Mary shuffled, avoiding looking at her boss.

"Is that what you've been doing for him?" Ada glanced from Michael to Mary.

"No, ma."

Ada frowned. "Okay, go ahead for today."

Emily's highchair was positioned right beside Ada, who chopped up a few pieces of sausage for Emily, but Emily picked up each piece and dropped the food to the floor.

It was time for Ada to put her plan to work.

"Sing with me, boys," she instructed.

"What should we sing?" Ikenna asked. "*Cry, baby*"?

She shook her head. "No, please." She rubbed Emily's cheeks. "Little Ada, what do you want us to sing for you?"

Emily stared.

Ada was determined. "Boys, drum for me."

Ahanna jumped right in and began a rhythmic beat on the table. Ikenna started clapping. Almost at once, Emily grinned and moved with them until she was smiling.

Ada was ready. She scooped a tiny piece of egg into Emily's open mouth. Emily was not expecting it and looked as though she was about to cry, but the boys made more noise to distract her. Emily frowned, but the tiny scoop of egg stayed in her mouth.

Ada took Emily out of her chair and held her loosely to calm her, while the other children resumed eating. Saliva poured down Emily's lips, but the egg stayed there. Ada used a kitchen towel to clean out her mouth.

One bite. One bite was something. The magic may not happen at once, but it would happen eventually.

Ada's plan developed further as she held Emily over breakfast. She would reduce Emily's bottles from four to two a day to allow her to get hungry. That would make for an effective transition.

When Ronke arrived around noon, Ada was so relieved, she wanted to hug her like an old friend. They sat in two chairs in the foyer to catch up, where Ada recounted the drama of the night before, and Ronke apologised profusely for not fully explaining the significance of the alarm system. Soon, the hilarity of the situation had both women holding their stomachs laughing.

Ronke wiped tears from her eyes. "Thank you for being such a good sport."

"I'm not, really," Ada said. "But this whole thing is too big in my head for me. I have left it to God. I will be taking one step at a time, and I won't stress myself anymore to get it all perfect at once."

Ronke's laughter subsided. "You're right, my dear. But I wish you didn't have to do it alone. Is there anyone you would like to invite over for a while? A relative, perhaps?"

Osas's face came to mind, but Ada quickly shut down the thought and emotions that came with it. It was the only way she could cope. She'd explained everything up until that point in the long voice note she left for Osas – she would do the rest of it on her own.

"No, no one."

Ronke nodded. "Very well." She looked hesitant and finally said, "Just so you are aware, I have booked an appointment with the school tomorrow. The kids have been scheduled for assessments. The school year starts on Monday. Luckily, no one says no to a request from Wande Badejo, so they will be allowed to enrol."

Ada's eyes widened. "Oh, okay." Admittedly, she hadn't thought of the new school year yet. "Will they need to study? We haven't prepared—"

"There's no need. This assessment is to see if there are any areas the children may struggle with since it's a different educational system. You'll get the results the same day. You also get a tour with the principal when you get there. Special circumstances and all that."

"I'm guessing he doesn't act as a personal guide for every new family," Ada noted wryly.

"Now, you're getting it."

Ronke pulled out her phone and began to scroll through it. Ada watched and chewed on her lip, wondering how she was going to bring up the next topic. When Ronke looked up again, Ada blushed.

"There is something else I want to ask," Ada said, "since you seem to have a strong relationship with the school."

"Yes, anything."

"Will you let them know ahead of time that I don't want to be addressed as Mrs Badejo?"

Ronke raised an eyebrow. "May I ask why not?"

Ada twisted a piece of her *boubou* in her hand absent-mindedly. "My boys aren't aware of the… arrangement."

Ronke's eyes widened. "They don't know you're married?"

Ada winced, and even though she knew they were alone in the room, she double-checked that no one was lurking at the fringes. Once she was sure they were alone, she settled down and plucked at the edge of the leather seat.

"I don't want to confuse them. How will they understand an arrangement like this, only three months after their father's burial?" Ada rested her head against the back of the chair.

Ronke saw her lips quiver. "I will tell the school that everyone is to address you by your first name."

Ada let out a breath slowly and sat forward. "Thank you so much."

"Not a problem. I'll see you tomorrow." Ronke got up, then turned to her again. She gave Ada a brief, sympathetic once-over. "Er, are you sure you don't want me to expand your wardrobe a bit? Maybe another colour? I only ordered the five black *boubous* and scarves you asked for."

"They will serve their function. Remember, I am still officially in mourning for my first husband. I don't want to forget that."

"I understand." Even though Ada could see Ronke did not.

When they arrived at the school the next day, the principal, a huge Caucasian man with a booming voice, was waiting for them in the parking lot along with the Vice-Principal for Academics. The principal introduced himself as Walter Thornton, an Englishman who had taken over the headship of the school seven years ago.

As they toured the school, Ada saw state-of-the-art computer and science labs, art rooms, and sporting facilities with games she had never heard of – what in the world was cricket? It was all a bit overwhelming. Her boys would be taught here? Experience all this? Her own children?

"Father, thank you o," she whispered as she fell behind the group.

A tiny flicker of excitement began to form. Maybe, just maybe, all of this would really be worth it.

Chapter Ten

Every day that passed, Ada felt lighter as she watched her children settle into their new environment. They took to school without any hiccups.

The only discomfort was that Ikenna and Ahanna had to be separated. The school said it would be better for the boys to develop as individuals. Surprisingly, Ikenna took the separation the hardest; he was forced to make new friends without Ahanna. Ahanna, on the other hand, began to thrive as soon as he had to stand on his own.

Tobe's teachers, meanwhile, fulfilled the promise the school had made, and encouraged his intellectual gifts, keeping him challenged. Ada thought nothing could be so rewarding as watching him explore his potential.

As for Timi, Timi didn't say much. And he didn't say anything to Ada at all.

While everyone else was settling down, Ada continued to work on Emily. Every mealtime, the boys entertained the little girl, and Ada and Michael strategised over a solution to her eating problem, focusing on introducing easy foods to swallow. They tried mashed potatoes, cereal and soft-boiled eggs. Nothing worked. Ada researched how to make a child swallow, and all the information she found overwhelmed her.

When the breakthrough finally came, it was unexpected, and it had nothing to do with Ada.

On the evening in question, Ada was preoccupied with Timi. His refusal to join them for meals, coupled with his decision to remain in the gaming room all day and sometimes late into the night – along with his general attitude, of course – was grating heavily on her nerves.

That evening, as Michael served dinner, she called the gaming room and Timi picked up. In a cheerful voice, she told him dinner was ready, but Timi swore at her and slammed the phone down. Ada was staring at the handset, her eyes bulging at his audacity, when Emily gave a piercing scream from her high chair.

"Little Ada. What is it?" Ada glared at the twins, who sat nearby. "What did you do to her?" The twins stayed silent.

"She wants their noodles," Tobe eventually offered.

"Did she tell you?"

"They were teasing her with them."

"So, she started crying when they stopped?"

"Yes."

Michael, who came to see what the fuss was about, listened to Tobe and raised an eyebrow.

Ada lifted both hands in the air in surrender. "Let's try it."

They retrieved a small bowl of noodles, and once they were cool, Ada asked the boys to recreate the scene.

"But our food has finished. We need more to show you," Ahanna said, mischief all over his face.

Ada gave them a second helping without arguing. She wanted to see this with her own eyes.

When the portions were ready, Ada stepped aside and allowed them to do their thing. They touched a strand of noodle against Emily's lips, then pulled it away. Emily licked her lips, then burst into tears.

Ada, ready at once, dropped a noodle into her mouth. The twins, now invested in the experiment's success, mimicked chewing motions with their mouths, moving their jaws up and down with exaggerated movements. Emily copied them, mimicking the sucking noises. She chomped on the noodle over and over until it turned to mush in her mouth, and instinctively, she swallowed.

When Emily finally opened her mouth, there was nothing there, and everyone shouted for joy. The ruckus in the kitchen even drew Cynthia downstairs with baby Obinna. Ada pulled Emily out of her chair and swung her round and round.

"Adanne! Adaeze! Ada'm ooo! I knew you could do it. All you wanted was something delicious. We were boring you with all the bland food. My Ada is a real African queen!"

Emily did not understand what the fuss was about, but she giggled.

Finally, Ada settled her down and tried again. Emily kept the food in her mouth, soon started chewing, and then swallowed. She loved the clapping and the attention, and demanded more.

She was eating. Not only eating – she was eating well.

Mealtimes changed after that. Ada made sure the twins were always present when Emily was eating. They entertained her till she laughed, and then the feeding began.

Within a month, Emily started looking less emaciated. Milk feeds were reduced to once a day, and finally, only a small bottle at night.

The real difference showed in her physical capabilities. She fed off the twins' energy, and whatever they did, she wanted to do. Over time, she kept pushing herself to do more, and her speech also underwent a vast improvement. Emily mimicked everything she saw and heard, and with so many people in the house speaking all the time, she started to join in the chatter, becoming increasingly coherent with each passing day.

On the other hand, Timi became bolder in his rebellion. Ada complained regularly to Ronke. Even worse, Wande had gone incommunicado. Since the day he'd left for Singapore, he had neither called nor answered any of Ada's calls or messages. At first, Ada had been relieved to be left alone, but his continued silence, especially in the face of her problems with Timi, frustrated her terribly.

"Does he intend to abandon me and his family like this?" she often moaned to Ronke. "What do I do with his son? He should at least call and talk to his boy. Timi's attitude is something else."

Ronke always promised to pass her messages on to Wande, but Wande didn't seem to care. He never responded.

"Everybody, take your things upstairs. No more dropping your property around and expecting Mary and Cynthia to clear after you, you hear?"

Ada pulled her ear for emphasis and received a mixture of yeses and grunts in response as the kids loped through the hallway and hauled their school bags and sports kits up the stairs.

Timi came in last and dropped his stuff on the floor, allowing the contents to spill out. The racket caused everyone to turn around and look at him. Once he had made a sufficient scene, he proceeded to climb past Ada and her gaping-mouthed children to his room as if nothing had happened.

Ada swallowed hard. A vein throbbed in her right temple. She gripped the banister tightly, not saying a word until she caught her breath.

Addressing her boys, her eyes overly bright and her voice high-pitched, she said, "You all have to take a bath. The stench I endured coming home with all of you could kill an elephant. Nobody eats till they smell like humans again."

They grumbled some more. Ikenna grumbled louder than the rest.

As she shepherded them to the bathroom, she said, "Don't worry, lunch is worth the wait. Uncle Michael has prepared beans with lots and lots of juicy, succulent fried plantain."

When the boys heard 'plantain', it elicited the expected reaction. Tobe and Ahanna raced to their rooms. Ahanna called, "Dibs on the bathroom!" and stuck out his tongue at his brother, provoking more grumbles from his twin.

"Ikenna, it's okay. *Oya*, use my bathroom so you don't have to wait for him to finish," Ada said.

Fifteen minutes later, the three children were in the kitchen eating with gusto. Ada poured each of them a drink of water, but when she bent over Ikenna's shoulder to pour him a glass, she wrinkled her nose.

"*Bia*, Ikenna..." Ada stepped back from him. "Did you say you had a bath?"

"Yes." Ikenna didn't stop eating.

"Tell me the truth. Your fresh clothes cannot hide the smell of sweat. I'm asking you one more time: did you have a bath as I told you?"

"I did. You can ask Ahanna."

Ahanna scrunched his face. "Please don't involve me o."

"I'm talking to you," Ada said to Ikenna. "You said I should ask your brother. Okay. Wait for me." She clicked her fingers. Tobe and Ahanna looked at each other but kept quiet.

Ada went upstairs to investigate her bathroom, and was back in less than five minutes, her face clouded.

"If you had a bath in my room, why are my floor and towel completely dry?" She tapped Ikenna's shoulder to get his attention.

"*Ahn, ahn,* what is it? Leave me!"

Ada staggered, her palm on her chest, and she cocked her head. "Ikenna Obidiegwu Okeke, who are you raising your voice at? Are you drunk?"

He continued to ignore her. Tobe glanced at his brother, his forehead creased. Ahanna held his fist over his mouth, trying to catch his brother's attention across the table.

Something snapped in Ada. How dare Ikenna treat her this way? Lie to her face, and with such a brazen attitude?

Every eye looked up when she grabbed Ikenna by the ear. Tobe and Ahanna got out of their seats and followed them to the door of the kitchen. They watched their mum drag Ikenna up the stairs without a word.

Ada pushed him into the first bedroom and he landed on the floor.

He struggled to right himself while holding onto his throbbing ear. "Mummy, what is it now?" His earlier bravado wavered just a little.

Ada stared at him in shock. Then fear took hold that if she didn't put a stop to this attitude right this minute, her son would become – Ada trembled at the notion – like Timi. The first strike brought a scream from Ikenna and tears to Ada's eyes.

Suddenly, it wasn't Ikenna on the floor; it was Timi. Timi, who had mocked her; Timi who so often threw his contempt and rudeness and disobedience in her face.

Well, not anymore. Today, she was going to teach him a lesson he would never forget.

Ada's arm came down hard one more time.

A fierce knock on the door snapped her out of her frenzy. Ada shook her head; she felt like she was underwater, fighting to come up for air.

Ikenna writhed in pain in the corner. He peered at her with horror and shrank back.

Ada looked at her hands like they belonged to someone else. This was not her way. This was Emeka's way.

The knocking persisted. "Madam! Madam! Open, please." It was Michael. He never came upstairs.

Ada's limbs worked in slow motion. Still shaken, she opened the door.

Michael took a step back when he saw her drenched in sweat, Ikenna crouching behind her.

"I do not mean to disturb you…" He sounded winded. "But Emily needs you downstairs."

Ada could hear no cry of distress. The entire house would be aware if Emily wanted something. She could not bring herself to look Michael in the eye.

He was there to save her from herself.

"Thank you. I'll be down soon."

Michael departed quietly, and Ada turned to her son who was still huddled in a corner. The attitude had gone, and all that was left was Ikenna, her bold and brassy boy, who often spoke without thinking but was always ready to apologise if he knew he'd hurt someone.

Choking back a sob, Ada rushed to his side.

"Mummy… I am… sorry," he said through his sobs. "I lied… Sorry, Mummy… and I was rude to you. Sor… ry. I will never… do it again."

Ada pulled him closer. "I know." She took the edge of her *boubou* and wiped his tears, rocking him until his sobs subsided.

After a while, she realised he had fallen asleep. She got up slowly. Her boy was getting too big for her to carry, so she led him to bed.

When she came out, Ahanna and Tobe were waiting outside their rooms in the hallway.

Tears filled Ahanna's eyes. He stood by his door and did not approach her.

"Is he all right?" Tobe asked.

"Yes, he just fell asleep."

"Can I see him?"

"He is sleeping, Ahanna."

"I know, but can I? I won't wake him." Ada said nothing, and Ahanna walked past her into the room.

She hadn't seen her children so subdued since the first few weeks after their father's death. She turned away, but not before she noticed Ahanna gently take his brother's hand, then crawl into the bed and lie beside him, careful not to wake him.

Later, the kitchen was empty save for Michael, who rested in his armchair with his feet up on a small stool. He straightened when he saw Ada.

"*Oga* Michael, please relax."

He leaned back once again in his seat. She dragged a chair next to him and sat down, not looking at him, not speaking. Michael waited.

"I don't know what happened," she said finally, blinking back tears. She looked up to meet his gaze.

"Can I speak freely, ma'am?" He smiled at the warning look she gave him, even with her misty eyes. "Not addressing an issue is like sitting with burning coal on your lap and pretending it isn't there. A reaction is inevitable, and you reacted today, but just to the wrong person."

Ada wasn't ready to admit how close to the mark he was. Her head hung downwards. Michael set his lips in a firm line. "I love Timi with all my heart. Like his father before him, I carried him with these two arms when he was a baby, but I must admit his behaviour of late has been reprehensible, and he is asking for a well-placed kick in his nether regions."

Ada would have smiled if she could have.

He continued softly, taking both her hands in his. "And I am also aware you have taken the brunt of it. But, my dear, it's time you dealt with it."

"Me?" Ada felt a tightening in her stomach. "That's his father's job. I've been trying to reach Wande for an entire month now. I've left countless messages."

"That must frustrate you, but this is not about Wande. Pause for a minute to hear me." Michael leaned closer. "It's about loving another child the way you love your own."

"I don't understand. I'm still bungling with my own."

"*Pah!*" He waved his hand in a shooing manner. "You are an amazing mum. Tell me one parent who hasn't done something they wished they hadn't, and I will show you a liar. Parents make mistakes, and at least your boys have a mother who loves them.

Timi isn't lucky enough to have the same, and he is busy digging a hole for himself that he may not be able to get out of. If it were Tobe making wrong decisions, wouldn't you want someone to help him so he doesn't fall into the pit? Even if he resisted?"

"Maybe… I guess."

"Then, that's all I am asking. Do the same for Timi."

Doubt flitted across Ada's face. Michael smiled, then shuffled to the back of the kitchen to his quarters.

Ada sighed deeply and sank into Michael's chair.

Quietly, she began to pray. "Father, I feel so bad. I didn't realise how much anger I had against the boy until I poured it all out on my own child. Forgive me. I know Timi is only thirteen, but I really want to strangle him right now." She hesitated. "I'm sorry. I don't mean that a hundred per cent. I just don't know what to do."

Love him.

"But he doesn't even—"

Love him. The way I love you.

Ada knew the scriptures; she knew what God expected. To give the way she had received. It was hard, but she was willing. "Then put a love for him in my heart. Love him through me. In Jesus's name, I pray."

Ada stayed silent. Then she added, "Please give me strength." She had a feeling that she would need it soon.

Chapter Eleven

Ada sat on the steps in front of the house, gazing at the fountain as its lights changed slowly from red to blue to orange and back again. The kids had gone to bed, and she needed to be alone.

Timi kept playing on her mind. She had ignored him in the few days since the incident, not allowing anything he said or did to get to her. But at the back of her mind, she knew what was coming: a full-on confrontation. Her insides turned at the idea.

Timi frightened her, but like Michael said, she could leave him or help him, and to help, she had to face her fears. There was no time like now.

"Jesus, give me strength."

Resolutely, she dusted off her dress and marched into the house. Her hands clenched as she made her way to Timi's room. *He's just a little boy, he's just a little boy…* A plan was forming as she got closer to his room.

She knocked, waiting until she heard a faint, "Yeah?"

She hesitated, rubbing her sweaty palms on her clothes, took a deep breath and opened the door.

Without bothering to turn, Timi threw a casual, "Thank you, Aunty Mary" over his shoulder. Maybe he thought Mary had brought in his laundry.

Timi was at his desk with headphones on and his laptop open. This was Ada's first time in his room. She glanced around, expecting a mess, but it was surprisingly neat. Not as much planning had gone into this space as in Emily's bedroom. A well-made bed with innumerable fluffy pillows rested against the wall. A beautiful seascape hung above the headboard. The brown oak desk even had an armchair. Tasteful, for sure, but austere. Not what she imagined for a thirteen-year-old boy.

She cleared her throat. Whatever he was listening to must not have been loud, because he spun around, snatching the headphones off his head, startled. A veil of annoyance clouded his features.

"What do you want?"

"To talk." Ada clasped her palms behind her to stop herself from wringing them.

"I have nothing to say to you." He returned to the screen.

"I am expecting you in the game room in fifteen minutes."

"I'm not coming."

"You are," she said, raising her voice to get his attention. "I've got something you need."

"What?" He twisted to face her, but she had gone.

Her plan had been set in motion. She marched to the game room. Pacing the wide, noisy space, she imagined what Osas would have said if she were there. *Calm down, Ada. You are not entering the lion's den, are you? Which one be all dis shaking?*

At the thought of her friend's reaction, Ada didn't know whether to laugh or cry. This would have been a piece of cake for Osas. Sternly, Ada reminded herself that no matter how Timi acted, he was just a child. She was the adult.

Twenty-five minutes later, just as Ada became certain he would not come, Timi barged in, seething.

"Did you disconnect the Wi-Fi?"

"Yes," Ada said, her outward calm belying her inner stress. "Now can we talk?"

"Put it back on!" he said, his hands forming fists at his sides.

Ada gestured in his direction. "Timi, I will not have you speak to me like that."

"Ha!" he sneered. "I don't have to listen to you. You are nobody!"

"I may be nobody, but the Wi-Fi is off until we have a conversation. You can do this the easy or hard way. It's up to you."

Timi swore and walked out on her.

Ada stared after him, rubbing her arms to still the shaking and stop her impulse surrender. Then she remembered Ikenna, the words Michael had spoken, and the Lord's instructions, and she remained resolute.

It was past ten thirty at night. Ada was double-checking the doors before bed when Timi came storming down the stairs and met her at the kitchen door.

"I'm guessing you're ready to have that conversation?" she asked.

He just stared at the door.

She opened it again and he followed her inside.

Ada made herself comfortable in Michael's chair, drawing strength from it.

"Do you want to sit?" She pointed to the chairs behind Timi. He folded his arms and glared, ready for war. Ada was ready, too.

"Timi Badejo. For as long as I have been here, you have shown me disrespect. You have done things I would never tolerate from my children, and I will no longer accept it. From now on, I have rules you must follow, or there will be consequences." Ada took a breath. She didn't want to get emotional.

"First," she said, counting off one finger, "no more taking your meals in your room like a prisoner. You are a part of this family—"

"We are not family!" he snapped.

"What is Emily to you, then?"

Timi looked away.

"As I was saying, you are part of this..." Ada spread her hands around the kitchen. "Whatever you want to call us. So, mealtimes and family outings are compulsory. Obeying my instructions is non-negotiable. If you backtalk or break any rules, I will take away your phone for a day. I will also take away your gaming privileges and cut the allowance which feeds that preoccupation."

"That's ridiculous. You can't do that." He backed away, glaring.

"I can, and I will. Watch your tone."

"I will not listen to your rubbish!" he shrieked. "I'll tell my father about this, and he'll have all of you thrown out of here!"

"Go ahead, please do. And when you speak to him, inform him I'm trying to reach him. That will be three days of gaming privileges gone."

Timi's eyes flashed, and he launched a vicious verbal attack filled with obscenities that sent a chill up her spine. He stomped his feet and pointed at her. It was not just the words; it was the venom with which he spewed them. If he aimed to shock, he succeeded. Ada's stomach tightened at the onslaught. She swallowed hard, working to maintain an impassive stance. She was grateful she was sitting – she did not think she could have remained steady if she were standing.

He went on for a full minute until he ran out of insults to hurl. Then, he stood with his legs apart, panting, his fists clenched. The overhead light bounced off his face, and Ada noticed the shine in his eyes.

Something else was clearly troubling him, and he was lashing out the only way he could. Her heart suddenly overflowed with compassion. He was indeed just a child. A new desire welled up in her to hold him, to tell him everything was going to be okay.

"Contrary to what you may think, Timi," she said gently, sensing how different emotions warred within him, "I am not doing this to be mean. Your outburst just now has cost you your phone and gaming privileges for a month. I expect you to give me your handset in the morning. The new rules take effect at once. And if you are not down for breakfast with the rest of us tomorrow, you will not eat."

His shoulders sagged, and he leaned against the kitchen counter. "I hate you so much." He did not wipe away the tear that slid down his cheek.

Her heart bled for him. *Father, how can I reach this boy?*

"I'm sorry to hear that. Let me assure you that the feeling is not mutual. I would like everyone to get along. To be a family, or if not, let's just be the best… us."

She rose to move towards him, but he stepped back and left the room.

Ada had to credit Timi for his stubbornness. He did not drop off the phone as she asked, and he missed breakfast and lunch. She knew he was alive because Mary said he answered her when she called him down at mealtimes.

Luckily, it was a weekend. If he were at school, she might not have been able to follow through with her threats.

Steeling her heart, she informed Michael of her plan and held onto the keys to the pantry and the kitchen when she locked up at night.

Around midnight, Ada stayed awake to find out if the hunger strike had made an impact. When footsteps scurried past her door and thumped up the stairs shortly after, she stifled a laugh.

Michael, anticipating the same move, had also stayed up. He came out of his room when he heard the rattles of the pantry door. He found Timi attempting to undo the latch.

"Young man, what are you doing? It's late."

"Sorry, Uncle Mike. Can you please open this door? I haven't had anything to eat today."

"Why not, my boy? Everyone else had a feast. I should know, I prepared it." He gave a little smile.

Timi hesitated. "I... I wasn't hungry then, Uncle Mike. Can you please open up? Even the fridge is locked."

"I don't have the keys, son. Tobe's mother has them."

"Ugh!" Timi balled his fists. "She has no right! I hate that woman!"

Michael's countenance stiffened. "Hey, young man. You will not speak that way in my presence. Your annoyance is understandable, but your behaviour is certainly not. Your mum would be so disappointed. What's the matter with you?"

Timi's face crumpled. Michael wrapped his arms around his shoulders and drew him close.

"Get a grip, son. Now, wait for me. I think I have an apple in my room; I'll be back."

Timi's eyes lit up. Michael quickly returned with the shiny red fruit. Gesturing to the kitchen table, he handed him the apple. Timi took a bite as he sank into the chair. He closed his eyes as he chewed, savouring each morsel.

"My boy, listen," Michael said. "You are a smart young man. If your aim is to send this woman away, the alternative may not be as great as you think. Who loses?"

His strength now restored, Timi's attitude followed suit. "If she leaves, no one loses. Good riddance!"

"That's where you are wrong," Michael said. "Your sister loses. Haven't you seen the miracle that's been happening right under your nose?"

Timi looked away, and Michael rose to return to his room.

"Don't let your hurt ruin her chances at a better life, my boy."

On Sunday, Mary reported that Timi would not be coming down for mealtime because he was sick, and requested his food be brought up to him.

When Ada heard that, she sighed with relief, then chuckled… Sick, but still hungry. Good one. Even Michael shook his head at the request.

Emboldened, Ada went up to Timi's room and tapped on his door. Timi opened it instantly. His disappointment when he saw her was palpable.

"Timi, come and eat," she said. "Uncle Mike has prepared quite a spread. He made fried rice with plantain and sautéed chicken. There is a carrot cake waiting to be devoured, and I am allowing all of you to have ice cream with it. We would love for you to join us." She stepped back to leave before saying, "Remember to bring your phone when you come. The month starts from the moment I receive it. Besides, I know it's useless to you now, anyway."

"You cancelled my subscription."

Ada nodded; she knew it would be the final blow. "Yes, yes, I did. You can decide how you proceed."

Timi held out until dinner. When he finally strolled into the kitchen, the surprise from everyone could not match Ada's relief. By then, she wasn't sure she could have gone on one more day knowing the silly boy was starving himself.

Ada stretched out her hand, and he dropped his cell phone in the middle of her palm before joining the others at the table.

At first, the conversation was stilted, but soon, the twins regained their mojo, and their lively chatter filled the kitchen once more.

Ada gave Timi a double helping. Tears stung her lids as she saw him wolf it all down. *Silly, stubborn child*, she thought as she added another serving to his plate. He only paused eating when it was time to feed Emily.

"Adanna! Adaeze! Adanne! Adaora! Adaugo!" the boys chanted, clapping enthusiastically while Ada made a production of flying the spoon of tasty food towards Emily.

As Emily swallowed, every single adult and child, save Timi, erupted in cheers. Nobody had forgotten that Emily hadn't been eating at all less than a month ago.

Timi finished his dessert and got up to leave, but Ada stopped him before he reached the door.

"Timi, after a meal, we acknowledge the adults in the room who made it possible. So, you say thank you to Uncle Michael, Aunty Mary and Aunty Cynthia."

The entire kitchen fell quiet. Ada held her breath. Any potential progress hinged on his response, and she prayed he wouldn't defy her. There was a limit to how much more aggression she could take.

Maybe it was the full stomach, or maybe he too was tired of the conflict – or maybe he just wanted his phone back – but within seconds, his features smoothed out.

"Thank you, Uncle Michael. Thank you, Aunty Mary. Thank you, Aunty Cynthia."

Ada released her breath in a silent whoosh. She was happy enough to dance a jig, but instead, she simply said, "Goodnight, Timi."

Tobe peeked into the gaming room, where Timi sat in front of the large screen. His mum had released Timi from his game room prohibition a week early for good behaviour. He had since returned to spending all his free time locked in virtual battle.

Tobe hesitated, then walked in. Timi did not look up.

Tobe sat down and watched him play. He had never had an interest in going in there before, and with the door locked for the past three weeks, he couldn't have – even if he wanted to. But now, he wondered what Timi was so captivated by in the giant space.

Tobe wondered at the older boy's absorption; Timi's eyes never left the screen. His fingers worked by themselves, pushing the joysticks back and forth rapidly. After five minutes of intense concentration, Timi leaned back in his seat, a satisfied grin on his face.

"So, you won?" Tobe asked.

"Can't you see? It's taking me to get my rewards. I obliterated the computer."

"Oh, sorry. I couldn't tell. I just saw gun flares and everybody running."

"That's funny. So, you don't play Fortnite, I'm guessing."

"No… no, I do not."

"I could teach you if you wanted."

"Really?" Tobe pushed his glasses up the bridge of his nose. "You'll do that? I mean, I would like that… Well, it's not my thing, but I'd like to see what you love so much."

"Whoa, nerd guy." Timi shook his head and smiled. "A simple 'okay' would have been enough. Let's do this."

After an hour of coaching, Tobe understood the basics and even found the experience a little thrilling. He asked questions to clarify moves, and Timi was patient in explaining.

"Want to go another round?" Timi asked.

Tobe was surprised again. Timi seemed like he really wanted him to stay.

"Sure, but let me tell my mum where I am." Tobe got to his feet and stretched, sniffing the air. "Ah, Mummy is making cookies. Should I get one for you?"

Timi hesitated. "No, no, thank you." Timi picked up the PlayStation console.

Tobe sat again. "Can I ask a question?"

"If you must," Timi grumbled. Gone was any semblance of the pleasant companion Tobe had enjoyed for the last hour.

"Why don't you like her?" Tobe's gaze did not leave Timi's face.

"Who?"

"My mum. Why don't you like her? Ever since we got here, you've been horrible to her."

"Hey…" Heat flooded Timi's face and he dropped the console. "I'm not sure you should talk to me like this. I'm older than you."

"I always wanted a big brother," Tobe said. "So, coming to live with you was such a bonus, till I got here and met you. You're so rude, with no thought for anyone but yourself. You only play with your sister because my mum forces you to—"

"You can stop now." Timi's lips tightened, and he looked away.

"I would have apologised for that if I weren't telling the truth," Tobe said. "But you know what?"

"There's more?"

"You're not a terrible person. When we go out, you're cool with my brothers and me, even giving us swimming tips. And you just taught me that game. So, it's only my mother you can't stand. Why?"

Timi leaned back on the couch with his arm thrown across his face, covering his eyes.

Tobe stood to leave when suddenly Timi spoke. "I don't… hate her. I just… I just didn't want this." The silence stretched.

Tobe spoke first. "None of us wanted this. We didn't want our dad to die, and we didn't want to leave our school, but now we're here. We can all decide to make it work or make it really difficult."

"Hey," Timi said, laughing. "You're eleven, right? Why do you talk like an old man?"

Tobe shrugged. "I'm twelve, and what's that supposed to mean? *Like an old man.* Is that a good or bad thing?"

"I don't know… it's just different."

Tobe smiled as he got up and walked to the door. "My mum's chocolate chip cookies are very nice." He turned before the door closed and gave an exaggerated nod. "Very nice."

The atmosphere in the kitchen was merry. Music was playing, and Emily, as usual, was attached to Ada's hip while the twins chased each other. Obinna sat in a highchair watching the boys race. Tobe held the oven door open for his mother while she pulled out the trays.

Suddenly, Timi stood at the door, shifting from foot to foot. Ada's hand flew to her chest; she had just been thinking of him, and by some miracle, he was here of his own accord. She breathed a prayer of thanks. She knew she had to play it cool.

"Just in time," she said. "Want to try one?"

He hesitated for a moment before reaching out for a cookie. He bit into it and chewed. The intense explosion of flavours was so unexpected that he flopped over in the nearest chair, eliciting laughter all around.

"I told you, didn't I?" Tobe said, taking a piece for himself.

Timi nodded, grinning. "May I have one more?"

"Sure." Ada gave him a piece from the second tray. She would have given him the entire batch if he'd asked for it.

"Tobe." Timi always pronounced it *Toby*. The twins gave their usual smirk. "Wanna play some more? There are a lot more games on the PlayStation I could show you."

Tobe's grin nearly split his face in half. Ada's emotions matched his expression.

"Mummy, may I?" he asked.

Ada swallowed hard and nodded. When the boys reached the kitchen door, she called out, "I'll bring more cookies and milk up for you."

"Can we go too?" Ikenna asked.

"No way!" said Ada. "I'm not letting you eat upstairs. Finish and clean up, then I'll see."

Chapter Twelve

Two weeks later, they were all seated for dinner when Ada's phone beeped. Silently, she read the email, but glanced at Timi furtively, chewing on her lower lip. The message was from his principal, requesting a meeting with her.

She had to work to stay calm so as not to disrupt their uneasy truce. Things had improved since the day he'd come down for the cookies. He'd stopped giving her a look of hatred when he passed her in the hallways, and spoke to her directly, using phrases like *good morning*, *thank you*, and *please*.

She cleared her throat. "Timi, do you know why your principal is asking to meet me tomorrow?"

He did not stop eating and gave a dismissive shrug. "I dunno. Why don't you ask him?"

"Watch your tone." Ada's voice held a warning. "Do you not have any idea what he might want to speak about?"

"Stop with the questioning! You're not my mother!"

Tobe's head dropped till his nose was almost touching his food. Everyone else at the table stayed quiet. Ada's heart sank, so much for the truce.

"I don't see anyone else here," Ada said. "Do you?"

Timi got up and pushed his chair so forcefully it fell back. The noise startled the younger children, and the babies started crying. Ada reached for Obinna while Cynthia carried Emily. Timi left the kitchen, glowering.

Ada tried to lighten the mood by offering dessert. It worked on the twins, but Tobe's face was strained with worry. Rubbing his arm, Ada gave him a reassuring smile.

After dinner, Ada made sure everyone followed their night-time routines, all the while thinking about her impending conversation with Timi. She delayed it by playing with the twins until the boys were so sick of her excuses, they shooed her out.

When she arrived at Timi's room, she knocked but got no response.

"Timi." She knocked again. "Open the door."

Still nothing. Ada was not going to spend all evening dreading the confrontation for nothing. Eventually, she shoved the handle and went in.

Timi shot out from under his blanket, eyes wide, his shirtless torso glistening with sweat. His headphones dangling haphazardly off his head.

"Get out of my room!" he yelled. He threw whatever he had in his hand at her.

Ada jumped to escape the flying object – a magazine – and stepped out in haste. On her way out, the magazine landed on the floor. On the cover was a smiling, generously endowed naked woman.

Out in the hallway, she leant against the door, her hand over her mouth. She squeezed her eyes shut, grimacing, trying to stop the scene from replaying in her head as she made her way back to her room.

Later, when her mind had cleared, she knew she was being silly. Timi would be embarrassed enough for both of them. Besides, she still had unfinished business with him.

Ada, it's no big deal. You can do this, she said to herself as she made her way back to his room.

She knocked on his door – extra loud this time. "Timi, I shouldn't have barged in. I apologise."

No response.

She coughed. "But I need to speak to you tonight, regardless. Meet me in the game room. I'll be back if you don't show up."

She listened. She wasn't even sure he was still there. Finally, she heard the thump of feet on the other side of the door.

When he arrived a few moments later, he couldn't look her in the face. The discomfort was mutual. She made a decision not to refer to the incident again; there were more pressing matters at stake.

"Timi, the email sounded serious. If you'd rather I didn't speak to the principal, I understand, but it means I will have to involve your father."

"What's the use?" Timi leaned back on the couch and stared at the ceiling. "It's not like he's going to come."

"What does that mean?"

"He never comes. Not any of those times I was in trouble, did he?" Timi gripped the side of the sofa, and Ada's heart sank. Had he been giving her hell to get his father's attention?

"If you're referring to your behaviour with me, I never told him."

"What?" Timi's eyes went wide. "Even when I was—"

"Rude and exasperating? No, I didn't."

Timi looked almost pleased with her. It amazed Ada that Wande's blatant ignorance might turn into something positive.

"I'm on your side," Ada said, "whatever or wherever that may be." Timi frowned and threw his hands up in the air.

"Why doesn't he come to see us? Back in the UK, it was the same. No matter what I did, the principal kept on saying I was off the hook. One day, I gave up breaking rules." Timi rubbed his hands together, his head down. There was a tremor in his voice. "What is it about us he doesn't like?"

Ada's eyes filled with tears.

"Your daddy is busy, Timi, that's all. Even I can hardly reach him." It was half true. "He misses you children so much, and the few times we have spoken, it's been all about you guys."

Ada was happy Timi's head was still bent. She had never been the best of liars. *Father, forgive me.*

"But right now, this isn't about your dad," Ada went on. "I may not be your favourite person, but I'm responsible for you. Unless you tell me I got that email because you're being honoured as a top student, I need to know what's going on." She gentled her voice. "What happened today?"

Ada's mind raced through imagined scenarios, ranging from exam malpractice to drugs. She had no idea what Timi was capable of. Could he have unleashed the attitude he'd shown her on teachers at school?

Finally, he spoke. "I pushed a girl and she fell."

"Timi!" Ada's eyes widened. She looked around the room even though no one else was present and whispered loudly, "You were fighting a girl?"

"I didn't fight her." He shifted uncomfortably. "It was an accident. I just touched her a little, and then she was on the ground on her back. Her friends made a stupid fuss, and the maths teacher came. The girl tried to explain, but he wouldn't let her. Once he found out I was involved, he started on about kids from overseas being unruly. 'That is not the way we do things in Nigeria.' *Yada yada yada.* He doesn't like me."

Ada's heart slowed. It was nothing unfixable. "That's ridiculous. But first, *biko*, explain how you touched her."

Ada's mind flashed back to the magazine and prayed silently that it wasn't what she thought.

"I was passing her and her friends when I sort of play-punched her shoulder. I didn't realise she was so close to the edge." He turned slightly towards her. "Honestly, Aunty Ada, it was an accident."

He'd said her name. *Stay calm, it's no big deal. So what?*

But it was a big deal. It was like a long drink of water after an arduous journey, or a hug when she needed it most. She wanted to draw him close, but rubbed his shoulder instead.

"I believe you. Thank you for telling me. But, we still need to sort this out. This teacher must have told the principal some version of the story." She paused. "Do you have this girl's address?"

"Er, no. We just see each other at school."

Ada raised an eyebrow. "Why were you 'sort of' punching her?"

Timi covered his face with his hands. Ada wanted to laugh. Now, she understood what had happened.

"We need her mother's number urgently. I'll get your phone." She saw Timi perk up and added, "Text me the number once you get it." She scratched her palm, her brow creasing while a plan formed in her head. "We need to kill this quickly. Set your alarm for an hour earlier tomorrow."

By the time Timi arrived downstairs the next morning, the aroma of Ada's cookies permeated all the way through the house. Ada was alone in the kitchen, dressed in her black *boubou* and scarf, but this time around, she looked different to the young boy. Brighter.

She held several boxes of cookies, and she looked like she was ready to leave.

"Where are you going?" Timi asked as he dropped his backpack on the kitchen table.

"I'm taking you to Emmanuella's house this morning."

"What? No way…" Timi stepped back.

"What did you think I wanted the address for?" Ada said. "Come on, let's go."

"I thought *you* were planning to go."

"I didn't play-punch her," she teased. She rustled the cookies. "Nothing like a few of these to smooth ruffled feathers."

"They smell delicious," Timi admitted. "Even I forgive myself." He gave a cheeky smile.

He stretched out his hand to sneak one away before she caught him and whacked him with a napkin.

"Don't you dare."

Ada grinned. They were talking – like normal people!

She hoped this intervention would be successful. The girl's mum had been willing to meet briefly at her home before school, and Ada had not been ashamed to use Wande's name to her full advantage. The other mum's tone changed slightly after Ada introduced herself as *Mrs Badejo, the wife of…*

It was the first time Ada had ever referred to herself like that, but helping Timi was as good a reason as any.

Lagos was truly a city that never slept. Emmanuella's family lived in the Lekki Phase 1 suburb, which was close to Banana Island, just over the Lekki Ikoyi bridge. Even as early as 6.30 a.m., the number of commuters going to and from the island was astronomical. Despite traffic on the bridge, they arrived at the girl's home just in time.

The security guard flung the gate open once the driver mentioned who was in the back seat. They'd obviously prepared for their arrival.

A woman wearing a dark suit, maybe in her fifties, was already coming out of the front door, followed by another lady in a nanny's uniform carrying a bag and files.

Behind the nanny was a girl dressed in the same uniform as Timi. She was fair-skinned and as tall as Timi, with long braids that framed her round face beautifully. She was bopping her head to something coming through her headphones, lost in her music. Ada thought she might have seen the girl at swim practice once or twice.

When she noticed their car, the girl's startled expression was comical. She stopped short on the drive.

Ada felt Timi stiffen beside her. She didn't need any other confirmation that this pretty girl was Emmanuella.

Before they got out of the car, she turned to Timi and said, "Remember what I told you to do?" He nodded. "Please don't forget," Ada added. "They are a Yoruba family. No matter how rich they are, they appreciate proper greeting protocol, and we want to make a good impression."

"But what if my uniform gets dirty?"

"Greet the less formal way then, where you bend forward and touch your toe. Okay?"

He nodded, and she was glad he wasn't arguing.

Ada turned forward again. "Hmm, your Emmanuella is beautiful." Timi did not crack a smile, and a bead of sweat formed over his top lip. She patted his leg. "Please, instead of staring at her while I speak to her mum, introduce yourself. Apologise for the accident. And finally, don't even think of approaching her until you have gone and prostrated for the mum and said good morning."

Timi seemed suddenly incapable of speech.

The car door opened, and they approached the two ladies.

Soon, Ada offered her baked goods to Emmanuella's mother, and within ten minutes, laughter rang out all around the yard. The cookies changed hands, and there were smiles from the adults and the teenagers, who were also making conversation.

Before they knew it, they were back in their cars, heading off to school. Emmanuella's mother had graciously offered a ride to Timi so as not to duplicate a journey for Ada. Timi's eyes had lit up at the suggestion, and he could not hide his disappointment when Ada declined. Ronke had insisted on clear security protocol for the children, and Ada wouldn't break any rules, no matter how cute or convenient.

Once they settled back in the car, Timi still had a goofy grin on his face.

"That was cool."

"It was, wasn't it? Talking is so much better than fighting, *abii*," she teased. "So, what did she say?"

"Well, she knew it was an accident and accepted my apology. For the rest of the time, we talked about music and stuff."

"Nice."

Timi leaned back in his seat. "What did you tell her mum?"

"Luckily for you, your new friend had already done the challenging work for us and told her it was all a misunderstanding. I just layered on top of that. Now, she thinks you're an amazing young man."

Ada didn't think he would appreciate the fact that she'd used his mother's passing to garner more sympathy for him, so she didn't mention it.

"You're quite the diplomat, aren't you, Aunty Ada?" Timi said. He stared at the remaining boxes of cookies sitting on the seat. "So, who else are you going to work your magic on with the rest of the cookies?"

"I'm starting from the top and working my way down, from the principal to the vice-principal, then to that maths teacher."

"No way. He doesn't deserve cookies. He's horrid."

"That may be so, but what's the alternative? I could challenge him and get him reprimanded, but what next? He'll still be your teacher, and with an even bigger chip on his shoulder. That won't be good for you." Ada shook her head. "No, let's go the honey route first. No one messes with one of my own, okay?"

Once they arrived, Ada spent an hour spreading gifts and goodwill around the school. The maths teacher preened as she praised him for being such a marvellous instructor and doing a stellar job maintaining discipline; she even told him the words came from Timi, himself. It amused Ada that he didn't flinch at the thought that Timi, a boy he had picked on since the first day of school, would praise him so. By the end of the conversation, he was promising to look out for Timi personally.

Ada beamed on her way home, feeling like a supermum, quenching fires and smoothing out roads for her boy. Every day she was surprising herself a little more.

Timi had swim practice every Wednesday for two hours after school. Usually, Ada dropped the other kids at home and then returned to wait for him in the car park. But today, she arrived early and took a seat on the bleachers. She heard voices nearby in the changing room and was about to call out to Timi to let him know she was there when she caught the drift of a heated conversation.

The boys had stopped by her side of the bleachers to get out of the sun. From her viewpoint, she saw only one boy clearly – a stocky lad with a shaved head. Ada remembered him from swim trials. What he lacked in height, he made up for in speed. Though not as talented as Timi, he was a strong swimmer.

His voice floated towards the bleachers: "Don't you find it embarrassing, repeating the same fib all the time? 'My dad is the Wande Badejo'." He spoke with a mocking nasal twang, trying to mimic Timi's accent, and he lifted his shoulders with an exaggerated swagger. "Just because you share the same surname doesn't mean you can claim him as yours. You've been here for almost a term, and no one has seen him... not even once. Only your nanny."

Ada's lips curled. *Nanny?*

"It's getting embarrassing," another said. "Why don't you just tell the truth?"

There was a chorus of agreement from the other boys.

"But it's true!" Timi didn't raise his voice, but Ada heard its tightness.

"Don't be shy. Show us proof!" a different boy sneered. "A picture of you together."

"Okay, I—"

"No, that won't work," the stocky guy said. "Not when there's such a thing as Photoshop. I want real-life evidence."

"What do you mean?" Timi asked. Ada wanted to rush in and help, but she knew he wouldn't appreciate it.

"What's one thing no father would ever miss?" the other voice said.

"Yes! I've got it," the stocky guy said. "Inter-high finals. Next term. With you as the touted golden swimmer, it'll be an event no actual father would miss. If he doesn't show for that, then you are officially a liar."

"That's not a problem," Timi said. "My dad will be there."

"*Aaight mate. Oh well, pip pip cheerio!*" he mocked.

The rest of the boys burst into laughter as they headed towards the car park. Six of them, all dressed in navy blue and silver Nike tracksuits with their names printed on the back, their matching sports bags loosely slung over their bodies. Ada's eyes narrowed. She would have loved to wipe the self-satisfied smirks off their faces.

Her mind went to Timi, and she alighted from her perch. She found him leaning against the gym wall with his eyes closed. When she touched his shoulder, he jumped.

"How long have you been here?" he asked.

"Long enough." She pointed towards the boys. "When did all this start?"

He pursed his lips and looked away, digging his hands deep into his pockets.

"When I joined the squad." He rolled his head from side to side. "During one of the team-building sessions, they asked us to talk about our family. I mentioned that dad was Wande Badejo of Badejo and Badejo and all hell broke loose."

"No wonder you're always asking Aunty Ronke when your dad's coming home."

"He won't show and they'll call me a liar." His shoulders sagged as he kicked the dirt at his feet. "The worst part is, I wish I was lying. It's better than the truth. My dad is Wande Badejo, and he doesn't care enough about me to bother to show up for anything."

Ada's heart broke. They were not so different from each other, her and this boy, both plucked from the only environment they once knew and dumped in a new place with no help to navigate their new lives. Ada felt ashamed for her earlier abruptness with him. Again, she had the overwhelming desire to give the tall, little boy a hug, but still, she kept her distance.

"Don't worry, Timi," she said. "I don't know how, but we'll fix this. I'll find a way, even if I—"

Timi reached out and touched her shoulder briefly. "Thank you, Aunty Ada."

She tilted her head in his direction. "What for?"

"For everything." Sincerity shone through his eyes, but he looked away quickly.

"It's okay." Ada pushed down the sudden lump in her throat. She coughed, and fumbled through her bag, pretending to search for something.

Today was her best day by far.

Chapter Thirteen

"You can't keep blowing me off. Not this time." Ada tried hard to maintain her composure. Ronke was not the enemy, but this was the fifth conversation on this matter in a week. Ada was tired but needed this woman on her side for the plan to work.

"Ronke, I consider you my friend. I value your support. Believe me when I tell you I would not call this man again if it weren't important. This is different – he needs to come home now."

Ronke chewed her bottom lip, her forehead creased with worry. She slouched over the table, cradling her phone. Ada was on the other end of the line.

"You know I can't force him to come."

"I know that, but I can. Will you help me?"

"If the situation is as desperate as you say," Ronke said, "I'll do anything. I'm listening."

Ronke didn't move from where she stood at the side of Wande's desk. "Sir, your wife called. Again…"

"My who?" Wande looked over the rim of his glasses.

"Your wife, sir… Ada."

"I thought she'd stopped those weekly phone calls. Have you missed a payment, or…?" His eyes never left the screen in front of him. He reached for his notepad and his gold-plated Mont Blanc pen to jot something down.

Ronke shook her head. "No, sir. I do not miss payments," she hissed. "Your wife says she needs to talk to you urgently. About your kids."

He slammed his laptop shut and pushed his chair back. "What happened?" His movement was so quick that she barely had time to raise her hands to stop him.

"Nothing has happened, sir. She wants you to come and see them."

"What?" Wande craned his head forward and narrowed his eyes. "That's what the urgency is about? A visit? Does she realise what I do? Is my work a joke to her?"

"Sir, she says she will leave if you don't come home by Friday."

Wande threw his head back and laughed. "She's lucky I'm in a good mood today." He let out another hearty laugh as he settled once again in his chair. "Mrs Coker, for these people, it always boils down to money. Tell her to name her price, and let's move on." He dismissed Ronke with a wave of his hand.

Ronke went back to her desk and placed her head in her hands. So much for being magnanimous. How could a man be so clueless about what was important in life?

She almost wanted to hit up the side of his head as she'd done once when he was a teenager. In those days, he always apologised quickly. But he wasn't a kid anymore, and that was no longer an option.

"God," she spoke aloud, "I am here again. Ada says she is praying about this. I am joining my faith with hers for you to help us in this matter. I ask in Jesus's name."

She sighed and went back to work. Not long after her exchange with Wande, she was startled by a shout and the bang of a fist on a table.

"Mrs Coker!"

She returned to Wande at once. He sat by the window, arms folded, shoulders hunched. His war pose. She could only wonder at what happened in the five minutes she had been gone. She braced herself for whatever was coming. His eyes were on fire.

"I pay that woman good money to do one job! Who does she bloody think she is? There are millions of women out there who would kill to earn what she does! Forget what I said earlier. We are not offering her a dime more." He turned back to the window, but Ronke clearly could see the unsteady rise and fall of his shoulders.

"Sir, may I speak freely?" she asked.

"No," he said gruffly. "I don't want to hear anything. We have a contract. I swear, if she sets a foot out that door, I will destroy her!" Still panting, he leaned on his table and waved a hand at her. "Go ahead. What did you want to say?"

Ronke hoped she hid her amazement well. Why was he so riled up? She often vacillated between minding her own business and plunging into the deep end with his antics. This time, she decided on the latter, hoping her three decades of service would speak for her.

"Sir, I have been with you for a long time. I served your father and now you. In all that time, I have never interfered in your private lives. Not with him, nor with you."

"What's with the history lesson, Mrs Coker?"

Ronke stopped herself from rolling her eyes. "Sir, I interact with your new wife regularly. The last time I was there, Emily invited me to tea with her dolls; Ada's boys were riding Timi like a horse."

Wande felt a tiny tug in his heart. "Okay, so she is doing the job. What else?"

"Really, Wande?"

Her tone made him turn. She'd stopped calling him by his given name the minute he had taken over as CEO after his father's death. She squared her shoulders, ready for an outburst, but instead, he leaned against his desk and folded his arms, glaring.

Taking a deep breath, she continued. "Mr Badejo, your kids are happier than they have been in a long time because of that woman. If she says you should come home, I think you should listen. For two reasons. One." She stretched back a finger. "She has never asked this from you before. Two, I don't know if you will find anyone else like her, and three—"

"You said two."

It was Ronke's turn to glare. "Sir, there is nothing you do that your division heads cannot handle. You spend so much to hire the best, and you refuse to let them do anything." She calmed herself and spoke more gently. "Please go home, sir, maybe for a week? See what she wants. You'll be back at work in no time."

Wande shrugged, and she saw a tiny bit of the boy he used to be. "Why the urgency?"

"She's been calling every day for the past week on this matter."

His brow furrowed, deep in thought. Then, he brightened suddenly and clicked his fingers. "Maybe we call her bluff? That money is too good. She isn't going anywhere, trust me. Tell her I am busy, and I can't say when I'll be back." He looked smug – nonchalant, even.

Ronke shook her head and left his presence. She couldn't stand it.

The minute Ada bought the tickets to Port Harcourt for herself and her boys, she called Ronke to let her know.

Ronke in turn, called her boss at once. "Sir, she has bought tickets for Friday. She wasn't bluffing."

Chapter Fourteen

Wande's annoyance at Ada's summons mounted as he walked into his three-bedroom apartment in Knightsbridge. He'd had time on the way back from work to mull over the situation, and as he did so, his ire only increased, sticking like a burr in his side.

Who did she think she was, making threats and giving ultimatums? It sounded like she was on some sort of ego trip in his house, surrounded by servants whom he paid for. Maybe he should remind her who was really calling the shots in this arrangement.

He promptly called the head of his protocol team for West Africa and asked him to get the jet ready. He would not wait till the following weekend, as he had told Mrs Coker. He had to deal with this matter at once and on his own terms.

So, within the hour, Wande was dressed and headed for the airport. He left the private terminal before midnight.

He let himself in just after eight the next morning. His million-dollar home looked like a nursery had exploded inside. Pieces of clothing, building blocks and other toys were strewn all over the place. A rubber seat that resembled a potty had pride of place by the stairs. A bowl of half-eaten food sat on his Boca do Lobo handcrafted-marble side table with a drop or two of a mystery mixture on its surface.

His slow-burning annoyance quickly grew into a raging inferno.

"What in the devil's name is going on here?" His voice reverberated around the house. At the same time, the door opened behind him, and there she was, standing with her mouth and eyes wide open.

What was it about this shapeless black dress she always insisted on wearing?

"Cat got your tongue?" he asked. "What are you staring at, woman?"

"I… I… What are you doing here?" Ada looked around as if searching for answers in the air.

"What am I doing in my house? Is that the question you should be asking?"

"I… I was… just…"

"Just what? Now I have a question for you." He spread his hands around the space and spoke through gritted teeth. "Can you explain to me why *my* house has been converted to a pigsty?" His voice was raised as he advanced towards her. "Is this why I brought you here? So you can turn my home into this? God knows I pay you enough, and the least you can do is not treat my home like you do yours in whatever backwater village you come from. I mean, look at this. What is this?" He spun on his feet to assess the mess again. "If this is how you treat my home, then what state are my children in?"

Ada felt a sharp pain in her head and a sense of *déja vu*. His voice almost sounded like Emeka's.

Wande's nose crinkled and his lips curled. "What was that stupid message you sent through Ronke? Dictating to me where I should be and when? Nobody tells me what to do!"

Ada stepped away from his venom, stumbling into Cynthia, who had been standing behind her throughout this tirade, stunned into silence.

Ada knew she should say something. Tell him about the morning routine. Tell him how Emily never wanted to be far from her, so they would bring her and Obinna, and their deluge of toys, downstairs, and the nannies would do all they could to entertain them, while Ada focused on the older boys, checking homework and coordinating after-school schedules. She should tell him that once she returned from the school run, the house was always restored to its pristine condition.

But no words came. Instead, she hung her head in shame. "Mummyyyyy!"

The scream put a stop to the tirade as all eyes turned to the first floor. Emily was struggling to get out of Mary's arms.

"Little Ada, wait," Mary said. But Emily was insistent that she wanted to get down.

Mary looked at Ada helplessly. Ada came to life at the sound of Emily's cry and moved to the foot of the stairs. She nodded to Mary to let her go.

Emily held onto the poles on the banister, grinning from ear to ear.

"Mummy, *shii*!" She waved with her other hand, looking at her feet to see each step. "Mummy, *shii miii*!"

"I see you, baby." Ada knelt at the foot of the stairs; her arms outstretched to receive the little girl.

Wande's eyes widened, and he moved forward slowly like he was wading through a marsh.

Who was this child? This child, whose face glowed, her cheeks round and chubby, with deep-sunk dimples that made her look like a doll. A thick afro on her head was held in place by a yellow ribbon that matched her yellow-striped onesie. Her smile looked like his late mother's.

"Mummii, *shii*!" Emily had three more steps to go, but suddenly, she threw herself into the air.

Instinctively, Wande jumped for her. His right leg made contact with a truck on wheels, and his foot slid forwards against his will. His arms worked to steady him, but the floor rushed towards him faster than he could catch himself.

The crack as Wande's head made contact with the marble floor made Ada feel sick to her stomach. Silence reigned as his body lay unmoving.

Then, everything went crazy.

Michael reached him first, even though Ada was nearer.

Her eyes widened in terror. She handed Emily to Cynthia and knelt beside Wande.

Michael lay his head on Wande's chest. "He is breathing. Call security, madam."

"Yes, yes." With shaky fingers, Ada dialled one on her phone.

The call was answered immediately, and Ada tried to explain what had happened, but the details spilled out of her mouth without reason, and the operator sounded confused.

Michael snatched the handset away, raising his voice above Emily's screaming. "We have a medical emergency. Wande Badejo has collapsed."

He dropped the phone, turning back to Wande's body on the floor. He loosened Wande's tie and the top three buttons on his shirt, stopping intermittently to place his head on Wande's chest to ensure he was still breathing. His hands were swift and sure as he arranged Wande's body in the recovery position.

Ada stepped back as she watched Michael work on Wande.

This was all her fault. She'd insisted he come.

Her harried thoughts were cut short when a loud blasting noise came from above the house. She grabbed Michael by the arm.

"It's the medical chopper. Open up for the personnel," he said gruffly.

Ada had never seen a helicopter up close. She stood mesmerised, blocking her ears, as the huge contraption descended on the front lawn. Three men in white medical garb got down from the chopper. The first was an elderly man, judging by the grey on his head. The other two were younger and carried a stretcher. More cars arrived from the private security unit, including two uniformed men on blue-and-white motorcycles. Security agents guided the paramedics into the house, speaking quickly into their walkie-talkies. Ada stepped aside to let the entourage pass.

After a few minutes, there was another flurry of activity as everyone rushed back out of the house. Ada barely caught a glimpse of Wande on the stretcher, carried downstairs by his personal guards and the two young paramedics. Her hand flew to her throat.

The older gentleman stopped next to Ada on the way out. "I assume I'll see you at the hospital?" He didn't wait for a response before joining the rest of the crew in the helicopter.

Ada clung to Michael in the doorway, allowing her tears to fall as he wrapped his arms around her, steadying her.

"Is he dead?" she cried.

"Don't fear," he shouted over the whirr of the helicopter blades. "Medically speaking, he is in the best hands in the country. We will ask God to do His work while they do theirs." He pulled her close. "You should go to the hospital."

Ada nodded, reluctant to leave the safety of Michael's arms. He led her to a waiting convoy of three black SUVs, which took off from the drive promptly, flanked by men on motorcycles.

The usual bottle-neck traffic on Alfred Rewane Road and Akin Adesola Street in Victoria Island opened for them as they sped through. Any trip to the island would normally take anywhere from thirty to sixty minutes during rush hour, but they arrived at the hospital in only fifteen.

Ada had never had to use the hospital in the three months she'd been in Lagos. Emily's paediatrician made house calls, so the place was all new to her. It wasn't somewhere she'd hoped to have the occasion to visit.

The convoy drove past the entrance to the back of the building. Ada got out, at a loss for what to do or where to go.

She sighed with relief when one of Wande's guards came out of the massive glass building and led her to a side entrance signposted 'Private'. He entered a lift, and Ada followed in silence. Together, they went up to the fifth floor.

"Badejo," was all the guard said to the nurse at the nursing station. The nurse rose promptly and escorted them to a door at the end of the corridor.

The room was unlike any hospital room Ada had ever entered. The space was furnished to the same standards as an exquisite living area, with thick, wall-to-wall carpeting, and a full lounge set and coffee table. A flat-screen TV mounted on the wall was tuned to CNN, but the sound was off. Art was strategically placed all around the room. The most noticeable difference from the usual hospital atmosphere was the smell, and sure enough, there was a lavender-scented diffuser in the corner of the room. Soft instrumental music drifted through surround speakers in the ceiling.

This can't be right, Ada thought, and was ready to turn back when she saw the same grey-haired man from the helicopter by the window.

"Doctor?"

He turned around, startled.

"Ah," he exclaimed as recognition dawned on him. "You're the lady from the house. I didn't hear you come in; my hearing aid must be getting wonky." He laughed heartily, his whole body shaking. When he recovered, he introduced himself.

"I am Dr Nnamdi Okoro. I have heard everything about you and your progress with little Emily from Dr David Jones. You're the lady working with the children, right?"

Ada nodded. She couldn't help but smile at the portly physician. He reminded her of a smaller version of Father Christmas.

"I am sure you are anxious to see Wande. Come with me."

He led her through a double door to another room with a hospital bed bigger than any she had ever seen. There was an IV station beside the bed, with heart and chest monitors lining the walls and a small sitting area in the corner.

"All his vitals are great; we have done a full blood count and will get results soon. I am not worried. He is in excellent health." Ada heaved a sigh of relief but still glanced worriedly at the figure on the bed. She walked over to him slowly, while the doctor continued to murmur medical jargon.

She stood by Wande's bed and studied him as he lay still. In every one of their encounters, he had always seemed larger than life. But here, in bed, she could see past his bluster and his scars. He looked at peace without his frown lines; she had once thought them a permanent feature. He looked… vulnerable.

Without thinking, her hand went to his face, and she cupped her palm gently beside his ear. "Please be okay," she whispered.

She shuddered, remembering how his words had made her feel when he arrived in the house. Another man who thought she was useless.

But she pushed those thoughts aside, too. For now.

Father, please let him be alright. Even if he has to come back as horrible as he was, just let him come back.

She moved away from the bed and returned her attention to the doctor, who began asking questions about Emily. Ada brightened. This was a conversation she could have confidently.

Wande opened his eyes slowly, trying to adjust to the stark light in the room. He winced. He felt like sharp shards of glass were piercing his skull, but familiarity slowly dawned on him. He recognised where he was at once: in his family's wing of the Radcliffe Hospital in Victoria Island.

Wande had spent more hours than he liked in this room: first, with his father when his mother's health was declining, and then when he'd watched his father follow suit six months after her death. He felt a heavy weight of sorrow on his chest. He did not need this; he had to get out of here. But his whole head seemed to be in some sort of vice, and he couldn't move. He fought the panic that welled up in him.

Voices spoke loudly in a far-off corner of the room. Wande tried to push himself off the bed, but a sharp pain on his right side caused him to cry out.

A face loomed large over him, but in the glare, it was difficult to make out who it was.

"Hello, young man."

Wande would have smiled if he could. No matter how old he got, he would always be 'young man' to Dr Okoro.

"Glad you could join us. You gave us quite a scare."

Seeing the familiar face of Dr Okoro, the top cardio surgeon in the country, did little to calm Wande's nerves. Dr Okoro had operated on his mother.

"What happened?" Wande's voice cracked. "Can you get this thing off my neck?"

Quickly, the doctor released Wande's brace. "Sorry, just a precaution. First, can you tell me who I am? And who you are? And what date it is?"

"You are Dr Nnamdi Okoro, I am Wande Badejo, and today is the…" He scrunched his face as a fierce headache hit him and winced. "Today is the 15th March 2019."

"You pass with top marks, my boy."

Nearby a woman sighed. Probably a nurse.

"How are you feeling?" Dr Okoro continued.

"Everywhere hurts." Wande tried to adjust his body in the bed. "Ugh, my leg… my right leg."

Concern flashed across the doctor's face. "Madam, please excuse me. Let me examine him."

Ada took a step back and Wande's scowl fell firmly into place.

"What are you doing here?" he growled.

Dr Okoro looked from one to the other. Ada squirmed.

"Why, Wande, she is here to see you; we were all concerned."

"Get her out of here, now." He didn't want anyone to see him like this, in bed helpless, and definitely not her.

"Sorry, I just—" Ada stepped towards the bed.

"Now!" Wande fell back on the bed, heaving from exertion. If his body weren't so weak, the sheer force of his anger would have raised him from the bed. This was all her fault, after all.

Soon, he would deal with her. He needed to get out of there first.

Chapter Fifteen

"The trip will take much longer without the escort," said John, the driver, as he drove out of the hospital grounds and straight into traffic. Ada preferred this way of travelling anyway; it made her feel normal again.

Why did I insist he come? She had been turning over the question in her mind for some time. Seeing Wande in the hospital had inflamed things even further. Unable to untangle it on her own, she dialled Ronke.

Ronke sounded tired when she picked up. "I just got a call from Wande breathing fire and brimstone."

"He showed up, unannounced," Ada said. "I thought you said he was coming next weekend."

"He said he was. You can imagine my surprise when I heard he was about to touch down in Lagos, and that I should join him there today. I'm so sorry. I should have told you."

"I know. *Chaii*, Ronke. It was a disaster. None of us were ready, and the house was in its morning chaos! He went crazy."

"Oh o... You know how he is about cleanliness."

Familiar anxiety from her previous marriage filled Ada's body. The constant cleaning and cleaning, all so Emeka didn't find something to complain about.

"Maybe it would have been different if I'd ever had a chance to get to know him." Ada's voice wavered. "He... was screaming at me in front of the staff, and I... We were all settling down in a good space until then."

Ronke's voice was soothing. "There's no need for all this. He is there now. Wande takes a bit of getting used to. And now, at least, Timi can see his father."

Ada sighed. "You're right." She sat upright as if to echo her resolve.

"I'll see you in the morning," said Ronke. "We have a lot of work to do. A room needs to be set up for him somewhere downstairs before he gets home tomorrow. It seems he has either sprained or broken his left ankle."

Ada's heart plummeted and she bit her knuckles.

Ronke went on, "And that's just the easy part. The doctors are more concerned with the knock on his head, and they're insisting he stays overnight for observation. That will be a tough one. Wande hates hospitals."

"He's going to kill me when he wakes up," Ada muttered.

"Snap out of that. We have bigger issues to consider. Wande needs a downstairs space converted into a bedroom-cum-office for the next few weeks. Think of a location and let me know what you decide ASAP. Chidi will be right over to handle the renovation. The work needs to start immediately."

"Chidi?"

"Yes, Chidi, the designer."

"Wait," said Ada. "Renovations? Why can't he recuperate in his bedroom like everyone else?"

Where he won't disturb us. The idea of Wande sequestered there for weeks until he recovered sounded like a much better scenario than him staying downstairs, able to witness most of the family activity.

"Unless Wande is in a coma, he will be working, and his work involves lots of meetings. Do you really want people traipsing through your home?"

"I didn't think of that," Ada said. Her flicker of hope died quickly.

"It looks like he may have to be there a while. I think you've got your prayers answered, my friend."

Ada dropped the phone with a sense of dread.

Back at the now-spotless house, Ada quickly gave the staff a rundown of Wande's condition and the changes that were going to be necessary. Mary and Cynthia glanced at each other when she mentioned that Wande would be there for a while. She knew how they felt; she was not looking forward to it either. Only Michael seemed unperturbed, and Emily, who had found her way back into Ada's arms, was blissfully unaware of all that had happened or her role in it.

Ada's next assignment was to find a room on the ground floor for Wande. She had already decided that it would be too much to rearrange the two living rooms. So, she checked out the library to assess its merits.

She loved the space. When she walked in, light burst through the large windows. Wall-to-wall shelving held books from first-edition classics written by African and international authors to books on science and all types of religions, as well as biographies of famous and not-so-famous individuals. At the centre of the room was a coffee table surrounded by four fabric-covered bucket chairs, great for snuggling up with the perfect book. She'd found Tobe in such a position many times.

She shook her head to clear it.

"No, this won't do," she said with disappointment. It was too narrow and furnishing it as a bedroom and office all-in-one would be awkward.

Next, she went into the study, a room that was off-limits to the children and that she herself almost never entered. One end of the space was set up like a sitting room, with a three-seater leather couch, a coffee table, and two additional armchairs. Bookcases and cabinets spanned the length of the room. At the other end, a workspace with a desk tucked into the corner. There was a wet room just off the nearest hallway, only steps away.

It was ticking all the boxes so far.

Ada spied two framed pictures on the navy-blue wall behind the desk. One was a portrait of an elderly man and a young teenage boy, and the other was obviously of a very young Wande. She smiled; it was not difficult to see the resemblance between grandfather and grandson. She took a few pictures and sent them to Ronke.

Within minutes, Ronke responded: 'Great choice. Chidi is on the way. Chat later, about to board the plane.'

Twenty minutes later, there was a call from the gate saying Chidi had arrived.

Ada stood at the front door waiting for him. A red sports car swung into the drive at an alarming speed and parked right outside like it owned the spot. A yellow heel stepped out of the driver's side, then the rest of the owner followed.

This was Chidi? Chidi was a *she*? Not just any she, but a gorgeous she.

Chidi's bright pink-bustier top exposed her flawless ebony skin and well-toned arms. The hems of her wide-leg Ankara pants floated over the stones on the driveway as she walked, her braids brushing past her calves, her yellow sandals clicking with high tempo.

"Hello, Ada," she said brightly as she climbed the steps two at a time. She removed her matching, oversized yellow designer shades and smiled.

Ada smiled shyly. "Please come in."

Chidi breezed past her into the foyer and did a perfect spin to face Ada again. "I hear we have quite the emergency."

"Ah, yes. He may come home as early as tomorrow, and we need to be ready."

"I'm thinking the study will be the best place to tackle first."

"Oh, yes." Ada found herself walking faster to keep up with Chidi's long strides.

Chidi needed no directions, and she was soon at work with her measuring tape, notebook and pen.

"I suppose we should plan for a wheelchair," Ada said. It was difficult to imagine Wande doing anything other than walking through the front door.

Chidi shook her head. "He's not gonna like that."

"You know him well?"

"Very." She gave a knowing chuckle.

Ada didn't know what to make of it. It was difficult not to wonder about Wande's reasons for hiring such a beautiful designer. Did Chidi know who she was?

Ada's hand went to straighten her scarf, then stopped. Why should she care? Wande's personal affairs were none of her business.

Chidi took a call, speaking in rapid Yoruba. In less than an hour, a truck full of men, materials and furnishings arrived. Chidi changed into shorts and sneakers, and wrapped her hair in a bun at the top of her head. They set to work.

Timi sat in the front seat. He stared forward out the windshield as Ada shared the news.

"Your dad is still in the hospital for now," Ada explained. "But he's improving. And when he gets out, it sounds like he will be staying with us for some time."

Timi took a deep breath but said nothing till they all got down from the vehicle. Ada wasn't prepared for the hug she received. He held her until she was breathless. As she laughed and rubbed his back, he turned away, brushing his fists across his eyes.

Her apprehension began to fade. She would take anything Wande threw at her to keep this boy happy.

Her next big task was to keep the boys away from the workmen and Chidi. It was as if the boys had never seen a woman before – and certainly not a woman wielding an electric saw.

Ada understood their fascination. Even she was intimidated by Chidi's beauty, her strength, and her ability to command her ten-man team. But the site was too dangerous for the boys, and eventually, Ada had to ban all of them from coming down to visit. In return, they were allowed to watch movies and have dinner upstairs.

While the men worked, Ada and Michael made sure refreshments were available throughout the night – food, drinks, coffee. Security also showed up to monitor the situation. By the time Chidi left at midnight, Ada felt thoroughly exhausted from the all-day event.

The next morning, the boys were shipped off to school, and the house grew quiet. While everyone was on tenterhooks waiting for Wande to arrive, Ada stood by the door of the study. She could not believe the transformation. What had once been a stuffy, disused space was now a tranquil studio. There was no way Wande would not appreciate the effort. He might even tone down his attitude, and maybe the situation would be tolerable after all.

Ada had to hope.

Chapter Sixteen

"How exactly am I supposed to get *up* these stairs? Did any of you dimwits consider that when you were spending my money on renovations?"

Wande's booming voice reverberated from the front drive. He was entering the house for the first time – in his wheelchair – and Ada stood at the top of the steps, every muscle clenched, trying her best to fade into the wall. She had been dreading this exact moment since Chidi finished renovating the study.

Wande's security team stood nearby, looking at each other, none of them entirely sure how to respond. Finally, they gathered around him.

"Not a problem, sir." Kunle, Wande's personal driver, signalled to his second. "Dipo and I will take you up." They squatted to lift the chair and its occupant. Ada watched them with fascination. That wheelchair looked like a miniature car. Apparently, their muscles were not just for show.

Wande closed his eyes, his jaw grinding until the guards set him down at the top of the stairs.

"Stop gawking," he muttered when he saw the entourage waiting for him there: the nannies, Michael and Ada. "I am not a circus animal."

Ada and the nannies stepped back into the foyer, but Michael remained in place as the men wheeled Wande towards the converted study.

Ada ran ahead to open the door for them. As she surveyed the finished project, she felt proud. Now, when Wande entered, he would see the office portion first. The imposing desk had been replaced with a smaller one, easier for manoeuvring with a wheelchair. Chidi had installed automated blinds and floating artwork for visual flair where the workspace used to be.

Behind a curtain, where no one could see, a whole new bedroom set had been brought in, positioned in the centre of the room for easy access. Even the carpet had been replaced with hardwood floors to make it smooth for Wande to traverse.

It was truly remarkable what Chidi and her team had done in a single night. Even the air conditioning wafted the scent of vanilla around the room.

As Wande rolled forward, Ada watched his face carefully for a reaction. He wheeled himself into the room and went straight to his desk. Then, he adjusted his chair to fit the height of the table and asked for his laptop.

Her heart sank. She could find no trace of anything other than frustration in his features.

"All of you… get out," he barked, his eyes boring into Ada.

Wande's presence was felt even through the walls of the house. Emily and Obinna played more quietly than usual, while all the adults spoke in whispers. Ada busied herself with the babies, trying not to think of the man downstairs, but it was hard, and she kept checking her watch every few minutes. Cynthia would soon be home with the kids.

Before long, the intercom buzzed to announce Chidi's arrival, so Ada went downstairs to meet her. Chidi wore her braids in a tight bun, her body encased in a skin-tight charcoal-grey skirt suit. Today, her ruby heels matched her red sunglasses. She looked very corporate – how many versions of her were there?

"Chidi," Ada greeted her. "We have been admiring your amazing work today."

"Thank you. I'm glad you like it, but I've come to hear it from the horse's mouth." She waltzed past Ada, heading to Wande's suite.

"Chidi, wait." Ada turned to stop her, but she was moving with considerable speed. "He isn't in a good mood."

Chidi gave Ada a pitying smile. "I can handle it." Ada watched, mouth agape, as Chidi opened the door after a perfunctory knock and shouted, her voice raised, "The king has returned to his castle!"

"Silly girl."

Ada stiffened. Was that laughter she heard? Laughter disguised in Wande's voice?

Chidi had left the door slightly ajar, and Ada craned her neck as she passed, to see Chidi bending to peck Wande on both cheeks.

Ada quickly looked away and headed for the staircase. There was obviously… more to their relationship. It was none of her business, of course, but how would it look to the children? Should she have a word with him about keeping his affairs private?

She shuddered at the thought of attempting to communicate that kind of thing to him. They were barely able to exchange civilities.

Ada went to hide upstairs with the children. A few minutes later, she heard the study door shut. The now-familiar click-click of Chidi's heels followed as she headed for the door.

That was a short visit. Ada balanced Obinna on her hip and led Emily by the hand as they made their way back down the stairs. When they got to the last step, Ada released Emily's hand to let her jump off.

"Whee!" Emily clapped for herself as she landed safely on both feet.

Ada smiled as she sat down on the bottom step and placed Obinna in front of her. Now that he could support his own upper body, he loved sitting up to view the world. His round brown eyes darted back and forth, absorbing everything. Now, they watched Emily, his constant companion, as she jumped from one floor tile to the other.

When the big boys arrived, Emily's smile was broad, and even Obinna kicked his chubby legs in excitement.

"Ikenaaah! Ahaaanaah! Tobiiii! Timiii!" she called. One by one, they entered and dropped their backpacks, sports bags and whatever else they were carrying to hug the squealing babies.

Timi stopped in front of Ada, his eyes wide and searching. "Is he...?"

"Yes," she said with a smile. "He arrived an hour ago." Timi didn't let her finish before he ran up the stairs. "Wait."

Timi was already on the first landing. He turned around, impatient.

"Remember his leg?" Ada said. "He's in the study now. Be gentle with him."

Timi flew right down again and rushed to the study door. Ada watched him rub his hands on his trousers and straighten his uniform before knocking.

Eventually, a shout came from inside. Timi hesitated before entering.

Ada tensed. Her boy was walking into the lion's den.

Wande was in the middle of sending an email when he heard the knock. This had better be good.

He was irritated already with everybody. Mrs Coker still hadn't turned up. Legal had goofed one of his contracts. He was going to fire someone today, for sure.

"Come in!" he growled.

Part of him hoped it was that pesky woman. It was her fault he was where he was, his whole life was disrupted because of her mess. Just the sight of her got on his nerves, but if she showed her face, at least it would give him a chance to remind her of her place.

The door opened slowly.

"Dad?"

Wande felt his ire slip away.

Timi had grown taller since he had seen him last, his features more mature. In all the bustle of his arrival, Wande realised with a twinge that he had forgotten to greet his son.

"Oh, Timi. I didn't know it was you, lad." Wande managed a smile, his frustration disappearing.

"Hello. I heard you got hurt." Timi approached the table but did not go around to hug his father.

"Yeah, my ankle is a bit out of joint, but it'll heal."

"Dad, you're strong – like Superman." Timi smiled shyly, but Wande didn't miss the look of pride. A familiar twist of guilt resurfaced.

"Not quite that super, lad."

"But close. Do you know how long you're going to be here for?"

"Not sure, son. I still have companies to run."

Timi's eyes shone. "I know, but you have to stay till you're better, right?"

"I guess. It may be best." Wande nodded in the direction of the door and hesitated, but the words tumbled out anyway. "I have to get back to work now."

Timi dropped his gaze. Wande chose not to pay attention to the slump of his son's shoulders.

"Okay," Timi said. He went to the door and paused. "If you need anything, just let me know. I can get it for you."

"There are plenty of people around to tend to me, lad," Wande said.

Timi gave a small nod and left.

Wande stared at the closed door after he had gone. Their stilted conversations always left him feeling tense. He knew he would never win Father of the Year, but he just… didn't know how to change it now. His late wife had done the majority of the parenting. When she was alive, he hadn't needed to think about any of it. Now, things were different.

Timi had his mother's large brown eyes. She could stare for minutes without blinking, and so could Timi – almost like they could see into Wande's soul. Wande couldn't shake the feeling that whenever he looked at Timi, it was his late wife staring back at him through those very same eyes.

Wande turned in his chair and looked up at the portrait of him and his father.

If that man could see the state of Wande's relationship with Timi, he would be disappointed – more than disappointed. 'We Badejo men must stick together'. It was his favourite line, especially in an argument with Wande's mum.

Wande had loved hanging out with his dad, but even when Wande was young, their conversations had always revolved around business: strategies, tactics, and stories from his father's days at work.

What could Wande talk to Timi about? Where would he even start?

An email alert pinged. He allowed it to distract him.

Later, the boys showered and changed for dinner. They stood with Ada in the foyer, ready to go into the kitchen, when Tobe cautiously asked if they might be able to meet Wande.

Timi hesitated. The discomfort of his exchange with his father had not quite left him yet. "Uh, I think so. Why not?"

Before Ada could stop them, her three older sons walked across the hallway with Timi to the study and knocked on the door.

And before Ada could hand Obinna to Cynthia and rush after them, they were already making their way back.

Their faces were blank. Ada searched Tobe's eyes for some indication of feeling, but even he was expressionless.

"That was quick," Ada said. "Perhaps he didn't want to be disturbed."

"No, we saw him," Tobe said.

"Yeah," Ikenna said as he settled on his chair. "We just said our names and nice to meet you. He said nice to meet you too, and that was it."

"He's huge…" Ahanna said, his eyes wide. "Timi, are you going to be that huge when you grow up?"

Timi laughed. "How am I supposed to know, squirt?"

"Well," Ikenna joined in, jumping off his seat, "I am going to be the tallest person in the world and huge like your dad." He stretched his arms as far away from his body as he could and began to strut around the kitchen. "I'll be like the Incredible Hulk."

Everyone laughed, and he returned to his seat. Ada breathed a quiet sigh of relief. Wande's irritability had not dampened their spirits, at least.

As Ikenna took up his fork to start eating, he couldn't resist a jab at his brother. "We're still waiting for Tobe to grow. He's a midget."

Ahanna, never one to allow a tease to go unappreciated, fell off his chair onto the floor and laughed hard.

"Stop that right now." Ada waved the serving spoon at them. "We do not laugh at people's physical appearance. Tobe is the perfect height for a twelve-year-old. Timi is blessed with extra height, that's all." She smiled at Tobe, who nodded and went back to eating.

Timi suddenly spoke up. "Sometimes I wish I wasn't so tall. Everyone keeps assuming I'm in a higher grade, so they look at me weird when I say I'm in grade nine. The next thing they think is that I got held back and that I'm dumb."

Ada's brow creased. Timi wasn't one to share his struggles at the dinner table, especially when the other boys were in such a good mood. She studied the serious set of his features.

"I didn't know you felt that way," she said gently. "But you know what? Let them keep assuming. Something tells me certain girls in your class don't mind tall guys." Ada winked for good measure.

Timi buried his head in his meal, blushing. Ikenna and Ahanna broke into a random song with lyrics that suspiciously rhymed with 'Ella'.

Meanwhile, Michael passed the table holding a huge tray on his way to the study. Silence fell at the table as everyone's eyes followed him.

"Mummy?"

"Yes, Ikenna."

Ikenna stared towards the study. "Won't he be lonely there by himself?"

"I don't think so." Ada didn't want to think of Wande at all. She returned her attention to her food, but the boys continued to stare.

Timi quietly set down his fork. "If it's okay with you, Aunty Ada," he said, "I'd like to go and eat with my dad."

Ada frowned. "Of course, Timi."

"Can I go too?" Tobe asked.

"You stay here," Ada said. "Wande might feel overwhelmed with too much company."

"Aunty Ada, let him come, please," said Timi.

Ada's frown deepened. She could see unease in Timi's eyes.

Reluctantly, she agreed. As the boys got trays to leave with their food, the twins expressed their displeasure at being left out and asked Timi if they could come, too. Timi invited all of them to join him and his dad.

With the kitchen emptying, Emily and the baby began to fuss. Ada knew she wouldn't be able to feed either of them when they were in such a state. So, she left Obinna with Cynthia and followed the older kids with Emily, dreading what Wande would say as the entire troupe made their way into his makeshift studio.

Wande was eating and reading a document at the same time. His fork paused on its way to his mouth as the entourage came in carrying trays of food. Ada entered last, with Emily in one arm and a highchair in the other.

Wande dropped his fork and asked dryly, "To what do I owe this honour?"

Ada tried not to bristle at his tone. "The kids thought it was unfair that you were in here all by yourself. They decided to join you."

"Oh, that's not nec—"

"Daddy, please." Timi stared at his father. "Let's eat together."

Ada held her breath as Wande's jaw stiffened. He glanced from Timi to Emily, and then back to Timi. Slowly, he relaxed. "Okay, then. Silence, please. I'm still working."

Ada let out her breath.

With the blinds drawn tight, the whole space was open to the children. Timi and Tobe took the chairs, Timi moving his chair nearer his father's desk. The twins sat on the floor, but Ada had to stop Ahanna from attempting to climb on the bed. As she pulled him away, she saw Wande's eyes darken.

For several minutes, strained silence stretched through the crowded room, but soon, Ikenna and Ahanna forgot about the instruction to stay silent and began a steady stream of whispers. When the other children joined in, the sound echoed loudly off the walls. Wande's frown deepened with every peal of laughter, but he didn't say anything.

Meanwhile, Ada struggled to get Emily to eat. She was fussing.

Ikenna said loudly, "Mummy, let's sing for Ada so she can eat."

Ada's eyes travelled to Wande's bent head and back to her son. "Er, no. I'll keep trying." She prayed that Emily would, for once, go without her usual performance.

Wande lifted his head and looked towards the twins. "You sing for her to eat?"

"She likes to be entertained before she opens her mouth," Ada explained.

"Entertained. Huh." Wande leaned back, his eyes narrowing. "This I'd like to see."

Ada shifted uncomfortably in her seat. It wasn't exactly the way she'd hoped to introduce Wande to their routine.

Ahanna started a beat on the side of his tray. Ikenna took his plate off his tray and drummed on it upside down for a fuller sound.

They chanted, "Ada oo Ada! Ada ooo Ada… Adaeze, Adaugo, Adanna, Adanne…!" Timi and Tobe joined in to clap.

Wande sat forward, resting his chin in his hands. Emily was loosening up, but she still didn't open her mouth. A quizzical look appeared on her face as she moved her body, waiting to join in the chorus. With Wande watching, Ada suddenly felt silly. But Emily had to be fed, and this was how it always happened.

Ada joined the singing and even danced, and Emily's grin widened as the chant became louder. Finally, she opened her mouth, and Ada popped in a spoonful of mashed potatoes. The boys erupted in cheers, and Emily waved her little arms in the air as she chewed, grinning happily.

The incredulity on Wande's face was comical as he watched them go through the process a second time.

"This is ridiculous," he said finally, drawing silence from the room. He looked at Ada. "Why do you sing your name for her?" Ada coughed, the discomfort swiftly returning. "Ada is the name reserved for the first daughters of the family. She is... your family's Ada."

"No, her name is Emily," Wande said sharply.

"I know that, I just—"

"I don't think you do. I gave my daughter a name. I would like you to respect that name without confusing her."

Ada bristled at the rebuke. All the kids had stopped eating and were now looking at them. Ada gritted her teeth and said, "I apologise. Emily."

"Thank you. And this singing thing is ridiculous. Find another way to get her to eat."

With that, Wande turned his attention back to his computer.

Ada stared with her mouth open. How dare he? Did he have any idea what they'd had to do to get to this stage?

The two older boys looked at each other. Timi bent his head down and shook it slowly. Ada regained control of her expression and gave them a reassuring smile.

"Maybe, we should leave you to eat in peace, then," Ada said stiffly to Wande.

"That would be best."

She pressed her lips tightly and glared at his bent form, wishing somehow her stare could translate to a smack on the back of his head.

"Boys, come on. Let's go." Subdued, her boys got up to leave.

Tobe pulled on Timi's sleeve and said, quietly, "Hey, let's go."

"I want to stay," Timi said.

Wande looked up to see the group huddled at the door waiting. "Timi, go with them."

"No. I want to stay with you."

"Go," Wande said again.

Timi's whole body deflated. He took his tray and joined the other boys in the doorway.

The remainder of the meal in the kitchen was a far cry from normal. Gone was the levity that was present a few moments before.

When everyone had left to watch TV, Ada remained alone. She hugged herself, vigorously rubbing her arms to ward off an internal chill. Still smarting from the reprimand over Emily, Ada wondered again what she had brought upon herself. She had been so disrespected in front of the children! Her heart thudded with dread as the thoughts took root.

How was she going to survive 'The Beast' if he was to be caged in his study for six more weeks?

Chapter Seventeen

The Easter holiday began, but the children still needed extra lessons. Timi and Ikenna were struggling with maths, and Ahanna was a little behind in English, so the principal suggested they take classes at school over the holidays.

Unwilling to make the boys attend school over the holidays, Ada put in a request for a home tutor, instead. The school was willing to assign one to each of the boys for a fee. She even signed up Tobe; he relished the extra opportunity to learn.

Ada was learning an interesting lesson in the world of the rich: always ask for what you want. People were willing to do more than she expected, and they were almost always willing to do it for the right price.

The school asked that each child be equipped with a laptop to simulate lessons in school. Ronke arranged for four MacBooks – already configured and set up with security features – to be delivered to the house. Ada ordered a kiddie tablet for Emily, as well. Surprisingly, they all took to their Easter lessons with enthusiasm.

Ada wished she could avoid Wande, but he seemed determined for the opposite, calling on her multiple times a day for reasons ranging from the totally unimportant to the outright ridiculous. No sooner was she seated to do something than the intercom would ring and, sure enough, it was him telling her to come to the study, to get a glass of water, to fetch a remote right beside him, to clear his used dishes, to polish his shoes. His favourite request: bring Emily. To Ada's annoyance, he would call her to his office only to tell her to fetch his little girl, making her undertake the long journey upstairs again.

In two days, he had called Ada in a dozen times just to see Emily. Because Emily was frightened of him, she would cling even tighter to Ada whenever he attempted to lift her out of her arms. So, Ada now had to sit with Emily on her lap while Wande stared at her.

On the third day, Ada tried to facilitate a conversation.

"This is Daddy. Say Da… dd… y."

Emily turned her lips down and pointed at Ada's chest. "Ada."

"Yes, yes. I am Ada." Ada copied Emily's action. She pointed at her chest, then at Wande. "I am Ada; this is Dada."

"Da-da," Emily repeated, looking anxiously at her father.

"Please," Wande cut her off, annoyed. "I am nobody's Dada. You call me Father or Dad. I'm not interested in any local nicknames." Emily hid her face in Ada's dress. "Just go," Wande muttered, waving Ada and Emily away.

Ada rose, gritting her teeth. Her normally placid demeanour was showing signs of wear.

"Where does he get the nerve?" Ada paced through the kitchen as Michael cleared the remnants of crockery after dinner. "I've just been summoned to empty his dustbin! I don't understand –

what am I here for? There are staff for everything in this house. His PA just left. The cleaning staff sit right outside his office for errands, and he knows this because I told him. Can you imagine me last night, at 3 a.m., coming downstairs to give this man water from a fridge which is right there in his office?"

Ada stopped at one end of the room and turned on her heel to pace to the other side.

"Then, the criticism of everything I do," she said. "The staff should be like this; this should be done like that. Where has he been for the past three months, *ehn*? Where was he when we were all struggling to find a rhythm? Now, he arrives like a warrior prince to take over his kingdom!"

She stopped, her eyes flashing.

Michael emptied the contents of the last dish into a Tupperware container and shut it tight.

"Ada," he said gently, "you are getting upset in the presence of the wrong person. Have you told your husband any of this?"

"Don't ever call him that," she retorted, giving Michael a fiery look.

He shook his head and stacked the containers neatly in the fridge.

Ada knew her anger was misplaced. She bit her lip. "I'm sorry."

"That's okay. But isn't that what he is, though? Technically?"

She rolled her eyes. "On paper, yes."

"So, that makes you a wife. Maybe not in all aspects, but at least when it comes to the basics: mutual respect, consideration, etc. What wife takes being treated like trash every day?"

Ada rubbed her ear and looked away, her thirteen years with Emeka flashing through her mind.

"So, my dear, the only problem I see here is you." Michael shrugged.

Ada froze at his words, and her eyes narrowed.

Michael raised his hands in front of him. "Your contract says you are here as Mrs Badejo, with all the rights and privileges that position upholds. You are to care for the children to the best of your ability, and in so doing, you will have fulfilled your end of the bargain. And in exchange… You know the rest."

Ada raised her eyebrows. "Have you read the document?"

Soon after she'd arrived, she'd confided in Michael the details of the arrangement with Wande, and he had asked to see the contract. They hadn't discussed it until now.

"Didn't you? It's the basis on which you're here, isn't it? You've forgotten that you are here as a mother to his children and his wife for all intents and purposes. Yet, you have allowed him to box you into the role of chief servant."

He went over to the sink and started washing the crockery. She joined him to help dry. It was something she did often, and he had given up trying to stop her. They worked in silence for a minute.

"Maybe it's because I'm not educated?" she said suddenly. "Maybe he thinks I'm stupid."

"Not educated?" Michael turned, confusion written all over his face. "What do you mean?"

She shrugged. "You know, like, I don't have a degree from the university."

"That, my dear, is hogwash." Michael paused. "You don't need a university degree to be clever. Or to be able to do this job."

Ada dragged a dishcloth around the fine edge of a plate. Slowly, Michael returned to washing, but not without a sideways glance at Ada.

"Perhaps *you* are worried you are stupid," he suggested after a moment. "Is it because you didn't go to university?"

Ada didn't respond right away.

Michael's expression softened. "Did you *want* to go to university, Ada?"

Her hand paused on the edge of the plate. "I couldn't," she said. "It was never in the cards."

"Why not?" Michael asked.

Ada grimaced. "We were poor. I only attended school when I could, I borrowed books to keep up. My father always planned for me to marry rich." She set down the plate. "One day, Emeka showed up – a man with wealth my father had never even seen. There was no way around it. I was sold. Emeka promised I could go back to school one day, but… well. It never happened."

Ada faced Michael again, her eyes burning. "I suppose it's all repeating itself." Ada sat down heavily in the nearby chair, her head down. "All I have tried to do all my life is be a good girl. A good daughter. A good wife. A good Christian. I don't know what else God wants from me."

Michael slammed the pot he had been scrubbing back into the sink full of soap-suds. Ada flinched. He rinsed his hands, then grabbed a towel, walking in a circle as he dried his hands.

"We aren't done with that yet," she said.

"I am. For now." His face was hard as he sat on the dining chair beside her. "Ada," he said, "I am afraid what I'm about to ask will hurt. Even so, it must be said."

A frown creased Ada's forehead as she shifted in her seat. "Go ahead."

"When do you plan to take responsibility for your own life?" he asked.

"What do you mean?" Ada said. "How could I have changed anything?"

"You are ready to blame every other person who has touched your life," he said. "Your father; your ex-husband; God. There are sixteen-year-olds everywhere living through worse conditions than you have described, surviving on their own terms. If you didn't want to be 'sold', as you put it, why didn't you walk out and forge a life elsewhere?"

Ada's lips trembled, and tears gathered behind her lids.

"Why didn't you end your unhappy marriage?" Michael asked.

"You don't understand," she said. "I've never been given a choice in my life. They all made me—"

"Stop that!" Michael said. "Maybe you've had to make difficult decisions in the past. Even so, they were *decisions*. And right now, you're making a decision to be here. To do this job. Nobody is forcing you, and you can leave right now if you want."

"But... the contract..."

"That you signed and didn't even read!" Michael exclaimed. "Who will you blame for that?" He banged his fist on the table, and she jumped. "Tell me, who do you blame now?"

Ada couldn't hold back the tears anymore.

It was Osas who had read the contract for her. Osas who had told her what to do. Osas who she had listened to.

Ada put her head in her hands.

"That's what I thought." Michael rose and slowly went back to the sink. "Walk away or stay – the choice has always been available. There are situations where one can say they had no choice. This is not one of them, my girl."

Taking deep breaths, Ada shook, perhaps from the cold breeze of the air conditioning, or perhaps from the quaking of her soul. She rose from her chair and stood in front of him. She pulled her hand across her face and nose, then wiped it on her gown.

"You don't know what it's like. To be me. To be a woman. A woman in Nigeria. It's easy enough for you to stand there and speak about forging a life."

"So now you are blaming your gender? Your country?" Michael resumed washing up. "When does it end?" He shrugged and continued scrubbing.

She glared at his back, readying her response, when he suddenly turned, his hands dripping.

"Your problem is up here." He spoke fiercely; his voice clipped as he viciously poked his head with a finger. "Stop thinking you are a mouse in a trap. Wake up! There is no trap! You're living in luxury and thinking like a pauper."

The room seemed to shrink in the aftermath of his words. Ada turned and ran out of the kitchen, her eyes blinded by tears.

She fumbled up the stairs before she got to her room, stumbling in only to find the twins and babies using it as a playroom.

"Cynthia, help me sort these children, please. I want no disturbance."

The nanny took one glance at Ada's face before giving a quick nod and herding the children out.

Once they left, and the room was silent, Ada wished they would return. She didn't want to be left alone with her thoughts. She didn't want to hear Michael say those horrible things again and again, on repeat in her head.

He had no idea what he was talking about.

After a while, when the anger had receded and self-pity had had its way with her, she was left with a single niggling thought.

Could he have a point?

Could Osas have had a point, all those many days ago?

Useless.

Could any of it – even a fraction of it – be true?

That night, she punched her pillow in frustration and cried bitter tears until she fell into a restless sleep.

Chapter Eighteen

Ada woke in a panic. Her room was eerily silent. The cribs were empty. She dashed to the intercom, and Mary picked up on the first ring.

"Mary, where is everyone?"

"We're in the kitchen, madam, having breakfast."

Ada released a sigh. "Without me? How did that happen?"

"The twins bring Emily, and Tobe carry Obinna. *You still dey sleep. They no wan disturb you since you sick last night.*"

Ada shook her head and smiled; deep sleep like that was very unusual for her.

Cynthia's voice came on the line. "Madam, we're okay. Please take your time and get ready. There is a surprise waiting for you."

Ada snorted. "Surprise? What kind of surprise?"

"Come and see, Ma." She could hear laughter in the background. Ada rushed through her bath and dressed quickly. Her phone flickered on the bedside table – probably spam from the telecom company, she thought as she picked it up – but it was a text from Michael.

All the emotions from the previous day rose to the surface. She sat down by the dressing table and opened the message, her fingers unsteady:

'You are so much more than you think you are, you just don't know it yet. Have a good night, and I'll see you in the morning.'

Ada smiled. His message soothed her aching heart. Michael still believed in her.

She went down the stairs feeling much lighter. As she walked into the kitchen, her entrance was met with joy as all the children rushed to her.

"Mummy, are you better?"

"Come and sit with us!"

Even Emily clapped and shouted for Ada from her safe and comfortable position in Cynthia's arms.

Ada's heart was full as she sat at the head of the table.

Cynthia, Mary and Michael were grinning. Usually, they all stayed away on Sundays on her instruction, but today, they were all gathered in the kitchen.

Ada realised this was the first time she had seen them out of uniform. The girls were in jeans and simple tops. Michael wore a tie-dye shirt with brown pants. Without his usual hat, she noticed his full head of black hair – not bad for a seventy-year-old man.

Each one of them looked thrilled to see her. That morning, nobody had a role, or a station, or a part to play – they were all just one big family.

"What are you all doing here?" Ada asked. Emily struggled out of Cynthia's arms and came running to her. Ada, distracted as she crouched to lift Emily, was caught off-guard when everyone broke out into the happy birthday song.

As the voices melted together, Ada straightened, Emily in her arms. Tears pricked at the corners of her eyes.

Apart from the few instances when her birthday had coincided with a school day in her youth, the day had never been acknowledged. Looking around the room at each bright face singing for her, Ada felt truly blessed.

Ikenna was first up to embrace her. "Happy birthday to the best mummy in the world!"

Ada's heart swelled, relieved again that her previous actions had not estranged her from her beloved firecracker.

She laughed as Ahanna jumped on her next, then Tobe, and drew in a sharp breath when she saw Timi standing shyly behind him.

When he stepped up to embrace her, she hugged him tight, holding on for a long time. Since his father's arrival, he had taken to eating meals with Wande. She had missed him, even when he was near.

Mary and a smiling Obinna were waiting, so she had to let Timi go. She gave Obinna a kiss and a hug and handed him back to Mary.

"Thank you, ladies," she said as she received a hug from Cynthia and Mary.

Those women had made her life in that house so easy. She wouldn't let them forget it.

Last in line was Michael. Ada rushed in for a hug, and he wrapped his arms around her.

"Happy birthday, Ada. May this be the year you learn to dream."

Ada couldn't speak. She just nodded against his chest, her tears seeping into his shirt.

Maybe this was what it felt like to receive an earthly father's love. Ada had never hugged her late father, and she would never know if her mother had been the type to show such affection.

She stepped away from Michael. Perhaps it didn't matter. She was here, now, with this family.

She reached for a kitchen napkin to wipe her nose. "How did you all know?"

"Tobe told me this morning, Ma," said Cynthia. "So, I told *Oga* Michael, and with help from all the kids, we came up with your surprise."

"Tell me, then. What's the surprise?" Ada looked around the kitchen.

"Madam," Michael said formally with a slight bow. "We all want to gift you a day off."

Ada laughed with tears still in her eyes. "What does that mean?"

"Exactly what we said, Ma. A day off," Cynthia chimed in. "Since we haven't had enough time to buy you presents, we all agreed that this will be our gift to you. We will stay and take care of the kids, and you go and do whatever you want."

"But... I don't need a day off. You shouldn't be working today. That's not fair on any of you." Her gaze swept across the three staff.

"We want to do this, madam," Mary added.

"John has volunteered to be at your service; he is already waiting by the car," Michael said.

Ada threw her hands in the air. She couldn't think of it. A day off, with all of them stuck at the house?

"But what will I even do? Where will I go?"

"Anywhere you want, Mummy," Tobe spoke from the corner. "Aunty Cynthia had to explain to me what a day off was. I didn't know it was possible. I have never had a day in my entire life without you there. That means you haven't had a day off in twelve years." His eyes shone.

Ada swallowed hard. "I don't mind, Tobe. You know that." He nodded but said nothing else. She looked at her twins. "Ikenna, Ahanna, you guys want me to go, too?"

"Yes, Mummy!"

"But, Emily…" Ada looked down at the little girl, hoping that at least she would refuse this outrageous plan. Her face was tranquil as she laid her head on Ada's shoulder.

"Emily will adjust, Ma." Mary hitched Obinna higher on her hip and smiled at Emily. "She is learning *small, small.*"

"Aunty Ada, I think you should go. Before we all change our minds." Timi grinned, and Ada rubbed his head.

"Mummy, we even made you a picnic basket." Ahanna lifted a light-brown wicker basket onto the table.

"All the children helped," Michael said as he pushed the basket nearer for Ada to see the contents.

"I washed the grapes," Ikenna said.

"I put peanut butter on the bread," Ahanna added.

Ada opened the basket. It was filled to bursting with snacks, fruits, and refreshing drinks – it looked bottomless. A strange sadness twisted in her gut.

She knew they were all waiting for a response from her. Forcing a smile, she said as cheerily as she could manage, "This is great, guys. Cynthia, come and take Emily."

Ada anticipated a fuss from Emily, but she reached out to Cynthia without hesitation. Ada felt bereft. The betrayal – Emily, of all people. Michael lifted the basket from the table and began to carry it out to the car.

It was really happening, then. Despite her protesting, Ada was really going to have a day off.

"Let me get my bag." Ada hurried to her room and quickly stuffed her Bible and notebook in her bag before heading back.

By the time she returned, the room was clear. Michael was standing by the kitchen door.

Wearily, Ada looked across to the study. "What about him?"

The trip suddenly felt far more complicated. What if she asked his permission to leave, and he said no?

Michael put his hands on her shoulder and gently guided her towards the door. "Don't worry, I will sort him out." As he closed the door, he called out, "Have fun!"

Ada stood on the drive, alone, feeling lost. Wasn't it something she'd always said she craved – some alone time? Now that she had it, she didn't know if she wanted it. How quickly they had all let her go. Even Emily.

"Happy birthday, madam." John's cheery voice cut through her dark thoughts. He stood by the open door of a gleaming black BMW she had never seen before.

The warmth of the sun and the shine of the car quieted her silly thoughts.

This time was a gift – her gift, from her family. She was determined to enjoy it.

John was also in mufti, as it was his day off, too. He wore a flowery shirt printed with oversized colourful flowers. It suited him.

"You're looking bright today, *Oga* John."

"It's for your birthday, madam." He put on his seatbelt before pressing the button to start the car.

"I'm sorry to take you away from your wife on a Sunday."

"Ahh, forget it. When I told her the reason, she practically threw me out of the house." He chuckled heartily. "Ah, my wife likes you *well well*. You are always so kind and generous to us and the children."

Ada blushed. She didn't know how to handle the compliment, so she quickly asked, "Where are we off to?"

"Anywhere you want, madam."

Ada hesitated. She had never travelled anywhere outside of outings with the children. "Any suggestions?"

"How about a drive around? You could go somewhere for lunch or breakfast, or, since you have such a nice picnic basket there, we could go to the beach in Victoria Island. It's not very exclusive, but…"

"Ah, I don't mind." She smiled as the Banana Island entrance gates came into view. "Luckily, I'm not such a princess."

She leaned back into the comfortable red leather seats, inhaling the leather polish used for the interior. "Why the new car?"

"It blends in," John explained. "After all, we are travelling without the security detail today."

"Wande Badejo's cars never blend in, John," she said, and they both laughed.

John talked as he drove, teaching Ada tidbits about each area they passed, and grumbling at all the new developments, which had grown exponentially over the past decade. The newbuilds struck Ada as shiny and modern, but John spoke as though he disapproved.

"I knew Ikoyi when it was made up of mostly family homes, the kind with large gardens, very typical of the era when the British still occupied Lagos," John explained. "All these high-rises are relatively new. I worry that the land cannot support all this infrastructure. Will the water and roads still hold up as they once did? I would take large gardens and trees over soulless concrete any day."

Ada was more than a little impressed by his passion. "You make a convincing argument, *Oga* John."

"You can understand why I was so happy when Sir and Lady Badejo designed their house to pay tribute to the beautiful landscape of those times."

He drove down the long stretches of Gerrard, Alexander, and Bourdillion Roads, talking as he went, lamenting the state of the Falomo Police Barracks as they passed them.

"It's terrible the way our police officers and their families are treated. That place is now a slum. And they wonder why they are taking bribes on the street. The leadership has failed them as well as us."

Ada followed the landscape with her gaze.

"Look." He pointed ahead to a set of dilapidated buildings. "That used to be Falomo Shopping Centre. Oh my, in those days, it was the place to go for everything."

Ada listened, distracted by the sights as they reached Awolowo Road, with its array of upscale shops and boutiques.

Still confined to her mandatory widow's black, she had not even thought of clothes in so long. She wondered what it would be like to shop in such a place.

"John, stop."

John parked the BMW along the side of the road, and Ada stepped out onto the curb.

"I'll wait for you," John offered with a smile. In front of her, a shiny sign read "GLAM DIVA" over a set of double doors, marking the entrance to a bright and airy clothing store.

Ada stepped inside; her shoes quiet on the light-brown wooden floor. She shivered as she was met with a cold blast of air conditioning. At ten on a Sunday morning, she was the only customer there.

Smiling shop assistants greeted her when she walked in, but none of them rushed to help her. Their distance was welcome; Ada wouldn't have known what to say to them if they asked. She'd never put much stock in fashion. Emeka had constantly monitored her wardrobe; he preferred traditional attire, the style and fabric always decided upon by him, always dull brown or dark blue. She had never cared for his taste. If she'd been allowed to choose for herself, she would have picked bright colours – oranges and yellows and pinks.

Ada turned to face one of the displays, and sure enough, there it was. Before her was a burst of sunshine. It was an asymmetrical high-low dress, with yellow, red, and turquoise shapes patterned over a white background. She reached out to touch it. A soft breeze from the AC blew at the same time, and the fabric floated forward to meet her.

A salesgirl came over. "It's the only one we have left. Chiffon, and great for our hot weather. It will go perfectly with your skin tone. Your size, too. Do you want to try it on, or should I pack up it for you?"

Ada licked her lips, contemplating what to say.

"Madam." A second sales lady came to join her colleague. "She asked, 'Do you want this dress?'" There was an edge to her voice.

Ada looked at the dress again. Then, she said, with deep certainty, "Yes, I do."

A relieved look passed between the two saleswomen. The second returned to her seat, while the first continued her sales pitch.

"I have a pair of yellow sandals that will go perfectly with that. And some gorgeous options for bags."

Ada remained silent, trapped in a dream, while the salesgirl began to build her outfit after outfit. Colours, styles, cuts, designs – all of them were sure to look fabulous on Ada, she said. All the activity sent Ada's head spinning; it had been a long time since she'd felt anything like it.

The salesgirl gathered everything at the counter, and Ada stood across from her, still fixed in the dream. After the girl finished calculating the final price, she told Ada the figure.

Ada exited her trance abruptly.

An uncomfortable silence passed before Ada informed the salesgirl quietly that she would need to put everything back.

The smile on the salesgirl's face slipped, her dreams of a huge commission draining away fast.

"Madam, *wetin naah*? What is the problem?" she said a little too loudly.

Anxiety rooted Ada to the spot.

Then, a tall, curvy lady came through the door at the back. She wore a silk leopard-print shirt tucked into a tight pencil skirt, paired with red high heels. She surveyed the situation at the counter for a moment before turning to Ada.

"Can I help you, madam?"

But the salesgirl spoke first. "Madam, *this madam no wan pay. I tink say she no get money.* She just wasted our time this morning."

"Henrietta, please don't speak to my customers like that. Excuse us." The curvy woman smiled warmly at Ada. "Please call me Uche. I own this boutique."

"My name is Ada."

"Ahh, Ada, *Anyi bu umunne nwanyi.*" Her smile widened. "We are sisters. My older sister is Adaku. So please, feel at home here. Is there a problem with the stuff we brought out?" She began to take the items out of the bags.

"There is nothing wrong." Ada lowered her voice. "I just didn't realise the cost when I was choosing."

Uche lifted her head. "Do you like them?"

"I love them. I have never had anything so beautiful." Ada fingered the fabric of the sunshine dress with a wistful look.

"Would a discount help?"

"Honestly, I am just thinking of everything I can get for the kids with that money," Ada admitted.

"Mothers!" Uche shook her head. "Always putting everybody first. How many do you have?"

"I had four," Ada said. She turned the fabric over under her hand. "But now I have somehow ended up with six."

Uche crossed her arms, but her face still held a smile. "When last did you buy yourself an outfit that you really wanted?"

Ada laughed, but tears filled her eyes. "I don't know."

Uche looked at the sunshine dress. "Did you try it on, at least?"

"No," Ada said. "I'd rather not... You see, I am still..." She looked down at her black dress.

"I understand." Uche nodded slowly. "How long?"

"Five months."

"I'm sorry for your loss. Well, if you cannot try it on, at least let me have an idea of your size." She crossed to the other side of the counter and pulled Ada's *boubou* tight at the back, grabbing as much fabric as she could to reveal her silhouette.

"*Chaii!* See the figure under there. Great proportion of bust and hips. A comfortable UK size 12. I can see you wearing a size 10 *sef. Meen*, if I had your body, Lagos wouldn't rest."

Ada stepped away, smiling despite her discomfort. Uche quickly checked the sizes on the tags of each of Ada's ill-fated dresses. She switched one dress for a smaller size and came back.

"Do you know what *Nne*? Go, I will keep this stuff for you. The three dresses, the shoes, and the hat. I will keep them for a month. If I do not see you again by then, I'll hang them back up. It will give you time to decide, and since you are a first-time customer, I'll throw in a twenty per cent discount."

"Why? Why are you being so nice?"

"My sister, I know people say it's just clothes, but I don't agree." Uche shook her head. "There is something about the right dress and the right pair of shoes that lets you take on the world. As far as I'm concerned, I am in ministry, solving problems one fabulous outfit at a time."

Ada had to smile. "*Ezigbo nwanne m nwanyi*. My good sister, you are so kind. Thank you."

Uche walked Ada to the door and waved her off. "See you again soon."

Once Ada had left the store, John came out of the car to meet her, surprised to see her empty-handed. Ada turned to wave at Uche, and she laughed at the confusion clear on her face as John opened the door for her.

Ada got back into the car, subdued. She didn't see herself ever going back to the store. She would never be one of those ladies who shopped in a place like that.

"Where to next, madam?"

Ada shook herself out of the doldrums. This was meant to be a fun day.

"I don't know. Let's go to the beach!" She rolled down the window so she could feel the breeze on her skin. The buffeting force of the wind tugged at her cheeks and clothes.

In that moment, as the car raced toward the coast, she wasn't a daughter; she wasn't a wife; she was not even a mother. She was just herself. Ada was finally having a day off.

Chapter Nineteen

They were soon at the entrance of the privately-owned Oniru Beach. John paid the entrance fee from his stipend. "For emergencies," he said, and they drove in.

When they pulled up along the shore, John opened the car door for her. The sound of the crashing waves made Ada feel like hopping across the sand like a little girl. She followed John across the uneven ground as he headed towards a man clad in a sleeveless top and cargo pants.

"My brother, happy Sunday o," John said. "We want to rent a tent and chair."

Within seconds, money had changed hands, and Ada was being led to a small blue, square tent with sun chairs underneath. She settled into one and took off her slippers, enjoying the feel of the cool sand between her toes. John stood nearby, half in and half out of the shade.

"John, you don't have to wait on me. I'll be reading a bit. Go and relax."

"If you insist, madam," he said with a twinkle in his eye.

As he walked away, Ada lay back and closed her eyes. She sighed contentedly, relishing the feel of the warm morning sun on her skin.

As Ada took off her scarf, her hand went to her head, and she picked at the tufts of hair. Her hair was coming back to life again, growing thick and fast.

Her attention turned to the waves rising and crashing before her, the sun shining so brightly, the palm trees swaying lazily in the breeze. *Three months ago, everything I knew was snatched away from me. I didn't think I would survive. But I am here. The boys and I are well – more than well, in fact. Lord, I just want to say thank you.*

Her phone beeped, and she checked the screen.

It was a WhatsApp message from Michael with a picture attached. All the children were in the pool, obviously having a good time.

She smiled, sent a quick reply, and set the phone back down again. She took deep breaths and distracted herself with the sights and sounds at the beach, getting lost in the rhythm of the water crashing on the sand.

In the distance, a solitary woman stood at the water's edge. She seemed to be teasing the waves, edging her feet forwards and backwards in time with the movements of the water. She yelled something at the water, then dipped a toe in the sand and ran away as the waves came in.

Ada laughed. She could identify with this strange woman; waves could be dangerous. Ada watched her play this game a few times until she suddenly stopped and faced the waves. Another was forming – a big roller. Ada sat up as the woman raced towards it.

What was she doing? It was too powerful, too dangerous. Suddenly, the woman jumped headlong into the water and disappeared. Ada's hand went to her mouth and she stood up.

Seconds passed, but Ada felt like she was searching for the woman for hours. Finally, she appeared, swimming through the largest wave as it carried her back to shore and deposited her on the sand, unharmed.

The woman had the widest grin on her face. Ada collapsed in her chair, out of breath, as if she had just experienced the whole thing alongside her.

This woman was now walking towards her, drying herself with her beach towel.

Ada blurted out, "Weren't you afraid?"

The woman turned, shading her eyes from the sun, and gave Ada a friendly, quizzical look.

Ada went on, "The wave, it was so big you could have drowned. Weren't you afraid?"

"No," the woman said. Ada knew it. This woman wasn't like her. She was like Osas. Bold, free… Audacious. "But, I was afraid the first time I tried it."

Ada looked up. "Really? What changed?"

The woman shrugged. "I got tired of being afraid."

Ada held her breath. The woman's face was serene and open. Ada waited for her to continue as though her words might contain the answer to all the mysteries that swirled in her head.

"I dug my heels in and told the wave to come."

Ada exhaled, disappointed. "That's all?"

"Yup. It got easier each time I faced the next wave. Now, I don't even think about it."

"You make it sound so easy."

"It's not easy. It's terrifying, especially the first time. That's life, isn't it? We jump in, even when we're afraid."

Ada nodded and waved to the woman as she continued towards the parking lot and disappeared.

Jump in, afraid? Surely fear was a sign to stop doing something. Ada didn't even know when she was allowed to jump.

Memories of her conversation with Michael came steamrolling back again. She allowed herself to consider whether Michael had been right, whether there was more she could have done to alter her path in life. Could she have jumped in? Defied her father? Left Emeka? Done the online course with Osas and been a graduate by now? Read the contract with Wande? Negotiated it, even?

It would have been tough, yes. But impossible? Maybe not.

She had allowed others to carry her for so long. She thought of Osas again with longing and shame.

Ada stared out to sea. "Father, give me strength," she whispered into the air. "Help me to be brave."

As the prayer left her lips, she stood up, dusted the sand off her clothes, and strode towards the shore. A wave had just receded and the water's edge pulled back. She dug her feet into the sand the way she had seen others do and waited for the next one.

The rumble of the incoming wave filled her ears as it gathered momentum, as if to test her resolve. It sent a challenge: *move, or I will move you.*

Her knees threatened to buckle, but somehow, she resisted.

"No more," Ada said under her breath. She gritted her teeth and crouched like a fighter in a ring, daring the wave to come.

It did. She screamed as it slammed into her, a wall of water rushing around her, drenching her completely. For a few seconds, Ada felt fear like she had never experienced.

Was this how she'd die?

Almost immediately, the water receded, leaving her on her hands and knees, spluttering.

Ada felt John's arm around her. He was saying something, but she couldn't quite make out what it was, her ears still full of water.

"John, I did it!" She grabbed his outstretched hand. "I was afraid, but I stayed. John, did you see that?"

His look of concern elicited a bubble of laughter from within her. She laughed even harder as his mouth hung open. Ada didn't care; as soon as she could stand up from the sand, she took off running, waving her scarf in the wind.

Let him think her mad. This feeling was exhilarating!

As she sprinted down the beach, Ada felt like a bird, wild and free, and a thought crossed her mind: *what else am I capable of?*

Chapter Twenty

Ada and the children were busy preparing *fufu* in the kitchen when the intercom rang. Cynthia picked it up to answer. "Ma, it's *Oga*."

The smile slid from Ada's face. She closed her eyes and sighed.

Wande had given her some respite that morning; until the call came through, she'd been hoping he'd found other ways to amuse himself.

"What does he want?"

"He says to tell you he needs a glass. Right now."

"Can't you tell him we're busy?"

Cynthia looked shocked.

Ada chewed her bottom lip as she continued to mould more balls of *fufu*.

She didn't understand his relentless requests. There was a cabinet in Wande's room stocked with everything essential he could possibly need, only inches from his desk. He could stretch and get a glass himself. Not to mention that Timi was right there having lunch with him; why didn't Wande ask him?

Michael watched Ada weigh the request from across the kitchen.

"Madam, what should I tell him?" Cynthia asked, shifting uncomfortably at the elongated silence.

Ada took a deep breath. *This is just another wave. Dig in your heels, afraid or not.*

"Cynthia, take a glass and drop it off for Timi's daddy."

"Er... Ma?"

"You heard me. Please don't keep him waiting."

As Cynthia hurried out with a glass on a tray, Ada caught Michael's eye. He gave her the smallest of smiles, but it did nothing to calm the storm within her.

What would Wande do now? She still had marks on her back from Emeka that she had earned just for airing her opinion.

When Cynthia returned with Wande's tray, Ada held back from asking about his response, or if there had been any. Instead, she concentrated on feeding Emily to keep her mind from wandering.

As the week progressed, she grew bolder. She refused to pick up the intercom at every opportunity. When Wande made a request, she sent a delegate to carry out his bidding. Even when he asked for Emily in the evenings, Tobe was the one to take her to him.

Ada avoided him whenever she could. She didn't feel strong enough for the inevitable confrontation that would follow if they were in a room together.

On Sunday, her luck finally ran out. At midday, Wande wobbled out of his office on a single crutch and held onto his door handle, watching the noisy parade of children and nannies passing on their way to the pool. Each quieted down when they saw him and directed a muted greeting his way. Ada grimaced and hoped he would just let her pass.

But it was not to be.

"Come. You!"

Ada forced herself to keep walking.

"Ada, I am talking to you."

Steeling herself, she walked towards him slowly, her gown swaying along with her. She kept her eyes on his, resisting the urge to avert them.

Wande blinked in surprise as she approached. "I don't know what game you are playing at, but I will not have you disobey me in my house."

"Let's talk in your office." She clasped her hands behind her to stop them from trembling.

Wande did not budge. "What if I want to stay here?"

She shrugged and nodded pointedly in the direction of the kitchen. He frowned and shuffled back inside his room.

The curtain separating his bedroom from his office was open, and although the cleaners had yet to do their rounds, his bed was perfectly made – not a pin out of place. Even his desk, with all its papers and charts and notes, was arranged just so.

Wande sat on his bed and placed his injured leg on the stool in front of him. He had parted the curtains to let in natural light, and the sunrays filtered through the trees outside, streaking across his bed.

He was in a purple golf shirt with his collar turned up and khaki cargo pants. Without his frown, Ada couldn't help but notice, he was an attractive man. She had never seen him look so… casual.

"No meetings today?" Ada asked as she took a seat in the chair opposite him, her heart beating wildly.

"I didn't ask you to sit down." Wande scowled.

Ada cocked her head and glared. "What exactly is your problem?"

"Oh, the mouse is learning to speak?"

Ada flinched. Arguing with him would not be the best approach. She made an effort to take calming breaths.

"I meant, why are you so angry with me? I don't understand what I've done to you."

"Are you blind, woman?" Wande scoffed. He gestured vaguely at his immobile self. "Look at me! I have to remain housebound – and worse, in a chair – like an invalid!"

"Invalid?" Ada said. "Hardly. You're not paralysed. You broke your ankle after stepping on a child's toy."

"Because you left my house in a mess! Who allows children to leave their things strewn all over the place like that? And besides, I was trying to save my child from the precarious position you put her in! She could have seriously hurt herself."

"I had everything under control. I would never be careless with Ad—Emily's welfare."

"I saw her jump off—"

"She always jumps!" Ada cried. She could see his jaw working furiously. She wanted to curl her fingers around his neck and wring it with all the strength in her hands. "She always jumps," Ada said again, more quietly. "And I was ready. As for the house, it's never in that state for more than an hour each morning, and if you had allowed me to explain—"

"I don't want to hear your excuses! I saved you from your miserable life, put you up like a princess, all for you to just start forgetting why you are supposed to be here. That is irresponsible, and it's high time you owned it!"

Ada recalled the surge of waves as they approached her on the beach. She remembered how she remained standing in their wake.

Now, she stood squarely in front of him. She wasn't going to put up with his bullying. Not anymore.

"If we are going to talk, we will speak as equals. Even if I were your servant – and I am not – I would not be spoken to this way." Ada swallowed hard, gripping the edge of the table for support.

Wande moved his head away, surprise freezing his words.

She used the silence to plough on. "You have been here, what? Two weeks? And you haven't even done the decent thing to ask me why I wanted you back so badly. You've been huffing and puffing all over the place, and you still don't know the reason for all this, do you?"

Wande grabbed his crutches and, ignoring her, wobbled to his desk and sat down. He opened his laptop and put on his headphones.

She stared in disbelief and slapped both hands on the table. He didn't look up.

Her voice was shaky. "*Chere biko*, what kind of work do you say you do?" She no longer cared if the whole house heard her. "What is this conglomerate you say you have built? What man worth his salt treats his own flesh and blood the way you do? As uneducated and poor as I am, I would never do what you do to your own children.

"Your kids don't even know you. You use work as an excuse and blame everyone else for being the reason why your daughter has not had a proper meal since birth, or why your son is miserable all the time, despite all the money you have thrown at him… If this doesn't bother you, then you are even lower on the human totem pole than I thought. You're a bully, a hypocrite, and a coward, and you have failed as a father. *You* own *that*!"

Ada inhaled deeply. Wande's expression was still blank. Her throat tight and her chin trembling, Ada willed her legs to stay steady.

Her mind was beginning to catch up with her body. What was she doing?

She left his room and headed for hers, desperate to be anywhere he was not. Once she was inside her own room, she closed the door and leaned against it, where she succumbed to the tsunami of emotions that overwhelmed her. She wandered over to her bed and flung herself down on the plush coverings.

"He's so annoying!" she cried as she punched her pillow in frustration.

Despite it all, she wished she had been bolder. She knew her courage came from the fact he wouldn't have heard what she said with his headphones on.

Well, thank you, God, for small mercies. She had gotten her frustrations off her chest without the consequences. He wouldn't have a reason to fire her and, best of all, she had nothing to apologise for.

|215|

In the study, Wande remained motionless. He took off his headphones slowly. He'd never got around to putting his laptop on.

He gripped the pencil in his hand so tight it snapped. Picking up his phone, he dialled. He didn't like people who forgot their place, and this woman was forgetting quickly.

After all, Emily was fine now, and Timi seemed okay. Her role was not crucial anymore. He growled when he got Mrs Coker's voicemail.

"Mrs Coker, I need you to settle the accounts with this woman. Pay her for one more month. I want her out of my house first thing in the morning."

Chapter Twenty-One

Even though Ada had set her alarm fifteen minutes earlier to wake up and receive the delivery of the children's computers, the extra time wasn't necessary, in the end. She shot out of bed at 4.30 a.m., shaking from the very real dream she'd just had, her heart pounding in excitement.

In her notebook, she began to write feverishly, her fingers trying to catch up with her brain as she replayed the scene.

It was a smart and stylish boardroom. Everyone there was talking quietly. A woman walked in, and everyone sat up to attention. Short braids framed her smiling face. She was wearing a charcoal-grey suit with a silver pin on the collar and a lovely scarf around her neck. Before she took her seat, she announced in a pleasant voice, "I am so sorry for keeping you all waiting. This morning alone I've had to put out two fires from our sister company, and I received a rather unexpected call from the Minister of Finance. And it's not even nine o'clock." She grinned.

I couldn't take my eyes off her. There was something so eerily familiar about this woman. As if she heard my thoughts, she turned and looked directly at me, pinning me to the spot with her gaze. The room began to spin, and I felt dizzy.

The face staring back at me was my own.

Still fizzing with excitement, Ada closed her diary and got out of bed. She needed to get her Bible study done before the children woke up. Her study for the day was Proverbs 31, titled *'A noble and capable woman.'*

As Ada read and took notes, she couldn't help but wonder about the woman the passage described. She was loved and respected by her husband and children, and she ran multiple businesses of her own, ranging from general merchandising and fashion to buying and selling land.

Ada scanned the text for any resemblance to herself, but only found one line that fit: *'She wakes up early to provide food and tells her servant girls what to do.'*

Well, she did that, but that was all.

You can do all things through me.

Ada's brow furrowed.

"That's impossible," Ada said out loud with a laugh. "I can't do all that."

The thoughts I have for you are good.

Her laughter died instantly. She turned around, startled.

"Who said that?"

There was no one there, of course. The image of the boardroom came back stronger.

Ada looked in the tall mirror at the edge of her room. "But that version of me doesn't exist. The woman in my dream knew what she was doing. She was intelligent, smart, charismatic…" She didn't voice the words that scared her the most: *I could never be her.*

The silence that followed was unnerving.

Conflicting words ricocheted around the room, bouncing off the walls and back to her consciousness. They circled through her body and her mind until they grew too loud for her to bear. *I could never be her. I can do all things.*

Clutching her head in her hands, Ada slid to the floor. One of those voices was going to win. She was going to have to make a choice which, and soon.

Chapter Twenty-Two

Wande heard a lot of noise coming from the dining room, which meant that somehow, despite his instructions, that woman was still in the house.

Wande grabbed his crutches. He thought he had been clear, but it seemed Ronke had been unable to do her job. Now, he had two people expressly disobeying him. As if one was not enough.

Ada stiffened when Wande entered the dining room, and even Tobe looked down at his computer.

Only Timi smiled at him. "Hey, Dad. How's your maths? I've got homework."

Wande forced a dry laugh. "Terrible, son. I've got a head for business, but don't ask me about equations or algebra. I can't help you there." He frowned as he caught Ada stifling a laugh. The cheek of her. Wande shook his head in disgust. If her sons weren't present, he would have fired her right then. Again.

"My mum is great with math," Tobe said to Timi. "She helps me when I don't understand."

Wande snorted. Indeed. The poor boy must be failing woefully. Wande felt sorry for him.

"How often is that? Tobe, you know far more than I do." Ada playfully pushed her son's head.

"Aunty Ada, the test is starting." Timi stared wide-eyed at the screen. He glanced at her with panic. "You have to help me. Please."

"Timi, I can't," she said. Her laughter quieted. "I won't help you cheat on a test."

"It's not a test; it's a revision exercise to see if we understood."

"And clearly, you didn't," she added gravely.

"Aunty Ada, please. Please…"

Ada's resolve was hopeless in the face of Timi's pleas. She sighed and folded like a reed in the wind. "Okay. Fine. But, on one condition: you will allow me to teach you the material today after school. Deal?"

"Deal." Timi gave two thumbs up in agreement.

"Okay. What's the first question?"

"Find the factors of $4xy + 7y - 32x - 58$. What does that even mean?"

Ada opened a fresh page of her notebook and jotted down the equation.

Wande leaned against the wall. She was really going all out with her performance. Her inevitable failure would be an even better reason to fire her.

"It's multiple choice!" Timi said.

"That makes it easier. Read the options." She listened as Timi read them out, then said, "C. The answer is C."

Timi clicked the option, and the screen lit up green before moving on to the next question. Timi gasped and sat up in his chair.

"Aunty Ada, you were right."

Wande adjusted himself. A fluke, probably. *How could she find those answers without even looking at the screen?*

"Why do you sound surprised?" Ada had that silly grin on her face.

"You didn't even finish solving it before you knew the answer," Timi said. "Can you try the next one?"

"Go on, and call out the answers, too."

"Factorise c3d3(c-d)6-14cad(c-d)."

"Oops, I should have written that down. Say it again, please, Timi." Ada scribbled and began working. "Is it A?"

Timi punched his hand in the air. "Yes!"

"Okay, quickly, the next one."

Wande leaned against a chair, his forehead creased and eyebrows raised. There was something wrong here. Maybe she had a book of answers nearby, but he could see nothing.

The twins had finished their work and were curious why Tobe had signalled to them to be quiet. They watched silently as their mum scrawled something down in her notebook.

Ada dropped her pen. "It's A."

"Whoa!" Timi and Tobe broke out in cheers and gave themselves high fives.

"Aunty Ada, you are amazing! Okay, last one…"

Timi read out the final sum, which seemed much more complicated than all the others. The whole room remained silent.

Wande, who prided himself on his inability to be surprised, was stunned. Never in his wildest dreams would he have considered this village woman capable of such astute brainwork. Timi was in grade nine, following a Cambridge curriculum. How in the world was she be able to do those problems – and so quickly?

Ada answered, and Timi keyed in the option. Tobe hunched over Timi's shoulder, watching the screen.

Both boys screamed, and Timi shot out of his chair to give Ada a hug, followed by Tobe and the twins. She'd aced it.

Ada was basking in the glory of her achievement when Wande's deep voice carried across the room, silencing everyone.

"I must say, I am incredibly surprised."

"Why?" Ada's eyes flashed as she turned to face him. "You thought I was stupid?"

He wouldn't have said it in those words, but – well – perhaps he hadn't thought her capable of such a feat. He was taken aback by the clear rebuke in her voice. Carefully, he began to speak, "I wasn't going to—"

"Well, let me tell you," she said, "I'm not."

Every eye around the room looked at her in awe. Her gaze locked with Wande's. He knew she was silently daring him to say something. She only looked away when Tobe wound his arms around her waist and hugged her.

"Mummy, you're incredible."

She smiled wide and hugged him back.

Wande slowly made his way back to his office, shaking his head as we went. On the way out, he turned back to look at her one more time.

Firing her was clearly not the best course of action. It was clear that she was... necessary, however inconvenient she might be. But Wande grappled with the dawning reality that she had many layers – plenty of which he had yet to see – and many, perhaps, that he wasn't ready to face.

Chapter Twenty-Three

Ada didn't have time to bask in her private victory before the children informed her that their homework needed to be scanned and sent back to their tutor.

This wouldn't have been a problem, except that there had been no mention of printing and scanning in the guidance documents the tutors had provided for the courses. Ada did not have such equipment readily available.

She shook her head and sighed. What was the use of online homework if the work was not a hundred per cent online?

Unable to solve the problem quickly on her own, she dialled Ronke.

"Not to worry," said Ronke over the phone. "I can get a printer across to you by the end of today."

"That won't work. Their teachers want it within the hour." Ada tried to stem her frustration. "I was also hoping you could talk me through the process. I don't even know how to scan."

"Sorry, dear, I thought I told you. I'm in Japan now. Wande has some business to attend to here, and he sent me to lay the groundwork. For now, I suggest you use the other option available to you."

"What other option?"

"Wande has a fully set-up state-of-the-art office right there."

Ada's heart sank. She had guessed she would say that. "Thanks, Ronke. Please push for the printer to come quickly."

"No worries, I'll get on it."

Ada started for the door of the study. In that instant, she would rather have travelled to another state on foot than go in there.

Wande was surprised to see Ada. He had spent the last several minutes thinking about her hidden intellectual aptitude and, in particular, what a benefit it would be to the children. As intent as he had been on getting rid of her, she was proving too valuable – in more ways than one.

He was still thinking about it when she poked her head through his doorway.

She spoke softly. "I'm sorry, I need… Well, the kids need help. I wouldn't normally disturb you, but apparently, Ronke is in Japan, and I am stuck."

"How can I help?" Wande spoke with caution.

"The kids need to print, scan, and send their assignments back to their tutors by email. Time isn't really on our side."

Wande felt himself relax. It wasn't the most complex of queries. "That's fine. I can give you a few minutes and you can use the printer here. Let me just…" He adjusted himself to get up.

"Don't, please. I will need your help to show me how it all works."

"You don't know how to use it?" Wande chewed the inside of his mouth to keep from saying more. He would have loved to topple her off her brainiac high horse, but he'd just made a resolution not to, so he kept quiet.

"You don't have to say it like that. I've never needed to use one. I don't suppose you know how to use a hoe and a cutlass or cultivate the yam you eat, do you?"

"Touché, I don't."

"Good. So teach me how to do this, and maybe one day, I'll return the favour."

Wande's right brow shot upwards. Was that true wit? What more lay hidden underneath her black turban?

For the next few minutes, Ada sat side-by-side with Wande at his desk, their legs almost touching, while he showed her the basics of printing and scanning. He concluded the presentation by explaining how to attach and send documents by email. Then, as he reached over to examine something on her phone, he caught a whiff of her musky perfume, and for a moment, he lost his train of thought.

As he gave her back her phone, their hands touched, and the split-second contact sent an unanticipated spark through him.

That was going to be a problem. He averted his gaze quickly and ducked his head to write something on a piece of paper.

"There, that's all there is to it. Now, have the kids send the assignments to me in separate emails. Do you think you can manage that?" He hoped she would rise to meet his sarcasm, but she didn't.

"Timi and Tobe, definitely," she said flatly. "The twins will need a bit of help. Let me go tell them. I'll be right back."

Wande watched her billow out of his office.

Hmm. It hadn't been so bad teaching her. She'd grasped the concepts quickly and asked intelligent questions.

Ten minutes later, she returned to tell him the emails had been sent.

"I can see one from Timi," Wande said, checking his computer.

Ada coughed. "Can I try it myself?"

"Sure, if you want." He closed all his tabs and turned his laptop towards her.

The email box was already open, and black lettering denoted an unread message. When she opened it, it took her a minute to remember where the print icon was before she clicked. She relaxed when she heard the gentle wheezing of the printer at the side of the room.

One step down, two more to go. She gathered all the papers and left the office to give them to the kids.

Wande did not take his eyes off her when she returned forty-five minutes later and placed the pages on the glass tray on top of the printer. She smiled in triumph once she was done.

"All good?"

"Phew! Yes, thank you."

She returned the laptop to Wande, licked her lips, and sat down in front of him.

"Yes?" he said. "What is it?"

"Can we talk?"

He sat back in his chair and nodded. It felt dangerous.

"So, what do we need to discuss? My first yam planting lessons?"

She laughed, and Wande's eyebrows lifted again. She had a pleasant, full-bodied laugh, and not for the first time, he noticed the wide curve of her lips, their warm expression. He made himself refocus on what she was saying.

"We obviously got off on the wrong foot, and I would like to start again," she said. "So many things hinge on our ability to get along. We have a contract to work together for a purpose. My kids now have financial stability and a great education, and your kids are benefitting from emotional stability and proper care. That being said..." Her eyes glanced sideways. "I still want us to look again at the terms of the agreement."

Wande flung the pen he was holding onto the table. A sudden look of disgust marred his features.

"As usual, it always boils down to more money."

Ada's mouth opened in indignation. "It has nothing to do with money. It has to do with our roles."

Wande scrunched his eyebrows and tilted his head to the side. With a suspicious glint clouding his eyes, he sat forward, hands clasped on the table.

"My role is already clear: I provide."

"And that is no longer enough for me," Ada said. "I want more, and like I said, I do not want money."

Wande sat back, his brows still raised. "What more could you want?"

Ada moved her chair nearer but kept her hands hidden under the table. "We both want what's best for the children. I propose we do this together, or we don't do it at all."

"Are you threatening to leave again?"

She shook her head vigorously. "I don't want to leave; I want us to do it better."

"Go on. Explain." Blind curiosity controlled Wande's speech. He was incapable of ignoring whatever she had to say.

"How will any of this work if we can't work together peaceably? You don't speak to anybody in the house except Timi, and when you do, it's with a frown or a glower and only to complain. You make people uncomfortable." Ada swallowed. "For your information."

"Oh, do I now?"

"Yes," Ada said. "And then there's Emily. There is no way you two can bond if the atmosphere isn't right. Rightly or wrongly, you are still a scary stranger to her. The friendlier you are to us, the more she will warm up to you. And I know you want to have a relationship with her. I've seen the way you look at her."

Wande fought off a blush. "What is that supposed to mean?"

She smiled. "You know what I mean. So, what is a stable family worth to you? Can you handle a bit more time with us?"

He allowed the family statement to slide and instead decided to focus on her other comment.

"What exactly does more time entail? You know I have a business to run."

Ada started to speak and stopped again, before finally continuing. "We are all aware of how busy you are, but we still have to make this work. You, as my fake husband, and me, as your fake wife – both of us together." She gestured at the space between them. "As real parents to the kids. We need your one hundred per cent participation in the affairs of the family.

Mealtimes are family times; so, join us for at least one meal a day. We eat together in the kitchen, where it's cosier. Maybe you'll like it."

"Okay." Wande couldn't begin to explain what he was agreeing to. He only knew that he was saying yes.

Ada smiled at his concession, as though the answer was unexpected.

Her voice light, she pressed on. "And you have to give us a minimum of an hour of your time, once in a while, aside from mealtimes."

Wande didn't want to admit she looked even more attractive when she asserted herself. "That is asking a lot," he said.

"And," she continued, without missing a beat, "if you want to criticise me about anything, and I mean anything, you say it to me privately. Mutual respect—"

"On both sides," Wande cut in. The tides inside him began to turn. He could feel the inevitability of it.

"Agreed, on both sides."

Silence hung between them. Wande sighed. "Is there anything else Her Majesty wants?"

Now, Ada was really smiling.

For Ada, she would recall this moment as the first time there had been a total disconnect between her heart, mind, brain, and mouth.

She had turned to leave, thinking the day was already won. She had gotten Wande to agree to joining the family at mealtimes and donating his time outside of that, too. What was the sense in asking for more?

In the back of her head, something whispered, *Is there anything else you want*? And at the same time, she remembered Michael's words: 'you are living in luxury and thinking like a pauper'.

With her hand already on the door handle, she turned and suddenly blurted, "I want to go to school."

"What?"

Ada stared at him as if the words had not just come from her mouth.

"I... I want to go back to school." Hearing it out loud, it sounded fantastic.

"I'm going to assume you mean university," Wande said slowly. "What do you want to study?"

Ada was stumped. The words had tumbled out before she could think it through.

What *did* she want to study? Acing Timi's math review had sent a feeling like liquid gold racing through her veins. She remembered the woman from Proverbs 31, who ran all those businesses. She remembered Mrs Nwafor and her unmatched cunning.

"Business management," Ada said.

"An undergraduate course in business management. Interesting." Wande seemed to be genuinely mulling the idea. She was still in shock that he had not rejected it at once. "Are you sure you can handle the house, the kids, and the academic workload?"

Ada gulped. She wasn't sure about anything at this point. She was swimming in uncharted territory. "Y… Yes… I think I can."

"Okay. I'll get Mrs Coker to get in touch."

Ada stared at him, blinking. Were they having the same conversation?

"You'll do it?" she said. "You'll find me a school and pay for it?" She held her breath, waiting for his answer.

Wande just gave a small shake of his head. "Isn't that what you just asked for?"

"Yes. I… I just…"

She released the breath she was holding, staring at the chair she had just vacated moments earlier, and with great embarrassment, she burst into tears.

Wande tried to get out of his chair, but Ada waved him away and headed for the door. She needed to get out of there before he changed his mind.

Was it really going to happen? After years of yearning? She couldn't sit still. To let out her nervous energy, she joined the children, who were flying their kites out on the front lawn now that their schoolwork was complete.

The kids were delighted to see her. Usually, Ada would sit and watch them, laughing as they ran around, but this time, she ran alongside them as fast as they did, waving the kite that the twins had made for her.

Later, panting heavily, Ada went into the kitchen to organise cold drinks for the children. There, she found Michael hard at work, chopping up vegetables for dinner. She tapped him on the shoulder.

"What is it?" he said. "You're looking as if you want to burst."

Ada did feel as if she were about to burst. She wanted to scream out loud that the impossible was about to happen – that her greatest desire was coming to pass.

But just as she was about to share the good news, another thought came: *What if?*

What if Wande changed his mind? What if he was like Emeka, who always said what she wanted to hear only to rescind it at a later date as punishment?

Ada forced a smile at Michael.

"Nothing, just happy to see you." She quickly turned away and took a pack of juice boxes from the fridge before leaving the kitchen. When she returned to the children, she sat in the shade, feigning tiredness, and tried to fight the dark cloud that was beginning to swell inside her.

Not too long after, Cynthia came to tell her that Wande had asked to see her immediately.

Ada's stomach sank. There it was. He was going to walk back on his promise.

Her body seemed to weigh a thousand pounds as she got up and took herself back to his office. Once there, Ada knocked quietly, taking deep breaths.

However this goes, it's okay. He made a mistake; he changed his mind. The day may not be today, but that day will come.

He called for her to enter. "Have a seat."

Ada sat down, rubbing her palms over her dress.

"Are you okay?" he asked. "When you left here, you were in quite a state."

Ada had been trying to shove away the memory of her tears.

"Please, let's try and forget about that, shall we?"

"Right then," Wande said. He glanced at his computer. "So, I have been doing some research. There is a school in Virginia that has a fast track preparatory six-week session for older students starting a first degree – like a foundation course, of sorts. For international students, sessions are held over Skype. If you can go through that, fulfil your duties here, and pass, then I will be willing to pay for your full-time programme. You start next week."

Ada began to inhale deeply and exhale slowly through her mouth.

Wande looked up from his laptop.

"Is there a problem?" His forehead creased.

Ada swallowed the lump that had wedged in her throat. She shook her head but didn't speak.

"Good," Wande said mildly. "That's all. I just wanted to let you know it's been sorted. Mrs Coker will call you soon with the details."

Ada nodded and left the office. By the time the children trooped into the house, chatting excitedly, she had managed to collect herself. They didn't notice her flushed face.

"Cynthia, please help me sort the children for dinner," Ada said. "I need to make a call."

Cynthia nodded, and Ada's heart warmed as none of the kids fussed over her planned absence. Even Emily waved and called out, "Bye-bye, Mummy."

"Adanne, I'll be with you soon." Ada waved back.

The children seemed ready to let her go. Or, at least, they seemed content to carry on with their lives even in her absence. Maybe it was time, indeed.

She called Ronke immediately to impart the news, and Ronke's effusive congratulations made it all feel even more real. Ada couldn't help but burst out laughing.

"I can't believe it, Ronke. You have no idea what this means to me." She was grinning, though her eyes glistened with tears. "And it's happening so quickly. I hear the course starts next week."

"Yes, you made your request just in time, but we have a bit of work to do. You'll need an international passport for ID purposes. I'll need your year of graduation from school, as well as the name of your secondary school to get your high school results."

"They weren't good." Regret washed over Ada. "Will that be a problem?"

"No, your acceptance isn't based on those grades, but the school still needs the records."

Ada let out a slow breath. "Oh, okay. Ronke, this is real, right? He won't change his mind later and stop me, will he?"

Ronke's voice was almost amused. "Ada, Wande is many things, but if he gives you a gift, he won't take it back. You have done the hard part by getting him to agree." She laughed quietly. "Anyway, I have sent you all the information you'll need. So, Ada, the only thing left to say is, welcome back to school!"

While the kids slept, Ada devoured all of the information that Ronke had sent about the school and the programme. She had already started planning how she would shift responsibility for the children's evening routine over to the nannies. There would be more to consider, but Ada was working through each step slowly.

The school's taught sessions were held for three hours each evening from six until nine. Assignments were due at the end of each week. She figured she could handle the weekly workload and then study for a few hours every weekend.

Ada excitedly shared her plans with Ronke the next day over the phone, as she and the kids made their way back from taking passport photos. Ada figured that if she needed to get one, the children might as well benefit from the same. Ronke also arranged for Cynthia and Mary to be added to the application as staff of Wande Badejo. The ladies could barely contain their excitement.

As Ada continued to babble down the phone, Ronke slowly went quiet. Suddenly, Ada was conscious of herself. "Ronke, am I talking too much? Why are you so silent?"

"I don't think you're planning with the correct timing. The class starts at 6 p.m. Atlantic time, not 6 p.m. Nigerian time."

Ada's heart thudded. "What does that mean?"

Ronke explained the time difference to her. The class would start at almost midnight. "How could that happen?" Ada asked.

"I thought it was strange when Wande asked specifically for schools on the East Coast in America. But you know, it's Wande," Ronke said. "You never know exactly what he's thinking."

Ada felt a slight weight settle around her. It was odd. Too odd. It could only mean one thing: Wande was setting her up to fail.

Even though she'd expected as much, she still felt a little betrayed. She knew they were not friends, but for him to deliberately sabotage her like this left a sour taste in her mouth.

Despite her disappointment, it was still an opportunity. If this was the stumbling block she had to overcome for her dream to be fulfilled, then so be it.

"That's okay, Ronke," she said, her voice light. "It will all work out."

"Are you sure? We could always find another school."

Ada struggled with the idea. Maybe that's what Wande wanted – for her to make a fuss so he could use it as an excuse not to carry out his promise. She would gladly disappoint him.

"No, don't bother. The fact that he asked specifically must have been for a reason. I'll handle it."

"Are you are sure?"

"I am," Ada said, resolute.

Chapter Twenty-Four

"Hello, Wande."

"Yes?" he said gruffly.

Ada wanted to drop the phone and run, but she wasn't ready to have him mess up the confidence she had worked so hard to construct. Besides, the children deserved to have a harmonious home. That was what it was all for, anyway.

"It's time for dinner." She heard the click of the intercom and stared at the handset in disbelief.

How annoying that she'd have to wait till after dinner to have it out with him. So much for trying to be harmonious. Of course, she could not take him at his word. She'd been a fool to think so.

The children's plates were piled high with delicious-looking yam pottage and a side salad. They had all just joined hands to pray when the kitchen door opened and Wande hobbled in. The kitchen chatter came to a standstill.

Ada hadn't prepared the children for his arrival, and she almost laughed at everyone's shocked faces. Even her mouth briefly hung open. So, he really had decided to come. Her annoyance dissipated like the last froth of waves on a beach.

Michael stepped up and asked, "Do you need anything, sir?"

"No, Michael, thank you."

The silence stretched for a few seconds, but it felt much longer, with Wande looking around, seeming lost, and everyone else waiting to hear the reason for his presence.

Ada felt it was best she took charge of the situation. "Timi, move over. Let your daddy sit next to you."

Timi eagerly changed seats, but the other boys just stared.

Once the meal had been served, the air in the room turned stiff. Even Emily didn't demand entertainment, slowly opening her mouth to receive food while sneaking furtive glances at the big, bearded man who usually lived in the other room.

"So, everybody." Ada finally broke the silence. "How was the tutoring today?"

Wande gave a slight smile. He knew the question was for his benefit, as she'd spent most of her day monitoring the children's lessons already.

But the kids were not biting, and silence reigned. Wande was halfway through his meal when he coughed to clear his throat. All eyes turned to him, including Ada's.

"So, To-beh…" Wande dragged out each syllable as if testing out the name.

Tobe looked up slowly from his meal.

"Yes, sir?" he said hesitantly. Ada wished she was sitting next to him to give him a comforting squeeze.

"What do you want to be when you grow up?"

Ada almost choked on her drink. *That* was the best conversation starter the CEO of the biggest conglomerate in Nigeria could come up with?

But when she looked at Tobe, he didn't seem to mind the question, and a tiny light shone in his eyes.

"I would like to go to space, sir. I love everything about space."

Wande gave a genuine smile. "When I was younger, I also wanted to go to space. I wanted to be an aeronautical engineer."

Tobe sat up in his chair. "Really, sir? What changed your mind?"

"Oh, I found out I like making money more." Wande dipped his fork into the pottage and filled his mouth with it, grinning.

Timi cracked up first, then Tobe, followed by the twins. Ada had no idea what was so funny, but all the boys were soon doubled over with laughter.

That became the joke of the evening. Ikenna said he wanted to be a soccer player, but he thought he liked making money more. There was another round of laughter. Ahanna followed suit with his dream of being a teacher, but he had changed his mind, he now wanted to make money. Another wave of giggles. Timi, Ada discovered, had dreams of writing a novel, but he would give it up. Why? The now-irritating line: he thought he liked making money more.

Dinner passed quickly after that. The boys all said goodnight to Timi's dad as they went to get ready for bed.

With Obinna on her hip, Ada spoke to Wande in the hallway as he made his way back to his room.

"Now, that wasn't so bad." She smiled.

Wande turned around at her voice. "I don't know if I can handle this three times a day. Children are not my area of expertise."

"But you had them eating out of your hand in ten minutes. You're a natural. As for three times a day, just imagine you're taking medicine. You may not enjoy it, but it's good for your soul. And you'll be happy you did."

Wande's expression was strange – almost pained. "Yes, ma'am."

He was halfway down the hallway when she called to him again. "Hey, thanks for coming. And making the effort."

Wande didn't like the fact that he felt warm at her appreciation. He didn't want to feel warm about anything that had to do with her or their arrangement.

While he stood at the end of the hall thinking, the baby kept fussing in her arms. On impulse, he walked back and rubbed the baby's cheek with his finger.

Ada sighed. "I think he's tired of me. I think he wants the attention of someone much higher up."

"What? Me?" Wande couldn't hide his anxiety. He looked at Obinna, with his brown cheeks, his round brown eyes and his cute nose, and something tugged in his heart. If he had little experience with children, he had zero knowledge of babies, having missed that whole period of Timi and Emily's lives.

On a whim, he sat down on a chair outside his office, dropped his crutches on the floor, and stretched his arms towards a surprised Ada, who handed over Obinna. The baby settled quickly in his arms and laid his head on Wande's chest. Wande stroked his back.

"I didn't know I was a baby person." He chuckled nervously.

"You never know until you try." Ada's heart warmed at the sight of her baby in his arms, though Wande looked truly nervous. Obinna lifted his head and grabbed a tuft of Wande's beard.

"Whoa, young man. Easy."

Ada tried to pry away Obinna's fingers, but Wande gently moved her hand aside.

"Don't worry. It doesn't hurt. Let him be." He spoke softly as he began to bounce Obinna a little. Ada stood back and watched Obinna's tiny fingers run through Wande's beard. Soothed, Obinna stopped blinking, and his eyes remained closed.

"Wow, thanks for that," Ada said. "I'll take him now. Let's get out of your way. It's well past his bedtime." She reached for the baby.

"Wait, give him a few minutes – I hate being disturbed when I'm falling asleep. He seems comfortable."

Ada raised her brows. "Okay, in that case, I'll go and see Michael about the menu tomorrow."

Wande didn't look up as Ada made her way to the kitchen. When she and Michael were finished, she found Wande with Obinna asleep in his arms. Wande remained still as he gazed at the baby, his face free of all anger, frustration and worry. He was almost unrecognisable.

Seeing Wande like that, looking at her boy, caused something to tug at Ada's heart. She shook herself and coughed, grabbing Wande's attention.

"I'll take him now, thank you," she whispered. "I usually have to sing and dance with him. But I can see that I found the new sleeping tablet – your beard."

Wande chuckled as he handed over the baby.

It had been pleasant. The whole evening had been surprisingly pleasant. Emily still looked at him like he had two heads, but the baby… he wanted some more of that. Maybe this medicine wouldn't be so bad after all.

Chapter Twenty-Five

There was still a slight tension in the air whenever Wande walked into a room, but with each day that passed, the tension dissipated, until all that was left was a quick glance of the boys' eyes in his direction. The kids were beginning to accept the fact that he was going to be around more often.

Ada had taken to sending messages to Wande prior to mealtimes suggesting questions he could ask the children – ones guaranteed to garner an enthusiastic response. Science for Tobe, sports of all kinds for the twins, and for Timi: music, movies, and swimming. Wande never responded to her texts, but she knew he'd read them when his questions and conversation referenced her prompts. Each child would light up as he turned his attention to them, and they loved nothing more than to ask him questions in return. It soon became clear that he was quite the storyteller, regaling them with unending anecdotes of his life in business. Ada was unsure of the truth of the tales, but it didn't matter: the children's smiles were a testament to his talent.

They discovered Wande's gift for a narrative one morning when Ikenna put a question to him at breakfast.

"Timi's daddy?" They often addressed him this way.

"Yes, Ikenna."

"How did you get your scar?"

Ada held her breath. She would need to have another talk with her son about asking inappropriate questions. It was too late now. Everyone's eyes were on Wande.

But he didn't miss a beat as he jumped into an incredible story of him fighting off eight deadly sharks in the middle of the Atlantic Ocean. Halfway through the astonishing account, the boys realised he was just making it up, and they enjoyed it even more.

Every few days after that, one of the twins, or even Timi, would ask the question, "How did you get your scar?" And it became a cue for another adventure story with Wande as the hero, fighting off lions, or tigers, or bears, or worse. The boys ate it all up, and they soon began to look forward to mealtimes with him.

Another win for Wande was his relationship with Obinna. Whatever the two had between them, the feeling was mutual. Wande would visibly soften once the baby was brought in during lunch, and Obinna would struggle out of the arms of anyone who held him, reaching for Wande, who in turn would open his arms wide to receive him. Wande had even taken to rushing through his meals so he could focus on Obinna and talk with the boys.

The only one not affected by his charms was Emily. She still refused to look in his direction when he came in and would always eat her food quietly without fanfare. The only good thing about her reticence was that no one needed to sing anymore for her to eat. This both relieved and saddened Ada, but Emily reserved her drama for other moments, so the "Ada" song was still needed to soothe ruffled feathers from time to time.

With the family dynamics improving, Ada's focus turned to her first day of uni. She ordered every book on the reading list, as well as new notebooks and pens, and she even plucked her eyebrows so that she was Skype-ready. Timi and the twins knew all about her new endeavour and showed their support in their own ways, but they could not understand her eagerness.

"Mummy?" Ahanna had asked one day at breakfast. "You actually *want* to go to school?"

"Like, nobody is forcing you to do this?" Ikenna chimed in.

"Yeah, Aunty Ada, I don't understand how anyone can be this enthusiastic about school," said Timi.

Ada laughed. "I have always enjoyed learning, and I haven't been able to do it in so long."

"Well, if you want to learn so you can teach, I'm all for it," Timi said. "You're the best math tutor I have ever had."

"Aw, thanks, Timi." She beamed at the compliment. "I don't know what your father will say to that, considering what he pays for your schooling and lessons." She and Wande shared a bemused glance.

Timi shovelled a bite of food into his mouth. "By the way, Emmanuella's mum is going to call you, too. I told her you're my new secret weapon."

Ada laughed. "I'll help any way I can."

That adrenaline kept Ada buzzing throughout the day as she finished helping the children with their schoolwork and monitored the boys' swimming lessons. She remained on an emotional high until it was time to prepare for her first class.

Her plans to get a nap first were futile. She couldn't relax and regretted the wasted time immediately as ten o'clock approached and her energy slipped away, replaced by a tangle of nerves. Sitting in front of the laptop in the library, she encouraged herself: *I can do this. I can do this.*

The ringer for the Skype call pierced the silence, and she wanted to scramble out of the room, especially when her inner voice said even louder: *You don't need to do this; you already have a great job. What if you fail? Think of the embarrassment, the disgrace. Remember your failure in your final exams?*

The fear was physically present with her in the room, sucking up all the air.

She breathed slowly. "Jesus, help me." By the time the smiling face of a lady came on the screen, welcoming them to the programme, the dark force had gone, and Ada felt much better.

Each of the lecturers took a few minutes to give an overview of their course. The teachers spoke fast, and Ada struggled to get the hang of what they said through their accents. She felt lightheaded until another student of Indian descent raised a hand and mentioned Ada's very same issue.

Ada wanted to hug him. The lady in charge asked if anybody else was struggling, and three-quarters of the class indicated they, too, were having issues. After that, there was a concerted effort by all the teachers to speak more slowly. Ada relaxed.

They went through the course outlines for all the subjects. This six-week preparatory course had only one exam at the end of the programme – a test written live and submitted within thirty minutes of the end of the exam. The results would be the basis of their admission into the university.

When the lecturers finished presenting, they asked the students to introduce themselves. The students had been briefed on the compulsory introduction in their welcome pack, so Ada was ready.

As they all spoke, the instructors made sure to pin a point of interest on each student, which usually got everybody else laughing. When Ada said she was a mother of six children, the teacher made a huge deal over the fact and congratulated her on being there despite her family commitments.

By the end of the session, everyone was laughing together like they were old friends. Ada enjoyed herself thoroughly, grateful that the children were all upstairs in bed and wouldn't be disturbed. She left the library at one in the morning, nervous but thrilled at what lay ahead for her. Tomorrow couldn't come fast enough.

There was one person not thrilled by her first class: Wande.

He was a light sleeper and the sounds coming from the library disrupted his much-needed rest. When he didn't have overseas appointments, he tried to be asleep by eleven. He now realised that was precisely when Ada started her classes.

"Serves me right," he grumbled, grabbing a pillow to cover his head. He would have to invest in some earplugs, or maybe he could tell her to move rooms. He didn't want to ask her for any favours, though, especially since the timing of her courses was all his doing.

It had been a petty move, and he knew it. After she had swanned into his office, demanding a new arrangement, he'd decided that he would give her what she wanted, but he wasn't going to make it easy. If she bothered to stay up late and study after midnight, he'd know she was serious about going back to school. There was a small, strange part of him that wanted to see exactly what she was made of.

But he obviously hadn't thought the plan through. If this was setting the tone for the next six weeks, he was in for a terrible time.

Chapter Twenty-Six

One such night, Wande had given up trying to sleep, and was scrolling through his emails, waiting for rest that he was sure would not come. He worked for an hour before deciding to go to the kitchen and get a snack.

The first thing he saw was fresh bananas. He didn't like bananas, but when he heard the library door creak open, he quickly picked one up. He met Ada as she was trying to close the door gently. After she'd made such a noise for the past three hours? What a joke.

"What exactly goes on in those classes that sends you into fits of giggles so often?"

Ada jumped when she saw him. "Sir?"

"You heard me. What kind of comedy club are you attending every night in there?"

Ada started laughing.

Wande wasn't joking, but the way she laughed with abandon, her shoulders shaking, drew a reluctant smile from him. He dropped his crutches and settled on the seat outside his office, peeling the banana.

"I'm sorry. There is a particular lecturer, Mr Mark Wilson, who is so funny. He delivers the only math course in the programme."

And off she went again, giggling. Wande rolled his eyes, waiting for her to compose herself. He took a bite of the fruit. Ugh.

"Let me guess, you're his star pupil," Wande said dryly.

"Well." Ada shrugged, hugging her books with a big grin.

The awkward silence lingered, and the smile slowly slid off her face.

Meanwhile, Wande speculated about this woman in front of him. Mr Walter Thornton, the principal of Timi's school, had just been telling him what a valuable support Ada was to the community. Ronke couldn't stop singing her praises, too. Now, she had admirers from across the seas. What did they all see in her, apart from perhaps her pretty face?

He realised with a start that he had scarcely had a conversation with her outside the topic of the children. Maybe it wouldn't hurt to find out what all the fuss was about.

But while he was thinking of something to ask, she beat him to it.

"So…" Ada looked everywhere but right at him, digging her toes into the carpet. "What do *you* want to be when you grow up?"

They locked eyes, and Ada's cheeks were round as she pursed her lips, trying to suppress her laughter. Wande's expression shifted from confusion to comprehension in a single second, and he also laughed, giving her permission to do the same.

He remembered his feeble attempt at conversation with the boys. He wagged a finger in her direction.

"Touché."

"How was your day?" she asked.

"Not too bad… Same old, same old." He shrugged.

"Nah, that's the kind of response I get from the boys. I'm not having it. Let's try something else." She had a twinkle in her eye. "What was the best part of your day?"

"What?"

"Come on, what was your high point? Is it such a strange question?"

Well, it was a strange question, but what surprised him most was that nothing he'd done in his entire day – neither the deals he'd closed nor the money he'd made – brought as much pleasure as the laughter they'd just shared over a simple joke.

"Ask another question," Wande said.

"Okay." Ada chewed on her pen; her forehead creased as she thought hard. "What's the current deal you are working on?"

Now, this was something he could answer. "How much detail do you want?"

Ada dropped her laptop bag and her books by the wall and went back into the library to fetch a chair. She plopped it down in front of Wande.

"Everything," she said, "*gist* me."

Wande was far from tired, so he decided to play along. He talked about his desire to build an alternative transport system in Nigeria. He was looking at water and overhead railway transportation systems, working with a Japanese company to make it happen. Currently, he was busy undertaking due diligence responsibilities and strategic planning tasks so he could make proposals to the different governors in all thirty-six states of the Federation of Nigeria.

Ada interrupted a few times to ask questions – intelligent questions, which prompted him to outline a process he had skipped over once or twice and clear his thoughts even further. He didn't know why he was surprised, but he still found it difficult to dispel the image of her as an ignorant village girl, even though he knew now that person didn't exist.

"All of it is truly amazing," Ada said when he finished his summary. "Can you imagine how much better living and working would be if we could sort out this issue of clogged roads and traffic? Think about the reduction on pollution. It would even encourage foreign investors—"

Wande chuckled. "I think you have got me confused with a philanthropist. I am in it for the money, after all."

"That's what you claim," she said, "but intentionally or not, in the end, it will make the life of the ordinary Nigerian citizen better."

"I suppose you are all welcome, then."

"I have one more question."

Wande grumbled. "What's with the interview so early in the morning?"

Ada laughed. His voice sounded gruff, but his eyes twinkled.

"Why are you up at this hour, anyway?" she asked. "Couldn't sleep?"

"Well, if you must know, I'm a light sleeper. Every night from your first giggle to your last 'good night, everyone', I can't sleep a wink."

Ada's eyes widened. She slapped her hand over her mouth. "Please tell me you don't mean that." She chewed on her lower lip. "I should probably apologise, shouldn't I?"

"Maybe."

"Or maybe, I should say it serves you right! After all, it was you who insisted on a school with such inconvenient timing."

Wande cleared his throat.

It was now obvious where Mrs Coker's loyalties lay. Wande had never been in a position to have his own crap exposed. Maybe he could slide past this. Perhaps it would be better to be honest.

"I should probably say I'm sorry." He gave a half-smile, but Ada's face was expressionless.

"Why did you do it?" she asked.

Wande suddenly felt small, like a tiny bug. It was the way she asked. If she had shouted or been angry, he might have blustered his way through some sort of answer. Instead, she just asked like she really wanted to understand.

How could he explain that he felt intimidated by her? As insignificant as he always said she was, he knew there were more guts in her than even she realised. He felt foolish now.

"I can only imagine how tough it is for you, taking it all on," Wande said. "I don't know how you get to class and laugh, regardless of how funny Mr Willy is." He was hoping she would smile, but she didn't. "Look, if you're struggling, I can find something else."

An uncomfortable silence fell between them.

"It hurt a bit," she admitted. "A part of me felt you wanted me to fail, which was odd, because you willingly agreed to the whole thing in the first place. I thought you were different."

Her disappointment sunk in like a well-placed blow.

"But you know what?" she went on. "You've given me something I've always wanted, and as stressful as it is, it was never going to be without challenges. This way, this time is all mine. I don't have to worry about the kids, and I can focus on studying. So, thank you. What you meant for evil has worked out for my benefit." Her lips curled with mischief.

Wande felt only marginally better. "Good one. I am now one of Joseph's evil brothers, right?"

"So, you know your Bible?" Ada said. "Well done. And besides, if the shoe fits…"

Wande didn't mind this sassy side of her. He smiled and let out a slow breath. He was no stranger to tough decisions, but he knew what he'd done had been mean, and regretted it. He was relieved they could laugh about it.

"So, I am off to bed. Thanks for the chat." She didn't wait for a response before she turned to go.

He watched her leave and wished he could tell her to stay longer. She probably would have stayed, too, if he'd asked. But he knew she had a full day the next day, and to see her come out of class after three hours smiling, able to spend time chatting with him and even asking about his day, was something else. He feared he had stumbled on something a bit extraordinary with this woman.

The next evening, Wande told himself he wasn't working past midnight, hoping for another chance encounter with Ada. His watch read a quarter to two. He shuffled back and forth from his door. What reason could he give to be out of his room? Everything he needed was right there. Even a bowl of fruit had mysteriously appeared in his room that morning. He cursed her attention to detail; her proactiveness in this instance was not appreciated.

With luck, he was by his door when he heard her familiar, "Good night, everyone", and walked out of his room just as she came out of the library.

"Oh, hello." Ada's smile was wide when she caught sight of him. "Do you need anything? I asked them to place a basket of fruit in your room today."

"Thank you," he said. "I don't need anything. I just needed to stretch. Leg's a bit stiff." *Good one*, he cheered himself. "How was your class today? No math lesson, I take it?"

Ada chuckled. "Unfortunately not, but I have Mr Willy tomorrow if you want to join me."

Wande laughed as he raised his hand in front of him. "No, thank you. I only work with numbers when they spell out a currency."

"Perhaps the problems were your teachers," Ada suggested. "My math teacher in secondary school was the best. Mr Nworie

Njoku. There was no one else who could explain problems the way he did."

Wande clung to the scrap of information from her past. It wasn't often she offered them up so easily, and that night, he found himself hungry to know more. "Here, sit a minute," he said. "I've got a chair for you." They sat side by side outside his office. "What was it like for you? Growing up?" he asked.

Ada checked her watch. It was late, but she found herself wanting to answer his question. He had so seldom asked for any information about her that finally giving it was like taking a breath of fresh air. She settled deeper into the seat before launching into the story of her life as a student at St Martha's Girls Secondary School in Umuahia.

"So, during the rainy season, everyone was suddenly allergic to grass to avoid clearing bushes... We would soak the *garri* in the morning, so that by break time it would have risen sufficiently to feed all of us... Mr Njoku was the only one to ever tell me I was exceptional."

As she told her stories, Wande watched her with great concentration, never breaking eye contact. He was a good listener when his head wasn't buried in his laptop.

"Only one teacher ever told you that?" he asked. "Surely your parents..."

She looked sad. Wande didn't like it.

"I lost my mum when I was a baby," Ada explained. "My father didn't care how intelligent I was, no matter how hard I tried in school. None of it ever mattered to him. I don't know what I would have given to hear him say, just once, 'I am proud of you. You've done well.'"

Wande found it difficult to relate to her. All his life, he had been the centre of everybody's world. He'd grown up in the knowledge that he was exceptional and had a gift – and he thrived on it. He wanted to tell her that her father was a fool for discrediting her accomplishments, but she immediately shone the spotlight on him.

"What was your secondary school like?"

Wande wanted to get her smiling again, so he found himself exaggerating his high school experiences as a boarder at the Nigerian Military School, Zaria. Ada's eyes opened wide at the stories he told of his adventures. Within ten minutes, she was laughing again, and he relaxed as he shared the horror of being a junior and the eventual freedom he earned as he grew in the ranks at school.

"I have no regrets now. Discipline was a high priority; I had a low tolerance for excuses and laziness then, and I still do now. It was there that I learned the number one rule of success: when you wake up, make your bed. I do it every day, regardless if I'm home or in a hotel."

"I'm impressed," said Ada. Her laughter quieted. "May I ask you a question?"

"You've been asking away. Why stop now?"

"What's the real story behind the scar on your face?"

"Wow, you went there." Wande grinned broadly. "Well, one bright sunny day in the jungles of South Africa…"

"Stop… Stop."

Perhaps knowing she would not get a real answer out of him, Ada lifted herself out of her chair and bid him goodnight. She was still laughing as she made her way up the stairs, and so was Wande as she disappeared out of sight.

He knew one thing. He wanted to do this again. He just needed a good reason to be out of his room at two in the morning.

Chapter Twenty-Seven

Wande had just finished a call to his partners in Belgium when Ronke Coker walked into his study.

"Sir, we are going to need a decision on the Goulders Green project. The director asked to change the wording on the contract just before signing."

Wande's attention was currently taken up by the fruit arrangement in his office. This time, a citrus bowl crammed with grapefruit, oranges and tangerines decorated his desk. Ada changed the contents every day, as if she knew he liked variety. He smiled to himself.

"Sir?"

Wande guessed from Ronke's expression it wasn't her first attempt to get his attention. He cleared his throat and pushed his glasses up his nose.

He had to find a way to stop his mind wandering to thoughts of Ada. It was the simple things that drew him in. The fruit bowl, or her daily texts with talking points for the kids. She was making him look good in front of the children, and he knew it.

"Sir!"

Not again. "Mrs Coker, I just need a few minutes to think it through. Tell me what the director changed again?"

Ronke released a deep, self-righteous sigh that spoke volumes. Wande deserved it, and he forced himself to concentrate as she rattled off the changes in the agreement.

Wande began to look forward to his midnight rendezvous with Ada. Luckily, she never asked why he needed a particular brand of tea, or why he needed a stretch, or why he had a craving for ice cream at 2 a.m.; she accepted whatever he came up with, and it always ended with them sitting down for a chat.

Often when they talked about her schoolwork, she would ask to hear his opinion, and he was able to give her practical examples from his experience in business. Sometimes, they talked about the children, sometimes their childhood, other times, his work.

One day, he could tell she had something on her mind, and was surprised when she suddenly mentioned an old newspaper article he had featured in long before.

"Why do they refer to you as 'The Beast?'"

"Why not?" he shrugged. "I am a beast."

"Don't say that. You're not."

"Everyone says I am… in business, and with looks to match."

"I don't care what they say. You're a handsome man with a scar, that's all. It's not a beast I see with my baby in his arms, and it's not a beast I see with his son or my boys. People don't know what they're talking about."

It was the passion and conviction with which she said those words that gently stirred a dormant warmth within him. He'd observed her enough to know she wasn't given to empty words or flattery like he was used to hearing. She meant it. Wande filed away the warm, buzzing emotion to analyse later.

Slowly, their talks grew in duration, from fifteen minutes to half an hour, and within a few days, they were spending up to an hour and sometimes more, talking about everything and nothing, until Ada had to stop herself from yawning and Wande would reluctantly insist that she go to bed.

While they held their clandestine meetings at night, they remained strangers during the day. Wande attended mealtimes, but his focus was always on the children. He never gave Ada more than a cursory glance, and Ada concentrated on whatever task she had at hand. They orbited each other like distant planets, bound tightly to their unspoken rules.

Ada didn't even need to look up to know when Wande entered a room. She was always aware of him, his clean and freshly showered smell. He used one cologne during the day and a different one in the evenings.

Today, he looked relaxed – that was good. It meant the meeting with Badmos had gone well. She would ask him about it after class. Now, she was sure he was going to ask about Tobe's big test, which she'd messaged him about earlier.

"Hello, Ada. How are you?"

The question came from him, straight across the table.

Her hand shook, and the fork that was midway to her mouth landed on the floor. Cynthia moved to pick it up for her, but Ada waved Cynthia away and bent to retrieve it herself. She exchanged the cutlery, still avoiding looking in Wande's direction.

"Mummy," Tobe said with a strained, grown-up look on his face, "Uncle Wande is greeting you."

She blinked and turned to Wande, uttering a strained, "Hello."

"I am good, and you?" Wande smirked. He was enjoying this.

She nodded. *Get a grip, Ada.*

"Just wanted to let you know the meeting went better than I expected," Wande said. "Thanks for the advice."

Michael paused in the middle of serving the food and gave Ada a look. She felt the heat rising in her face. This shouldn't be a big deal. Wande was the same person she'd been talking to every night for two weeks. But those late-night sessions were different; it was just the two of them, and no one knew about it. And when the sun came up, the magic was gone, and everyone went back to their usual roles. Now, though, he had brought their secret into the light and she didn't know how to react.

That night, Wande was waiting, seated outside his office while Ada's class was rounding up. He'd given up any pretence of needing anything. He just wanted to talk to her. That was it. He tapped to a steady rhythm on his thighs, looking towards the library door. She would be out soon.

He smiled and sat up straight. It wasn't like he didn't know exactly what he was going to see: Ada still trying to close the door quietly even after all this time. Then, a slow smile when she saw him, as if his presence was still such a pleasant surprise.

But tonight, there was no smile after she shut the door. She walked straight past him, her face blank.

"Hey, where are you going in such a rush?" he asked.

Ada stopped with her foot on the first step of the stairs, half turned towards him. "What was that you did at lunch this afternoon?"

"Me? I've had meetings and work."

He sat back in his chair as she marched over to him, her black *boubou* following after her. A slight frown now firmly in place.

"That stunt you pulled... Don't pretend."

Wande's eyes opened wide. "I'm truly confused. What are you upset about?"

When she spoke again, her words came out in fragments. "Since we started... it's always been... And we are... And then out of the blue..."

Wande forced himself not to laugh again. She looked cute, all riled up. He wanted to hold her and quell the panic on her face.

"Ada, you're going to have to be a little clearer than that."

"How could you..." She closed her eyes and took a deep breath. "How could you bring up our private conversation at lunch?"

Wande stared, bewildered and amused. So that was it. He wrestled with himself about how seriously to take this outburst. Referencing their meetings in front of the children had been an impulsive move on his part. He'd just wanted to talk to her; to get her to look at him during the day for once, to see her face in the warm glow of daylight.

But she seemed really bothered by his actions.

"You're upset I thanked you for your advice?" he said.

"It sounds silly, but you know what I mean. We have our midnight chats, and then we go our separate ways. Today was so random, you should have told me... prepared me."

Wande's struggle to stop the laughter bubbling within him was overcome by an intense but irrational desire to kiss her.

The realisation stunned him. He was back in the court-house again. He emitted a sound that was somewhere between a chuckle and a cough as he got up to meet her halfway.

"I didn't think I was breaking a code. I apologise. But now we are here, may I start greeting you randomly?" His eyes sparkled with mischief.

She chewed her lip and her eyes looked everywhere but at him. "Okay."

"Okay? Good, so will you come back and sit? I would love to hear about your class tonight."

"No!" she refused. "I'm tired. Since we can now randomly communicate with each other at any time of day, there's no need for me to stay up half the night. Is there?"

Wande lost the struggle with laughter as Ada stomped up the stairs, but as he stared at the closed door, he felt a twinge of disappointment.

Chapter Twenty-Eight

Wande noticed a slight movement on his right and looked up. His heart did a little skip. He put aside the notes he'd been reviewing and took off his headphones.

"I knocked," she said.

"Sorry." He lifted his headphones. "Classical music helps me concentrate. Come in – well, you're already in anyway."

Hesitantly, she moved closer and hovered by his desk.

"Sit down and make yourself comfortable. I don't bite, you know." That lovely twinkle returned to her eyes, so she knew he was teasing; still, she remained standing.

At the same time, Wande was trying to place the tumult inside him. Her classes had been cancelled the night before, so they hadn't had their usual conversation session, and he'd had an empty ache in his belly ever since.

A part of his mind registered that her lips were moving, and he snapped out of his daydream.

"Sir! The boys are done with their swim training and are playing a game of basketball. Emily and I are organising a picnic. Want to join us?"

"At 11 a.m.? No school today?"

"You know full well it's Saturday." Ada stepped a bit further into his room.

"Uh…" Wande looked at the pile of notes beside him and his list of things to do. He hadn't known, actually, but he was not going to admit that to her.

"Hey," her voice dropped, "just give us an hour, your paperwork isn't going anywhere."

As inconvenient as the timing was, he didn't know how he could refuse.

Wande shuffled his papers without looking up. "Okay, then."

Ada clapped her hands, excitement shining in her eyes. "We will meet you out back…"

She trailed off and left in her usual cloud of black. Wande stared at the door.

How exactly did he get to this point? Two months ago, the thought of hanging out with a bunch of kids, without a justified business reason, would have been unthinkable.

Despite coming from a stable home, he'd never had a desire to follow the happy family route, as shown by the dismal failure of his first marriage. Business, he understood. Being responsible for the emotional needs of other people was not something he felt he could successfully accomplish, so he avoided it. Now, he was becoming that same family man he abhorred, and actually, he was looking forward to it.

He changed into a pair of chino shorts and took off the shirt he had worn for the meeting earlier.

Luckily for Wande, the sports facilities were all at the back of the house and easily accessible in his new electric wheelchair.

By the time he arrived at the basketball court, a game was already underway.

Timi stopped playing to grin and wave at his dad, though the move cost him, as Tobe took the opportunity to hit him across the head with the ball. The boys went back to the game while Wande wheeled to the side and found a space in the shade.

His eyes rested on the scene in front of him. Ada and Emily were having a tea party with Obinna in the sun, their small lunch wares spread out over a bright picnic blanket. He longed to tell Ada to bring Obinna to him but didn't want to disturb the happy trio.

Emily was feeding Obinna imaginary food, and he was getting frustrated each time the empty spoon touched his lips. Ada saved the day, opening a tiny jar of pureed food for Emily to dip her spoon into and feed him. Obinna much preferred this new version of the game and was soon kicking his legs and giggling.

Intermittently, Ada broke off to shout words of encouragement to the boys or interrupt a potential argument between the twins. Emily got up to toddle behind Ada, playing with the silken threads from her scarf. When she got bored with that, she clasped her hands around Ada's neck, closing her eyes with a tiny smile. Ada continued talking to the boys but raised her hand to touch Emily's and left it there.

Wande felt a foreign melting sensation somewhere in the region of his heart. On impulse, he took a picture on his phone.

He settled back to watch the game, but his mind and eyes kept wandering back to Ada, her cheeks flushed from the heat and her voice raw from cheering on the boys.

Finally, she looked up and caught Wande's eye, her surprise and pleasure registering the moment she saw him. Without skipping a beat, she gave him a thumbs up and winked. When Wande smiled and returned the gesture, her face truly lit up.

Something about her radiance caught him off-guard. He rubbed his chest, unsure what was going on. Had she always been this pretty, or had she suddenly blossomed overnight?

As if Ada knew Wande wanted to play, she turned Obinna on his hands and knees to face him. Once Obinna saw Wande, the boy started rocking back and forth, smiling wide with his toothless mouth open, drool spilling off his chin. Wande laughed. The child looked like he was revving to take off somewhere until he moved a little too vigorously and fell face down into the blanket. Ada's hand went to her mouth, and she picked him up.

Emily stood behind her. "*Sowy*, baby, *sowy*," she said, rubbing his head.

"Bring him over here, please," Wande called out.

Ada did as he asked and handed the baby to him. Wande lifted the still-tearful Obinna and laid him on his chest.

"Big man. That's okay. But where were you revving to?"

He laid Obinna across his knees and blew on his tummy. The tears turned to giggles as Wande repeated the act. He was so caught up in entertaining Obinna and revelling in his joy that at first he didn't even notice the tiny hand reaching up to him.

Emily was holding on to his arm, smiling as he made her baby laugh, and for a minute, she forgot her fear and joined in.

Wande immediately became still. His eyes darted from Obinna to Emily, finally resting on Ada. Ada motioned for him to continue with Obinna. He tried but was now so aware of his daughter beside him that his attempt at making Obinna laugh was half-hearted. All his senses were trained upon this one moment. In the two months he had been home, this was the first time Emily had voluntarily come near him without looking frightened. Wande gulped hard and released his breath slowly.

"Me," Emily said so softly, he had to bend down to hear her.

"What?"

"Me!"

Wande looked to Ada, helpless.

Ada's eyes shimmered. "She wants to join in the game. She's saying, 'Me too'."

Ada took Obinna from him, while Wande bent to pick up Emily. He lifted her as though she was the most precious thing in all the world, not wanting to frighten her.

He put her on his lap, but instead of tickling her tummy, which was impossible with her T-shirt and dungarees all buckled up, he bounced her on his good leg with a little force that lifted her an inch off his knees.

As she squealed in delight, Wande found his eyes misting up.

"*Horseeeyyy!*" she cried as she rolled her head back and relaxed into the bouncing.

When he stopped, she fell against his chest and flung her arms around his neck, before climbing down and scampering back to the rug where her dolls and tea-set lay.

Wande and Ada exchanged looks. Ada gave him a wide smile. "Good job, Daddy."

"Did that really just happen?" he asked.

She sat on the grass beside him and rubbed his arm. "It did. And you were wonderful."

He didn't tell her he had never been so frightened of messing something up – never in his life.

"Do you think it will happen again?" He looked longingly in Emily's direction while reaching out for Obinna, who had begun to fuss.

"I think so but let her come to you a few more times before you bulldoze her with all your love."

He smiled and nodded. For a few minutes, he basked in the miracle that had just occurred. His heart was filled to the brim.

"Hey," he said to Ada.

She tilted her head towards him, her hand shielding her eyes from the sun that shone behind him, with a playful smile. "Yeah?"

But then, his phone rang. A sharp annoyance rose in him briefly, then dissipated. He put his finger up, signalling for Ada to wait as he answered the call.

"Hey, Chidi. What's up?"

As Wande listened to Chidi's unimportant questions with half his attention, he saw the playfulness in Ada's eyes die away as she took on a more serious look. He ended the call as quickly as he could.

"Hey, are you okay?"

"Of course," she said abruptly. Her eyes fell to the grass. "What were you going to say... before that call came through?"

"Oh." The pause had turned Wande's bravery to mush. "Well. I wanted to say thank you. For her, for him." He lifted his chin in the direction of the kids on the court. "You've done good with these kids, Ada. I'm sorry I'm only telling you now."

"That's okay." Her expression was complicated. The praise did not achieve the smile he was looking for. "I'm just doing my job... that you pay me for."

Before he could read her expression, she had turned away and refocused her attention on the grass by her feet.

What was that? Why bring up their arrangement now? Wande squirmed in discomfort, but he didn't want her to leave. He searched the library of his mind for a topic change as rapidly as he could.

"How are preparations for your big test?" he finally asked.

To Wande's instant relief, Ada came alive again at the mention of school. "I'm so nervous. What if on Friday I forget everything I have read? I pray God grants me success."

"If I were God – even if you didn't take the test – I'd still give you an A-star."

"If you were God!" Ada burst out laughing, but his words resonated. After years of being told how useless she was, and that nothing she did was ever good enough, it was so different to be acknowledged.

Chapter Twenty-Nine

Wande paced at the bottom of the stairs. What was keeping her? Her exam was due to start in half an hour. He looked up, and for the first time, regretted installing the number of stairs looming ahead of him. Even though he'd tried calling her on the intercom – and even on her phone, in a moment of madness – she wasn't picking up. He couldn't believe she'd fallen asleep. Not on a night like this.

Wande was no weakling, but he knew he wasn't in the same shape he used to be. The steps stared back at him.

She would not miss that exam. Not like this. He steeled himself and began to climb.

Ada paced up and down the edge of the room alongside Obinna's cot as he wailed, his face red. A sharp knock on the door startled her, and her jaw dropped when she saw Wande standing there, out of breath, his head resting on the door handle.

"What's going on?" He took in the situation briefly. "What's the matter with Obinna?" His frown deepened as he hobbled into the room.

"He isn't well. His nose is blocked. I can't leave him. I don't know what to do!" Obinna had been crying for almost an hour, and Ada's every attempt to soothe him had failed.

"What about the ladies?" Wande asked. "Why not call one of them? I know it's late, but this is a unique situation. You need to be downstairs in twenty minutes."

Ada shook her head, flustered. "They both left for the weekend today. It's a long story, but they'll be back tomorrow."

Wande released an expletive, and Ada shrank away from him.

"I'm not angry at you," Wande said. "The fact is you need to be downstairs now. Bring Obinna and everything he needs – he and I will sort ourselves out."

"Really?"

"Of course." He was already hobbling back to the stairs.

"I'll meet you at the bottom." Ada stared after him.

"Will you hurry up, woman?" he hissed.

Shocked out of her stupor, Ada rushed around the room, picking up Obinna's toys, blankets and bottles.

She met Wande halfway down the stairs. He held his crutch in his left hand and leaned his other hand on the banister, hopping down one step at a time. Ada saw the fierce determination on his face. With enormous effort, he reached the bottom of the stairs, then limped past her to his study.

Once inside, he motioned to Ada to put Obinna on the bed. "Obinna and I will be fine," he said. "You need to go."

Ada set Obinna in the middle of the bed and stood staring at him.

"Now," Wande said.

She nodded, but stood there, frozen. Wande came gently towards her.

"Ada," he said, lifting her chin, forcing her to look at him. Fear flickered in her eyes. "I promise, Obinna will be fine. The hours will pass quickly, and if I need to, I'll call the doctor."

"What if I fail?" she said, her voice barely above a whisper. "I'll never be able to go to university again."

She struggled to draw each breath, and Wande's heart lurched. He knew the onset of a panic attack when he saw one. He checked his watch; she had only ten minutes.

Ada followed Wande as he drew her over to the sofa, her head down.

Why was she being so silly? Surely, he would tell her to stop being foolish and get on with it. That was probably what she needed to hear, anyway.

"Hey," Wande said as she sat down beside him. He opened his arms. Too exhausted with fright to process what she was doing, Ada reached for the comfort she so desired. Wande was warm, safe. Why did this feel so familiar? The cologne she always smelt at a distance filled her senses, mingling with the sound of his voice – so gentle, gentler than she could ever imagine.

"It's just one test," he said. "If this doesn't work out, we will do it all again if necessary. I will get you into a university, even if I have to carry you in myself."

Ada's chest filled with a new emotion. Fresh tears spilled down her cheeks as the pressure fell off her shoulders.

"Please don't cry," Wande said softly.

Ada wanted to assure him that they were tears of gratitude – of relief, even – but she couldn't speak. She felt the warmth of his breath as he lifted her face to his and wiped her tears with his thumb.

The simple motion sent sensations she had never experienced rushing through her. His gaze held hers as he cupped her cheeks and lowered his head. Ada's body went completely still as Wande kissed her, and his lips silenced whatever panic or fear remained.

He broke it off first, but she could feel him trembling, which meant he could feel her shaking too.

"Now," he said, "go and dazzle them with your brilliance."

Ada burrowed into his arms and squeezed tight as if drawing all his strength into her, then turned and ran out of the room.

Chapter Thirty

Two and a half hours later, Ada shut her laptop and rested her head on the table. Done and dusted.

Her nerves had finally calmed around fifteen minutes into the exam. Using headphones, as Wande advised, she blocked everything from her mind but the sound of her tutor's voice reading out the instructions.

She couldn't believe it was over. Now, her mind could roam undisturbed as it unpicked all the events of the evening. Seeing Wande at her door like a guardian angel, talking her through her panic, not to mention the strange thought that it had all happened before, and finally… the kiss.

Her fingers touched her lips as the memory came back in full force.

She'd never had a kiss like that – of that, she was sure. She shook her head. It was all so confusing. Was Wande just trying to comfort her?

There was nothing to it. There couldn't be anything to it.

She needed to make herself remember that.

As her mind cleared, she realised Wande must still be with Obinna, and hurriedly left the room.

The silence outside was unnerving. She went to his office and found it empty. Tentatively, she crossed the divide to his bedroom and followed the sound of the running shower. Surely

Wande couldn't be having a shower at this time – and where was her baby?

The door to the bathroom was slightly open, steam seeping out. Her mind conjured up an entire horror sequence of things that could have gone wrong. They had fallen, they had drowned, they had—

She rushed over, pushed the door open, and stopped. Steam billowed from the running shower and the tap.

Wande sat on the toilet seat, his shirt off, Obinna asleep in his diapers across his chest. Obinna breathed calmly and freely.

Wande put a finger to his lips when he saw Ada.

Quietly, she grabbed a towel and sat on the floor in front of him, cross-legged, trying desperately to prevent her gaze lingering on his well-muscled chest. What was this man trying to do to her?

"How did it go?" he asked in a loud whisper.

"It wasn't bad."

"Good. Now, put it in the back of your mind and forget it. Obinna is okay. I checked on Google: it said steam helps to unblock the nose… Somewhere else, it said body heat. I thought, why not combine the two?"

Ada wanted to laugh and cry at the same time. "Thank you so much."

"It's okay," Wande said. "We're partners, remember?"

Ada was too drained to respond. "Let me take him now so you can sleep."

Wande didn't look eager to release the baby. "I don't know about that…"

"Wande, you can't spend the night in your bathroom on the toilet seat."

His expression was dire. "What if the cold air from the air conditioning blocks his nose again? It's too scary watching him struggle to breathe."

"I know," Ada said. "I'll sleep in the library. If I switch off the AC in my room, our little madam won't be able to sleep."

"There's no need for that. You guys can stay here."

"Where?"

"Here," Wande said, "in the room. I'll put the heater on. That way, we won't disturb Emily. I'll stay on the couch."

"I can't…"

"We can take turns with him in the night."

Wordlessly, Ada nodded in agreement. They moved into his room, and Wande increased the temperature. Ada went to the kitchen to get a bowl of water to keep the air moist.

Wande shuffled into bed with Obinna still on his chest. Obinna's small hand clutched his favourite tuft of Wande's beard.

"What is it about that beard that he loves so much?" Ada wondered aloud.

Wande had already closed his eyes. "A well-conditioned beard is the softest thing you will ever feel, my dear."

Ada thought about that a little too long and felt herself blushing. Thank goodness, he wasn't looking at her.

She lay down on top of the covers and tried to sleep, but his very presence made it impossible. She was acutely aware of him as he lay with one arm stretched over his head and the other holding Obinna on his chest.

Resting her head on her elbows, Ada studied him under the light of the single bulb. Probably, this whole thing was a manifestation of his soft spot for Obinna. But he'd been invading her thoughts a little too often lately, and she couldn't deny the way her heart fluttered when he was around. And then there was the undeniable fact of that kiss.

And yet, all to what end? Sure, he had softened from his initial impossible self. Now, he was polite and considerate to her and the boys. Perhaps what she felt in her heart was simply gratitude, but she couldn't help but wonder what he really thought of her.

As if she had called his name out loud, his eyes popped open.

Ada didn't know what to do. Pretend she was asleep? Who sleeps with their head propped on their hands and their eyes staring into another person's face?

Wande wasn't going back to sleep. Instead, he spoke. "Can you get the little red container in my medicine cabinet? It's by the mouthwash."

Glad for an excuse to move, Ada jumped off the bed and ran to the bathroom. She found the cylindrical container too soon and hovered at the bathroom door, too humiliated to go back in. She would surely be the first person alive to die of embarrassment. Perhaps there were worse ways to die.

Finally, she returned to Wande's side.

"I would do this myself, but I don't want to wake the little guy," said Wande. "Please take a little of the ointment and rub it on my scar. It itches terribly otherwise."

Ada scooted closer to get the job done properly, thankful to have something to do with her hands. She unscrewed the cap of the ointment and squeezed a small amount onto her fingertip, its subtle fragrance carrying a hint of coconut. Her hand hovered over his face. It would be simple, just like helping the boys.

"Go on," Wande said at her hesitation. "I promise, I won't bite."

As her fingers moved, spreading the balm with tender strokes, she felt an electric fusion of sensation and emotion. Embarrassed, she looked away as her fingers stroked the length of the scar, but Wande's gaze sought her eyes even as the silence resonated between them. Ada was finding it hard to breathe.

Wande's voice broke through. "I wanted tribal marks like my grandfather." He turned to face Ada, Obinna firmly in his grip. "When I went to the village one Christmas, I played with the grandson of the barber who used to make the markings for the older folks. It did not go well."

Ada, thankful for the distraction, tried not to laugh as she whispered, "So there were no lions or tigers or bears?"

"No." Wande struggled to hold in his laugh under Obinna's weight. "I just started telling stories to look cool in front of friends. People took me seriously after that. I never told anyone what happened."

"No one?"

"Never."

His eyes were closing again, and a smile lingered on his lips. As much as she wanted to, Ada wasn't going to make the same mistake twice, and rolled away, musing over the story and the implications of what he'd said.

After a little while, she heard a whisper behind her.

"Hey, are you asleep?"

Ada turned again and found Wande's eyes wide open. He was smiling.

"Yes, I am," she said dryly. "Why aren't you?"

"Sleep gone." He shook his head. "Tell me about you, before all of this." He readjusted Obinna on his chest and so that they were in a sitting position.

Ada sat up, too. Her chances of sleep now gone. She wondered how she was going to avoid looking at his torso and her baby snuggled there, with the gentle way Wande was stroking Obinna's back. She cleared her throat gently and looked at her hands instead.

"How far back do you want to go?"

"Who knows? Little Ada?" Wande asked. "I just feel like I should… know you better."

"Wow, way back." Ada shifted, uncertain.

"I want to hear you talk." And talk they did.

First, about both their childhoods. Then, about everything that came after. They avoided their first marriages and stayed on safer topics until finally, voices worn out, they both fell asleep.

Close to three in the morning, Obinna began to fret, so Ada gently pried him from Wande's arms.

Wande stirred, but Ada whispered to reassure him, "It's okay; it's my turn."

Wande waited long enough for Ada to confirm that Obinna was okay, then closed his eyes and fell fast asleep again.

Ada, wishing she could sleep as easily, decided to go back to her room. She didn't want Emily to wake up and look for her, or worse, have the twins see her coming out of Wande's room in the morning.

As Ada scooped up a still-sleeping Obinna, she looked at Wande. The rush of emotions that flooded her at once took her by surprise. Gratitude, excitement, confusion, deep affection, and more than a hint of something else.

"Thank you for tonight, Wande Badejo." Her face was barely inches away from his. His eyes didn't flicker. His stillness emboldened her, and she brushed her lips lightly across his cheeks, then quickly left the room.

Wande's eyes popped open, and with a slight smile, he went back to sleep.

Chapter Thirty-One

Even after all the excitement, Ada still woke at five o'clock as usual. The memories from the night before returning slowly, gradually sharpening into focus.

She found herself smiling as she read that morning's Bible verse, this time from Ecclesiastes: '*There is a time to weep and a time to laugh, a time to mourn and a time to dance.*'

Ada checked the calendar on her phone and counted the weeks backwards, resting her head in her hands. Over six months had passed since they had buried Emeka. She felt as if shackles had been broken off her. Jumping up, she twirled around the room, not caring for once if the children were awake. She laughed and danced and praised God, His joy filling her heart until it overflowed.

Once her excitement had settled, she brought out her notebook and jotted down her plans for the day. Everything in it centred on herself.

She held herself back from calling too early, but once the clock struck eight, she took a deep breath and dialled the number on the card. She couldn't believe she still had it after so long.

"Uche, my name is Ada. I was at your store a while back one Sunday. Oh, you remember…"

Ada found herself smiling. "*Nwanem…* I need your help."

Wande arrived at breakfast lightheaded from the night before.

The kiss with Ada had been on his mind all night, invading his dreams. He hadn't planned it – of course he hadn't – his desire had overpowered everything.

Her tears had almost sent him on a university-buying spree. The feelings he had from all those weeks ago in the courthouse had ballooned into something else – something bigger. He wasn't sure yet what it was, but he knew one thing: he wasn't going to hold back with her anymore.

His disappointment was palpable when he sat at the table for breakfast and she wasn't there.

"Tobe, where's your mum?" He hoped he sounded casual enough when he asked the question.

"She and Emily are having a girls' day out."

"What does that mean?"

"We don't know." Ahanna shrugged. "She just said they may be back by lunch."

Well, she could have sent him a text, at least. And to leave Obinna, who was so sick last night? It was true that both nannies had come back early, but who leaves a sick child and goes out without thinking? He planned to have words with her when she returned.

It wasn't a stretch to say he felt like a pouting child who had been denied his favourite treat.

Wande allowed the boys to distract him, but his mind kept wandering back to Ada. He couldn't even taste the food he was forcing himself to chew, and after a few minutes, he gave up trying to choke it down.

"Guys, I'm sorry. I have to go now. I have a packed day." He raised his hands to silence the groans and complaints from the boys. "But I do promise that tonight, we men are going out for pizza!"

The excited reactions were no surprise, but their joy pleased him nonetheless, and he threw his head back and laughed. He hadn't stepped out of the house since he'd arrived, not wanting to be seen in public with crutches and a cast. Tonight, he would make an exception.

Michael stepped forward from the edge of the kitchen. "Sir, you know…"

"Michael, I know… that you make the best pizza in Lagos, but you're included in the boys' night out, so no cooking for you tonight, either! You get the night off."

"Should I clear that with madam, sir?" Michael raised a brow and gave a slight smile.

"Tell her to come and meet me," Wande grinned. He brought his hands together with anticipation, "and I'll explain."

"Yeah, Uncle Mike, don't be afraid," Ikenna said. "Uncle Wande is bigger and stronger than Mummy. He has fought wild animals, you know?"

Michael *hmphed* and turned away. Wande winked at Ikenna, bid the boys goodbye and went to his office.

Hours passed as he worked, and he grew fidgety every second that Ada did not come back. When she had still not returned by lunchtime, Wande was even more put out.

"Have you heard from her?" he asked Cynthia, ducking out into the hallway to look for signs of Ada's arrival.

Cynthia nodded. "Yes, sir, she called briefly to check on the house. Wherever she was, I couldn't hear her well. It was very noisy."

So, she could call Cynthia, but not him? He shook his head and asked Cynthia to tell the boys he would be out by five.

The boys sudden screaming cut through Wande's concentration, rousing him from his seat. As he neared the door to his study, he caught the nannies' voices in the mix as well. The sounds sharpened, and it became clear these weren't screams of danger as he'd imagined; they were hollers of wild excitement. Their mum had returned. Finally.

His annoyance at Ada resurfaced, but he was more irritated at himself for how much he'd missed her.

When he stepped into the foyer, the full force of the commotion hit him. The boys were jumping up and down, and the nannies had their hands over their mouths, their faces frozen with shock. Michael stood there with his hands on his waist and chest out like a proud man. *But where was Ada?*

"Dad! Dad! Look at Aunty Ada."

There she was: a vision in their midst, holding Obinna and laughing, dressed in a white, blue, and pink halter-neck dress that floated around her body as if unaffected by gravity. She wore large hoop earrings, and her hair curled in tiny ringlets, covering her beautifully shaped head.

Wande's mouth went dry as his eyes locked with hers, and she gave a tiny hint of a smile. It was Ada but presented in a way he had never seen or imagined. His heart rate picked up erratically. As she glided towards him, he took a step back, unable to process a single coherent thought.

"Hey. Sorry, I took so much time out today," she said shyly. "I had a few things to do."

A few things – that was an understatement.

Ada, for her part, had released herself into the hands of Uche, who had decided Ada was due for a total makeover. Uche had immediately organised appointments for make-up, nails and hair; then, she and Ada had gone through the store's entire inventory to find styles she loved and was comfortable wearing. The suitcase Ada brought home contained outfits for all occasions. Ada had told Uche that she never went anywhere, but Uche insisted a woman could never be too prepared, so she'd matched the clothes with all kinds of footwear and jewellery Ada was sure she would never need.

Ada had enjoyed the experience, and was thoroughly exhausted, but seeing the entire family's amazed reaction at her restyle was worth every minute.

Wande tried hard to close his mouth as he looked her over. Everything caught his eye. She had hair... She had arms and legs. There were parts of her he never thought about because she had been covered in black from the first minute he'd met her.

"Daddy, why are you staring?" Timi was beaming. "Isn't it wonderful she isn't wearing black anymore? She says her mourning period is over."

Ada ruffled Timi's hair.

Wande looked at her sharply and their eyes met. For a brief moment, they were the only ones in the room.

"Mummmyyy!"

"Sorry, Adanne—" Ada gave a quick glance at Wande. "Emily. Let Daddy see you."

Wande reluctantly peeled his eyes away from Ada and turned to his daughter. Emily wobbled next to her, wearing a replica of Ada's outfit, her hair in a similar style. He reached out and she lifted her hands for him to carry her. As he playfully threw her in the air, her squeals of delight echoed between the walls of the foyer.

"I like your hair, Emily," Wande said. "What's this style called, anyway?"

"I think it's called finger coils," Ada said.

"Interesting. Well, you both look stunning."

Ada blushed. Obinna began to fuss, and Wande stretched out his arms.

"You don't mind?" Ada asked.

Wande shook his head and took a seat in one of the chairs at the edge of the foyer, still holding Emily, while Ada settled Obinna on his other leg. Wande caught a whiff of Ada's perfume, and his stomach did a somersault.

He had already started getting distracted around the old Ada; what was going to happen now she looked like she'd just stepped off the cover of *Genevieve* magazine?

He didn't have time to think as Obinna began playing with his beard.

"Itchy!" Emily cried, pointing at Wande's beard.

"It's itchy to you. Because you are a... *guuurl*," Ahanna stretched out the word, and all the boys joined him in chorus on the last word.

Ada turned to Wande. "Are you free? I need to get off my feet."

"Yes, my evening is open," Wande said, almost too quickly. "I would love to spend some time with you all." Everyone grinned at his words, but his eyes kept straying back to Ada. "Let's go to the family room. I haven't been in there since I returned."

"What family room?" Ikenna raised his eyebrow.

"The room with the piano, silly," Timi responded.

Ahanna and Ikenna raced to get there first, with Emily stumbling behind them.

Ada fell in step with Wande as the procession moved down the hallway. "We always call it the piano room."

Wande laughed. "You know, it's my fault that there are parts of this house that are still strange to you and the boys. I should have settled you in myself when you got here." His eyes softened.

"That almost sounded like an apology." Ada's tone was teasing.

Wande shrugged. "Maybe." He paused to lean down to her ear. "You look really nice, by the way." He swallowed. "Gorgeous, even."

Ada blushed all kinds of shades, but couldn't reply, as they had arrived at the door to the family room.

Despite the fact they almost never used the space, Ada had stolen a peek inside more than once, and it was one of her favourite rooms in the house.

Floor-to-ceiling windows led to a portico, which opened onto the rose garden. In the evenings, when all the curtains were drawn, the room was cosy and warm, with comfortable chairs spread out around the masterpiece that was the grand piano. It was a room where it was possible for seven people to do their own thing yet still feel connected. Ada could almost feel the happy memories that had passed through this place.

Two large, formal portraits of Wande, his parents, and grandparents adorned the walls; the rest of the photos captured candid moments between family and friends. Every picture depicted a smiling face.

All the kids settled into the room, but before Ada could speak, Timi said, "Aunty Ada, you said your mourning period is over."

"Yes," Ada said cautiously, attempting to avoid Wande's eyes, which watched her carefully from the doorway.

"Are you still sad?" Timi asked. "Do you still remember him, your husband?"

Ada's jaw clenched. "Of course I do," she said, tiptoeing over each word. "You can't stop missing someone…" She cleared her throat and gave the quickest glance in Wande's direction before continuing. "The mourning period is an expectation, something that you do when you are a widow. Sometimes widows wear white, sometimes they wear black – it depends. In any case, that part of my… experience is over… but the sadness remains." She paused before she asked the next question. "Do you still miss your mum?"

The atmosphere dimmed as all eyes turned to Timi. His lips wobbled as he struggled to respond. Ada moved over to sit next to him.

"I do," he said at last. "I miss her every day."

Ada shifted closer and Timi relaxed into her as she put her arm around him. Wande sat back in his chair and rubbed his hands over his face.

Tobe broke the silence. "I miss my dad, too. Sometimes, I imagine he's travelling and will be back next week, so I don't feel so bad."

"I remember how he used to rub our heads when he came back from work," Ahanna added.

"Yes. He would call us *Ndi agha m*," said Ikenna. The three boys smiled.

Ada looked at Wande. "My army." Wande nodded.

"He used to buy us biscuits and juice." Tobe nodded. The twins nodded too, each of them lost in their own memories.

Ada was happy for them – how they so easily erased the bad and concentrated on the good. It was not so easy for her, and she bit her lip to avoid saying anything uncharitable about their father.

"Tell us about your mummy, Timi," Tobe asked. Timi sat up in his chair and looked at his dad.

Wande gave a nod. He could see the struggle on the young boy's face.

"She was funny," Timi explained, "and she loved to laugh a lot. She was so pretty – like you, Aunty Ada."

Ada blinked rapidly; she didn't want Timi to stop talking.

"She always said I was special," Timi added. He relaxed some more as he began to share about his mum – the things she loved, anecdotes that made everyone laugh, how she would stop wherever she heard music and just dance.

"It didn't matter where we were. At home, walking on the streets, or in a mall. I used to be so embarrassed." His smile was marred with tears.

"How did she die?" Ahanna asked. "Our daddy was sick. He had cancer."

Ada held her breath. Judging by the expression on Wande's face, it looked like he was doing the same.

Timi frowned. "I... I... I don't know. She went to hospital to give birth to Emily and didn't come back. They say she died, but I don't know what happened."

Ada's head snapped up, and she caught Wande's eye. She couldn't understand why he looked confused, as well.

"Do you know what, guys?" she interrupted. "Let's pray. Everyone, hold the hand of the person next to you."

One by one, everyone in the room linked a hand with the person beside them. Wande held onto Ikenna on his right and Timi on his left.

Ada led the family in prayer, acknowledging the loss they felt over their loved ones and asking for God's comfort. She also thanked God for bringing them all together and for all the joy, laughter and tears they'd shared with each other. When she finished, everyone said their amens, and the atmosphere became decidedly lighter.

And, as if on cue, there was a knock on the door. It was Mary.

"Madam, the pizza is ready."

"What pizza?" said Wande. He glanced at Ada.

"Dad, you ordered already?" Timi said.

"Is this pizza for the girls or boys?" asked Ikenna.

Ada laughed at the confusion. "I brought pizza back with me to celebrate. What pizza are you guys talking about?"

"Uncle Wande was going to take us men out to eat," Ahanna said proudly.

Ada raised her eyebrows at Wande, who cleared his throat. "When you ladies took off for the day, we decided to do likewise this evening."

Ada cast a glance around the room and shook her head. "What does it matter? Pizza is pizza. Go on, all of you, it's in the kitchen."

The children rushed out, Emily hard on their heels. The noise woke Obinna, and he started crying. Wande stood up, crossed over to Ada, and began to coo in the baby's ear. The lingerings of a frown still clung to Wande's face. Ada frowned too, sensing the reason for his mild aloofness towards her.

Hesitating, she said, "By the way, I'm sorry that I didn't ask permission to leave today."

"Please don't do that."

Ada cast her eyes down to the floor. She felt Wande's finger under her chin, and he lifted her face till she was looking directly at him.

"Don't apologise for things you shouldn't," he said. "You have a right to go where you please and to do what you want. If I gave any indication otherwise, I am sorry."

Ada's stomach flipped at the intensity of his gaze. "I guess old habits die hard."

Obinna was wide awake now. Wande stole his attention away from Ada and focused on playing with the baby instead.

Wande was more and more like a gentle giant every day. Watching him whispering to Obinna made Ada's heart swell with an indescribable mix of warmth and tenderness. She could've stared at them all evening, but she knew she had to bring up what had been bothering her.

"Wande," she said.

He looked to her again. "I mean it, Ada. You do not need to apologise."

"That wasn't what I was going to say." Wande's expression shifted.

A river of questions about Timi's mother was held back only by Ada's tongue. Something strange had crossed Timi and Wande's faces when Timi raised the topic of her death. Perhaps it was not her business, but Ada could no longer prevent herself from asking the question.

"How come you never told Timi the truth about his mother?" she asked.

Wande's face steeled, and he drew an inch away from Obinna. He did not look surprised. "I must admit, it never crossed my mind to provide a detailed explanation. I thought he knew."

"But how would he? Who would have told him?"

"His mum was everything." Wande shook his head. "Afterwards, I could not face one more conversation about it. I... hoped that it could be left to someone else to explain it all to Timi."

"He misses her every day," Ada said. "Even if you didn't then, you need to do right by him now. He needs an outlet for all that emotion."

"I know, but how?"

"Well, you could start with apologising for not telling him how his mum died. Perhaps also for putting your work before him?"

Wande's eyes flashed.

Ada leaned back. This new ease with Wande was confusing. She didn't know when to remember that they were partners, not friends. Perhaps she had crossed a line.

"Mary," Wande said, addressing the nanny at the edge of the room but not removing his eyes from Ada, "take Obinna, please."

Mary did as he asked and whisked a crying Obinna away. Ada silently berated herself for overstepping, especially after they had been getting along so well. Now, she had upset him all over again.

Wande stayed still. "You're right."

Ada startled. It was not what she had expected him to say.

"The truth is," he went on, "I should not have married my wife. I didn't love her. She was simply available, and my parents were insistent. I respected her, but I was never around her or the children. She was lonely. She never said as much, but I could guess.

"When she died, I could not face my children – especially Timi, who has always been her twin. When I look into his eyes, I see every accusation she would throw my way if she were still here. Perhaps Timi agrees with her. Perhaps he, too, would tell me I'm a terrible father, if he could."

"He certainly would not." Ada stressed the words, desperate for him to understand. "He idolises you. He has raised you onto a pedestal that is so high, almost nothing could bring it down. He makes excuses for you at every opportunity. He loves you, Wande. Emily loves you, too, though she doesn't know you yet."

"I love them, too," he said. "But I have locked them away in a box in my heart, and I don't know how to get them back out."

"The lost years are nothing compared to the decades ahead. Don't waste any more time." Ada hesitated, but placed a hand on his shoulder and said gently, "This parenting thing is hard. We all learn on the go, but it doesn't stop us from retracing our steps when we mess up."

Wande dug his hands deep into his pockets and looked away.

"Gosh, I'd rather face a room full of Japanese investors than face my own son," he admitted with a quiet laugh.

"That's because you don't love your investors." Ada swallowed. "Love is terrifying."

The look Wande gave her made her want to look away so that she could breathe properly.

"You're a very wise woman."

Ada chuckled and tried to relax her body, which had wound itself into an impossible knot. "Ooh, two compliments in one evening? Sir, you have to stop."

Chapter Thirty-Two

After the children had eaten their pizza, they all stampeded upstairs to the arcade. Once the lower floor was clear, Ada stood sentry at the foot of the stairs as Wande went to retrieve Timi from the game room to speak with him.

While she waited, Michael emerged from the kitchen. He saw her silhouetted in her finery in the dim light of the foyer and gave her a wink.

"Why are you winking?" she laughed.

"It's either a wink or a whistle, my dear." He came over and grabbed both her hands in his. "I'm happy for you, Ada."

"Why? Because I have taken off the black?"

"Yes, but not just because of the clothes – they are only a symbol of what's been happening up here," he said, tapping his temple. "You have removed the darkness from your mind. I'm so proud of you."

Ada blinked as her eyes misted over. "You know, I suspect God used *you* to help me with that," she said. "So, thank you."

"Remember, it's okay for you to be happy, just as you make others happy," Michael said. "Jesus came so that you may have life and have it more abundantly."

"Thank you, Michael." Ada hugged him before he retired for the night.

With the kitchen dark for the night, Ada strolled around downstairs, finally settling back in the family room, where she curled up on the couch to wait for Timi and Wande to finish their conversation. Soon, the exhaustion from a very exciting day caught up with her, and her eyes began to drift closed.

"Aunty Ada."

Ada rose from the couch, momentarily disoriented. Timi was beside her. His eyes shone wide and red in the dark.

"Are you okay?" She held his face in her hands.

He nodded. He sniffed and asked, "May I microwave another slice of pizza to take upstairs?"

"You know the rules, Timi." She smiled at him as she rubbed his nose. "But I'll let you this once. Make sure you bring the plate down first thing in the morning, okay?"

"Thank you." He got to the door and then turned back to wrap his arms around her and give her a peck on the cheek.

Now, it was Ada's turn to be teary as he left the room and headed for the kitchen. She followed, but stopped when she saw Wande outside the door to his study.

"Thank you for waiting up. I hoped you would."

"Just wanted to make sure you both were okay."

"We are, thank you," he said.

Ada nodded and put a hand on the banister to head off to her room.

Wande looked at Ada and raw vulnerability shimmered in his eyes. "Ada, I know you are probably tired. But I... I won't be able to sleep yet. I was hoping you might be willing to take a walk with me."

"Now?" Despite her exhaustion, Ada's eyes lit up, and she tried to hide her smile.

The walk down the front steps was slow and careful.

"I'm not ready to cause another circus if I fall down these stairs," Wande said. They laughed, then settled into a slow walk in silence.

The air hung heavy with the scent of roses, and only the delicate chirrups of crickets accompanied them. The hustle and bustle of Lagos was so far removed from the grounds, it felt like they were the only two people left in the world.

"Let's sit at the fountain," Wande suggested. The fountain was enclosed in a wide stone lip, broad enough for comfortable seating. Ada helped Wande lower himself onto the cool slab, and she sat down beside him.

"I love it here," Ada said. "I used to sit here a lot when I first arrived. Whenever I felt overwhelmed – which was often, by the way – I'd come here to pray, and just be."

Hearing her words, Wande became sober and thoughtful. He shifted so he could face her, lifting one knee to balance properly.

"I owe you an apology for my behaviour then," he said. "You didn't deserve to be left to the wolves like that."

"I don't know. In a way, it did me good. I was forced to figure things out on my own." Ada smiled. "Maybe I should thank you."

"Are you always so gracious?"

"No, you caught me in a good mood today."

Wande didn't laugh as she'd expected. Instead, he opened and closed his mouth, as if he wanted to say something. Ada wondered what was bothering him.

"You know, we talked about you tonight," he said finally. "Timi and I. Do you know what he asked me?"

Ada's thoughts tripped over themselves as she imagined all the reasons they might have talked about her.

Wande's eyes twinkled as he watched her mind race. "He asked, 'Can we like her now'?"

Ada inclined her head, puzzled. She swallowed hard. "What did you say?" The crickets suddenly sounded louder, filling the silence between them.

Wande stood up and placed his hands on Ada's shoulders, running his hands down the length of her arms. Ada shivered. He pulled her closer – close enough that Ada could feel his breath on her forehead.

"I told him that he should feel free to like you as much as he wanted, because I like you, too."

Ada leaned back, breathless, but he moved towards her. His nearness and the scent of his cologne were wreaking havoc on her senses.

"Within a week, Ada, I'll get this cast off. And when I do," he said, "will you go on a date with me?"

Ada cleared her throat. "Um, like an outing? Will we bring the children?"

"No. Just you and me. No kids."

She shrugged. "Okay."

Thank goodness he couldn't see her insides. He would have witnessed fireworks going off and a marching band in full swing with Ada doing somersaults in the middle of the chaos.

Wande helped her up from the fountain, and they walked back towards the front steps without speaking. He leaned on her as he climbed each stair.

"Did I tell you how beautiful you look tonight?" he asked when they reached the top.

His every compliment kindled a tiny spark in her heart. The kiss from last night still lingered on her lips.

"And please," he added, "never wear black again. Get plenty more of these outfits so you're not tempted to revert to old habits. Don't worry about costs – I'll pay."

Ada leaned against the door, trying to stifle a fresh burst of laughter as he keyed in the code. "You already did."

He raised his eyebrows. "Ah, nice one. Money well-spent, I say." He stepped closer and rested his arm on the door, wedging her in.

She wasn't sure she could handle the way he was looking at her anymore, so she ducked under his arms and escaped into the house, only turning around when she was a safe distance away.

"I'm looking forward to the weekend!" she said as she ran up the stairs.

When she got to her room, she turned to find him still staring, and hastily closed the door behind her.

A slew of voices raced through her mind, and as the seconds ticked on, only a few of them sharpened into focus.

I can't feel this way for him.

He could choose any woman in the world. He wouldn't want me. This is a job. My job. What am I doing?

That instant, she decided not to think about the proposed date. The novelty of her new clothes and hair would wear off. Once he had gotten used to seeing her like this, they would revert to their previous friendly arrangement, and she would be nothing special. She was sure of it.

Chapter Thirty-Three

The next day, Ada and Wande sat out by the basketball court as the children wore themselves out shooting hoops. The boys' swimming trainer had just left, and now, they were charging around with abandon. Timi and Tobe were running the twins ragged, passing the ball over their heads and making baskets, while the little ones darted around clamouring for a turn.

Meanwhile, Emily was engrossed in feeding her dolls grass spaghetti, and Obinna slept in his little rocking chair, oblivious to the noise.

"Oh o," Ada said. She sat up suddenly from where she reclined on the grass, patting her dress on the side and looking around. "I think I left my phone in the house."

"What is it with you and phones?" Wande laughed. "What if there's an emergency?"

"What kind of emergency? Everyone important to me is right here."

Wande's heart did a flip, and a grin spread across his face as he leaned back in his wheelchair. Ada rose to check in with Mary as she headed back to the house.

He couldn't pretend that she wasn't important to him anymore, but in the hours since he had asked her on a date, he had become less sure of how she felt about him. She had been playing coy all morning, and their exchanges hadn't deepened beyond the occasional light joke.

Wande returned his attention to the children and marvelled at how much had changed in such a short time. With his cast coming off soon, he was expected to return to work in full swing, and no part of him was enthusiastic at the thought.

Things with him and Timi were in a good place. He and Emily were bonding, too. The other day, when Timi had called him 'Dad', she'd echoed it. It didn't matter that she hadn't repeated it since, the feeling was unmatched. Tobe, too, was an amazing kid, and Wande was also enjoying getting to know the sweet but rambunctious twins. Of course, the thought of Obinna always brought a smile to his lips. The little one had a special place in his heart.

"Daddy, catch!" Timi cried.

Wande had a split second to react. He caught the ball in his right hand just as it was about to whizz past his head.

The four boys hollered in appreciation and disbelief.

Wande laughed. "You don't know who you're dealing with, do you? Three-time All-State Champion here."

"Wow! Dad, that was amazing!" Timi said breathlessly.

"Truly, sir," Tobe said grinning. "I wish I'd caught it on camera."

"If you'd like, I can show you something else I used to do… At one point, I could make a basket with my eyes closed."

"Do it, Timi's dad! Let's see," Ahanna said, his eyes wide.

"Yeah, Dad, show us."

Wande rolled his wheelchair around to the back of the court and stood up. He steadied himself before closing his eyes and throwing the ball high into the air. Punching the air, he waited for the applause sure to come, but the ball hit the rim of the hoop, and instead, Emily gave a piercing shriek.

He turned to find her at the edge of the court with her hands on her head, screaming at the top of her lungs, while the ball bounced into the grass.

The four boys ran to her. Tobe lifted Emily and bounced her on his hip while the other boys chorused apologies all around, but she refused to be consoled.

Wande wheeled over to where the boys crowded around her. "Bring her here," he insisted.

Tobe handed the wailing child to Wande, who checked her over for damage. No bleeding. He heaved a sigh of relief.

"It's okay, Emily," he cooed. He looked at all the boys' stressed faces. "Hey, guys, don't look so worried. She'll be fine. A little stunned but not hurt."

Timi looked at Tobe. "Er, Dad, we can see she's okay. We just want to make it clear that this was your fault."

Wande looked puzzled, while Tobe and the boys nodded.

"Uncle Wande, remember, it was *you* who threw the ball that hit her," Ikenna said.

"C'mon, you guys know it was an accident," Wande said. He rubbed Emily's back while bouncing her on his knees. She was agitated but not resisting. "What are you afraid of, that she will have a concussion?"

"No, sir," Tobe said. "We're afraid what will happen to you when my mum hears what you did to her Ada."

"It was nice knowing you, Dad." Timi shook his head mournfully.

The seriousness on their faces was comical.

"Well, I'm not afraid of her." Wande adopted his most solemn expression. "Besides, the baby is fine."

The boys hurriedly abandoned him on the grass, as if staying near him would make them guilty by association.

Wande looked anxiously towards the house for Ada. An idea crossed his mind. What was it Ada did to console this little girl when she was upset? Ah, yes.

Once the boys were out of earshot, he began to sing, bouncing Emily to the beat of the song that had previously irritated him no end.

"Ada o Ada, Ada o Ada, Adaeze, Adaugo." He found himself laughing, and eventually, Emily gave up crying and snuggled into his chest. "Adanna, Adanne…" Even when he ran out of all the variations of Ada, Emily didn't seem to mind, smiling as she sucked her thumb.

Wande felt warmth all over as he gazed at his daughter. He marvelled at her rosy cheeks, her neatly coiffed hair. She looked like a doll wearing all the ribbons Ada insisted on adorning her hair with each morning.

A shudder ran through him as his mind went back to the day he'd walked into the house in London and found her unconscious. That day, she had looked like a tiny skeleton, the curdled bottle of milk at her side.

He drew her closer. "I could have lost you," he murmured into her hair.

There were no words for the terror of those days. He had been ready to do anything to keep Emily in a stable, safe environment – even if it meant forcing another marriage.

He looked again for Ada. Where was she? Plenty of time had passed, and she still hadn't returned.

Quietly, he asked Timi to get the boys to round up and return the equipment to the gym room. He handed Emily over to the nannies.

Wande wheeled his chair behind Timi and Tobe, heading along the palm-lined avenue to the kitchen. The three staff huddled in a corner stood to attention when he came in. He glanced around. No Ada. Wande checked the family room, but there was no sign of her. Baffled, he returned to the foyer.

Someone coughed behind him, and he wheeled his chair around.

"If you are looking for Ada, she's in your office, sir. I don't think she is okay," Michael said.

Wande thanked Michael, and wheeled faster than he knew he could across the foyer, and opened the door to the study.

Ada was hunched over the desk, sobbing. She lifted her head, startled, and her eyes were red and swollen.

Wande's mind raced through all sorts of scenarios. Mid-sob, Ada tried to say something, but the words came out in a jumble.

Wande got out of the chair and took her hand. Then, he sat on his couch and pulled her down beside him, drawing her close and allowing her to cry.

"Sorry… I came… here because I knew… the kids wouldn't… I just needed space."

"What's going on?" he asked softly.

Ada laid her head back. "It's Osas…" She was still heaving, and the words came out in torrents.

Wande froze; he had all but forgotten the name of the slender ebony beauty who had always been at Ada's side when they first met. She was the one who'd been a thorn in his flesh.

He cleared his throat. "Are you still in touch?" He was careful to sound neutral.

"No. Well, I didn't think so. Not since I wanted to leave Port Harcourt and everything there behind forever."

"What happened?"

"When I agreed to come here, I got a new phone and a new number, remember? Earlier, when I was looking for my phone, I thought of the old one. I found it in a box, and that's when they all came pouring in." Ada started crying again.

Wande shook his head. "What came pouring in?"

"All the messages. Voice messages. Text messages. Hundreds and hundreds. The inbox was full." Ada held her old Blackberry handset in her hands.

"What did she say?"

"She was crying in so many of them, and Osas never cries. And, she apologised."

"For what?"

Ada heaved a heavy sigh. "Before I came here, we got into a fight. Osas said some things… things I preferred to run from, rather than hear from her. I couldn't believe it. She is the most steadfast person I have ever known. I was so angry with her. But now, time has passed, and these voice notes…"

Ada burst into tears again. Wande pulled her into his arms and allowed her cry. She pressed a button on her phone, and the familiar voice came through the speakers.

"My friend, how are you? I know I should stop doing this, but I have no one else to talk to. Your voicemail is the only connection I have to you anymore… I am so scared, Ada. And sad. I had a cancer scare a few months ago. I'm alright – it's benign. But it got me thinking, what if something happened to me? *Na so we go be*? The thought of never speaking to you scares me more than anything. If, by some miracle, you hear this, *take your Jesus mind call me abeg.* Let me tell you how sorry I am, let me explain… After that, you can decide never to speak to me again."

The click at the end of the message sounded so loud in the silent room.

"She was my sister," Ada said quietly.

Wande was ashamed of the spark of jealousy he felt inside him. He quickly quashed the juvenile reaction and asked, "What do you want?"

Ada sniffed. "I'm so confused. She is so many things to me. For her to go through something that horrible – without me… It's not something I could have done. But, even so, I'm not sure I could ever forget what she said."

Wande resisted the urge to ask what, exactly, Osas had said to Ada. If Ada had wanted to tell him, she would have. He knew intervening would serve no purpose in the situation now. And yet…

"The kids are going to look for you soon," he said. "Go and wash your face, so you don't worry them."

Weary from crying, Ada got up and did as instructed.

Once she was in the bathroom, Wande shook his head slowly as he struggled with his own blossoming ideas. Things were going so well between them. What would it mean to have Osas back in their lives? Then again, what would happen to Ada if this went unresolved entirely?"

He picked up his phone from the bedside table and made three phone calls.

Ada came out with droplets still clinging to her lashes. Her face was a little less swollen, and she was no longer crying.

He patted the seat beside him. "I have my helicopter on standby. You can make the trip to Port Harcourt, or I can fly your friend down. Just let me know what you need. As for the children, I'll hold the fort till it's over. Are you okay with that?"

The sound that escaped from Ada's throat could either have been labelled as fright or pain. She threw herself onto Wande, her arms tightening around his neck. In turn, he wrapped his arms around her shapely figure and hugged her back. He tried not to let the sensations rushing through him get to his head. She was grateful, and he was merely a helpful presence.

She pulled away. "You are amazing."

Her face was just inches from his. He wanted to kiss her so badly, but instead, he moved away and cleared his throat.

Perhaps it wasn't such a good idea to get carried away with these feelings after all. The day's events had reminded Wande that he and Ada's ecosystem was more fragile than either of them had considered. All it took was a few voice notes from an old friend to send Ada into a state of pure devastation.

"You have held up your end of the contract; it's only fair I make your life as easy as I can." Wande's voice was detached when he spoke.

Ada deflated slightly at his words, and he felt guilty. While he longed for her approval, he knew he wasn't worthy of it. The last time he'd had a woman in his life, he'd made her life miserable. Ada didn't deserve that. Maybe they would both be better off if he managed to steer the relationship back into a safe emotional place.

"Thank you for your generosity, Wande."

"Of course." He coughed, and a slight awkwardness descended between them. The mention of the contract soured the air. They would need to be careful, because hearts, like contracts, could so easily be broken.

Chapter Thirty-Four

Sleep evaded Ada that night as she tossed and turned.

"Lord Jesus, I think the shock of those messages muddled my brain."

I am with you. Be at peace.

Ada couldn't find that peace.

Did she want to face Osas again? The impulse to call her back at every instance had all but disappeared, but she couldn't deny how many times she'd felt the urge to call and tell her what Emily had done, or talk about Tobe or the twins, or tell her how big Obinna was getting, or to share how she was feeling about Wande. It had been a near-constant desire since arriving at the Badejo household.

But the image of their last time together could not be wiped from the slate of Ada's mind.

Osas's face, contorted as she screamed at Ada. The look of exhaustion behind her eyes.

That night, Ada went to bed determined to tell Wande that she had settled the matter. There would be no need to rekindle dead friendships.

Morning dawned. It was the start of the week. The children all had tests that day, and Ada had promised Timi a special math lesson before school started.

Ronke came over for a meeting with Wande, and Ada greeted her in the hallway.

"This must be important," Ada remarked as Ronke came into view. "You're here so early."

"Well, Wande insisted on having Bukky Dada flown in today. She's one of his board directors."

Ada felt her stomach tighten. "You guys have never heard of Skype calls?" she questioned.

Ronke rolled her head back and laughed. "When next you see your husband, please bring it up to him. We all just obey."

Ada blushed at Ronke's casual use of the terminology, and if Ronke noticed, she didn't say.

Ronke also didn't say she had observed that neither Wande nor Ada called to complain about each other anymore. After years of supporting the Badejo family, Ronke hoped Ada knew what she was doing. Wande usually left women holding the short straw.

After the school run, Ada saw Wande at the door to his suite, giving an unfamiliar lady a peck on both cheeks. The woman was tall and elegant – less flamboyant than Chidi – but still possessed her own unique style. Watching them chat by the door, Ada had to admit they looked good together. Wande, dark and handsome, and the woman the epitome of corporate glamour, a perfect counterpart for him. They obviously shared business interests in common, and were clearly comfortable together. Ada didn't know whether to punch or applaud the woman, and she ducked into the kitchen before they saw her.

Ronke, Wande, and Bukky Dada remained in the meeting room all day. Breakfast and lunch were both served in the library and shortly before 5 p.m., Ada heard the click of stilettos across the marble hall. Ms. Dada was leaving, and as she went, she caught sight of Ada in the kitchen and gave her a friendly wave.

As the front door closed behind her, Ronke walked into the kitchen and sighed.

"Ada, do you think Michael has any wine hidden away – for medicinal purposes, of course?" Ronke found a bottle in the fridge and poured herself a drink.

"Long day?" asked Ada.

"Too long!"

"She looked like a cool lady, though." Ada almost whispered the words under her breath. "What, with her and Chidi, Wande has no shortage of professional, glamorous admirers on his doorstep." Her laugh was harsh and forced.

Ronke looked puzzled. "Is that jealousy I hear?"

"No. Just making an observation." Ada felt a blush spread across her cheeks.

Ronke smiled. "You know the saying 'A wealthy man will always have followers'… Well, sometimes it's true, but Wande isn't taken in by make-up and clothes. He knows he's a magnet for women looking for an easy life."

Ronke downed the remainder of her wine. "You need to stop worrying so much." With that, she swept out of the kitchen.

Ada frowned. Worried? She didn't have the right to be worried about anything. They were not a real couple – there was nothing established between them. Whatever Wande's feelings towards her, or any other woman, she wasn't entitled to know them.

When Ada next checked her phone, she found Wande had sent a text, apologising for missing breakfast and lunch but promising to make it up to the family over the weekend. Ada smiled. A month ago, Wande wouldn't have sent a message for anything.

She should be satisfied with being friends with Wande. To dream of anything more would just be greedy.

The kids were gathered in the family room after dinner when Wande appeared. He greeted the boys and asked after Obinna and Emily, who hadn't arrived yet and were on the way down the stairs with the nannies.

"Boys," Wande said, glancing at Ada, "could I steal your mum away for a moment?"

"Aren't you joining us for game night?" Ada asked. The boys began to warily shuffle out of the room to leave them alone. "They were setting up for Scrabble."

"No more questions." He reached for Ada and tugged her a little. She misstepped, falling into his arms. Before letting her go, he inhaled her scent deeply and suddenly felt lightheaded. "I don't know if I can ever get used to you in these bursts of colour."

Ada had on a bright yellow T-shirt and a pair of denim mid-calf pants. She laughed. "I am sure I still have one black *boubou* left. I could—"

"Never, ever, ever! I wasn't complaining. You look very pretty."

Ada didn't want to be affected by his words, but she couldn't help it. They were like a warm hug, comforting, affirming; she had used them as bricks to rebuild her once-shattered confidence. But she had to remind herself: *he isn't mine.*

"Did you send our children away just to discuss my appearance?" she asked.

"No, of course not. In fact, I have some news." His eyes twinkled. "Osas is here."

Ada stepped back, suddenly in desperate need of a chair. "What?" Overcome with fear, she grabbed Wande's arm.

"Ada," Wande's voice sounded far away. "Come and sit down." He led her to the loveseat by the door.

Ada gulped as much air as she could, still holding his hand for support.

"She's here? Really here?" she asked.

"She's outside in the car."

"How? Why? How can she be here?"

"I arranged it," Wande said. A lilt of pride followed each syllable. "For you to see her. So that you can repair your relationship."

"I… I… It was… Why would you do that? I didn't ask you to do that."

Wande's smile instantly disappeared. "I thought that was what you wanted." The words came out clipped and jagged.

"I'm not ready!" Ada cried. She began to struggle for breath again. Osas was there – really there – only metres away, just outside. What could Ada say to her? She hadn't had enough time to even conceive of it.

Wande swallowed thickly. "Say the word, and I'll have the driver take her back to the hotel."

Ada let out another breath slowly and felt herself returning to her body.

She could not send Osas away. Not after the long journey and, if she really had been ill, as her voice notes suggested, she would be exhausted. Ada would not be able to find it in herself to send her friend back to the airport.

But her fury still reigned. How dare Wande put her in this position? What did he know about their relationship? Despite his determination to control their own world, there were some answers that man did not have.

"I will see her," Ada agreed, but she aimed a searing gaze at Wande. "You had no right to do this."

A soft knock sounded on the door. Ahanna poked his head through into the room. "Mummy, Timi's dad, we're ready for game night."

Wande rose from where he sat beside Ada and gave Ahanna an easy smile. "I will be right with you. Your mother has a visitor now, so she will join us later."

Tobe appeared over his brother's shoulder. "What's happening? A visitor?"

"Mummy never has visitors," Ahanna said. His eyes lit up.

"Except Aunty Osas."

Ada stiffened and looked at Wande, before heading into the hallway. The boys caught on immediately.

"Is Aunty Osas here?" asked Tobe.

When Ada didn't reply, the twins screamed in delight and tried to pass by Ada, but Wande blocked their path.

"Let's give your mother some space," Wande said. "Come on. Back to the room for game night. I hope everyone is ready to lose!"

Tobe took one more look at his mother's tired face, waiting for her nod, before shepherding his confused brothers away.

Wande gave Ada a final glance. "I will tell the staff to bring her up the drive," he said quietly. And then he was gone. Ada calmed herself down, praying silently for guidance.

It was a moment she had imagined more than a few times, but she had never predicted it would play out here, in this way, under these conditions. The only thing she could do was breathe.

Wande watched Ada though the window. Ada was midway down the front steps when the car door opened and Osas emerged. She looked even thinner than before, but still just as stylish in a sweater over skinny jeans and a pair of heels. In the past, Osas would've been Wande's type, but not since... He put a stop to his stray thoughts as both ladies stared at each other as if frozen in time.

Osas moved first, sliding onto her knees, clasping her hands in front of her. Her action spurred Ada, who rushed down the remaining steps. Ada pulled Osas up, and they fell into each other's arms. Wande could see clearly enough to know that they were both sobbing. With no wish to intrude on their pain, he turned away and wandered down the hallway to join the boys for game night.

"It was a Friday night, about three months after I got back from my Master's programme in the UK. I had that new job, more money than I had ever dreamed of. I was living the life! But I was lonely. It's funny, while you complained about your circumstances, I envied you – at least you had Tobe. I had no one. Anyways, that night, I took myself to the club with one mission: to get blind drunk and find a man to keep me company." Osas looked to Ada for permission to continue. She nodded.

The two women sat in the privacy of the front room. After Osas had emerged from the car on the driveway, they had sequestered themselves there at Osas's request so that Osas could speak to Ada alone.

"By the time the general manager of my department walked into the club, I had accomplished my first goal. I was so drunk I didn't even recognise him at first. I spent the rest of my time at the club with him and his friend. They kept buying me drinks, and I kept drinking. By the time he pulled me into his car, I was totally wasted."

Ada listened quietly as Osas told her story. Ada occasionally checked her heart as Osas spoke, but each time, she felt no semblance of emotion. Nothing whatsoever.

"I woke up the next morning, and my body told the story of the horror it had been through. I was too ashamed to go to the hospital."

Ada nodded slowly. Memories of Emeka's force flickered through her mind.

Osas continued, "I just wanted to forget, but two months later, I realised I was pregnant. I wanted a baby, but not that way, and not with him. I considered an abortion, but I changed my mind at the last minute."

"What about this baby?" Ada asked. "What happened?"

Osas broke down again. Ada stared at her, confused by her sudden tears.

"I told you that I had a four-month training, and when I came back, I had lost the baby."

"How could I not have known?" Ada asked. "How could you not tell me this, Osas?"

"I wanted to. So badly. But you were going through enough as it was." Osas wiped her eyes with her sleeve. "Anyway, he was posted out of the country, and I thought I could move on with my life. But he came back around six months ago, wanting to start something together. When I refused, he went on the offensive. The more I dug in my heels, the more innovative ways he found to frustrate me. I put in a case to HR, and that was when he constructed an embezzlement case against me, determined to ruin my position in the company. The day I was formally charged was the day Ndidi threw you out."

Osas shook her head. "I had no excuse to pour my frustrations on you the way I did. I hope somehow, someday, you can forgive me."

Ada rubbed her arms, but she was not sure the air conditioning was to blame for the chill.

This was Osas, her friend – her sister, even. How could she listen to Osas, how could she look her directly in the face, and feel such a disconnect? More than anything, that hurt the most. Tears filled Ada's eyes.

"I can't believe I'm just hearing all of this now. What kind of friend was I to you? That you couldn't share this with me? I thought I knew you. Now, you have me doubting everything."

"Ada, you were going through so much—"

"So what?" Ada raised a hand to her forehead. "All these years. I feel like such a fool. I saw you nearly every day back then. How can you stay friends with someone and keep something like that from them?"

"I can't count how many times I wanted to tell you. But I was so afraid of adding to your hurt."

Ada was saved from having to respond by the sound of a cough. It was John, lurking in the nearby doorway. Osas jumped to her feet.

"Well," Osas said. "Must be time to go back to the hotel. I return to Port Harcourt in the morning for work." She smiled with great effort. "Wande was very generous with this whole thing, you know. The hotel is beautiful, and he even had me picked up in a helicopter."

Ada's stomach swirled with unease. Osas's smile, even as sad as it was, conjured memories of the best and worst parts of her life.

Osas wrapped her arms around herself. "I didn't know how this night would go," she admitted. "Thank you for giving me a chance to speak. I know I don't deserve your forgiveness, after the things I said to you. But…"

Despite what Osas said, Ada knew that she was looking for forgiveness or, at least, the prospect of such a thing in the future. But Ada could not put names to her feelings, and she definitely could not see through the fog of this moment to decide whether they could ever return to the way things were before.

Ada managed to give a weak smile. They had reached the car, and John opened the door for Osas.

Osas turned before she got in. "You look gorgeous by the way." She paused. "And happy."

"Take care, Osas."

Osas gave a quick nod and ducked into the car. Even in the dark, Ada knew she was crying.

Ada swallowed hard as the car drove away. For the second time, she felt like she was losing her best friend.

Ada had been sitting in the family room on her own for almost an hour when Wande arrived. When she saw him in the doorway, she unfurled herself; her body had been curled in a knot on one of the armchairs.

Wande leaned against the wall, his arms folded.

"I won't ask you what happened," he said. "I'm only here to apologise."

"You overstepped," Ada said quietly. She chewed her lip, her eyes on the piano in the middle of the room.

"I know," Wande replied. He hesitated. "I was afraid of what might happen if you never saw her again."

"What might happen?"

"She is an indispensable part of your happiness. I knew that when I first met the two of you."

Ada shook her head. "I'm not sure if that's true anymore."

Wande frowned. "Well, anyway. The kids are sorted and in bed. They are a challenge to quell when you're not there. Each one of them told me to 'do things how Mummy does'. Even my old boy, Timi."

Ada didn't reply right away. His anecdotes about the children did not raise her spirits in the usual way.

"I almost had to tackle the twins and Tobe," Wande added. "They really wanted to see her."

Ada had forgotten that the relationship with Osas was not entirely her own. Osas loved her boys, and they loved her; she had loved them as her own, and the children knew it. They had watched their mother sob in her arms too many times.

Ada sighed. "Look," she said, "I understand why you did it. Why you called her."

Wande waited for her next words with bated breath.

"I just… wasn't ready. I wanted more time to think about what I was going to say to her. Now, my head feels scrambled. I don't know which way is up and which way is down."

"I should have left it up to you," he said. "Again, I'm sorry."

Ada nodded silently. With a sniffle, she opened her arms to him. He went to her and nuzzled into her hair.

"I don't know what to do," Ada whispered.

"That's alright," Wande said. He rubbed her shoulder gently. "For now, we can just stay here, and not know what to do, together."

Together.

The word rang through Ada's mind with a brashness that shook her bones. So warm, and yet so frightening. She did not know how to feel about that word anymore.

Chapter Thirty-Five

The next day, Ada knocked softly on the door to Osas's hotel room. After a few seconds, Osas opened the door, and when she saw Ada standing there in the hallway, she covered her face with her hands.

Ada moved forward and gathered her friend into her arms.

"Ada—"

"Shh. Let me in."

Ada dropped her bag on the floor and went to lie on the double bed. Osas joined her, and they lay side-by-side as they had so many times, their faces turned towards each other.

"When you left last night, I got out my notebook," Ada said. Osas gave her a look.

"Yes, I now have a notebook." Ada gave a modest grin and Osas smiled through her tears. "I began to write down all the reasons why I should never speak to you again. I wrote one line. Then, I decided to write down the reasons why I should. I filled pages and pages… All the years you gave to me and my boys. That's why I'm here."

Osas wiped her eyes with the back of her hand, then slipped her arm through Ada's. "I really messed up, didn't I?"

"Yes, you did. I know you said you kept your struggles away to protect me, but it makes me feel like a worthless friend. I leaned on you heavily, and you never trusted that you could lean on me." Ada shut her eyes. "I guess you were right. I was useless."

"No, Ada." Osas shook her head. "You are as far from useless as a woman can be. I didn't mean anything I said that day. You'd just been through one of the most harrowing experiences a mother can endure. I should never have said it."

"But you were going through it, too. I didn't even notice. I was so consumed with my life and my worries."

"It wasn't like that."

"I should be saying sorry, too," Ada said. "I wasn't as good a friend to you as you were to me."

Osas tried to speak, but Ada stopped her.

"I am not just here to forgive you, Osas. I'm here to thank you." She smiled and reached out to dab Osas's tears off her cheek. "Let me carry *you* for once."

Later, after the two women had properly reconnected, Ada got her phone out to call Wande.

"Everything okay?" he asked.

Ada couldn't help herself, despite the tribulations of the night before, just hearing his voice made her smile. "Can I ask for a favour?"

"Anything you need."

"Osas needs the day off. She won't be leaving today. Do you know the higher-ups at her office?"

"Consider it done. When are you going to be home?"

Ada laughed and promised to be back for dinner.

As Ada hung up the call, Osas grinned. "Your Mr Wande Badejo turned out to be something else. It's a wonder that he would do all this for me, especially when our last meeting ended in such a disaster."

"I know it's hard to believe," Ada said, "but underneath all that concrete is a caring individual."

Osas sat up, giving Ada a bemused look, and clasped her hands together in prayer.

"Lord Almighty, I need to hear the full *gist*!"

Ada punched her in the arm. "See this foolish girl… what *gist*?"

An image of Wande came up in Ada's mind, and her heart did a small somersault.

"*Ehen*, see the way your eyes changed. Is Beauty falling for the Beast?" Osas whispered mischievously.

"Don't ever call him that again!"

Far from being upset, Osas burst into laughter. Ada rolled her eyes.

"Ada," Osas giggled, "have you forgotten that this is a job? You are being paid, you know."

"I haven't forgotten." Ada shook her head slightly. That truth had made itself more known over the recent days. "It's still a job. We have only agreed to be civil to each other."

"Civil? Yeah, right." Osas laughed again until she had no more air in her lungs.

"That's what you get for *misyarning*."

Osas closed her eyes, Ada rested her head on her pillow, and the women lay arm-in-arm in silence for a while.

If Ada closed her eyes, she could almost believe things had gone back to normal.

When the car drove into the compound, Tobe, Ikenna and Ahanna were already in the driveway, jumping with delight, zigzagging around with huge handmade kites that were nearly the same size as they were. The kites were inscribed with welcome messages: *'Welcome, Aunty Osas! We love you, Aunty Osas!'*

Osas was already in tears before she got out of the car and was enveloped by their hugs.

Timi hung back, watching until Ada introduced them. Osas quickly pulled him into a tight embrace.

"You must be Timi. I've heard amazing things about you. Thank you for inviting me to your beautiful home." She gave him one of her electric smiles.

Timi stood straighter and smiled broadly, as if he'd built the house with his own bare hands. Soon, he and Tobe were fighting over who got to carry her suitcase into the house.

Ada smiled. Osas had not lost her magic. Soon, everyone was under her spell: the nannies, drivers, and even Michael. Only Emily held back, just a little.

Osas's one-day stay turned into two. On the night the helicopter took off from the Badejo residence, the bitter-sweetness of it all had everyone looking solemn-faced. The two ladies clung to each other for a few minutes before they let each other go. Their friendship resting firmly on new foundations, they promised to keep in touch.

Chapter Thirty-Six

"What is this wretched route?" Wande snapped as Kunle drove him home. "It will be the middle of the night before we arrive."

"Sorry, sir," Kunle said. "There was traffic on the main stretch."

Wande sighed. He shouldn't have spoken to Kunle that way – he was raised better than that – but all the commotion with Osas's arrival and Ada's attention on her old friend was making him antsy. He wanted to get home – to see her.

Finally, the pilot sent word that he had touched down at the helipad in Port Harcourt with Osas in tow.

Wande experienced a secret wash of relief. Osas was no longer in Lagos, and Ada was free.

His cast was off, and he was feeling less stiff as each day passed. Still, he had not been able to get the thought of his date with Ada off his mind.

As he drove in, he noted the paediatrician's car parked on the drive. He had visited once before to check on Emily, but Emily was in perfect condition now, so why was he here again?

Wande jogged up the steps. Big mistake. By the time he opened the door and walked into the foyer, his foot was protesting.

But his heart protested more when he saw Ada and Doctor Williams immersed in deep conversation in the foyer. Ada was bent toward him, her head inclined just so, a smile beaming across her face. She looked radiant.

Wande was startled at the sight. He was not a jealous person. Usually. But today, his mind was already frayed – he had logged countless hours fixating on the existence or nonexistence of Ada's affections for him. And now, seeing this picture in his foyer, something bubbled like hot lava in his chest.

"*What* do we have here?" He dropped his suit jacket on the nearest table.

"Oh!" said Ada when she saw him. "Welcome home."

He detected a sparkle in her eyes, but in his exhausted state, he attributed it, if anything, to whatever conversation she'd been having with her visitor.

"Good evening, sir. It's a pleasure to see you again. How is the leg doing?"

"A little stiff, but I'll live. So, to what do we owe the honour?" Wande stepped up beside Ada and slipped his arm around her waist, pulling her close. She stiffened. Was his touch now repulsive, too?

"I'm here to call on the young miss Emily," the doctor said. "It's great to see she's thriving."

"Well, I must speak to your boss about how you go above and beyond your call of duty to make your patients happy. It is to be commended," Wande said, staring pointedly at the young man in front of him.

Doctor Williams quickly got the message. "Thank you, sir. I will be leaving now."

"That's a good idea. My wife and I usually like to have a quiet evening with our six children."

Ada looked at Wande with a frown, but he ignored her, while Dr Williams gave a slight bow before making a hasty retreat.

"Goodbye, Debo." She tried to follow the doctor to the front door, but Wande's grip was firm.

Once the door closed, she turned to Wande. All the light had slid from her eyes. Now, her face was wrought with confusion. "What's the matter with you? Why were you so rude to the doctor?"

Wande ignored her question and started the slow march toward his study. "What I want to know is, what was he doing here? As a married woman, you can't be entertaining single men at this hour. It's improper – you should know that."

"Excuse me? Entertaining men? The doctor came to check on his patient." Ada lowered her voice as they passed through the foyer.

Wande leaned on the wall for balance as he approached the study. He used to be able to run through these hallways without even breaking a sweat. Now, he felt like an old man.

"I don't care what pretence or excuse you use to meet each other," he said. "Just don't do it in my house."

"What are you saying? He just came to see Emily. He wanted to make sure she was still doing well."

"Okay, so the attraction is just on your side, then?" Wande's head was so clouded, he didn't know what to think. He was being silly and petty, and he knew it, but he couldn't help himself. He walked into his apartment and began to close the door on her, but Ada wouldn't let him, and she followed him into the living area.

"Don't shut me out. What is going on? You seem upset. Is this seriously about the doctor?"

"I am not upset; I would just prefer you to be honest."

"Oh, Wande." Ada looked away, biting her lower lip. "I haven't disturbed you over your friendships with Chidi and Bukky, have I?"

Wande was already midway into the room when he turned round sharply. "What?"

Ada shook her head. "Forget it. If you must know what we were talking about, I was just asking after his fiancée. I'm not interested in the doctor. Far from it."

She came closer and touched his shoulder, but he flinched and backed away. Her proximity to him was unsettling. This couldn't continue – he had to do something, and fast.

"I have to be in Cape Town tomorrow for business."

She stepped back, thrown off-guard by the sudden proclamation. "Wait, what?"

"I have lots of work to catch up on," he said, "and I would prefer you to leave me in peace so that I can prepare."

"Work? But you can work from here." Grabbing his arm in a tight grip, Ada panicked. Her voice was insistent. "You can't go, Wande. Timi's swim finals are on Saturday. It's extremely important to him that you be there."

"You'll be there. He doesn't need me." Wande walked to the mini-bar and grabbed a bottle of whisky. He poured a glass and drank it in one shot, squeezing his eyes shut as he swallowed, relishing the burn.

"Look, this isn't me. This happy family man thing. I've just been playing a role. And now, it's over." He poured himself another.

Ada's eyes narrowed. "This isn't about you. Timi needs you there on Saturday. His teammates think he's lying when he tells them you're his father because they've never seen you with him."

"That's ridiculous."

"To you, maybe, but not to a thirteen-year-old."

"Look, I've neglected my business for far for too long. Timi will grow out of this phase. If I don't work, how will I preserve his inheritance, the way my father preserved mine?"

She grabbed his arm again, this time forcing him to look at her. "Inheritance? What about Timi? And Emily? All the progress you've made will be gone, just like that." She hesitated. "What about us... as partners?"

"Look, woman, don't push me."

His eyes were like ice, and she recoiled.

"I won't." She stepped back, her arms akimbo. "Don't do this, please. They need you. I need you. Wande, this whole thing doesn't work without you."

Her eyes started to fill with tears, and he felt his insides unravel; it was the unmistakable feeling of losing control. Wande never allowed himself to be vulnerable with anyone, but here, now, he wondered what it would be like to just let go. To hold her and kiss her lips to stop them from trembling.

But he couldn't. With a sense of urgency he didn't fully understand, he dialled a number on his phone, hardening his heart to the pleading look in her eyes.

"Mrs Coker. Cape Town in an hour."

"Wande, please don't do this – not to Timi."

Wande turned his back on her and didn't move until the door clicked shut. He caught sight of his reflection in the mirror. For the first time in a long time, his scar looked darker, and he could feel the faint throb of it under his skin. He really was the Beast, and they were all better off without him.

At dinner, Ada felt as though all her insides had been scooped out and cast aside. She was a shell of herself as the children tucked into their food around the table.

Finally, the inevitable question came.

"Aunty Ada, isn't Daddy coming to eat?" Timi asked.

"Your father had to travel on short notice," she answered quietly. She had been rehearsing the line ever since she'd walked out of Wande's study. "He left the house a little while ago."

Four pairs of eyes turned to her, each displaying varying degrees of surprise, but the worst was the disbelief and hurt on Timi's face.

"He got a call. The company had an emergency, and he had to fly out. He was sad to go."

She cast her eyes down to her plate and forced herself to chew the food that had now lost all its flavour. *Thank you, Wande, for making me a liar.*

"Will he be back before Saturday?" Tobe asked, looking at Timi's crestfallen face.

"He... He can't make any promises."

At that, Timi rushed out of the room and slammed the kitchen door.

Ada wanted to slam something, too. Later, in the tense quiet of the fractured household, she thought about calling Osas, then changed her mind. How easily she had fallen back into her old habit of running to Osas for every little thing – but even Osas could not fix this.

Chapter Thirty-Seven

Ronke watched Wande continue to stare out the window. The high-rise office in Cape Town was in the middle of the V&A Waterfront, with a stunning view of Table Mountain. But Wande had been in that position for the last ten minutes, and it was a view he had seen countless times. She crept away without disturbing him.

The past two days, he had been thoroughly distracted and making unusual mistakes, acting even more temperamental than normal. She'd just sent one of the secretaries home after Wande had nearly bitten her head off over a misspelled word.

A few hours later, she tried to approach him again. He was seated at his desk this time, head in his hands. He was engrossed with something on his phone. A familiar voice came through the speakers.

"Well done, Timi! You're going to be wonderful on Saturday. Guys, wave for the camera." The sound of splashing and Ada's voice continued with her commentary. "And that's Emily getting ready to join the big boys in the pool. Emily, say hello…" Emily's voice piped up: "Heyooo!"

There was a few seconds' delay, then Ada's voice again. "I wish you could be here for Timi's competition. It would mean so much to him. He misses you… We miss you. Truly. This doesn't work without you."

Wande rested his head on his arm. Ronke smiled.

Under her breath, she said a word of prayer for him. Then, she said another for Ada and the rest of the family.

By ten that night, she got a call.

"Mrs Coker, sorry to bother you so late."

Sorry to bother you? Ronke took the phone off her ear to double check the ID of the caller.

"Ask Lydia to move all my scheduled appointments till next week. I'm going home."

Wande checked his watch again; he would be home in exactly five minutes. He was still trying to map out exactly what he was going to say.

On the flight back from Cape Town, he'd taken some time to work through his emotions. As always, he had rushed headlong into his work, thinking he could jump right back into his old rhythm. After two days of sputtering and starting again, he realised that at some point in the past few months, he had lost the old Wande. Nothing made sense.

Then Ada had sent him that video. He was so upset by it at first, but he found himself watching it on repeat. He felt a hunger to return to them, a pull so strong that it compelled him to get on a flight and go back home straight away.

He just hoped it wasn't too late.

As the car pulled into the driveway, he saw the kids all dressed in their bathing suits, playing a game of football on the front lawn.

"Stop the car."

"Sir?"

"I said, stop the car." His confused driver quickly pulled up.

"Take my things to the house and let the staff pack them away." He got out of the car and slid out of his suit jacket and tie, took off his cufflinks and threw them into the car on top of his suit, then proceeded to jog to the field, rolling up his sleeves as he went. Happy shouts and laughter and excited shrieks followed as the children spotted him. Warmth filled him from head to toe.

Tobe saw him first and stopped mid-tackle. "Timi, your dad!"

Timi went completely still and blinked slowly. His dad was approaching, sleeves rolled up, jogging towards them.

Timi, Ikenna and Ahanna took off towards Wande in delight, yelling and whooping. Emily joined them without even knowing what all the fuss was about.

Ada stood up to get a better view of the reunion. With no one around to censor her, she allowed the tears to fall. Wande had a twin in each arm until Emily arrived to greet him. Then, he dropped them and picked up his little girl, throwing her in the air… He continued to hold her as he hugged Timi tight. Tobe hung back, but Wande waved him over and pulled him into a big bear hug.

After a few minutes with the screaming kids, Wande made his way towards Ada, disentangling each child from his body with every slow step. As Wande closed the distance between them, her heart sped up. He took Obinna from her, and the baby wrapped his chubby arms around his neck; Ada wanted to do the same.

"You came back," she said.

"You asked me to."

"This will mean so much to Timi…" Swallowing hard, she pushed the lump down her throat along with her unspoken words.

Wande reached out to her and wiped away the rogue tear that was still finding its way down her cheek. He looked like he wanted to say something, but the boys surrounded him, all speaking at once. Wande handed Obinna back to Ada, gave her a smile and jumped into the match.

Chapter Thirty-Eight

Saturday dawned bright and clear. It could not have been a more perfect day for the swim meet. The five top swimming teams in Lagos state had gathered to compete at Timi's school, which was packed full for the occasion.

Timi sat with his school's swim squad in a special booth. The team was all decked out in custom black tracksuits, the word 'ELITE' printed on the back in gold. Timi was the youngest member of the team, and sat proudly among them, knowing he had put in the work and training every day.

But what made that particular day extra-special was the sight of his family in the stands. He was both proud and slightly embarrassed by their exuberant show of support. Ada had made T-shirts for the whole family with 'TEAM TIMI' stitched across them in bright gold lettering.

Once the principal spotted Wande, he came over personally to greet him, and acknowledged his presence during his welcome speech, also thanking Wande for sponsoring the swim team with their Nike apparel. Ada lifted an eyebrow at Wande, but he just shrugged and smiled. When the applause was over, the principal asked if Wande would be willing to say a few words.

Wande trotted down the stairs, looking fit and toned in his Team Timi shirt, Nike sweatpants and sports shoes. He waved to the parents and children as they applauded him.

"I once heard a quote from a good friend of mine, Michael Phelps, from the United States – something tells me you all kinda know of him too." The stands hummed with laughter. "Well, he said: 'I want to be able to look back and say, I've done everything I can, and I was successful. I don't want to look back and say I should have done this or that.' That's what I want from you today, boys and girls. Leave the pool with no regrets. Forget everything else, give it your best, and make yourselves proud."

The applause was thunderous as all the swimmers gave him a standing ovation. On his way back to the stands, he took a detour and passed by Timi's teammates. They all stared at him with wide, starstruck eyes. Wande got to Timi and pulled him into a hug, then bent to say something before leaving. Timi stood straighter, grinning from ear to ear.

When Wande returned, Ada nudged him, smiling.

"Good job, daddy."

"Just needed to clear the air." He coughed. "Speaking of clearing the air," he bent towards her, and Ada could feel his breath on her neck as he whispered, "Chidi and Bukky are just friends I work with. Never been anything more. Okay?"

Her gaze met his and held it. She nodded and Wande put his arm loosely around the back of her seat, his fingers lightly grazing her shoulders. It required mammoth strength for both of them to refocus on the competition unfolding before them.

Timi broke every single record held at that competition, even his own personal best times, leaving the second-place swimmers trailing far behind. Even the other parents joined in cheering during the relay as Timi flip-turned in the freestyle and led his team to another gold.

Wande, who had never attended Timi's events before, was filled with remorse and regret for all the years he'd missed. But he also felt pride. Timi was an astonishing athlete.

"He's on fire today," Ada observed when Timi broke yet another record. "Wande," she said, eyeing him suspiciously, "what did you tell him at the start of the competition?"

He had a wide smile on his face. "I told him to obliterate them!"

Wande was called to present the medals, and he did so with a flourish every time Timi's name was called.

A very excited Badejo family made their way out of the school grounds. Wande had instructed his security to drive in the second car, while he drove with Ada in the passenger seat, Timi and Tobe in the middle, and the twins in the back. Before heading home, they stopped to order ice cream from Cold Stone Creamery on Admiralty Way.

When all the children stumbled out of the car at home, Wande held Ada back with him on the driveway.

He placed both hands on her waist, drawing her towards him. She glanced around and held her breath, but with no children in sight, she allowed herself a tentative sense of calm.

"My cast is off."

"It's been off a while now," Ada said, unsure where the conversation was heading.

"I believe you owe me a date. Tonight. I'll pick you up at seven."

He left her staring after him, trying to calm the racing of her heart.

Ada ran upstairs and called Uche from the privacy of her room.

"*Nwannem*, remember all those things you told me about what to wear and when? *Biko*, forgive me, I wasn't listening. I never thought I would need all that information."

Uche laughed, and Ada sighed with relief.

"What's the occasion?" Uche asked.

"Erm, it's a dinner."

"Okay, what kind?"

"Are there different kinds of dinners?"

"Ada, of course there are different kinds of dinners." Uche laughed. "Let's forget the occasion for a moment. How do you want to *feel* tonight?"

Ada trembled as she contemplated the question. "I want to feel confident; I also want to feel…"

"Beautiful?"

Ada licked her lips, afraid to agree out loud. "Maybe," she said eventually.

"You don't need clothes for that, Ada. But, there is a light-blue dress I packed for you. Off-the-shoulder, fitted, floor-length with puff sleeves. I included earrings, bangles, and a neckpiece that will match nicely."

Ada held the phone between her shoulder and ear while she dragged the suitcase to the bed and unzipped it, listening as Uche dished out instructions.

"Wear the silver sandals that match the bag. For makeup, you don't need much. Apply it the way we taught you. Remember the mascara, and let those lovely lashes do the work God created them for. When you blink, everyone around you will feel the breeze."

"*Chai*, Uche! Thank you so much! What would I have done without you?"

"My darling sis, I told you – it's a calling."

"Saving your sisters, one outfit at a time."

Seven o'clock came around too quickly. Ada had just finished picking out her hair with a toothed comb. The coils were softer and no longer stood up straight on her head; instead, they formed more of a halo around her face. She marvelled at how large her eyes looked with eyeliner. Pursing her lips, she finished the look with a light-pink lip gloss.

When she heard the knock on the door, she assumed it was one of the girls coming to tell her Wande was ready.

"Come in." Ada bent over, trying to buckle her sandal.

"Hey, Mummy."

Her head shot up. Tobe stood at the door. Earlier, she had told them she was going out with Wande, but she hadn't elaborated beyond that. Now that she was dressed up, she was anxious about what Tobe would think.

He walked in slowly. "Mummy, you look beautiful. Are you ready? Uncle Wande is."

"Thank you. I just need to buckle my shoes."

"Let me..." Tobe bent down to help while Ada smiled at the top of his head.

When he was finished, Tobe sat back on his haunches. "You know, Uncle Wande asked me if it was okay if he took you out tonight."

A rush of blood flooded Ada's cheeks. "He asked you that?"

"Yes, like an hour ago. He called Timi to his room first, then called me up after."

"What exactly did he say?"

"He said he wanted to take you out on a dinner date, and he asked me how I felt about it."

As long as she could remember, Ada had tried to be as open with her boys as she could, but this was new territory for her. Did adults really involve children in such conversations? Wande obviously thought differently.

"And do you mind?"

Tobe shrugged. "I never saw you smile with Daddy the way you smile with Uncle Wande. So, I told him it was fine by me. I want you to be happy, Mummy, always."

"*Nnnam*!" Ada drew him into a hug. "You children make me happy. And that's what's important. There is nothing between Uncle Wande and me…"

"But if there were… I wouldn't mind," he said, his voice resolute.

"Okay, then. I'll remember that." Ada kissed the top of his head. A thought crossed her mind, and she shivered. "Did Timi's dad call in the twins too?"

"No, just me."

Ada sighed and relaxed. She wasn't ready to field questions from those boys.

"Let's go and meet him, then." Tobe stood up and put out his hand to help his mother stand.

Wande stood at the bottom of the stairs, looking debonair in a navy-blue dinner jacket and talking quietly to Timi, who still had all his gold medals hanging around his neck. Ada's heart softened as Timi helped his dad straighten his tie. Wande play-punched him, and Timi pretended to duck. How far they both had come. How far they *all* had come.

Timi noticed Ada first and stepped back, his mouth open. Then, Wande looked up, and Ada felt the flutter of butterflies that people so often spoke about. She had never experienced it before. She held onto the balustrade, afraid she would melt from the intensity of his gaze.

In that instant, Ada knew one thing: that no matter how this evening turned out, her heart already belonged to this man.

|348|

Wande blinked. His physical reaction to Ada took him by surprise. He had almost gotten used to seeing her wearing new flattering colours, but tonight, well – Wande wasn't sure how someone could look so beautiful during the day and become even more beautiful at night. He wiped the corners of his mouth to stop the drool he was sure was forming. Each time she took a step down the stairs, it felt like pliers were loosening the nails that had closed his heart to women all these years. He wanted this woman in his life way beyond the words of a contract, and he was ready to risk it all. That night was as good a time as any to move that idea forward – if she agreed.

By the time he stretched out his hand to help her down the last step, his breathing was under control.

"Wow!" He moved towards her, but noticed the boys in his peripheral vision and reluctantly stepped back.

"Aunty Ada, you should be a model," said Timi. "You're so beautiful."

"I agree," Tobe said.

"Okay, boys, enough with that," Ada laughed. "Get back to the rest of the family, and remember, bedtime is ten at the latest."

"Yes, sir," they said with a mock salute, and they left to join the others.

"So, we shouldn't wait up then, sir?" Michael appeared from nowhere with a huge smile on his face. He looked between Wande and Ada.

"No. Nobody should wait up," Wande said emphatically, causing Michael to smother a chuckle.

Ada hid a smile and turned away, embarrassed but pleased.

"On that note, have a good night, sir, madam." Michael bowed.

Wande ushered Ada out the door and shut it behind them.

He faced her and, for the first time in his life, he felt unsure.

"I don't want there to be any confusion," he said. "This is not a dinner between business partners. Tonight, I am just a man having dinner with an incredibly beautiful woman. Are you okay with that?"

She caught herself watching his lips as he spoke, and quickly averted her gaze, focusing instead on the potted plant beside him.

"Yes, yes, I am." Secretly, she was more than okay. Feeling emboldened, she also had a request. "May I ask a favour?"

"Anything."

"Do you mind if I hold onto you this evening?" she smiled. "If you let me go, I may fall flat on my face in these heels."

Wande smiled, gazing into her eyes. "I will never let you go, Ada." His words sent a current surging through her.

A red convertible waited for them at the bottom of the stairs. Wande opened the door for her, making sure she was settled before going around to sit beside her.

"Top open or closed?" he asked as they got inside.

"Open," Ada said with a grin. "No security tonight?"

"They're around, but they're tucked away."

Just as Wande put the car in drive, his phone beeped. He ignored the tone, but it beeped again. Then again. Wande grumbled.

"Why don't you check it before we leave, in case it's important?" Ada said gently. His distress was no secret.

Later, Ada would wish she had kept her mouth shut.

It should have been a relatively quick problem to solve. Wande was supposed to have signed and scanned a document back to his office in Nepal earlier in the day, but it had completely slipped his mind.

Together, they went to his study. Ada lounged in his office chair while Wande booted up the printer. After a few moments of muttered frustrations, it became clear that the printer wasn't working.

Annoyed, Wande turned to Ada. "Do you remember how to print a document off of that computer, the way I taught you before?"

Ada nodded. "I think so."

"Good. Can you send this one to the boys' school printer? As soon as it's done, we'll be on our way. I promise."

He gave Ada the password and promised he would be back as quickly as he could with the document.

Ada did as she was instructed and logged into the computer. Wande had said the file was in a folder on the desktop. She just had to click…

Ada's eyes strayed to the other folders on Wande's desktop.

Merger with abc…

Tax policy for xyz …

Title deed for Ndidi Okonkwo…

Ada stopped scrolling. Ndidi Okonkwo? Her sister-in-law? True, the first name and surname were common Igbo names, so it could have been anyone, but the hairs standing on the back of Ada's neck told her otherwise.

She clicked on the tab.

The first document Ada found as she leafed through the folder was a deed of assignment. She clicked on that, and there it was, in black and white:

'Deed of ASSIGNMENT between:

Ndidi Gladys Okonkwo AND BH Limited'

BH stood for Badejo Housing; Wande had told her that during one of their many talks.

'In respect to property situated at…'

Ada sat back in the chair, as if held down by a heavy weight, as she realised the property in question was Emeka's house. Her home – the one that Ndidi had so callously thrown her out of. Did it belong to Wande now?

A memory of the conversation she'd had with Ndidi came back to her in slivers.

'Ada, the matter is out of my hands. You must leave the place right now. The new owner wants immediate occupation.'

The new owner – that was Wande? The truth dawned with sudden clarity.

Of course. It all made sense. He'd been unable to convince Ada to agree to his schemes on his first attempt, so he'd silently forced her hand by stripping her of a place to live – he had manipulated the whole thing to make sure she capitulated under pressure.

Ada looked around, suddenly unsure about everything. All at once, the study was foreign to her. Was any of it even real? What was his game? The contract had her in his employ for three years. Why buy her house, too, on top of everything else?

Perhaps it was all to make sure she stayed. Maybe he was pretending to like her so she, a poor, foolish village girl, would think he'd offer something more, and so he could keep her around as long as he wanted. And even if she was wrong about all of it, the fact still remained: he had her house, and he had never spoken a word of it.

She clicked away from the deeds and printed the document Wande had requested.

She looked around the room; this room that had seen all of her tears and laughter, and unbelievable frustrations with this same man. So much had passed since her arrival. And all of it had been more or less a lie.

Ada curled her fists at her sides, digging her nails into her palms, and fought viciously against the tears that threatened to come. No more crying, Ada. Not for anyone, and never again for him! As soon as the document had gone through, she reached down to take off her shoes and flung the silver sandals across the room.

Wande sped back to the study, greatly put out at the unexpected delay in his evening. But his anticipation still ran high. All he had to do was send the document, and he could go on to have the best night of his life.

He stopped short at the door to his office when he noticed Ada staring into space at the computer. When he touched her shoulder, she jumped.

It was her eyes that frightened him.

"What's the matter?" He tried to draw her to him, but she shrugged her way out of his arms before heading towards the door.

He hurried after her and caught her arm. "Ada, are you ill?" He saw her pale face, and worry flooded him. "Let's go to the hospital."

"No. I can't go out anymore. I need to go to bed." She made a break for the stairs. He grabbed her arm, frightened at this sudden change. This was not how the night was supposed to go.

Her voice was shrill as she pulled away from him. "Don't touch me!"

"Ada, wait. Please. What happened?"

Panic flooded him as she turned away. He searched his mind for what had happened to her in the few minutes he'd been in the other room. What could he have done when he wasn't even there?

"Leave me alone!" Ada ran up the stairs without looking back.

Chapter Thirty-Nine

Ada stood on the front porch of the house, dictating the arrangement of the children's luggage in the car to Mary. They would not be walking out of that house naked. At least, not quite. In the many months since their arrival, they had acquired new clothes, toys, and sports equipment, but Ada was determined to allow them only the bare necessities until she could shop for them on her own. Anything that reminded her of the Badejo household would be staying there.

Early that morning, she'd woken the boys to explain that they were leaving. The conversation had been, as anticipated, a total disaster. None of them understood why they had to leave, and Ada couldn't satisfy their questions without revealing too much. Timi stood by holding back tears. It had been impossible to separate him from the other boys, so he found out just as they did.

Emily was happily oblivious to the changes, playing in the front yard while Ada packed the car. Among the staff, only Mary was aware, as Cynthia had not come back yet from a weekend off. Ada sent a brief text to inform Michael of the situation before she ran upstairs to get Obinna's things.

Wande woke up to the loud ring of the intercom. He had finally fallen asleep around four in the morning, having given up waiting for Ada to call. He jumped up immediately at the noise and heard the gruff voice of Michael on the other end.

"What? What do you mean?" Wande slipped into his bathroom slippers and grabbed his pyjama top. "I'll be there right now."

Moving more quickly than he had in the past several weeks, his mind raced at the news: Ada was leaving. They were all leaving.

He saw Ada standing by a taxi out front and almost slipped down the front steps. Ada was dressed in her old black *boubou*, strapping Obinna into his car seat. When she saw him, she frowned tightly, her eyes betraying nothing.

"Hey," Wande said as coolly as he could. He guessed it would not pay to sound overly emotional. "Feeling better, I see. Sneaking off somewhere?"

"There is nothing sneaky about leaving the house at seven o'clock, in full view of the world."

Wande was momentarily distracted as Emily rushed to him. Wande scooped her up. He looked at Ada again, but she was busy telling the twins to get in the car.

"Ada, I'm talking to you. Where are you going? Where are you taking the boys, and why are you dressed in… in… that?"

"I'm done with this. With all of this."

Wande tilted his head, and his eyes narrowed as his mind scrambled to make sense of her words. He took a slow breath as he approached her, taking his time, as if stalking a wild animal that could spring at any moment.

"Come inside. Let's talk. Yesterday, everything was fine, and you just…"

She stepped back with her hands held out in front of her like a shield. "Yesterday, I found out exactly what kind of person you are, sir. I want nothing to do with you ever again."

Wande's mind went into overdrive. Yesterday? Everything had changed when he'd left her in the office. He couldn't put his finger on what could have caused such a rapid change. Did she get a call?

"Does Osas have anything to do with this?" he asked finally.

"Osas?" Ada shook her head. "No. No one has anything to do with this. I saw it!" She closed her eyes tight, her lips pressed against each other, pushing the words out like they tasted too bitter in her mouth. "I saw the deed of assignment. Between you and Ndidi!"

Wande froze. How could she have found that?

"You kicked us out of our house! We were on the streets with nowhere to go – because of you!" Her eyes were like burning coals.

Wande stepped back as the force of her anger hit him squarely in the face. Even Emily shrank back in his arms.

"Maybe Ndidi would have changed her mind about us, eventually, but you made sure that never happened. You had me cornered like a rat. When I didn't agree to your… proposal, you… You tightened the noose around my neck."

Wande was saved from responding, because just as he opened his mouth, Tobe came down the stairs, carrying his laptop bag and basketball. He wasn't smiling, but when he saw Wande, his eyes lit up with hope.

"Good morning, sir," Tobe said. He looked from his mother to Wande, but the glower on his mother's face remained. Whatever was wrong between them, he knew it hadn't been fixed.

"Tobe, how are you?"

"Not good, sir," and Tobe, seldom afraid to speak his mind anymore, blurted out, "I don't want to leave, sir." His mother glared at him, but he ignored her.

"You don't have to," Wande said. "This house will always be your home."

"Don't say that, Wande!" Ada snapped. "And as for you, Tobe – and your big mouth – go and drop those things; they do not belong to us."

Emily started crying at her outburst, and she struggled out of Wande's arms towards Ada. Ada picked her up without thinking.

"Mum?" Tobe asked, shocked.

"You heard me. Go and drop them. We will leave the way we came."

Tobe went back in the house, his steps slow and heavy, as though his feet were made of lead. Ada stared pointedly past Emily's head at Wande, and he felt his insides curl. She wasn't joking.

Worse, he had no reasonable explanation he could give her about the deeds – not one that would convince her to stay, anyway. He knew what he'd done and why, and he'd done it without remorse. He never guessed she would find the documents. But now, faced with it, he could see how wrong it was. He could see all the sordid facts of the deal that had been invisible to him, back when the only thing he wanted was the right mother for his children.

"Ada, please let me explain. I know how it looks—"

"You have nothing to say that I want to hear. We're leaving."

"Will you leave her?" He nodded at Emily, who was snuggled in her arms.

Ada turned away from him.

She felt like she was being torn apart from the inside out, her heart in shreds. Leaving Emily and Timi was going to be far more difficult than she'd predicted.

"Look," Ada said, more quietly, "it would have happened eventually. The three-year contract would have flown by, and besides, I warned you this would happen, didn't I? But you had everything planned exactly to your wishes. So, you deal with the fallout."

Tobe reappeared, got into the car, and slammed the door behind him. Ada put Emily on the ground, and she scampered off to join the twins in the car, but instead, the twins got out to keep her company.

"Ada," Wande said. His voice sounded as if it was being dragged over sandpaper. "If you leave this place, the contract dictates that you forfeit any income earned. Do you really want to do that to the boys?"

The words were laced with desperation, but the ice in her eyes froze him in place, and he knew instantly it wasn't the right thing to say. He shouldn't be reciting the details of their agreement. He should be begging her to stay with him, because he…

"Mary!" Ada shouted.

Mary came running. "Yes, ma."

"Take Emily right now!"

Wande knew what real panic felt like. "Ada, wait. Please. I shouldn't have said that. Forget the contract. I can explain the situation with the house."

Ada stepped forwards, anger etched along the lines of her face.

"Why should I forget the contract? It's the only honest thing we have between us, isn't it? Take your money if you want. Sue me, strip me of everything. I've been in this same position before. Ikenna and Ahanna, get in the car!"

The boys rushed to do their mother's bidding. Emily squirmed out of Mary's arms and ran after them.

Ada went on her knees to grab her, and hugged her so tightly she thought her heart might explode.

"My Ada…" she murmured. "I love you so much." Ada held onto her and let the tears fall on Emily, and Emily, not knowing why her mummy was crying, cried with her.

When Ada released her into Wande's arms, Emily screamed at the top of her lungs. She, too, could feel the wrongness in the air. Why wasn't she in the car with everybody else?

As the car doors slammed shut, and the taxi drove away, Emily clung to him, still screaming for her mummy.

The atmosphere in the car was bleak. The twins were sniffling. Tobe had his face turned towards the window. Only Obinna seemed unaffected in his car seat, sucking his thumb.

They approached the massive gate to the compound, but it remained closed. Ada wound down the window on her side.

"What's going on?"

"We just got a call from the main house that you should go back," said the attendant at the gate. "You forgot something, madam."

Ada looked at her phone. She had several missed calls from Wande.

"Ma'am, what would you like me to do?" asked the taxi driver.

Ada chewed her bottom lip to keep herself from screaming. She knew what Wande was doing. Muscling in again, making sure everything went his way. It had to stop.

She knew she had no choice. "Go back!" she snarled to the taxi driver through bared teeth.

When the car stopped at the front of the house, Ada got out and slammed the door. The boys exited slowly, unsure of the status of the departure. A sombre Wande stood waiting at the bottom of the steps.

"Who do you think you are?" Her eyes flashed, every fibre in her body vibrating as she clenched her fists. "You may rule the world, but you do not rule me. Tell them to let me out!"

"Boys." Wande's voice was calm and steady. "Go inside the house." He nodded at Ada. "Your mum and I need to talk before you leave."

Ada noted with fresh anger that none of them looked to her to confirm this before obeying him. When they went inside, Wande took a step towards her.

"I'm not stopping you from leaving," he said. "I apologise for locking the gate. But help me out here a little, Ada. Look at the kids – they're a mess. Look at us. Let's not end it like this."

Ada's breathing was calming, so he forged on. "I promise, when we are done talking, I'll take you to the airport myself and make sure you get to wherever you want to go."

"That won't be necessary," Ada spat. She turned to the driver, who stood by his car, contemplating deeply whether he had wasted his time this morning. "Driver, wait. He will pay you three times what I'm paying you."

That, at least, pleased the cab driver.

Wande led the way to his study, walking past the children in the foyer. The twins and Emily were already watching a programme on her tablet, while the older boys sat in silence. The atmosphere was heavy, and Wande felt a deep sense of regret; this was not how it was supposed to be.

"Will you have a seat?" Wande asked as soon as they were alone in the study.

"Say what you need to. I don't have time for this." Ada hugged herself and stood next to the door.

Wande saw the fear scrawled across her features, and his heart sank.

"I won't force you."

Reluctantly, she sat on the couch. She tried not to focus on the details of the room – a room where she had known something close to happiness for the first time in years.

"Ada," Wande said gently, "I didn't push you out of that house. The house was already on the market before I met you. I have told you this already."

Ada shifted on the couch, uncomfortable. She did remember.

"I got involved in the sale after you made the call to me," Wande explained. "I knew the potential new owner of the property, and just offered him more money, instead. The transfer details are in my name because it would have been too cumbersome to shift the property twice."

"But you knew—"

"I heard you were thrown out after the fact," Wande said. He sighed. "I confess at that time, I didn't care much. I was desperate to find help for Emily, and you were it. You were the one."

Silence descended between them.

Finally, Ada spoke. "The day we lost that house was the darkest day of my life. My boys and I had no one; we had nothing." Ada swallowed hard, trying to fight against the memories of her terror as Ndidi had thrown their things into the truck. She began to tremble.

Wande knelt before her and wrapped his arms around her. "You will never know how sorry I am."

Ada shook her head vehemently. "I never want things to be like that again. I never, ever want the fate of my boys and me to be in the hands of another human being… for someone else to determine if we have a roof over our heads or… or… if we get to eat."

"But, Ada—"

"I'm not stupid."

"No. You're not—"

"I have a brain, I have two hands, I have God…"

"Yes, I know." He reached upwards and used his thumb to wipe away her tears.

"I can make something of myself… I'll work hard." She sniffed.

"I know you can. But, Ada, why not work here? This is also a job. I… I'll pay you double."

She gave him a soft, sad smile. "That's the problem. This has not been a job to me for a long time. I'm your employee, but I can't work for you when I feel the way I feel."

Wande grabbed her hands. "Then let's forget the stupid contract. We can make this work."

"I'm sorry," she whispered. "I have to leave. I have to find my way."

She removed her hands from his grip. "I… I'm not doing this to hurt you or the children. Really, it isn't even about the house, or you. It's me. I need to step out for myself, to find out who I am outside our contract. I need to do this for my heart to be okay."

Wande sat back on the floor and leaned against the couch, his head in his hands. Her words stormed within him.

He knew he could force her to stay. He hadn't become a successful businessman without understanding the art of getting what he wanted. But, at what cost?

"Okay." The single word was like a shard of glass as he spoke it, and it pierced his heart.

"So, you'll let me go?" she said. "No strings attached?"

Wande bit into his lower lip until he tasted blood. He was grateful that she couldn't see his face.

"I will let you go, no strings attached."

He heard her release a breath slowly. Then, he got up and went to his desk to retrieve a single folder. Ada knew without being told what the folder contained. He took a cigarette lighter and the extra-large ashtray from his desk, the one he kept around for smoking guests, and he crossed the study to throw open the balcony door.

Wande snapped the lighter and brought the flame to the corner of the folder. Both of them watched it burn to ash.

"You have fulfilled all the terms of the contract," Wande said once there was nothing left of it. "Everything you and the children have acquired during your stay here is rightfully yours. You have earned it all multiple times over. It would be foolish to leave anything behind."

Ada's eyes flickered to his face. He was not letting her go empty-handed. She opened her mouth to say something, but he stopped her.

"It would also assure me that you do not consider me your enemy."

Ada found it difficult to swallow past the lump in her throat. She loved this man; she loved Timi and her little Ada. Her release from their agreement was what she knew she needed, but not what she wanted. She wished she could somehow let him know, but he continued speaking.

"If we are going to do this, let's do it properly. Let the boys pack all their stuff and allow John to drive you to the airport."

Ada could not speak, and she barely nodded.

Wande called the kitchen from his desk and dished out instructions for Michael. They sat in silence each lost in their own swamp of regret and fear, until Michael called to say that the packing was finished.

The children were playing in the hallway when they came out of the study. Timi and Tobe passed a joyful Obinna back and forth between them. The twins were chasing Emily. They all stopped and looked expectantly at the adults, and then at one another. Surely, they hoped, the misunderstanding had been cleared up now, and everything could go back to normal.

Ada straightened her shoulders and tried not to let her apprehension slip into her words.

"Tobe, Ikenna, and Ahanna, we will be leaving now."

"What?" Timi choked out.

"Mummy!" Tobe cried.

Ikenna started crying. Ahanna just stared.

Wande raised his hand to stop them from protesting. There was an immediate hush in the room. He took Ada's hand in his.

"Boys, your mum was always going to be here for a limited time. We will respect her wishes and support her in any way we can. Timi, Little Ada and I will miss you all terribly."

As they all stood together in the foyer, Ada realised it was time for everyone to say their goodbyes. Properly, this time.

First, she faced Timi, whose shattered heart was stitched directly onto his sleeve.

"Please don't go," he whispered. "I promise, I'll do better. I'm so sorry for how I treated you when you arrived."

"Timi, look at me." Ada spoke softly and waited for his eyes to meet hers. "This has nothing to do with you. You've been an amazing brother to my boys and Emily. I have loved nothing more than watching you grow, and I could not be prouder of you." She stepped back to look at him properly, cupping his face with her hands. "You have my number; you call me and tell me how school is… How our friend is…" She gave a watery smile. He hung his head low and wiped his arm across his face.

"But…" he trailed off.

"It won't be the same? I know. But we will still be in each other's lives. Port Harcourt is not on Mars – it's an hour away by air. Who says you can't come for a visit?"

"What about little Ada? She won't understand."

Ada allowed the tears she had been holding back to fall. "You're going to look out for her. You and your daddy. You'll make sure. Promise me."

Timi finally nodded. "I promise."

Ada sniffed and then coughed to clear her throat. "Please keep Ada in the house while we drive off, okay?"

Timi agreed, and he stayed inside with Emily as the rest of them walked out in silence.

Outside, Wande had his arms around Tobe. They were deep in quiet conversation. Raising her hand, Ada shielded her eyes from the glare of the sun. When they saw her, they broke apart.

Mary had been packing as much as she could into the car for the children and Ada. She now stood by, wiping tears from her eyes. Michael had still not come out. Ada suppressed the slight sting of his absence.

Timi rushed out to give Tobe a brief hug. Wande lifted the twins up one after the other. Then, the twins joined Tobe in the car, their shoulders hunched, sitting in silence.

Wande took Obinna from Mary, who had been holding him, and walked away from the car with the baby in his arms. No one could hear what he said to Obinna, or if he said anything at all, but he soon returned and, with stoic resolution, placed Obinna in his car seat and buckled him in.

Ada turned to face Wande, and, as if in witness to the moment, a dark cloud suddenly shrouded the sun.

"Goodbye, Wande," Ada said, "and thank you for everything."

"Goodbye, Ada, and thank you. I am so, so sorry." What they really wanted to say was:

I loved you, Wande.

Please don't go, Ada.

But neither of them spoke the words out loud.

Chapter Forty

It was past midnight when Wande gave up any attempt at sleeping. He left the room quietly so as not to wake Emily, who had clung to him all day.

He was surprised to see the kitchen lights on. Wrapped in his house coat, Michael was there, stirring something in a small pot on the stove. Wande quietly slid onto a stool at the island, hesitant to disturb his process. Minutes passed in silence between the two men.

Then, Michael filled two mugs with the thick brown liquid from the pot and plopped a few mini marshmallows into one of them before pushing it in front of Wande.

"You know how old I am, right?" Wande chuckled as he grabbed the mug, the warm aroma taking him back to simpler times. His throat tightened and he coughed.

"I found out one is never too old for comfort." Michael took the seat opposite Wande.

"How did you know I would come here?" Wande asked as he sipped the hot chocolate.

"I remembered how you used to roam the corridors of this house when you were unhappy. So, I prepared for your arrival when I heard you doing the same today. Some things have not changed."

"No. Many things have not changed."

Michael took sips from his mug and skimmed through the open Bible in front of him. "Was it your fault that they left?"

It was a simple question, an open invitation to talk. Wande no longer had the energy to resist it.

"Yes." Wande hung his head.

"What did you do?"

"Ada found something. Something I did before they came. I needed help for Emily, and there was a situation with Ada's house…"

"Let me guess, you followed your father's philosophy: 'Do whatever it takes'."

Wande sighed and bent over his mug, chewing his bottom lip. "His success was built on those four words. That's why we are sitting on the empire we are today. The results have always spoken for themselves."

"Until now."

Michael placed his still-full mug on the countertop beside him. The silence between them was heavy.

"May I speak freely, sir?" Michael asked.

"Please stop with the 'sir', Uncle Mike. We're alone. Of course you can speak freely."

Michael closed his Bible and placed it beside the mug.

"This matter with Ada and her boys is a result of the bigger corruption that is going on in your soul."

"What do you mean?" Wande straightened and shifted uncomfortably in his seat, pushing away the mug.

"Where is the Wande of old? The boy who put everyone else first? Where is that young man who told me, in this very kitchen, that his one desire was to be like David, a man after God's own heart?"

"You still remember that?" Wande rubbed the back of his neck and tried to avoid Michael's steady gaze.

"I weep for that boy." Michael's voice rose now, firm in his rebuke. "In your bid to please your earthly father, you have become this pride-filled, success-driven, power-drunk caricature of the man you were supposed to be, running roughshod over people like they are nothing just to get what you want."

The accompanying slap Michael gave to the top of his Bible could just as well have been across Wande's face. The old man took a breath and released it slowly.

When he resumed talking, his tone was gentler. "God has never stopped loving you, even when you stopped loving Him and went your own way. But He doesn't change who He is to accommodate any of us. It's up to you to choose which side of the divide you want to be on."

Michael picked up his things and went to his room, leaving a speechless Wande staring into his mug, watching his hot chocolate grow cold.

Chapter Forty-One

"Ada, if I hear Ikenna mention again how small my house is, I will spank him o." Osas sat heavily on her couch and rested her tired legs on the coffee table.

Ada looked out of the window, comparing the view of buses, kiosks and pedestrians to the old vista of the rose garden and pool from her bedroom in Banana Island. "I gave the children a taste of the best and snatched it away so cruelly."

"Hey, snap out of that," Osas said. "No regrets, remember? Let's refocus. You said you had a plan?"

Ada came alive again and sat beside Osas. "Yes, I do." She brought out a tiny notebook from her back pocket. "As we speak, I have just under seven million naira in my account. I am putting four million of that in treasury bills. I don't have the stomach for the stock market."

Osas lifted her brows as Ada continued, "I've found a place two streets down. No comments, please – we are not staying here. You need your own space." Ada went back to her list in her notebook. "I've found a private school I can afford for the boys, Obinna included. I haggled for a good discount, as well."

"Look at you go." Osas nodded, impressed.

"Now, how do I pay for all this and still survive?" Ada continued. "I've listed the things I know I can achieve with minimal expense. In fact, I've found out I'm an amazing teacher, and that will be my primary income stream."

Osas's eyes widened as Ada took the pencil from her ear and ticked items off her list.

"I spoke to a mum from Timi's school while I was in Lagos about tutoring her daughter. I told her I can tutor one-on-one for an hour in maths, biology, physics, and chemistry, and for every parent she brings me, I will reduce the fees for her daughter. So, she's gone on a marketing spree for me." Ada started laughing.

"But how much can a private tutor charge? It doesn't sound like it will be enough."

When Ada told her what she planned to charge per hour, Osas screamed.

"Apparently, Cambridge tutors are in high demand. I just followed the pricing online and gave a discount." Ada looked up from her book and winked at Osas. "I'm not certified *yet*, but she agreed. I plan to tutor for five hours a day, five days a week, from four until nine. If God can just fill those slots, then I'm sorted."

Osas shook her head in wonder. "Ada, I may just resign and start this business with you."

"Except how will you afford all your designer clothes?" Ada smiled. "Anyway, the second idea is baking. Remember? I'll make some delicious samples you can take to work, and you can help me with the Instagram marketing. My third idea is a catering service. There must be other people, like you, who want good food but refuse to cook – young executives who are in the office all day. I will cook to order: a pot of stew for the week, or soup or rice or beans – whatever they want. I can bake weekday mornings when the kids are in school and do the bulk cooking over the weekend."

Osas clapped gleefully. "I love it! I'll be your first client. Only, don't you hate cooking?"

Ada sighed. "I do hate cooking, but…" She smiled wistfully. "*I love making money more.*"

Ahanna entered the living room as she said this and started laughing. "Timi's dad used to say that."

Osas's brows lifted but she remained quiet until the little boy had left the room.

"Don't say anything." A frown had replaced Ada's smile.

Osas raised her hand in the air. "I am not saying anything o." Suddenly, tears shone in Osas's eyes. "I remember the last time we had a notebook in our hands. Now, you've mapped out plans for three income streams. You have so much to be proud of."

Ada smiled. "I know. I'm learning a lot about myself, who I am, and the things I'm capable of. Apparently, I was the only one holding myself back. But, don't worry. I know I'm not Superwoman. I don't plan to kill myself in the process of finding myself."

Together, they laughed. The future seemed bright, finally. If only Ada could find a way to chase away the lingering shadows.

Chapter Forty-Two

For the first time in his career, Wande Badejo cut off from the office completely. Across the globe, meetings were rescheduled, portfolios reassigned, and power truly delegated. The official statement on the matter said that Wande had to attend to a family emergency. No one would have believed the real reason: Wande was busy being a father.

Every morning he dropped Timi off at school and came again to take him home in the afternoon. He was a permanent fixture at all his son's after-school activities and school events. He and Emily spent their days together before Timi came home, reading and playing outside or playing pretend with her dolls.

Wande did everything he could to distract her from the gloomy silence that had descended on their home. Emily moved into his room because she would cry for hours in hers now that Ada and the baby were not there. The three of them spent most evenings in Wande's apartment; they had many years of togetherness to catch up on.

One evening, Wande went to say goodnight to Timi, as he had taken to doing every night since Ada and the boys had left. Just as he was about to knock, he heard a conversation through the slightly open door. His hand froze.

Timi sat at his desk with his laptop open. "Aunty Ada, I will work on it, I promise."

"Just do the extra page and send it to me. I'll have it marked and ready for when we talk tomorrow."

The sound of Ada's laughter came bubbling through the speakers, and fresh longing tore through Wande's heart. He sank to the floor outside Timi's room and cradled his head in his hands.

"Timi," Ada said, "you know how groggy you get in the morning when you don't sleep on time. So, goodnight."

In the background, another chorus of goodnights followed between Tobe, the twins, and Timi. He clutched his chest, imagining all their sweet, lovable faces. He waited a few minutes, then slowly rose to his feet and knocked on the door.

When Wande entered, the boy was under his blanket and only his head was visible.

"All ready for bed, young man?" Wande hoped his voice sounded neutral. He sat on the edge of the bed.

"Yes, Dad." Timi glanced sideways. "I kind of thought you weren't coming tonight."

"You know, it's okay for you to catch up with your Aunty," Wande said.

Timi bit his lip.

"I just wonder why you thought you needed to hide it from me."

"Honestly, Dad?" Timi hesitated. "I was worried that you might get upset about it. And I don't want you to leave us again. I'm sorry."

Wande pulled his son into a hug. "I should be sorry. I've been a poor example of a good father and a good human being. I'm working on that, I promise. But to be clear, I will never, ever leave you or your sister – ever again."

Timi nodded. They sat in silence for a bit.

"How are they doing?" Wande finally asked.

"They're okay. Aunty Ada has found a place. They're moving in soon. They've been staying with Aunty Osas."

"I'm glad she has someone to help." A part of Wande meant what he said. The other familiar, old part of him had been hoping she would be unable to cope with the changes and would plead with him to come back. But she had not. And now, she was getting a place of her own, which meant she wasn't planning to come back anytime soon.

"The boys miss home… They ask after you and little Ada – sorry, Emily – a lot. They want to see her, but Aunty Ada says it may not be best. It would just confuse her."

Wande agreed. Emily still woke up screaming for Ada and Obinna at night. He felt another lurch in his chest as he remembered his little cherub, Obinna.

"Dad, is there anything you can do to bring them back?" Timi asked, his eyes wide. "I've been praying like Aunty Ada says I should, but I'm wondering if Jesus needs our help somehow."

"Ah, my boy." Wande couldn't help the chuckle that escaped. "I think Jesus can handle things by Himself. The real problems arise when we try and get involved. I'm learning that myself. But please pray – maybe I'll do the same."

After Wande left Timi's room, he went outside and sat by the fountain overlooking the front lawn.

Images of the time he'd had with Ada came rushing back. This was where he had asked her to go on a date with him. The date that never happened but still changed everything.

Wande leaned forward and rested his elbows on his knees, allowing his thoughts to go to places he usually did not allow them to travel. He'd been struggling with the image of himself that Michael had painted, running away from its stinging truth. But now, hearing the same from his own son.

He wrestled with the legacy he would leave for his children, and had to admit he did not want them to follow in his footsteps. He needed to do better, to be better, and he knew only one person who could help.

Without waiting to get to his room, he spoke into the night sky, right there by the fountain.

Dear Lord Jesus, it's been a very long time…

For the next couple of weeks, Wande spent a lot of time in prayer and self-reflection. It brought a lot of pain to the surface, but it refreshed him in ways that were both surprising and comforting. He studied his Bible more and tried to obey the thoughts in his heart that aligned with the Word of God. He found himself apologising more to his staff, often leaving shocked faces in his wake. He also found himself relapsing into his old ways, but as Michael often reminded him, that was to be expected. Such a transformation did not take place overnight.

Wande even enjoyed talking over business ideas first with God, before putting them forward to his board members. He made Lagos his headquarters and navigated most of his business dealings through that office. Ronke kept calling to make sure he was okay. Wande wasn't sure what part of him she was concerned about – the woman saw too much.

Life began to take on a familiar peaceful rhythm, and he was grateful, but at night, when he lay in bed, thoughts of Ada would come flooding in. He found himself praying for her, for her success, for her to be fulfilled, and for the boys to be happy. It wasn't easy at first, but eventually, he felt lighter in spite of the knowledge that the more independent she became, the less likely it was that she would ever return.

In Port Harcourt, Ada had been going nonstop. The move to the new apartment took up all the hours in her days, and online tutoring eclipsed her evenings, with her allotted timeslots already three-quarters full. Ada still pinched herself whenever a parent sent in their payment for the month. This was income she'd earned all by herself.

Her weekends were filled with creating sample dishes for the catering side of her business. Osas took the food samples to work, and already, a few friends were asking for more. Busier and more fulfilled than ever, all Ada had ever wanted was on the horizon, and yet something seemed off.

She started counting the number of times a day her mind drifted to Wande. Her calls with Timi were great, but she couldn't ask about his father. It was an unspoken rule. Plus, she longed to see Emily just one more time.

During the early days after she'd left, if there had been one reason to go back, it would have been Emily. If, for any reason, Wande had shipped the children off to somewhere unknown, or hired a terrible caretaker, or if Timi had complained, Ada would have thrown in the towel and gone running back immediately. But, according to Timi, they were fine, and their daddy didn't seem to be changing the status quo as yet. Ada suspected he wouldn't be able to stay at home too long, though. Emily, she heard, was asking for her a little less every day, and she had stopped running to the door whenever the doorbell rang, hoping it was Ada.

Lord Jesus, protect all of them, she prayed every day. *Love them for me. Keep them from all harm. I miss them. Please, let me see them again one day.*

One would assume that after five months, Wande would be over Ada, but it was just getting worse. God didn't seem to be hearing his prayers or helping him move on.

One Friday in October, Wande was having a particularly hard day. At a quarter to four that afternoon, Mrs Coker arrived to drop off mail, which was strange, because she usually scanned and emailed all official correspondence to him. When Wande picked up the large manilla envelope, addressed from Virginia, USA, he turned it over and suddenly got chills.

'To: Ada Badejo

c/o Badejo Corporations'

In all the goings-on of the last few weeks, he'd forgotten Ada's six-week foundation course. He was holding her certificate in his hand:

'Adaora Badejo Certificate of Completion With Distinction'.

Wande punched the air and jogged around the foyer in a victory lap. He knew she would ace it. He thought his heart would burst with pride, and he was overcome by an overwhelming desire to tell her how proud he was of her. A plan began to form in his head. Before it progressed too far, he stopped himself.

Lord Jesus, I don't want to overstep any boundaries here, but if this is not a sign from You, You are going to need to hit me over the head because everything in me wants to deliver this personally, and if by some chance...

Wande was afraid to pray the rest of what was in his heart. It was surely too much to ask.

Chapter Forty-Three

As was typical, Osas came to spend the night in Ada's apartment and delivered her a breakdown of orders that had come in that day.

Every day, Osas had been helping with Ada's Instagram accounts. They'd even made some advertising clips in Ada's glossy new kitchen, which had been a surprise success, and a few offices had contacted Osas for sample tasting sessions.

Despite making endless lists for her business and ticking off the items one by one, Ada's mind went wandering again. What was Wande doing? Was his leg giving him issues? Was he thinking about her? She usually snapped out of that line of thought by reminding herself of his failings, but recently, she was finding it difficult to sustain the hurt anymore.

Today, thoughts of Wande would not leave her mind. She caught herself just staring at her open laptop when Osas called her name sharply.

"Ada. Where are you right now?"

"Nowhere?"

Osas sat at the table facing Ada. "You've been a bit off lately. What's on your mind?"

"I told you," Ada said, "it's nothing. Everything is on track. For the first time in my life, I'm earning an income, and I can plan a future for myself. I have three viable income streams – a fourth if this new dry-cleaning idea takes off."

"And you should be proud. You've done well, my friend. Though I am hearing a 'but' in there somewhere."

"There is no 'but'."

"But there is a 'but'." Osas tilted her head. "Don't forget, I know you."

"Stop that." Ada closed her laptop and pushed it away from her. She pressed her lips tight and avoided Osas's direct stare.

"Hey, it's okay to miss him," Osas said. "You were in love – that doesn't just go away."

Ada groaned. Osas knew her too well. When she put her arms around Ada's shoulders and hugged her, Ada covered her face with her hands, not even bothering to deny it.

"This is so silly of me."

"It's not silly, and if you feel like crying, you should. You've been on autopilot since you landed here."

Ada sniffed. "I should find a way to move on, right? But even if I can, what about Timi and little Ada? I feel bad about keeping our tutor sessions a secret from Wande. If Tobe and the boys did that, I would hate it."

Osas drew her hand back and looked around the room, avoiding Ada's eyes.

"What? What is it?" Ada asked.

"Well, Tobe may not have cut off completely."

"What?"

"Well, it wasn't his fault… He and Timi were talking one day and Wande walked into Timi's room. When Wande knew it was Tobe, he asked Timi if he could say hello. So, they got talking."

"How do you know this?"

"I walked in on Tobe." Osas frowned. "Ada, before you react, can I just say something? You know how Tobe absorbs stuff and doesn't let it out, but that afternoon, he was crying. He said he missed Wande and Timi; he missed the life you all had together. He is grieving that loss – they all are – and you've not allowed anybody to mention Wande's name in this house. This evening is the first time you've let me even bring him up without biting my head off."

Ada wiped her eyes. "So, it's my fault now? *He's* the one who made us sign a contract."

"Yes, he did. But that was *before* you guys had… whatever it was you guys had. Why can't it be different now?"

There was silence between the two women.

Ada's voice quavered. "He is controlling. He can be manipulative and that scares me. I can't fall into the hands of another Emeka. Never again."

"Please, let's not get things twisted. I don't see Emeka bringing your best friend all the way from a different state to mend a friendship that was important to you. The man I met in that house would have done anything to make you happy. But I can't speak for him." Osas sighed. "I know I've done some crazy stuff in my time. Do I wish I could go back? Yes, I do. But I can't. So, I have learned to live with my regrets and try to make better choices every day. Reach out to him or not? It's up to you. But decide with a clear eye so you won't have regrets tomorrow."

"Why are we even talking about this?" Ada asked, exasperated. "I was just a solution to his big problem. He hasn't made even one attempt to get in touch with me."

"But, Ada, you said—"

"I know what I said. But Wande is a powerful man with the resources to do anything he wants. He could have found me by now if he'd really wanted to. He has my number, and I haven't got a single text."

"Ada, you wanted him to come get you?"

"No... I don't know... But he didn't even try. He just moved on." Ada stood up. "I don't have time for this. I need to check on the cookies in the oven."

Osas stared after her friend, then looked down at her phone. She too was tired of keeping secrets. She made a decision, dialling the number quickly.

"Wande, do you have a minute? We need to talk."

Chapter Forty-Four

"So, when my friend starts receiving guests from Lagos on a regular basis, should I not be excited?"

Ada was in full teasing form. Osas had told her to come over by one o'clock to meet her guest, whom Ada assumed was the handsome young man Osas had been seeing. They'd met and hit it off when she was in Lagos.

"Ada, please leave me." Osas was genuinely embarrassed. But today was not about her, she reminded herself. Today was about Ada, and she only hoped her plan to help her friend wouldn't backfire.

Outside, the gate creaked. Osas peeped out the window and hurried towards the door.

"Fifteen minutes early – I like that!" Ada shouted after her.

"It reminds me of…" The words died on her lips.

When Timi walked in, Ada was convinced she was hallucinating, until her boys' screams confirmed that he really was there. She started walking towards him as if in a dream, when Osas appeared with Emily in her arms.

Ada's hand went to her mouth as she tried to hold back her sobs. Timi untangled himself from the twins as they focused their attention on Emily. He gave Ada a hug, and she tightened her arms around him, his slim body shaking slightly.

"I've missed you so much, Aunty Ada," he said.

"What are you doing here?" She was laughing and crying at the same time, running her hands over his shoulders and arms.

Emily's piercing cries brought fresh tears to her eyes. "My baby," she whispered as she stepped back from Timi. Osas put Emily on the floor.

Ada knelt and opened her arms. "Ada m ooo." Emily ran across the room, screaming, "Mummy!"

Ada scooped her up and squeezed her tight, getting lost in the soft warmth of the little girl in her arms, until she noted with sadness that Emily had lost a bit of weight.

As they moved around, she sang, "Adaeze, Adaugo, Adanne, Adanna," intermittently kissing and hugging the little girl, who soaked it all up.

Tobe was watching, bemused. "Where is Uncle Wande? Is he here as well?"

Ada's heart stopped, now fully grasping that for the children to be there, it meant he was there, too.

Tobe must have read her mind, and he led the charge downstairs with the twins. Ada stayed behind, soothing Emily, as if to calm herself before facing him.

"Timi, is your dad here?" she asked.

Timi nodded. "Aunty Ada, he talks about you all the time. He didn't think you would want to hear from him ever again."

Osas jumped in. "I knew we should have told him that you were miserable and pining away for him."

"I wasn't pining," Ada insisted.

"*Abeg*, be quiet. Let me go downstairs and see that busybody madam Felicia's face as she comes out to inspect the car."

"Osas, wait," Ada said quietly. "Do you think he is here just for the children's sake? Maybe he needs me to take care of them again."

"Don't be crazy," Osas said. "You're going to see him. Timi and I will take the children for a drive. I'm guessing you and Wande will want to talk privately."

She winked at Ada as she and Timi headed out the door.

Ada straightened her dress and looked at herself in the mirror. She barely resembled the woman she was all those months ago when she first met Wande at Osas's flat. And here he was again, this time by choice, rather than out of necessity.

Ada made a quick exit, her heartbeat matching her steps.

Wande was leaning against the car door, the sun hitting his shades. She stopped to take in the sight of him. He was here. He was really here. He straightened when he saw her. He had lost weight, too.

"What are you doing here?" she asked.

"I know you may not want to see me, but I have three very good reasons for being here." He paused. "No, four."

Ada folded her arms and waited for him to speak.

"Ada," Wande said, "if I could go back in time, I would do everything differently. I'm sorry for hurting you."

Well, Ada had not been expecting that. She swallowed the lump that formed in her throat as something heavy shifted within her. She looked into his eyes and saw that he truly meant it.

"There is nothing to forgive, Wande." Ada fought to keep her voice even. "Things are okay with the boys and me. God is really helping. I bear no grudges against you."

"I know, and I am sincerely happy for you." He kept staring at her until she started to fidget. He shook himself, then bent into the car and brought out two envelopes. "Reason number two: this came for you, and I knew I had to deliver it myself."

When Ada held the certificate in her hands, she held nothing back; she screamed and flew into Wande's arms, and he whirled her around.

Ada felt lightheaded. She didn't know if it was from the spinning, or the excitement of the results, or Wande's closeness and his whisper in her ear: "You've done well, Ada. Very well, indeed. You took on a university-level course while handling a home, six children and one insufferable invalid. I'm so proud of you."

Ada smiled. "And you were the one who sat with me, night after night, reviewing my class notes and explaining topics in practical terms, so I could understand. It was you who gave me a chance…"

As they spoke, memories of their time together flooded her mind, and she hugged him again. The familiar fragrance of his aftershave, along with the feeling of his arms around her, sent her emotions into a tailspin. His embrace was too comfortable, too much like home. Even Wande seemed caught up in the magic as his head inched closer.

Just in time, Ada remembered where they were and why he said he was there. She removed his arms and stepped away from him, her breathing unsteady. He, too, seemed a little shaken.

"You said there were other reasons you were here."

Wande still looked dazed.

"You're holding another envelope," Ada pointed out.

"Oh, yes. This also belongs to you."

Ada took the second envelope and opened it. Mixed emotions flowed through her as she studied the contents.

"The house rightly belongs to you and the boys," Wande said. "That's why all of your names are on it. When I bought that property, it was purely for selfish reasons, but I'm glad I now have the opportunity to do this for you. Now, you guys have a place to stay that no one can ever take away."

Ada looked at the documents, which clearly stated that she and the boys were the legal owners of Emeka's five-bedroom house with a double garage and space enough for whatever business she wanted.

But she felt no joy. In fact, she experienced overwhelming sadness at the realisation that Wande wished her to stay in Port Harcourt. He didn't want her back, not even as a nanny.

"What's the fourth reason? Why are you here?"

Her sadness was thick enough to form a wall between them.

Wande could nearly see it swirling around her body. "Did I say something wrong? I don't—"

"I'm grateful," Ada said quietly. "Truly. It's... very kind."

"Ada. Do you think by now I don't know when there is something you're not saying?"

She hesitated for a moment before she asked again, "What brought you here?" She paused. "It certainly wasn't the fact that you missed us so badly that you wanted us to be a family again. You wouldn't be here, giving us a house in Port Harcourt, so far away from you all, if that were true."

Wande stepped back. Ada's frown deepened. What was he playing at? Her apprehension intensified when he drew her into his arms and held her there.

"Ada," he said, "the fourth thing I wanted to tell you was that we are moving here. To Port Harcourt."

It was now Ada's turn to push back. "I don't understand."

"You made us into a family, and as a wise woman once told me, this whole thing doesn't work if we are broken up. So, if you want to stay here, we will come here, too. I'm currently looking for property near yours."

She fell back into his arms again, unable to fight any longer.

"You would do that?" she whispered.

"Truth be told," Wande murmured, "I would do anything."

They held each other for a moment. Ada savoured every second. Still, niggling thoughts distracted her mind, what-ifs blossoming among them.

"When I made the decision to come here," Wande said, "I promised God, and myself, that I wasn't going to impose my will on you." He stepped back from her so his face was in full view. "I am afraid what I want to say isn't what you want to hear."

She hoped he couldn't feel her rapidly beating heart. Did she want to go down this road with him? For once, the cautionary voices that usually plagued her went silent, and all she felt was peace. She decided to let the chips fall and trust God for the outcome.

"Why don't you try me?"

Wande closed his eyes and drew a deep breath. "You're an amazing woman, Ada: strong, kind, even when you don't have to be… You're a great mother. You are so full of wisdom; it blows my mind. You're the best pretend wife anyone could have."

That made her laugh.

"You've also become a friend," he went on. "Someone I've grown to respect, admire and… and… love from the bottom of my heart."

Ada allowed the words to flow over her.

"You were the singular catalyst for turning this beast human again. You brought such joy, such colour to my world. And then you left, and the pain was real, and nothing was right again. Ada, from our first midnight conversation, I have been falling incredibly, irrevocably, in love with you." He hesitated. "If I'm honest, it was way, way before that."

Ada was silent for a moment. "Then why didn't you come for me?" she asked. "When we left? Why didn't you chase after us?"

"I thought you wouldn't want me to."

"I thought you'd forgotten me," she admitted. "All this time we've been here… to never hear from you, not even once – I thought you were done."

"I was anything but."

Wande hugged her again, and she relaxed into his arms. Ada knew she was not capable of the same sort of flowery speech, but she could – well, she could tell the truth.

"I love you, Wande…" Her voice broke as she tried to say what was in her heart. "So very much. I was so scared I was never going to see you again."

Wande wiped her tears and held her in an embrace that said, without words, that he was never going to let her go again.

Wande had booked a suite in a nearby hotel. The children did not want to be separated from each other again, so they alternated, sleeping in both Ada's cramped two-bedroom apartment and the hotel over the next two weeks. Meanwhile, Wande's office oversaw the purchase of his new Port Harcourt property. During those nights, Ada regaled Wande with stories of her various business enterprises, and she basked in the effusive praise that followed. She craved his approval more than she cared to admit.

"This is about more than money for me," she explained during one of their quiet conversations in Wande's suite. The kids were asleep, and the hour was late. "I've never felt as vulnerable as I did when Emeka died, and I was faced with the reality that I could do absolutely nothing about my circumstances. I moved from my father's house to my husband's house, and then to yours. I never want to feel like I need someone to save me."

"I understand that," Wande said. "I can promise you now that I will fully support any endeavour you put your mind to."

"There is one more thing," Ada said with only a teaspoon of hesitation. "You have to promise not to try and take over. I know it's all new for me, this running-a-business thing, but let me do it on my own. Let me make my mistakes, and if I need your help, I'll come to you."

"I promise." Wande gave a reassuring smile. "This is all your own. But what if I want to come in as an investor?"

Ada's face must have betrayed her uncertainty, but he continued. "Hear me out. I'm not a fool. This idea of yours – tutoring students who want to do IGSCEs and A levels – is brilliant, and you already have a clientele that has grown organically by word-of-mouth. That is gold. Why shouldn't I want to give you money to *make me money*?"

Satisfied with the proposal, Ada preened under the veiled praise. "As long as I can work on it for two years straight, on my own, then I'll consider outside investors, if the need arises."

"Deal. Anything else?"

Ada smiled as her heart lay at rest.

Two days later, on Sunday evening, Osas popped by the hotel for a surprise visit, and Wande insisted on taking everyone out for dinner. When they returned from the meal, they all went to hang out by the pool. Every few minutes, Wande looked at his watch.

"Do you have somewhere you need to be?" Ada asked. She no longer felt the familiar frustration at his business-related distractions. He had given them plenty of his undivided attention in the recent days. "If so, the kids and I are good."

"Nope." He grinned. "I'll be back."

Ada watched the kids splash each other in the pool.

A few minutes later, Wande returned. "Ada, can I steal you for a moment?" He looked at Osas, who shooed Ada away with a wide grin on her face.

"Are you okay to watch all of them?" Ada asked, nodding to the kids in the pool.

"Go," Osas insisted. "I've got Tobe and Timi to help."

Ada followed Wande upstairs into the complex, puzzled when he refused to answer why they were leaving the rest of the family behind.

As they walked into the suite, Ada noticed a scattering of rose petals on the floor, then the flicker of dozens of candles, along with huge flower arrangements and the subtle scent of jasmine in the air.

"What's going on?" she asked, looking around. The hotel living room had been transformed into a fairy tale garden. Wande led her through the path of red, pink and white petals to the centre of the space.

Against the wall was a floral decoration spelling out the words, *WILL YOU MARRY ME*?

She gasped, and as he dropped to one knee, the world seemed to pause, Ada's heart quickening in anticipation.

Wande's eyes shone up at her in the candlelight. "Ada, will you make me the happiest man on earth, and marry me?"

"But, Wande, we—"

"We have a piece of paper, yes, but we both know that means nothing. I want a new beginning for us. This time, when I stand with you in God's presence and say those words, I will mean them with every fibre of my being. So, Ada, will you marry me?" Wande smiled. "Again?"

Tears welled up in Ada's eyes. She was momentarily speechless, caught between the reality of the present and the shape of the dreams that had led to this very moment – a shape that was slowly coming into focus.

"Yes, Wande," she said through her tears. "Yes!"

Wande rose from the ground and lifted her into a hug so tight it felt like he wanted to absorb her into himself.

"Thank you, Ada," he whispered into her neck.

His lips found hers, and Ada responded with passion she didn't know she possessed.

So, this was what love felt like. This was what it was to be desired. She felt it in every cell in her body, and just as she was sure she couldn't remain on her feet much longer, he pulled away. Breathing hard, his eyes were bright with the promise of pleasures to come.

They sat together for several minutes in the suite. Wande's business-inclined mind could not leave their new reality alone for long, as soon, he was asking Ada about all the particularities she desired: Did she want a planner? How many guests? How long did she need to decide what she wanted?

"Can I tell you what I really want?" Ada asked.

"Please," Wande said, "anything."

"I want it to be just the two of us. I want it without fuss." Ada paused. "And I want it now."

"Wow." Wande appeared truly stunned. "Mrs Badejo, I did not expect that at all. What about the dress? The flowers? The—"

"All that means nothing to me. I want to start my new life with you – that's all I want. And…"

"Yes?"

"I know you have put in a lot of effort into moving to Port Harcourt, but the truth is…" Ada had been holding the admission back since he arrived. She wasn't sure how he would react. "I really want to go back home."

Wande heaved a sigh, and Ada felt cool relief course through her. "I would love that, too," he said. "Anything else?"

Ada looked at Wande with a new worry in her eyes. "We should tell the children. Tell them everything."

The suite was silent as the children absorbed the news that their parents were already married. Their swimsuits, still wet from the pool, dripped intermittently onto the plush carpet. Osas busied herself fetching more towels.

"Do we get to go back to Lagos?" Ikenna asked.

"Of course. Lagos will be your new home." Wande smiled at him.

"Forever?" Ahanna asked.

"Forever, Ahanna."

The twins high-fived and left the room to join Aunty Osas in her search.

Timi and Tobe were not so easily mollified. They had more questions. *Why? When?*

"Mummy, is your name different from ours now?" Tobe asked.

"Yes, I'm officially Ada Badejo."

"So, are you our mummy, or Timi and little Ada's mummy? Or both?"

Ada went over to him and hugged him tight. "I will always be your mother. It's just my official name, that's all."

Wande came over and pulled him into a hug. "Your mother loves you boys so much. Nothing – no one, no house, no name – can change that. In the future, if you want, we can all have the same surname, if it's important to you. But no pressure."

Timi joined in, as well. "Hey, you know one good thing? This means we're real brothers, after all." That elicited a smile from Tobe. Timi pulled him up, and they left arm in arm to join the other children.

As they left, Ada began to cry, this time only happy tears, for the future that was still to unfold.

A week later, the couple stood before a pastor. Their voices, thick with emotion, echoed in the quiet church auditorium as they spoke their vows. They were witnessed only by their six children, who were seated in the front row. The kids looked on as Wande and Ada made the promise: "to have and to hold, forsaking all others as long as we both shall live."

Later, as their three-car convoy drove into Love Legacy Lane, Ada's heart raced. The gates opened, and she remembered arriving for the first time a year ago, cloaked in fear and uncertainty. Now, Wande squeezed her arm, and she turned to see him staring at her, his eyes bright with mischief. She was sure he was remembering, as well.

The boys, who were in the car ahead of them, tumbled out into the waiting arms of the nannies. Michael and Ronke stood slightly apart on the drive, awaiting their turn amidst the excited circus. Ada laughed as the children hugged the staff. Everyone was happy to be there.

The nannies ran to Ada's side of the car, bouncing on their toes impatiently. Ada opened her door, and as Obinna disappeared from her hands into Mary's, she was engulfed in a brief but heartfelt hug.

"Welcome back, Ma."

"We missed you, Ma."

"I have never come back to such a reception before." Wande's deep voice carried as he put his arm across Ada's shoulders, smiling at the girls.

"Welcome back, sir," they chorused as they curtsied, more subdued but still smiling.

"Now, I need you ladies to sort out all the luggage and take your madam's things to the apartment upstairs," Wande asked. "My old apartment."

The ladies' eyes darted from Ada to Wande and then to each other, their smiles growing wider. "Yes, sir!"

Ada could hear their giggles as they rushed to do his bidding. She wasn't sure if she felt embarrassed or shy.

She caught Michael's eyes and started to walk across the drive to meet him.

Wande held her back. "I would like to do this introduction properly this time." He held her hand in his and walked to the foot of the steps where Ronke and Michael had been patiently waiting.

Wande cleared his throat. "Mrs Coker, I would like to introduce you to my wife, Ada Badejo. Ada, this is Ronke Coker – she runs my Lagos office. If you ever need anything from her, she is just a call away. And Mrs Coker, if you ever need to get in touch with me and can't reach me… Ada will know exactly where I am."

Ronke nodded in approval to Wande, then faced Ada, grinning from ear to ear. "Please call me Ronke."

"And please call me Ada," Ada responded, equally amused. Both women burst out laughing as they hugged each other.

Wande moved on to Michael. "Uncle Mike," Wande began, the warmth in his voice indicating a familiarity and respect Ada had never heard before. She looked from one man to the other in surprise.

Michael looked up, his eyes crinkling at the corners as a smile spread across his face.

Wande continued, "I want to introduce to you my wife." A touch of pride sugared his words as he stood behind Ada and placed his hands gently on her shoulders. "She is the most wonderful woman you could ever meet. She is kind, compassionate, so beautiful, and for some reason, she agreed to marry me."

Ada looked up and smiled with tears in her eyes, unable to speak. She reached for Wande's hand and squeezed it gently.

"Ada," Wande now said to her, "this is my Uncle Mike, the closest person I have to a father – and in some ways, even better."

Michael looked away and shook his head rapidly. After a few moments, he faced them again with his usual composure. "Wande, you're a very lucky man." Michael's voice did not falter as he repeated the words from long ago. "My name is Michael, I am the…"

But Ada did not let him finish as she threw her arms around him. "I have missed you, *Oga* Michael."

"Welcome home, Ada," he said. "Welcome home."

Epilogue 2024

Ada's eyes opened at exactly five o'clock in the morning. Careful not to wake Wande, she gently lifted his arm, which lay across her, and slid out of bed, closing the pink draperies behind her.

She tiptoed out of the cold room and sighed with relief at the warm air on the balcony. Wande liked the air conditioning to run colder than she did, but according to him, he balanced it by making sure he kept her warm all night.

Raising her hands high in the air, she stretched and took a deep breath as she tried to touch her toes. Not so easy anymore. She smiled.

Usually, after her stretches, she would take to her Bible and have her time with the Lord, but today, she was distracted, thinking of all the big changes ahead for her and the children. Timi was heading off to university after the holidays – the first time the family would be broken up. Tobe now wanted to complete his A-levels in England so he could be near his brother. She wasn't sure how she was going to handle it.

Ada was startled when she felt her husband's strong arms wrap around her, but she quickly relaxed into his embrace, enjoying his warmth.

"I tried not to wake you."

"You know that never works." Wande bent to give her the lightest of kisses at the base of her neck, making her shiver.

"Once you leave me, every fibre of my being feels it instantly."

"Oh, really?" Ada turned to face him.

"Yes." He continued his ministration on her neck, knowing exactly how it made her feel and enjoying her response. "You're my happy place. And, by the way, thanks for last night."

Ada couldn't help but blush. It was something he always did: thanking her, when she should be the one thanking him. Wande was a considerate and gentle lover, and over their years together, he had shown her a different side to the marriage bed. He had been patient with her as she slowly shed her inhibitions and began to enjoy the gift of sex between a husband and wife.

Giggling into his chest, she said, "Thank you right back."

He pulled her even closer. "I guess I won't be able to hold you like this for much longer." They laughed as he stepped back to kiss Ada's slight bulge. "How are you feeling today?"

"Much better, thank you. At least there's no more nausea first thing, which will make for a better workday. Osas and I have a bunch of meetings this morning. We decided to take your advice about diversifying the company bank accounts."

"Glad to be of service." But quickly, Wande's smile turned to a frown. "So, what I'm hearing is that I haven't convinced you to close up shop so you and the kids can fly out this evening?"

"You know I can't." She went up on her tiptoes to plant a kiss on his lips. "Keep the bed warm for me in Paris. Besides, the kids still have school."

Wande refused to be pacified. "The last week of school is a waste of time, and Osas can cover for you."

"Usually, yes, but that won't be fair on her, and you know it. She's carried so much weight these past few months with me being so sick." She tugged lightly at his beard with a sparkle in her eye. "It's only the twins who would love to play truant. Little Ada wants to finish primary two strong, with her graduation ceremony on the last day of school. We have a dress picked out and everything."

"Graduation from primary two," Wande mused. "That is such a huge joke."

"You laugh, but it's a big deal – and don't think I didn't see that tear you let slip at Obinna's graduation from baby school last week."

"Obinna's graduation made sense. He's going to Big School. My baby is going to primary one!"

Ada threw her head back and laughed with Wande. She sometimes had to pinch herself that it was all real. This peace, this joy, was really all hers. She allowed the happiness to wash over her. It was always a warm bath for her soul.

Ndidi Okonkwo arrived for her ten o'clock appointment twenty minutes early and sat in her car with her eyes closed, gripping the steering wheel of her burnt orange RAV 4. She took deep breaths as she listened to her daily affirmations before stepping out of the car.

Everything was riding on this meeting being a success. How difficult could it be to convince the owner and head marketing manager to open an account with her bank, especially with her as their personal banker?

Her boss had thrown her a lifeline this morning, and she couldn't afford to mess it up. He said the chairman had already made the connection; all she had to do was seal the deal. Just one more big account and she could keep her job as chief marketer.

She'd risen in the bank rapidly after she'd brought in all the money from the sale of Emeka's properties, and she had ridden on the coat-tails of that achievement until now. How did she get here, desperate for money again? Six years ago, with over 250 million naira to her name, she was sure she would be rich forever. But living the high life was expensive: renting the right homes, school fees at the right school for her children, the right type of car – it all added up.

But that wasn't all. With wise investments, she would have been okay, but her husband, who had not worked in years, spent his time financing businesses that always promised huge returns right before going bust. The final hit was his last investment – the money earmarked for the purchase of their own home – which he handed over to a group of money-doubling associates who assured him the oil wells they were buying in Saudi Arabia would set them up forever. He was going to be an oil baron; his family would be the foundation of a new dynasty.

Ndidi had pleaded with him not to do it. She'd had a bad feeling about these new friends, who always seemed to crawl out of the shadows wearing flashy clothing. But he didn't listen, and he still spent their money like the pot of gold would never end.

But now, the gold in the pot was dwindling. Ndidi was almost fifty years old, and the job market was not kind to older job seekers.

She sat in the reception area at the exclusive tutoring centre. With over one hundred students enrolled, it had a stellar reputation, with centres in every major city in Nigeria. Apparently, the owner of the school also owned the bakery and restaurant next door, as well as two huge dry-cleaning outlets in Lekki and Ikeja. Ndidi hadn't had time to properly research before rushing out that morning, but from what she gathered from Google, the real owner was not the manager advertised on the websites, but the wife of a billionaire businessman.

Ndidi lifted her nose in the air as she looked around the glamorous reception, with its stunning display of fresh flowers and complimentary refreshments. What else would one expect from a billionaire's wife? That sort of woman would've never done a stitch of real work in her whole life.

She checked her watch. Ten more minutes.

The secretary informed her that Mrs Badejo sent her apologies and would be a few minutes late.

Well, at least she has small manners, Ndidi thought, unlike some of these other rich people she had to schmooze for accounts. The name rang a bell, but she couldn't quite place it.

She was sipping on the free juice when she caught sight of two women talking beyond the glass entrance. One wore a lovely teal skirt suit and black pumps, sporting fashionable glasses and clutching a pretty handbag by her side. The owner, Ndidi guessed.

Ndidi stood up, adjusted her jacket and ran her hand over the front of her skirt. The first woman was focused on whatever the other lady was saying, so Ndidi turned her attention to her as well. She must be a member of staff, probably a cleaner, judging by her dark blue jeans, sports shoes and green polo shirt with the Eden Educational logo across the front. She also looked vaguely familiar.

Ndidi's eyes widened as she realised who was standing only a few metres away.

She had tried very hard not to think of her late brother's wife or his children. Actually, she preferred to imagine they'd never existed. It was easier than the alternative: imagining them living and breathing after what she'd done to them. But seeing Ada here, in front of her, looking well – more than well, in fact – triggered a rush of familiar emotions. The green-eyed monster that always accompanied any thought of Ada rose up, and Ndidi quickly fought to quash it. She had to focus on what had brought her here.

"Ndidi?"

Ndidi's eyes fell on Ada's slight but obvious baby bump, and she felt the bile rise in her throat, threatening to choke her.

"Ada Okeke, I can see you have been busy," she said, looking pointedly at her stomach. Her lips curled in a sneer. "Exactly what my brother feared. Where are my nephews?" She circled Ada, eyeing her from head to toe. "I'm sure you've abandoned them in Port Harcourt, and you're here jumping from man to man."

The secretary stood up to join them. "Excuse me, madam…" she said, addressing Ndidi. "I'm afraid—"

"Cynthia," Ada stopped her. "Don't bother, I'll handle this."

"What or who do you think you are handling?" Ndidi pushed herself up in Ada's face. "*Mu wa bu Ndidi*? You want to *handle* me? You still don't know your place, do you?" She turned to a bewildered-looking Cynthia and waved a hand at her. "Don't worry, I know this useless woman from way back."

Ndidi took her seat again and crossed her legs. "Ada, continue with whatever it is you do here. You will be lucky I won't mention the kind of woman you are to your boss and get you thrown out of here as well."

Ada stepped back, folding and rubbing her arms. *Yes*, Ndidi thought, *let her be afraid of what I may do. The useless mouse.* She refocused her attention on the door, anticipating Mrs Badejo's return, ignoring the shocked look of the secretary who stood there with her mouth open.

"Ada, so sorry I'm late."

Ndidi heard another familiar voice, and her stomach churned. The only person she disliked more than Ada was her big-mouthed best friend. What was she doing here?

Osas, wearing the same T-shirt as Ada, came in from a door at the back as quickly as a heavily pregnant woman could manage.

"What happened? Why are all of you…?" She stepped back. "Witchy Ndidi, what are you doing here?"

"*Ashawo!*" Ndidi's lips curled. "I can see you have followed your friend from across the country. What happened? They sacked you for sleeping with all your bosses, hmm? So, you're now a cleaner, too. *Eyaa.*"

"Did she say cleaner?" Osas glanced at Ada, grinning.

Ndidi was determined not to let Osas get to her. This meeting was too important to lose focus now.

Osas turned to Cynthia. "Has the lady from Tulip Bank arrived?"

Ndidi turned around in time to see the secretary nodding in her direction. How could Osas know about her meeting? A frown creased Ndidi's features, but she barely had time to register the thought when the lady in the teal skirt walked in.

Finally, someone useful. Ndidi rushed forward with her arm outstretched.

"Good afternoon, ma'am. Mrs Badejo, I presume?" Ndidi switched on her brightest smile and grabbed her hand, pumping it vigorously. "I'm from Tulip Bank. I'm here to discuss you opening an account with us, madam."

"But I'm not—"

"I'm sure you will be very pleased with what we can offer you as our premium client."

Osas turned to Ada, eyes wide. "No way! She thinks...?" Ada slowly nodded.

"Please, can you stop making noise in public?" Ndidi hissed at them. They were creating a scene, and she could see how uncomfortable Mrs Badejo looked. "I'm sorry, madam. Can we go into your office and talk privately?"

The woman gave an exasperated sigh. "I've been trying to tell you, I'm not Mrs Badejo. She is!" The lady pointed at Ada.

Ndidi blinked rapidly, looking from Ada to Osas. She suddenly felt as if the room were devoid of air. She was sure that she had misheard and was about to ask the woman to clarify her statement when a voice arrested all their collective attention.

"Babe, you forgot your…" Four pairs of eyes turned as Wande Badejo walked in.

Ndidi felt a chill as he made his way not to the lady in the suit, but to Ada. He slipped his arm around her waist. "You forgot your phone again." He bent and kissed her firmly on the lips, ignoring everyone else in the room.

Ndidi tried to swallow the lump that had formed in her throat.

"I apologise for interrupting. I'm Wande." He stretched out an arm to shake hands with Ndidi, and she mumbled a response. Her mouth felt like it was full of cotton wool.

Wande turned his attention to Osas. "Osas, you look about ready to explode." He greeted her with a huge smile and wrapped her in a hug.

"Just wait, your wife will soon be as big as I am." Osas laughed as she returned the hug.

"Cynthia," Wande said to the secretary, "it has been a while. We don't see you at the house anymore."

"Good morning, sir. I apologise sir," Cynthia said grinning.

Ada cut in. "With work, and her final year in school – and a certain brother James – Cynthia is so busy these days."

Cynthia blushed profusely.

"Good, good," Wande said. "Well, I must go now." He gave a brief nod in Ndidi's direction and kissed Ada again on the cheek. "See you later, babes."

Ada nodded after him, and silence descended on the room once more.

Ndidi came back into her body and felt an emptiness in the pit of her stomach – true fear. She stared at the women she had just insulted. Osas was sneering, while Ada almost looked sad.

"Oh, you can keep quiet, *abi*," Osas said. "You have stopped talking? Yes, she is Ada Badejo. Owner of this establishment, the one next door and the one next to that and the ones all around the country."

"I don't understand," Ndidi muttered.

"What don't you understand, you evil woman?" Osas's voice raised another decibel. "You thought she would be begging on the streets of Port Harcourt with your nephews, naked, the way you left them?" She turned to Ada. "I fear your God o. See how He has disgraced your enemies! I can't even deal with this; I don't want evil vibes around me. I'll see you inside." She went through the door that led further into the building.

Ndidi turned to Ada – Ada, who she had always envied, who she had hated for her beauty and innocence, who had lived in luxury in her brother's house while Ndidi had to skimp and beg for everything in life.

Part of Ndidi knew Ada might not have been happy in her marriage, but she didn't care; Ada had what she'd wanted – financial security – while Ndidi had to work tirelessly with a useless, abusive drunkard of a husband, too afraid of what people would say if she asked for a divorce.

Ada then turned to face Ndidi. She seemed taller, stronger. Ndidi stepped back; this was not the Ada she knew. This woman showed no emotion. Her face betrayed nothing as she spoke.

"So, Ndidi. David, the chairman of your bank, asked me to give you twenty minutes of my time. You have now used up your twenty minutes. Cynthia, have security escort this woman off my property immediately."

Ndidi left the office flanked by two colossal security men. The enormity of the situation hit her as she tried to start her car and found her hands were shaking too much to even insert the key.

Ada walked as quickly as she could, shaking off the last thoughts of Ndidi and the parts of her past still tangled up with that woman.

The divisional heads of all the tutoring centres were waiting for Ada to address them and let them know her expectations for the year ahead. She was already fifteen minutes late, and she hated keeping people waiting. She brushed her hand down her freshly pressed, lavender-coloured suit. All her clothes were getting snug at the waist. She was going to need a new wardrobe soon.

Cynthia passed in the corridor and gave her a thumbs up, confirming everything was ready for her in the meeting room.

Ada stepped inside, and she smiled as she noted everyone present there, waiting for her.

"I'm so sorry for keeping you all waiting. This morning alone I've had to put out two fires from our sister company, and I received a rather unexpected call from the Minister of Finance. And it's not even nine o'clock."

The words left her mouth with an echo, and Ada looked around the room. Where had she heard those words before? She shook her head to clear her mind and continued her presentation. At the end of it, the attendees gave her a warm and rousing round of applause. Ada smiled, an unspeakable joy bubbling up in her heart.

THE END

Acknowledgements

Love on the Dotted Line owes its existence to many individuals.

Mapaseka, you were the very first to read this book – in its roughest form back in 2020. You championed it wholeheartedly until you convinced me it was a story worth telling. *Ada's Story*, as we called it for so many years, will always be your baby. Thank you.

Obiageli Olajide, do you remember that manuscript I sent you, out of the blue, during lockdown? Well, this is it. It took five formative years, but here at last! Thank you for all your help.

To my ARC readers – Joy Idakwo, Tomiwa Adabanjo, and Anita Arume – you went from 'just' reading my work to becoming some of my greatest supporters. You gave me the courage to share this book with the world. Thank you for your invaluable feedback and support.

To my writers' group, 'The Scribblers' – Caroline, Tracey, Annie, and Alex – you are truly an amazing bunch! Your unwavering consistency kept me going even when I didn't feel like writing anymore. Your feedback on *Love on the Dotted Line* changed the book's trajectory and pushed it to new heights. I can't wait to celebrate all of our forthcoming publications together!

To the best editing team a writer could ever ask for: Tracey McEvoy and Annie Borelli. I appreciate you both. Tracey, you encouraged me when I was worn out and never let me drop the ball. You poured your heart into turning my rough draft into a truly readable manuscript – you deserve a medal. Annie, you made magic with these pages, elevating every word to capture exactly what I intended. Both of you took Ada and Wande's story to heart, and it showed. What more could an author want? This book is every bit as much yours as it is mine.

To Joy Iwendi and Chidinma Maduka, my ride or die. You keep encouraging me to be the best me. Thank you for being my friends as well as my sisters. Love's Legacy lives on.

To my children, Dara and Ibukun, thank you for the daily encouragement and prayers. You guys make it all worth it!

To Damilola, where do I begin? Thank you for loving and pushing me; for hugging and for holding me up always. Thank you for believing in me even when I no longer want to believe in myself. I stand on your shoulders to do all that I do. Love you boo!

Now, unto the King Eternal, Immortal, Invisible, the only wise God, my Father and my Creator be honour and glory forever and ever. Amen.

OGUGUA AJAYI is a Nigerian contemporary fiction author, screenwriter, producer, and entrepreneur. She holds a Bachelor of Laws degree from the University of Ibadan and a Master's degree in Creative Writing (with Distinction) from the University of Kent, United Kingdom.

Ogugua began her writing journey in 2019, and her short story *He Touched Me*, which explores the impact of domestic violence on mental health, was longlisted for the *SA Writers' College Short Story Prize* in 2020. She has since published two novellas: *Blessings in the Dark* and *Full Circle*. *Love on the Dotted Line* is her debut novel.

When she's not crafting stories, Ogugua enjoys taking long walks and indulging her love for all things chocolate. She currently resides in Kent, with her husband and two children.

www.oguguaajayi.com

Made in United States
Orlando, FL
23 May 2026

81751140R00246